Dead Iron

"Featuring a cursed hero, fabulous secondary characters, a world torn between machines and magic, and a plot that hooks your interest from the very first chapter, *Dead Iron* is a must read."

—*New York Times* bestselling author Keri Arthur

"The action is superb, the stakes are sky-high, and the passion runs wild. Who knew cowboys and gears could be this much fun?"

—*New York Times* bestselling author Ilona Andrews

"A novel and interesting take on the steampunk tropes, with generous nods to other genres and plenty of odd but human characters and Mad Science."

—*New York Times* bestselling author S. M. Stirling

"Werewolves, witches, and creatures of both flesh and metal clash. . . . Beautifully written and brilliantly imagined, Devon Monk is at her best with *Dead Iron*."

—*New York Times* bestselling author Rachel Vincent

"A magical steampunk history . . . a magnificent tale. . . . The reader will be drawn ever deeper into the ticking, dripping iron heart of this story."

—Jay Lake, award-winning author of *Green*

"The mix of magic and steampunk worked very well. . . . Curses, magic, werewolves, zombies, and the Strange . . . they were all fascinating."   —Fiction Vixen Book Reviews

continued . . .

"It is a novel filled with chases and explosions, shirt-twisting tension, and near misses. *Tin Swift* also boasts an entire cast of wonderful characters . . . all fascinating, troubled, and determined, and I couldn't help but be drawn into their struggles. I'm absolutely hooked on this series and cannot wait to root for Cedar and his companions again and again."
—That's What I'm Talking About

"An exhilarating adventure."   —Genre Go Round Reviews

"If you enjoy the steampunk subculture, like alternate histories, or appreciate stories that blend fantasy and science fiction elements, *Tin Swift* provides a thrilling read that's tough to put down."   —Fresh Fiction

BOOKS BY DEVON MONK

The Allie Beckstrom Series

Magic to the Bone
Magic in the Blood
Magic in the Shadows
Magic on the Storm
Magic at the Gate
Magic on the Hunt
Magic on the Line
Magic Without Mercy
Magic for a Price

The Age of Steam

Dead Iron
Tin Swift
Cold Copper

DEAD IRON

The Age of Steam

DEVON MONK

A ROC BOOK

ROC
Published by the Penguin Group
Penguin Group (USA) Inc., 375 Hudson Street,
New York, New York 10014, USA

USA / Canada / UK / Ireland / Australia / New Zealand / India / South Africa / China

Penguin Books Ltd., Registered Offices: 80 Strand, London WC2R 0RL, England
For more information about the Penguin Group visit penguin.com.

Published by Roc, an imprint of New American Library, a division of Penguin
Group (USA) Inc. Previously published in a Roc trade paperback edition.

First Roc Mass Market Printing, June 2013

ISBN 978-0-451-46427-9

Printed in the United States of America
10 9 8 7 6 5 4 3 2 1

PUBLISHER'S NOTE
This is a work of fiction. Names, characters, places, and incidents either are the
product of the author's imagination or are used fictitiously, and any resemblance to
actual persons, living or dead, business establishments, events, or locales is entirely
coincidental.
    The publisher does not have any control over and does not assume any
responsibility for author or third-party Web sites or their content.

ALWAYS LEARNING   PEARSON

For my family

ACKNOWLEDGMENTS

To my amazing agent, Miriam Kriss. Thank you for not telling me I was crazy when I first described this story to you and said I was going to write it. Your wisdom and advice made this book what it is. To my fabulous editor, Anne Sowards, who not only gave this book a chance, but also called and guided me through the trickiest turns with a steady hand. To the incredibly talented artist Cliff Nielsen, who brought Cedar Hunt to life with this gorgeous cover. And to the many people within Penguin who have gone above and beyond to make this book beautiful and strong. Thank you.

My deepest gratitude goes out to: Mom and Dad, for telling me your stories. Dean Woods, a virtuoso storyteller and brilliant brainstorming partner, for lending me your imagination. Dejsha Knight, for all your wonderful insight and help; Dianna Rodgers for reading this on the shortest deadline ever; and to my entire family and all my friends, who listened patiently while I whined and worried, yet still offered unflagging encouragement every step of the way. I couldn't have done this without all of you. To my husband, Russ, and sons, Kameron and Konner, you are the best part of my life. Thank you for helping me make my dreams come true and for letting me be a part of your dreams. I love you.

Last, but certainly not least, I want to thank you, dear readers, for giving me the chance to spin this tale for you.

CHAPTER ONE

Cedar had stared straight into the killing eyes of rabid wolves, hungry bears, and charging bull elk, but Mrs. Horace Small had them all topped.

With dirt brown hair piled in a messy bun on the back of her head, and a pinch of anger between her brows, the storekeeper's wife always seemed half a tick from blowing a spring.

"Two dollars," she repeated, her fist stuck wrist-deep in the fabric at her hip, her jaw jutted out like a bass on a hook.

"Cornmeal, coffee, and a bit of cheese," Cedar said mildly. He knew better than to let his anger show, especially this close to the full moon, in a store full of townsfolk eager to get their hands on the fresh supplies and gears from the old states. "Might be I'm missing something." He looked back down at the receipt with Mrs. Small's tight penmanship. "How again do they add to two dollars?"

He knew math—knew it very well. He'd spent four years back East in the universities and had plans of a teaching life. History and the gentle arts, not the wild metal and steam sciences of the devisers. He'd done his share of tinkering— had a knack for it—but did not have the restless drive of a true deviser, who couldn't be left in a room with a bit of rope, metal, and a hammer without putting them all together into some kind of engine or contraption.

No, his needs had been simple: a teacher's life filled with a wife and a daughter, and his brother, Wil. But that life had been emptied out and scraped clean six years ago, when he'd been only twenty-two. Leaving him a changed man.

Leaving him a cursed man.

"It's written plain enough," she said. "You do read, Mr. Hunt?"

"The part there that says 'fee,'" Cedar asked without looking up. "What fee is that?"

"The rail takes its due. You aren't part of the railroad, Mr. Hunt. Not a farmer, miner, rancher, or deviser. Not a member of this good community. I've never seen you in church. Not one single Sunday the last two years. That fee for the rail is less than all those months' dues you owe to God."

"Didn't know the collection plate took hold to my provisions," he said with a little more irritation than he'd intended, "and I don't recall offering my wages to the rail."

The mood in the general store shifted. The men in the shop—the three Madder brothers, dark-haired, dark-eyed, all of them short, bull-shouldered, and strong—were listening in. They'd stopped pawing and chuckling at the new metals and bits in the straw-padded crates, and were waiting. Waiting for him to say the wrong thing. Waiting for a fight.

Rose, Mrs. Small's seventeen-year-old adopted daughter, stepped down off the stool where she'd been dusting. She darted behind Cedar and out the door, silent as a mouse fleeing danger. She had good instincts. He'd always admired that in her.

Mrs. Small lowered her voice and leaned over the counter between them. "You are a dirty drifter, Mr. Hunt. Any man out this far west with no plan of settling down isn't drifting toward something—he's trying too hard to drift away from something. The good folk of this town want you to be moving on. You've brought enough bad luck down on us. First the Haney stock got drug away by wolves. Then the little Gregor boy goes missing. Trouble like you needs to be moving on your way."

"Trouble like me?" He tipped his hat down just a bit. "No offense, ma'am, but I took care of the wolf before the Haneys lost the rest of their stock. If I recall, there wasn't another man out tracking it. And if I'd known about the Gregor boy wandering off, I would have been looking for him too. Animals aren't the only thing I am capable of hunting."

This time he did look up. Met her eyes. Watched the fire of her indignation go to ash. It never took much, no more than a glimpse of the thing that lived just beneath his civilized exterior, to end a conversation.

Days like this, he liked it. Liked what his gaze could do. But it was easy to lose his grip, to go from staring a person down to waking up with a dead body at his feet. He didn't want that to happen. Not today.

Not ever again.

Cedar blinked, breaking eye contact with Mrs. Small. He pushed the bloody memories away and gave her a moment, because he knew she'd need one.

He took a moment too. He'd meant it when he said he'd look for the boy, would have been looking at the first sign of his getting lost. But Hallelujah wasn't made of trusting folk. They'd seen too much hardship to think a man who kept to himself and came to town only rarely would go out of his way to do them any good.

Except for the dandy rail man, Mr. Shard LeFel. Rumor had it all the town held him in high esteem. Rumor had it, when he or his man Mr. Shunt walked by, folk fought a powerful need to bow down on their knees.

Cedar hadn't yet met a man he'd be willing to bow to.

The Madder brothers swaggered up, caulk boots hollow on the shiplap floor. The brothers worked the silver mine.

Breaking rock all day never seemed to satisfy their need to bust their way through a man's bones every time they crawled out of the hills.

"How I see it," Cedar said, hitching his words down low, quiet, "I've been some benefit to this town, me and my drifter ways. Hunted wolves, mountain lions, and nuisances for ranchers and working folk alike. I'll be hunting for the lost boy. You can tell the Gregors that when they next stop in."

He dug in his pocket and pulled out a silver dollar and enough copper to settle the bill. Fee included. He placed the coins on the counter, plus a penny extra, and plucked a jar of ink from the shelf.

Mrs. Small raised one eyebrow, but said no more.

The silver filigreed bird perched on the edge of the high window sang one sweet chirp. Its head was the size of a child's thimble. The gears and burner inside it were so tiny, it chirped once every hour and needed only a half dropper of water a day to power it.

Valuable, that whimsy. He wondered where she had come by it. That delicate of a matic, a fine thing of little practical use, never survived this far west for long.

Beautiful things got crushed to dust out in these wilds.

Outside, the steam clock blew the pattern for ten o'clock. Town was mighty proud of that whistle. The blacksmith, Mr. Gregor, had put it in place of a clock tower right over his shop at the north end of town. Not half again as nice as the steam bells back East, it was still Hallelujah's pride and joy and could be heard clear on the other side of Powder Keg Bluff.

"Is Mr. Hunt troubling you, ma'am?" asked Cadoc, the shortest and widest of the Madder brothers.

Cedar picked up the flour with the two smaller bundles stacked on top. He tucked the ink into his pocket and nodded at the brothers, who all wore overalls, tool belts, and long coats loose enough to cover whatever it was they kept stuffed in their pockets. "Just a discussion of good citizenship is all, gentlemen," he said. "Afternoon."

He headed out onto the stretch of porch that gave shade in the summer, and the chance of shelter against rain and snow in the other seasons.

The Small Mercantile and Groceries was set on the corner of Main Street—the only street with real gas lamps in the town. The other buildings, thirty or so of them with pitched roofs and walls of milled or plank wood, were laid out in neat rows following the curve of the Grande Ronde River north.

A bustle of people were on the streets this morning, come into town for the new shipment, to pick up mail, or to trade harvest goods to settle their bills. It brought back his memories of the big cities, though there were more steam matics trundling about in the East. Horses, carriages, wagons, and folk on foot added to the clatter of the place, added to the living of the place, and reminded Cedar of things long lost.

Even the ringing of a hammer on wood reminded him of the civilized life that was once his.

He glanced up the street. His gaze skipped the bakery, butcher shop, tannery, and mill, drawn, as it was always drawn, to the clock whistle atop a turret made of iron and wood and tin, sticking up like a backbone above the blacksmith's shop. A coil of copper tubes wrapped through the structure and supported a line of twelve glass jugs, round as pearls and big as butter churns. Water poured from the top of the tower downward, like sand in an hourglass, and filled the glass jugs one at a time, until they spilled over into the next and turned the gears inside the tower toward the next hour.

Town needed a thing to be proud of. Needed a thing more than wool and timber and silver to keep it alive. Needed something beautiful. Needed hope.

Cedar looked past the tower to the mountains that cupped

the valley, two ranges of snow and hardship, blocking Hallelujah from easier lands and the great Columbia River. He knew there was ground enough between the town and the rise of the Wallowa Mountains that an airship could land and lash, but he had never once seen a ship venture over these mountain ranges—not even to deliver supplies or drop mail.

Hallelujah was in dire risk of being forgotten by the world that traveled easier roads to brighter skies.

A song piped out from near his elbow, soft and breathy. Cedar looked down.

Rose was on the porch, her back pressed tight against the clapboard siding, one toe of her boot propped on the lower rung of the whitewashed railing. She was talking to herself or maybe singing, her head bent, amber hair beneath her bonnet catching the gold out of the sunlight and falling in a loose braid over one shoulder, hiding much of her profile from him.

Around her neck was a little locket the size and shape of a robin's egg. It looked to be made of gold and silver, though it might just have been the shine of the morning sun upon it. He'd never seen her without that locket around her neck.

She balanced a small wooden plate with gears set flat atop it on the palm and fingers of her left hand. A tiny tin top with a copper steam valve followed the spokes of the wooden gears and gave off a sour little song that changed with its speed as it followed the height and width of each cog. Rose pulled a gear off the plate and replaced it with another from her apron pocket, sweetening the song, all the while talking, talking.

Clever, that.

He'd bet she fashioned it herself. She had the look of the deviser's knack—a quick mind that trawled the edge of madness, and clever, busy fingers. She had practical smarts too, though, like knowing how to stay away from the back of her mama's hand.

"Reckon I put your mama in a sour mood, asking her about the Gregor boy," he said. "I don't suppose you've heard when he got himself lost?"

"Last night is all," she said, stopping the top with her finger and slipping it into her apron pocket. "Didn't run off, I heard."

"Didn't run? Think he flew out the window?"

She tipped a glance out from behind the brim of her bonnet. Those eyes were blue and soft and wide as the sea. She smiled, the corners of her mouth tucking dimples into her tanned cheeks. Folk around town had their opinions of the girl abandoned when she was a babe. Thought she had too many wild ideas spinning through her head than was proper for a woman. He'd never seen her be anything but kind and steady in the years he'd been here. Deviser or not, madness or not, she had a good heart; that was certain.

Didn't seem the other men in town thought the same. A woman her age and unmarried was almost an unheard-of circumstance.

"No, Mr. Hunt," she said. "I think he got took."

"Took? That what his folks are saying?"

She shrugged.

"They saying what took him?" There wasn't a night predator brash enough to cross a closed door, and there wasn't a soul foolish enough to go without a lock or brace in these parts. Maybe the boy wandered when he should have been sleeping.

"Said it was the man."

"What man?"

"The bogeyman."

Cedar blinked and went very still. She wasn't lying. That was clear from the curiosity in her eyes. She'd heard someone say that, someone who meant it. He just hoped whoever had said it didn't know what they were talking about.

Under his sudden silence, Rose clutched the wooden gear plate tighter and pulled her braid back so it fell square between her shoulders. She did not look away, but lifted her chin and studied his face, his eyes, the angle of his shoulders, his clenched fists. She weighed and measured his mood as if he were made of parts and the whole, more curious than cautious, though she rocked up on the balls of her feet, ready to bolt if need be.

And for good reason. He'd been staring at her. He knew what she saw in his gaze. Knew the beast that twisted inside him. He looked away.

"Mr. Hunt?" she asked. "Are you not well?"

Like he thought, she had good instincts. Cedar found a smile and gentle tone left over from better days.

"Well enough. Thank you for your time, Miss Small."

"Do you think it was?" she asked. "The bogeyman?"

"I think a lady like you shouldn't need to fret about the bogeyman."

She did not smile. "They say he came in the night," she said. "Slick as a shadow. Took Elbert from his bed. Didn't even leave a wrinkle in the sheets. No one saw him. No one heard him. No one stopped him. Not even his daddy. It's unnatural." She nodded and looked him straight in the eyes. "Strange. I think that might be worth a fret or two, don't you?"

Mr. Gregor was a big man. A strong man with hair and beard as red and wild as the fire he toiled over. Probably looked like a giant from the eyes of a girl growing up in this town.

A crash from inside clattered out; then Mrs. Small's holler drifted through the doors. Rose flinched, tucked back down into herself, her hair falling once again to cover her face. He didn't sense fear from her. No, he sensed frustration. She took a breath and let it out like a filly settling to the chafe of bridle and cinch.

"Don't worry yourself, Miss Small," Cedar said. "You're safer here in your home than if you hid away in the blacksmith's pocket." He lowered his voice to a conspiratorial whisper. "I'm of a positive considerance not even the bravest bogeyman would dare cross the temper of your mother."

That tipped a laugh out of her, sweeter than the top's song, and Cedar couldn't help but smile in response. There was something about Rose that made a man want to smile.

"You have a way with words, Mr. Hunt. I best be going before that temper is aimed my direction." She started across the porch and opened the door just as her mother yelled for her.

"Rose, get the broom and pan. And I'll have you fetch the papers from city hall before the day's gone dead. The rail man's expecting them tomorrow. Are you listening to me? Rose!"

"Coming, ma'am," she called back.

Cedar watched her step through the doorway, caught for a moment as a lithe silhouette between the light and darkness, a graceful girl—no, he reckoned she really was a woman now—who paused just long enough to glance over her shoulder at him and give him a curious smile.

Then the Madder brothers came walking out, each calling a hello to Rose, and each fixing Cedar with a hard look.

Cedar got moving, down the steps and out into the busy street. He'd come to town on foot, wanting the walk. But he didn't want to deal with the brothers. Not today.

A cool breeze pulled down off the mountains and pushed a few clouds across the sky. Signs that summer was back would soon be broken by frost.

No time left to plant, to harvest, to spend the days hopeful and hale. The season of the dead was coming round the way. Maybe the storekeeper's wife was right. Maybe it was time for moving on to better hunting grounds before winter took hold. Maybe it was time to run again.

Cedar could feel the restlessness in the little Oregon town. Everyone twitching for a bit of sunlight that gave off enough warmth to last a day. Twitching for moving on, moving up to a better place in the modern world, to a better bit of luck. Before winter caught hold and locked the town tight between the feet of the Wallowa and Blue mountains.

The people of Hallelujah had been holding out against hard times for too long now. Killing winters, broken supply trains and routes, sickness. They hung their hopes like threadbare linens on the iron track that was being laid, tie by tie, coming their way with the promise of a new tomorrow and all the riches of the East and South.

No wonder they bowed to the rail man. He was all they had left to hope for.

Cedar strolled down the street, dodging a slow horse and a passel of kids chasing after a pig that must have gotten loose from its pen. The dirt under his bootheels was still hard from a season of sun, and he made good time crossing one street, then another.

Didn't matter how busy town was today. The Madder brothers followed him like a pack of dogs scenting meat.

He stopped at the end of the street. The western edge of forest crowded up here, making homesteading more difficult. His cabin was about three miles into those trees, up the foothills a bit, by a creek that flowed through the seasons. If the Madders had some business with him, he'd rather deal with it here than at his home.

He didn't want a fight, and he didn't want to draw his gun. But he'd do both to keep the brothers off his heels tonight.

"There something on your mind, boys?"

The middle brother's name was Bryn. Cedar could pick him out of the pack because he was always covered in dirt and grime from the mine—except for his hands, which he kept scrubbed from the wrist to fingertips, clean as a preacher's sheets. He stepped forward.

"We think maybe you lost something." He stuffed one of his clean, calloused hands into his overalls pocket and drew out a pocket watch. He gazed down at it longingly until the oldest, tallest, Alun, said, "Go on now, Bryn. Make it right."

Bryn Madder looked away from the watch and held it out for Cedar. "It's yours. As much as. I . . . found it. A while back. Broken. I cleaned it. Didn't fix it, though. Wouldn't take to fixing, and that's a curious thing."

The watch swung like a pendulum, stirred by the breeze: a silver disk, an accusing eye, cold and hard as hatred.

"A lot of men carry a watch." Cedar's throat felt like he'd just swallowed down ashes of the dead. That watch was not his. But he would know it anywhere. It was his brother's. And he'd last seen it on him the day he died.

Bryn nodded. Tilted his chin so he could look at Cedar through his good left eye. "This one you lost. We found it. Maybe eight months ago when that rail man dandy came to town. Thought about keeping it . . ." His voice trailed off on a note of longing.

"But it's not the sort of thing we'd need," Alun said, more for his brother than for Cedar. "Now, if it had been something useful to us, like say that striker we've seen you carry a time or two . . ."

"Is that what you want for it?" Cedar could not look away from the watch, gently swaying like an admonishing finger.

The brothers paused.

Cedar glanced at the oldest, Alun, who wore a heavier beard than the rest. "How much?"

Alun did not look away. Instead, he did something very few could do beneath Cedar's glare. He smiled.

"Our blood comes from the old country, Mr. Hunt," he

said. "Before Wales had that name. And our . . . people . . . have always been miners. A man sleeps and breathes and sups with the stone, he begins to understand things."

A wagon pulled by mule, not steamer, rattled past, taking crates and sacks and barrels of food, nails, mended shovels, and hammers out to the rail work twenty miles south of town.

"All things in this world eventually soak into the soil and stone," Alun said once the wagon had taken its noise up the street a ways.

"It gets to be where a man, one who knows what to listen for, can hear the stones breathing. It gets to be where a man knows what the stones have to say."

"The watch." Cedar didn't care if Alun thought he could hear rocks conversing. Hell, for all Cedar knew, he was telling true and he could talk to stones. The brothers had strolled into town a year ago, just ahead of the rail man, and quickly struck the richest silver vein in the hills. Maybe they'd gone out and asked the mountain where the metals were hid.

And maybe the mountain had sat down and told them.

Talking to rocks wasn't near the strangest thing Cedar had encountered on his walk across this country. He had seen the Strange—the true Strange—creatures that hitched along from the Old World, tucked unknown in an immigrant's pocket, hidden away in a suitcase, or carried tightly in the darkest nightmare. He had seen what the Strange could do when set free in this new land. He had seen it more clearly than someone fixing to blame the bogeyman for a missing child. He had seen the Strange personally, been touched by them.

And he still hadn't recovered.

It looked like the Madder brothers' Strange had done them benefit. They were wealthy by any man's standard, even though they never spent much, never left the hills much, and lived like they didn't have a penny between them.

They had a way with metal; that was sure. It showed in their buckles and buttons, each carved with a symbol of a gear and wrench, flame and water. It showed in the glimpses of brass and copper contraptions that rode heavy in the pockets of their oversized coats.

And it showed in the customized Colt pneumatic revolvers glinting in handworked silver and brass, holstered at their hips.

He was of a mind they were also devisers, though they'd never come out and said such. Made him curious why they didn't want to admit to their skill. A deviser could make things of practical applications that stretched the imagination. Yet folk in town always turned them a blind eye, while looking instead with hope to the rail man, LeFel.

"The watch isn't yours, is it?" Alun Madder said. "Stones say this belonged to someone close to you. Someone gone. A brother?"

Cedar held out his hand for the watch. "Those stones of yours talk too much."

That got a hoot out of all three of them.

"What is your asking price for the watch?" Cedar said.

"The striker. And a favor."

"What favor?"

The Madder brothers all shrugged at the same time. "Don't know," Alun said. "Don't need a favor yet. But when we do, you'll answer to us and pay it."

Cedar paused. He didn't like being left owing to any man, much less three. But that was Wil's watch. Rightfully his now. He wanted it. More, he wanted to know how it had suddenly appeared, all the way out here, almost four years after his death.

"One favor only," Cedar said, "not one for each of you. I'll do nothing that brings harm to the weak, the poor, or to women and children."

"Yes, yes." Alun rubbed his meaty hands together. "And the striker."

"You'll have it next time I'm in town."

"Agreed," Alun said.

The Madder brothers leaned in and extended their right hands as one, palms pressed against knuckles so they all shook Cedar's hand at the same time. Practiced, unconscious—they'd probably been sealing deals that way since they could talk.

Cedar held his hand out for the watch again. Bryn released the chain and sighed as the watch slipped through his fingers into Cedar's.

It should be cold, made of silver and brass with a crystal face. But the watch was as warm as if there were a banked coal tucked inside. It didn't tick, not even the second hand. It was still, dead. And warm as a living thing.

He tried hard not to look surprised or look away from the brothers.

"Just a watch, you say?" he asked.

Bryn answered. "So much as. Broken when we found it. Not much of a timepiece if it can't tell a man the time." He shrugged.

Alun was still smiling. "Enjoy your time, Cedar Hunt," he said. "Don't forget our striker. Come on now, Bryn." He punched Bryn on the shoulder—a hit that would have staggered a much bigger man, though Bryn barely seemed to notice—and the two of them started back into town.

Their brother, Cadoc Madder, lingered behind as Alun and Bryn angled south toward the saloon and the boarding-house, whose rooms hadn't been full since the gold rush. Next to that stood the bordello that had never needed to worry about an empty bed now that the rail, and its workers, had come to town.

Cadoc, who had been silent all this time, finally spoke.

"If you ever want to know what else the stones say about . . . things and such . . . you know where to fetch us up."

"Didn't figure your rocks were quite so conversational," Cedar said.

Cadoc rolled his tongue around in his mouth, pushing out his bottom lip, then his top, as if washing the grit off his words before using them.

"The railroad is coming. Can you hear it, Mr. Hunt? Crawling this way on hammers and iron. Breathing out its stink and steam. Thing like that brings change to a place, to a people. There'll be more metal above the ground than below soon.

"Leaves a hollow that needs filling. Scars more than stone deep." He paused and studied Cedar a little closer. "But then, you know about the things that can change a land, or a man, I reckon. You and your brother."

Sweat slicked under Cedar's hatband. He didn't know what Cadoc knew about Wil. About the change. The curse. Didn't even know how the Madders could know. Cedar had not spoken of his brother in nearly three years.

The wind laid a phantom hand between his shoulders, pressing there, telling him it was time to move on, move away, move west. Before his past caught up with him again.

Before there was blood.

But it was Cadoc who left, rambling down the street to join his brothers, not one of them with a care to look back at Cedar.

Cedar fought the urge to go after them, to force them to explain the watch, and what they knew of his brother's death. To tell him why the metal was warm as spilled blood.

Instead he stood there, a sack of flour on his shoulder, his fist clenched around the only thing of his brother's that remained, while the Madders bulled down the street through the crowd, looking like they'd welcome a brawl just for laughs.

He'd come back later with the striker. He'd see if their talk was crazy, or if they knew something more. Something true. By then he'd have a firm hold on his anger and his hunger. By then he'd be less likely to do them permanent harm.

And he would find out just exactly what their rocks had said about his brother.

Cedar took a deep breath, trying to calm the beast within him.

In the distance, the pump and chug of the steam matics working the rail set a drumbeat as the brown jug whistle sounded out lonely and hollow, like dreams coming this way to die.

He crossed the road to the trail that led to his cabin up in the hills. He'd cook up some coffee, fry up some bread, and have a meal before the moon rose. After the moon set, he'd hunt for the boy.

Because that was what a man did. And Cedar intended to remain a man for as long as he could.

CHAPTER TWO

It had been years since Mae Lindson called on the old ways. She promised Jeb she wouldn't use them anymore. Not out here, so far west, where there was no coven to hide her. It was enough trouble, he had said, for a man of color to marry a white woman. Telling people she was a witch would only bring them quicker to their doorstep with torches in their hands and hanging in their eyes.

But it had been three months. Three months waiting for him to come home. She was done waiting. Done wondering if he would ever come home to her. When she made a vow, it could never be unbroken—so was the way of her magic within the sisterhood. She had vowed her heart and soul unto this man, until death did them part. That vow, that promise, should have guided him home to her by now.

She pushed the basket of dirt sprinkled with rose hips and wormwood closer to the hearth where the light of the rising moon would soon find it. The fire was crackling hot and strong enough to burn on to morning.

The whistle and pop of the steam matics working the lines had quieted since nightfall. All the world of man had quieted. Now was the time for magic.

Mae glanced at her door. A strong bolt made of brass and springs held it tight. That, Jeb had given her as a wedding gift. He had fashioned it with his own hands, as he had fashioned all the other beautiful things of wood and brass that filled the shelves alongside her pots and dishes and herbs and books. Just as he had fashioned her spinning wheel and her loom. He was never without a gear or fancy to carve, but only ever showed his creations to her.

Still, the bundle of protective herbs wrapped along dried grapevines and rowan above the door did as much to keep her safe as Jeb's bolts and devices. Herbs and spells to keep the Strange at bay.

She pulled her shawl close around her shoulders and knelt next to the basket of dirt. The people of town were beginning to whisper about her. When she walked to town to trade her weaving for supplies, people talked. Said her husband had long left her. Said he was dead.

But they were wrong. She still heard him, heard her husband's voice in the night, calling her name.

Mae rolled up her left sleeve, exposing her wrist and forearm, strong from tending the field, strong from tending the sheep and chickens. She placed her fingers in the basket of dirt and stirred, fingers splayed, counterclockwise. The dirt warmed slowly, soaking up the heat from the hearthstones. She hummed, settling into the feel of this soil beneath her hands, between her fingers, and breathed in the scent rising off the soil—of summer giving its life away to autumn.

She sang the song slowly, words forming the spell that would find Jeb. Little matics and tickers on the shelf hummed along with her, echoing to the notes of their tuning.

"My hand touching this soil, this soil touching all soil. All soil beneath my hand. All soil I know. The heartbeat, the soul of two who have vowed until death do us part. Jeb Lindson, husband, lover, soul."

She closed her eyes, held her breath. Pushed away the awareness of the wind outside the door, pushed away the sound of the fire scratching across the wood. Pushed away everything except the one clear need to feel Jeb's heartbeat, somewhere, anywhere, in this world of soil and stone.

After a long, long moment, there, beneath her palm, she felt a slow thump.

Never before had one man been so difficult to kill. Mr. Shard LeFel watched with detached interest while Jeb Lindson balanced on one good leg and one bad ankle on top of a bucket. The rope around the man's neck was thick and strong. So was the limb of the oak over which it was thrown.

Plenty strong enough to bear the weight of the man, even though he was twice the size of LeFel and the opposite of him in every way. LeFel's silver white skin rivaled alabaster, his features so fine and fair, artists and admirers begged to paint his likeness. His hair was moon yellow, left long and sleek with a black ribbon holding it back from his high, white lace collar.

He wore no facial hair, nor powders, and dressed in the finest clothes, no matter the occasion. Suit, tails, and top hat from Paris, black gloves from Versailles, and one of his favorite vanities: a blackened and curved cane, carved from the breastbone of an African elephant, and plied tip to tip with catches of gold, silver, and deep, fire-filled rubies.

But even if all those things were stripped of him, it would still be his eyes that held him apart from any other man. Glacier blue, heavily lidded, they drew people to him witless and wanting, as if they had suddenly seen their dreams come alive and breathing.

It had proved a useful thing. In many pleasurable ways.

The big man atop the bucket shifted again, his unbound hands reaching into the night as if the shadows could aid him. He was stone dark, skin and hair and eyes, his wide hands blistered and calloused from a life of toil, his trousers and plaid shirt torn and stained—even before the five bullets ripped holes through his coat—directly over his heart, which continued to stubbornly, slowly beat.

LeFel had killed him twice. Once with a knife, a rotting scar he bore at his neck. Once with a gun, the small bullet holes in his coat belying the amount of lead burrowed in the meat of his chest. Each time, LeFel had watched his servant, Mr. Shunt, bury the big man. Each time, Jeb Lindson had found a way to crawl out of his grave and go walking.

Not much of a man left to him, really. Still, something drove him. Away from death and toward the living world. A heart like his, a soul that strong, was rare.

And it was a great inconvenience to LeFel's plans.

LeFel glanced at the canopy of limbs above them. The moon would be up soon, full and strong. Strong enough to make sure Jeb Lindson stayed dead this time.

"Please . . ." The big man's voice scraped low, ragged. Too much the same as it had been in life.

"You beg?" LeFel tapped the toe of his Italian boot against the wood bucket the big man stood upon. Not hard enough for the bucket to shift. Just hard enough for the hollow thunk to make his eyes go wide. It reminded him he was about to die. Again.

LeFel smiled. It was a lovely thing to see that even in death there was still fear.

Mr. Shunt, waiting at the edge of shadows, shifted, the satin and wool of his coat hissing like snakes against his heels. Too tall, too thin, Mr. Shunt kept his face hidden beneath the brim of his stovepipe hat that seemed latched to his head as if stitched there, and his turned-up black collar. His eyes, if ever they were seen, evoked fear, showing just what kind of creature lurked within the layers of silk. A very Strange man, indeed.

Next to Mr. Shunt crouched a wolf. Common as scrub

brush, that wolf was Shard LeFel's newest and most useful toy. It wore a collar of LeFel's own devising—brass and copper with crystal and carved gears—and a leash, which Mr. Shunt held in the crook of one finger.

Next to the wolf stood a small barefoot boy. No more than four years old, the child wore nothing but his bed shirt. His skin was death pale, his hair a shock of red. He made no sound, nor did he seem to see the world around him. He gazed off in a middle distance as if still walking his dreams, untouched by the night, or the cold, or his company.

"What do you beg for, dead man?" LeFel mused. "What is there left to you? Not life. Only a mockery of that rattles in your chest. What sweet dream pulls you from the smothering rest eternal?"

"Mae . . ." The single word fell from his swollen lips like a prayer. "My Mae."

LeFel frowned. "The witch?" He rapped the bucket with his toe again. "She has lied to you, sung you sweet falsities. You thought her magic was yours to keep, but I alone shall have it. Not even the vow she cast between you, the binding of your love, will hold her safe from my *needs*." He kicked the bucket hard enough it shifted.

Jeb swayed, but stubbornly held his balance on his battered legs.

"There are things I require in this world. Isn't that true, Mr. Shunt?"

Mr. Shunt chuckled, the sound of dry bones rattling.

"And when my brother saw to it I was exiled to these foul lands, for nothing more than killing his only heir, I had thought myself without recourse. But he did not know, could not know, the beauty of turned metal. Could not know the power harnessed in steam, could not know the primitive magic inherent in this land, nor the most *interesting* abilities of those who devise.

"And he certainly could not know that others of our . . . kind . . . would find each of these things pleasing as a midsummer feast."

Mr. Shunt chuckled again. The wolf at his feet laid his ears back and bared teeth at the sound. The child did not seem to hear.

"You could have given in to me, Mr. Lindson. But you refused. Even in death. And now you, my poor dark man, stand like a mountain in my way. Stand like a mountain between myself and your beautiful living wife." He aimed another blow at the bucket, but allowed only the softest tap of his boot.

"Mountains cannot stop me. I have hammered iron and silver across this land. I have broken every mountain that refused my harness."

Jeb, silent, stared at him with a gaze that held too much hatred for a dead man.

"Just as I shall harness Mae—"

"Mae . . . ," Jeb echoed. "My Mae . . ."

LeFel snarled. "She is mine!"

He slammed his boot into the bucket, shoving it sideways. Jeb rocked, the rope against the tree limb creaking beneath the strain.

Mr. Shunt sucked in a hopeful breath.

But Jeb somehow remained standing, silent, hatred in his eyes.

LeFel stepped back, pulled a bit of perfumed silk and lace from his coat sleeve, and wiped his lips in a circle, over and over again, the motion soothing, calming.

All would be well. He would kill this mortal man correctly this time. He would kill him so the tie of magic binding him to his wife would be broken, so Jeb Lindson could not return to his wife, could not lay claim to her soul, her life, or the magic at her hands. The binding that held them together, and kept Mae's magic out of LeFel's reach, would be broken.

"You," LeFel said, his voice shaking, but calm, "are a very lucky man, Mr. Lindson. You still have a small time left to breathe this air. To gaze upon this land. To ponder the life that is no longer yours before I take it from you a third time. Your death awaits the rise of the waxing moon. Poetic for a third and final death, don't you agree, Mr. Shunt?"

"Sweet as a lullaby," Mr. Shunt whispered, placing his hand gently on the child's head.

Shard LeFel tipped his face skyward, and gazed at the velvet night caught between the tangle of branches. Soon, soon, the witch would be his.

Cedar threw the brace of wood across his door, and pulled to be sure the hinges were secure. He had already banked the fire, leaving a heart of oak to parcel out heat for the next eight hours, and set a pot on the hook above it. He had already hung the bucket of water up on the ceiling hook in the corner of the room and shuttered the cabin's single window.

The last thing, the most necessary thing, he did not want to do.

A heavy iron chain thick as his wrist lay across the bricks of the hearth, one end welded through the iron ring pounded into the stone, the other end connected to a wide leather collar.

Cedar knew the chain and collar were unbreakable. He had fashioned both with his own hands.

He turned away from the door and paced in front of the fireplace, careful not to disturb the chain at his feet.

The missing Gregor boy weighed heavy on his mind. There was little information he could rely on. Grieving parents could conjure any sort of story to explain how their child had gone to death—wolf, wandering, or even the bogeyman come stealing in the night.

If the boy had been taken by beast, there would be no hope he was still alive. If the child wandered off, there could still be time to find him. And if it was the bogeyman or some Strange thing that put hands on that small a boy and stole him away . . .

Cedar rubbed his hand over his face. If it was a thing of the Strange, he hoped the child was lucky enough to receive a quick death.

He stopped pacing and took up a cup from above the fireplace in front of the small mirror there. He swallowed the last cold dregs of coffee. He hated the chain, hated the collar. And hated that he'd have to wait out the moonrise to begin his hunt for the boy.

Cedar placed the empty cup on the mantel next to his brother's pocket watch, then crouched in front of the chain, taking it up in his hands. The call of moonlight in the air burned like whiskey in his blood. He knew just how long he could resist the change. Had spent four years tied to the moon, ever since he'd hunted the red wolf Bloodpaw in Pawnee country, and instead caught the attention of the Pawnee gods.

There was no time left for memories, no time left for bucking fate. He was losing control. Even now, his hands stretched wide, his joints and bones loosened for the change. A haze of luxurious pleasure clouded his eyes and mind like opium, promising unearthly pleasures.

It was a lie. He knew what would happen after the change. The beast inside him would be free. He would kill. And he would not remember any of it until he woke in the morn.

Cedar bent his head and, with clumsy fingers, fastened the collar around his neck.

He stood and stared at his reflection in the small mirror there.

Still a man's face, strong nose, hard jaw, his skin tanned with something more than pure European heritage. His eyes were his own, hazel, with long lashes, above them dark brows and waves of thick walnut hair. Lines at the edges of his eyes hinted of past laughter, while other lines, at his mouth and forehead, mapped his sorrow. Clean-shaven, he was not a plain man, nor an old man, nor an unhandsome man.

He was, however, a cursed man.

The moon rose, inching higher, pushing his heartbeat to quicken. Fast. Faster.

One single silver ray poured through the shutter. Cedar moaned, not from pain, but from pleasure and sin, as his body twisted, stretched, changed. He clung to humanity, clung to the mind of a man, as long as he could.

But moonlight loosed a flood of quicksilver heat through him and dragged him down with the weight of an ocean. He drowned in moonlight, drowned in the need for blood, flesh, death. He threw his head back and yelled as his humanity shattered. The only sound that escaped his throat was a blood-hungry howl.

The first finger of moonlight slipped like a serpent's tongue through the canopy of trees. Shard LeFel smiled.

"This is your end, Mr. Lindson," LeFel said. "Your third and last death by my hand. They say a man can kill another man only three times in this world. Therefore I have gone through considerable measures to see that you stay dead."

LeFel slid his fingers into his coat pocket. He withdrew a palm-sized silver box and a tiny wrought iron key. The silver box was fine lacework. Held just so, it seemed as if the lace fashioned the box into a tree: thicker silver lines creating the trunk at the base, and thin, beautiful arcs of silver reaching out in branches, leaves, and crown that wove together to make the cage whole.

Within the box was a tiny clockwork dragonfly, gold and crystal wings thin as paper, glinting like dying sunlight as they fluttered beneath the cage that held them. The unearthly green light of pure glim—the rarest of all things—shone out from the dragonfly's body, blending with the sunlight-flecked wings.

"This trinket is worth more money than you have ever known, Mr. Lindson. Kings, emperors, a history worth of conquerors, have fought for this treasure, have torn kingdoms and civilizations down to splinters and dust to possess it.

"Rare . . ." LeFel's voice, for just that moment, lost its anger and hatred. For just that moment, his voice was a thing of unearthly beauty, clear and full of song. The animals in the night paused at the sound, and even the trees bent to be nearer him.

Mr. Shunt moaned softly, and LeFel seemed to remember himself.

"I think it a shame, really," he said with cold disinterest, all the song gone from his words. "A shame that it will be wasted on a scrap of meat such as yourself."

LeFel held the box by its corners, pinched between the black silk fingertips of his gloves.

"This treasure will be the last thing you will ever feel, Mr. Lindson."

LeFel slammed his foot into the bucket, kicking it free from beneath Jeb. The rope groaned beneath the man's full weight.

Jeb Lindson's swollen lips mouthed one word, even though no sound came out: *Mae*. His heart beat slowly once, twice.

LeFel turned away from him and stepped over to the child. "Such a dream, little maker," he cooed. "Such a strange and wonderful dream you see." He knelt and picked up the child's hand. "Can you catch the moonlight, little dreamer?"

The boy did not respond. LeFel had not expected he would. He didn't need his response. He needed his blood.

LeFel held the boy's hand toward Mr. Shunt.

"Mr. Shunt, if you please."

Mr. Shunt extended one long knobby finger, the tip of which ended in a silver needle. He pricked the boy's thumb.

The boy did not even flinch, but the wolf growled. LeFel met the wolf's copper brown gaze with his own. "You will play your part, my pet. But not now."

Then, to the child: "Just a bit of blood and shred of dream, little maker," he said. "That and moonlight is all I need this night."

LeFel pressed the boy's thumb against the silver box until one thick drop of blood fell upon the dragonfly, turning it slick and dark as rubies.

"Such a beautiful child." LeFel rose to stand in front of the boy. "And so useful." He held the box over his shoulder. "Mr. Shunt, your service."

Mr. Shunt stirred free of the shadows and lifted the box from LeFel's fingers. He crossed the short distance to the hanging man, coats of silk and wool licking his steps.

Then he stretched his arm out to touch Jeb Lindson.

Mr. Shunt's overly long, knob-knuckled fingers suddenly bristled with delicate tools, things meant for cutting, for hooking, for binding. He made quick work of tearing apart the last of Jeb's coat and shirt, digging a hole through the cloth to the skin beneath.

He took his time fastening the box into Jeb's flesh, savoring the dying man's gasps of pain, batting away his feeble swings.

Once satisfied with his work, he stepped back.

LeFel turned to face Jeb. He removed his own glove, and tipped his bare palm upward, catching moonlight. He closed his fist, pressed his lips against the knot his thumb and forefinger created, and whispered to the moonlight.

A spell. Not of the magic of this world. A Strange spell. Poison from a Strange man's lips. LeFel released the spell, blowing the captured moonlight like a kiss across his hand toward the man who was still not dead enough.

Moonlight poured into the tiny box in Jeb's chest, catching like dewdrops on a spider's web. The ruby clockwork dragonfly clattered faster, wings beating to escape a flame that burned too near, or to shake a poison swallowed down.

Silver threads from the lacework shot out of the cage and sank like roots seeking Jeb's lifeblood, digging deeper and deeper until they caught hold in his heart.

Jeb stiffened and no longer struggled against the rope.

"Now, Mr. Shunt."

Mr. Shunt fitted the wrought iron key into the neatly hidden slot in the silver cage. Then he turned the key counterclockwise: once, twice, thrice. The bloody dragonfly's wings slowed and slowed with each turn. Until it was still.

And then Jeb Lindson's heart beat no more.

Mae clutched the soil beneath her hands. Moonlight poured through the window, tarnishing her world with pewter light. She held her breath as Jeb's heartbeat went silent beneath her palms. "No," she whispered, "don't leave me."

The cold scent of winter, of death, drifted up from the soil and filled her with a bone chill. He was gone. Her husband, her lover, her soul.

Mae pulled her hands out of the basket. She wrapped her arms about herself and rocked and rocked until the fire died and the hearthstones beneath her had gone cold. She did not cry. Tears were for sorrow. And sorrow would wait until anger had its due.

In the deepest dark of the night, long before the dawn could grant light's mercy to the world again, Mae placed her fingers into the ashes of the fire and sang a much different song, wove a much darker spell, and vowed revenge upon her husband's killer.

CHAPTER THREE

Cedar woke facedown on the floor, his left arm curled up and numb beneath him. Half-remembered visions sifted like sand through his mind. Though he tried to hold tight to them, only fragments of the night remained, wrapped in old echoes of anger, fear, and the moon-crazy hunger for blood.

He took a deep breath and pushed all that aside, wanting to forget, for another day, the curse that plagued him, wanting with a sure desperation to be nothing more than just a man. But all the wanting in the world couldn't erase the beast within him. And every day he refused to slake the hunger, it took more to deny the beast's needs.

He rolled to one hip to get the blood flowing back into his arm, then lay all the way onto his back. He groaned at the stiffness in his muscles and joints. The chain next to him shifted and rattled against floorboards—a comforting sound. He dragged his right hand alongside his neck, checking to see if the collar was still there. Loose, but whole. He had not run free in the night.

Cedar blew out the breath he'd been holding and stared up at the ceiling. The light of dawn slipped the edge of the shutter, a single shaft of yellow burning down upon the floor like a gold coin.

But no coin could be more precious than the humanity morning provided—stiffness, aches, and all.

Clearheaded and hungry, Cedar savored the sense of revival the change always left upon him. He felt like he'd just plunged naked into a river in the brace of winter and come out the other side into summer's heat.

Except this time he'd also come out with a numb arm, an empty belly, and a headache banging away like a steam hammer.

Food. Water. Clothes. In that order. He knew the aches and pains would pass quickly once his most basic needs were tended. It was one of the only gifts to his curse—he healed rapidly during the full moon.

He should be healed and whole in just a few hours. And in that time, he'd go out to the Gregors', and talk to them about their missing boy. He planned to find little Elbert. He planned to bring him home if he was still alive.

Cedar sat and hissed at the pain that clamored through his skull and arm. He used his right hand to pull his left up on his thigh, and something slipped from his left hand and clattered to the floor. Something metal. A cup?

Whatever it was, it didn't move, and Cedar wasn't aiming to move either, until the grip of his headache eased off some.

A trickle of sweat licked down the side of his temple and jaw, then hit his thigh. He stared at the red splatter mark. That wasn't sweat. It was blood.

Cedar felt along the side of his eye and up to a lump and cut at the edge of his hairline. He sighed. Bleeding and hungry had to be two of his least favorite ways to start a day.

The cut and lump weren't more than he'd had before, but would need cleaning and a cloth to stanch the flow.

The headache settled a bit, so Cedar got to his feet. Like he'd thought, the stiffness was already fading, but his arm had taken to tingling with a toothy vengeance. He walked across the room to his trunk and worked the lock, trying not to move his left arm much. He lifted the lid, dug out a handkerchief, and dabbed at the cut. The blood was already slowing.

Good. He did not much care for doctors, nor to aiming their attention at his pain.

As he turned toward the bucket hanging from the ceiling, a flash of metal on the floor caught his eye.

His brother's watch. That must have been what slipped out of his hand.

What had he been doing with that in the night? He paced over and picked it up. Still warm, the watch didn't seem to have suffered. Not a scratch upon it.

Cedar rubbed his thumb over it, smearing blood across the crystal face. He swore softly. The last thing he wanted to see on the watch was blood.

Two steps toward the hearth and he stopped cold.

The watch was ticking.

He tipped it toward dawn's light. The second hand flicked from where it'd come to rest three seconds away from the twelve, and began its round. The watch ticked like a heartbeat. A cold chill washed over him. The Madder brothers had said it couldn't be fixed. Yet as soon as his blood touched it, the watch repaired.

Or maybe sometime in the night he had dropped it, thrown it, done something to shake the gears and springs free.

That was the logical answer.

But he knew it was not the true answer. Something broken didn't just fix on its own. Something had set the second hand tracking smooth and quick as a telegrapher's finger, but he did not know what that thing was. He rubbed the handkerchief over the watch, clearing it of blood. And still the watch continued to tick.

Far off, the steam whistle blew. An engine grunted like an old drum beating, slow, heavy huffs that never seemed to come nearer. The railmen were working, feeding great gobs of wood and coal into the matics that winched and lifted and dropped: giant, ingenious beasts ripping the land apart and stitching it back together with iron and steel.

The Madder brothers were right. There was a change coming. Coming on that rail.

Cedar set the watch on the mantel, where it should have stayed in the night, and took up his coffee cup instead. He hefted the bucket of water off the ceiling hook, drank until his stomach stopped cramping, and did his best not to think too hard about the rail. That wasn't his business. And he'd long ago learned it best to keep his mind on his own affairs.

He crouched in front of the cold fire and ate the beans and cornmeal and venison with the wooden spoon he'd left in the pot. It wasn't the food he hungered for—meat and marrow and blood—but it was plentiful and filling.

Feeling more civilized, he searched the one-room cabin for his clothes and found them, folded upon his bunk against the wall.

Folded.

He shook his head. The change from man to beast was never clear to him, and things like this woke a powerful curiosity within him. Did he linger in some sort of half state, where his hands were still those of a man, or did the beast take him on full? Did he change back into a man but have no conscious thought and sleepwalk his way through half a night? When, exactly, did he find the time to fold his clothing?

He didn't know, and there was no one to tell him. Staring in the mirror had brought him few clues.

The first change, four years ago, still held strongest in his mind's eye. He remembered the fear, remembered the painfully satisfying stretch of his body and bones reshaping into lupine form. Remembered looking over at his brother, who, even in wolf form, still carried his own scent and copper brown eyes.

He remembered most watching as Bloodpaw, the wolf he had been tracking, stood up and revealed himself as not a wolf, not even a man, but a god native to this land. The god had shaken his head and spoken in the tongue that the people of this land still spoke—a language Cedar did not know, yet for that one night, he had understood.

"Your people come like rabbits running from wolves. They spread far and wide," the god said. "Dark magic follows in their path. Poisons the rivers and the earth. Then come engines breaking the mountains down, punching holes from this world into the other.

"Strange things cross through these holes. Strange things hunt and eat and thrive in this world.

"But you are not a rabbit. You are a wolf. You will turn and hunt. You will drive the darkness back through the holes and send the Strange from this land."

The next thing Cedar remembered was waking far from that place, gripped by fever and nausea, the taste of blood and meat in his mouth. Wil was gone.

A bloody trail led Cedar to the carcass of a wolf, whose throat had been torn out.

He had killed his own brother.

The fever lasted a full week. When he finally came to, he was miles away to the west, just outside a small town. He begged clothing and supplies from a Mormon family, who took him in and nursed him to health. Since he was more recently out of the universities and handy with matics, he repaired their boiler to repay the debt. Then he kept walking west, putting his past behind him.

The jingle of a bridle and the sound of hooves brought Cedar back to himself, and his current state of nakedness.

He dressed quickly, trousers and shirt dark enough that the dried blood on his hands would not visibly stain them. He dipped a second handkerchief in the bucket, wiped his face, jaw, and neck, and washed his hands. Then he rolled the handkerchief and tied it around his head against the cut.

He didn't know who was riding past, but the only people who came this far into the forest were looking to either end trouble or start it.

He pushed his feet into socks and boots, lifted his hat from the hook. He left his goggles on the hook, and settled his hat over the kerchief on his head. Near the mantel he hesitated, and finally decided to tuck the watch into his pocket. He didn't want it out of his sight.

Then he took up his holster and gun, not a tinkered pistol, but a crystal-sighted Walker, gauged to the goggles he usually wore, and modified by his own hand for a faster reload. He strapped on the gun and holster and unbolted the door.

The door had gotten the worst of the night, claw marks gouged knuckle deep all the way up to eye level. Something else he'd need to repair.

Cedar stepped outside into the cool morning air that hung heavy with the honey spice of pines and pollen.

A gray saddle mule made its way through the buzz and brush of late summer. On top of the mule rode a yellow-haired, light-skinned woman. Pretty. No, more than that, stunning.

His heart skipped a beat at the sight of her and he felt as if a string had been plucked deep inside his chest, shaking off the ice that had numbed him for so long. Though it had been years since his marriage, and this woman did not resemble his wife, Catherine, an unexpected longing filled him.

She was beautiful. And he found he could not bring himself to look away from her.

Her eyes were deep brown, her face fine-boned and sweet. She wore a simple straw hat, with a sage-colored ribbon wrapped round it to match her paisley dress, as if for all the world she was out to enjoy a morning ride.

But as she drew nearer, there was no mistaking the anger that set her lips in a hard line. No mistaking the flush to her cheeks that looked more from crying than the meager heat of morning.

He didn't recognize her, which surprised him. He thought he knew all the people in town.

"Mr. Cedar Hunt?" she called out from a short distance.

He blinked hard to end the staring he'd been doing, then walked a bit away from the door into sunlight.

"Yes, ma'am." He tipped his hat and wished he hadn't. The band scraped the kerchief and got the cut bleeding again. "And who do I have the pleasure to be addressing?"

She pulled back on the reins and stopped the mule. Not too close, which said a lot. She was a cautious woman. She did not dismount to his level. He would bet she had a gun hidden in her sleeve.

Beautiful and smart.

"My name is Mrs. Jeb Lindson." She tipped her chin up, as if admitting such a thing usually brought on a fight.

Jeb Lindson. The Negro who kept to himself out a ways on the southeast side of town. Mr. Lindson was a farmer and sometimes hired himself out to work other plots of land. Cedar recalled he was a strong man, and didn't complain about hard labor, nor people's manners toward him, so long as it brought him a coin or a quart of fresh milk.

Cedar had done his share of roaming the area, and he'd seen the Lindsons' stead, a neat place with sheep and chicken and a team of mules. Ordinary, except for the plot of ground near the house carefully marked off with a white picket fence and a row of river stones around it. Green always seemed to be growing inside that fence, no matter the season. Green and blooms. He'd suspected it was tended by a woman's hand. He'd just never seen the woman before.

"Pleased to make your acquaintance, Mrs. Jeb Lindson," he said.

His reaction seemed to catch her off guard, and her stubborn mask cracked to reveal the grieving woman beneath.

It didn't take a scholar to see her pain.

"And yours," she whispered.

"What brings you out my way?"

"I am looking to hire your services."

"Trouble with your stock?" Wolves weren't the only thing he'd hunt, and hunting wasn't the only answer he had for vermin. Certain plants took care of grazers, certain fences repelled smaller varmints, and certain matics took care of both.

"Trouble with my husband's death," she said.

Cedar frowned. "Don't think I understand you rightly."

"My husband, Mr. Hunt, has been killed. Last night. Somewhere here in this valley. I want you to find his body and his killer."

"If you don't know where his body is, how is it you know he's dead?"

"I am his wife. A wife knows these things. A wife has . . . ways." She twisted the reins in her hands. Even though she had repaired her mask, her hands betrayed her grief.

"You don't think an animal killed him, do you, Mrs. Lindson?"

"No." She opened her mouth to say something more, then looked away from his gaze. "No," she said again.

Cedar took in a deep breath, and let it out quietly. This was something he could not do. The town didn't trust him, and if he killed a man among them, they'd just as soon hang him as listen to his reasons for it.

"I'm sorry for your loss, Mrs. Lindson," he said softly.

"But if it's justice you're looking for, you'll need to talk to Sheriff Wilke. I have little sway with the law in these parts."

"I am not looking for justice," she said, her hands gone cold as her face now. "I am looking for revenge."

He'd thought as much. Folk got it in their heads that once a man made his living by the gun, any target was as good as another.

"I don't hunt men, Mrs. Lindson."

"I don't consider my husband's killer a man, Mr. Hunt. I consider him a monster."

Her anger was fueled by sorrow, by a broken heart. He understood it. Understood what it was like to lose a loved one, a spouse. He knew what it was like to lose a child, and a brother too. He'd been at death's elbow all his life and felt death's chill sickle slice through his heart more than once.

"I'm sorry," he said quietly. "I don't hunt men."

She folded her hands calmly across the horn of the saddle. Stared at him with a widow's eyes. "I have money to pay you, Mr. Hunt."

"Money you shall keep, Mrs. Lindson. I have another job, a more urgent task, to fulfill this day."

"Well, then. If money won't change your mind, consider this: I see the curse upon you and I know how best to break it."

Cedar's heart kicked at his ribs. Was she telling the truth? Could she be a messenger, an angel from the god who had torn his life apart and cursed him with a beast's skin? Could she know some way to end his nights chained to the moon? Or was she just a woman gone crazy with grief?

"Find my husband's killer," she said again, "and I will free you from what ails you. I will wait until sunset."

"You'll wait for what?"

"For you to change your mind, Mr. Hunt." She clicked her tongue and turned the mule, urging it into a trot, then a ground-eating lope.

Cedar stared after her, his heart pounding so hard, he couldn't hear the mule's hoofbeats over the noise of it.

The ear-cracking pop of a rail matic expelling steam ricocheted through the hills. Then the low hum of the matic chugging, and another pop, finally shook Cedar clear of his racing thoughts.

Sunset. Just one day to decide if ending his curse was worth finding a man's killer, and abandoning his hunt for the Gregors' boy.

It seemed far too many decisions for such an early hour. Though he was sorely tempted to ride after the widow, he couldn't abandon the boy lost in the wilds, who might still have a chance at living if Cedar was quick enough to the hunt. Cedar decided his own curse, and what the widow Lindson knew of it, would wait a while longer.

He took a deep breath and nodded to himself. First, he'd go looking for the Gregors' boy. If he could find him fast enough, there might still be a chance he could talk to the widow, see what she knew about his curse. The boy, if he was still alive, didn't have much time left.

Cedar strode into the cabin and shut and locked the door. He lifted the lid on the trunk against the wall. His hunting gear was there, wrapped in a wool blanket. Everything a man could cobble together to aid in tracking, catching, and killing lay within those folds. Waiting.

Cedar removed the first wrapped parcel and placed it on his bunk, deciding his course of action.

Time was running out to save the boy. But the dead man would stay dead no matter how long the widow Lindson grieved.

Jeb Lindson did not like the dirt or rocks or worms. It was cold. It was too cold.

But there was a need pulling him. Like a sweet song calling. Something he should rise for, something he should fight for, on the other side of this dirt and cold that weighed his bones down. Something he loved more than life and wanted more than death.

His brain, not being all it used to be, took time to worry an answer free. By and by it came to him.

Mae. His beautiful Mae. She was the answer. She was waiting for him. Calling.

He had vowed to be hers until death did them part. And he was not dead.

It took time, maybe minutes, maybe hours, until his right hand found the silver box over his heart.

The iron key was there. Colder than the grave, silenced by the dirt.

It took time, maybe minutes, maybe hours, before he knew what to do. Finally, thick fingers dug away the dirt around his heart. And his thoughts singled to one slow chant: *The key. The key. Turn the key.*

He grasped the key between his fingers and thumb.

Cold. So cold.

But cold could not stop him. Death could not stop him. Nothing could stop him. Not even Mr. Shard LeFel.

He turned the key. Once. Twice. Thrice.

His heart rushed with something warmer than blood, liquid fire pulsing fast and hot as the clockwork dragonfly's wings rattled to life.

It fueled him. It strengthened him. Jeb Lindson pushed at the dirt and rocks above him, digging his way free from the stones, digging his way into the world of daylight, into Mae's world.

Because he had a new thought now. A thought that filled him with a different kind of fire. He was going to kill Mr. Shard LeFel.

Beneath the shadow of a tree, a small matic clicked and whirred. Sensing the tremble of stones and dirt falling from the dead man's grave, it rose up upon spider legs, balancing its portly copper teapot body. The gyroscope and compass set within its belly pointed the ticker east. It skittered off on quick, spindly feet. East. To the rail. To the man who had left it spying here. To Mr. Shard LeFel.

CHAPTER FOUR

Cedar gave the cinch on his horse, Flint, one last tug, then swung up into the saddle. It hadn't taken long to gear up. Guns and goggles in the saddlebags, canteen of water, and fry bread wrapped and warm. He'd hunt for the boy in the day, then find his way home before the beast took him.

He had two more nights of the change. Fight as he might, he'd never been able to push off the change for the three nights when the moon came full. For three nights a month, a beast he'd be. Empty of a man's thoughts, with nothing but a killer's hunger. And he was not going to spend this night or the next as a blood-hungry beast out in the forest. It would be too easy to kill the very child he was looking for.

Day was his charm right now. He'd need to talk to Elbert's father and ride by their house to catch a scent or sign of what stole the boy.

Cedar turned his horse's nose to the wind, and started off to town. It was still early enough that dew clung to the under-brush of the forest and birds sang and rattled in the high branches of the ponderosa pines. He could taste the green and sage of needles crushing beneath Flint's hooves, could hear the distant cluck of the creek over stones. Days after the change always made the world seem clearer somehow, like he'd been stretched out so far, he needed to take in the whole world to fill up his senses and the space inside him.

Days after the change, he still carried some of the beast close beneath his skin, keen sight, keen smell, keen hearing. Enough that hunting the boy would be easier for him than any other man. He didn't like it, but admitted it was the other gift the curse gave him. And he'd used it to his advantage more than once.

Slants of sunlight through the pine and Douglas fir promised an afternoon warm enough to melt the morning's dew. Far off, the clatter and chug of matics working the rail sent out a stuttering pulse. They were crawling closer every day, trees falling, rocks crushing, iron and spikes driving, as the rail pounded down.

He'd heard folk in town say the dandy was going to run the rail from Council Bluffs straight through town, and then clean over the seam between the mountains, breaking them in two. The track would snake onward, catching the mighty Columbia River, and opening the town to traffic from both the east and the Pacific Ocean.

If it was true, the rail would be a life vein to such a little town. But Cedar reckoned there were easier ways across this territory. A man didn't build and blast his way over a mountain unless he had a powerful need to.

And it made him wonder why, of all the little towns in Oregon, Mr. Shard LeFel was aiming to bust his way right down the middle of Hallelujah.

Cedar rode out from under the cover of the forest and made his way down into town. In contrast to the general commotion of yesterday, things seemed settled, folk going about their business of readying for the coming winter. About a dozen people halfway down Main Street surrounded a coach that was unloading three passengers and their trunks. One of the riders was striding off to the mercantile, a large letter bag with the wing and horseshoe patch clearly marking it as airtrail service. The month's mail had arrived from Portland.

Cedar rode on past. He knew there'd be no letters for him. There wasn't a soul in this world left for him, not a home that would welcome him in.

Folk looked up, and looked away as he went by, conversations dying out, then picking back up as if he harrowed winter's chill behind him. It used to bother him, back when he'd first been cursed. But he'd grudgingly accepted that he could no longer count himself rightly among civilized men and women. Surviving these untamed lands took having a healthy sense of self-preservation. And even though he wore a man's skin on the outside, folk sensed the beast in his soul.

They were wise to shun him.

He took his time riding to the blacksmith's shop. Other than the constant clack and clamber of the matics working the rail, and the occasional rattle of the smaller town-bound matics and tickers clicking through the simple chores of shucking corn or milling grain, the day was strangely absent of the sound of hammer and anvil. With the rail come to town, the blacksmith hired on a dozen men for repair and forging of the peculiar hex-headed spikes, bolts, screws, and fishplates the dandy LeFel required to hold the rail together.

That sort of work, and the added business in the saloon, bordello, and mercantile, had done the town some good too.

But there was no sound from the forge this morning. No sound since the blacksmith's boy had gone missing.

Cedar dismounted in front of the shop and hitched his horse. Shop was quiet as a boneyard. There was no heat radiating from the place, only a damp smell of oil, metal, and coal. The shush of water and clack of chains from the water tower a few yards off suddenly seemed too loud in the absence of the hammer.

Cedar walked into the open shop, expecting it to be empty. It nearly was. Only Mr. Robert Gregor was there, leaning both arms on the worktable, a bottle of whiskey at his elbow, his back turned from the light.

"We're closed today," he said to the sound of Cedar's boots on the packed dirt.

"Mr. Gregor, I'm here to offer you my services."

Mr. Gregor did not stir.

"I'm here for your son," Cedar said.

"My son is dead." Mr. Gregor turned, a tin cup in his hand, and squinted against the morning light. "Unless you are a preacher or a gravedigger, you'll do me no good." He took a long swallow out of the cup, then drew it down, empty. He twisted and refilled the cup. The bottle was well over half gone, though the sun hadn't half climbed the sky yet.

"Are you a preacher, Mr. Hunt?" he demanded. "A man of God?"

Cedar shook his head. "Just a hunter, Mr. Gregor. I didn't know your boy had been found. Last I heard, he'd gone missing." He tipped his hat. "I'll leave you with my condolences."

"Didn't say he's been found." Mr. Gregor straightened and took a few steps forward, looking like a man hoping to eventuate the conversation with his fists. "Gone the night into the wilds. We searched as far as he could have run. Farther. Spent the day and the night searching. No sign of him. Not a scent, a scrap, a sound. He's gone. My Elbert . . ." Mr. Gregor clenched the cup, but did not bring it back to his lips. He swallowed several times, choking his sorrow down, his face red, his eyes fevered.

There was no worse heartache than losing a child.

"Children have a way of enduring," Cedar said, "of holding on when there's scarce hope left to hold. Your son's a strong boy. I'd like to look for him, just the same."

"Why? Are you thinking a foolish man in his grief will be parted from his money? That you can plank me for a week's pay?"

"No, sir. I'm not asking you to pay. For all I don't mingle, I understand the death of a child, the pain of it." Cedar stopped, surprised at how hard that was to admit. He had spoken so little of his loss. Not even to his own brother. "If there's a chance I can find your son, or his body for burial, then my services are yours."

Mr. Gregor gave him a long look.

"A son?" Mr. Gregor asked.

"Daughter," Cedar said. It was more than he'd shared with anyone in the last four years, and there was no more he would say about it.

Again the long look. Finally Mr. Gregor said, "I'll show you his window. We looked for tracks, for . . . blood."

Cedar waited as the blacksmith paced out of the shop, then followed. The man was a good hand taller than Cedar, thick in the shoulders and arms. He stank of whiskey and sweat, but his stride was even and strong as he led the way around the back of the shop and to the house beside it, which, with the second floor above, comprised the Gregors' home.

Two tall, thin glass windows were fitted upon the ground floor of the house, with a taller, thinner window centered above them beneath the peaked roof on the second floor. The rest of the house, with a proper porch and a plot of garden gone to seed, spread off to their right. Mr. Gregor stopped between the bottom-floor windows.

White lace curtains, likely brought in from England, were closed behind the glass panes. The windows began about waist-high and rose a good way above Cedar's head. The wooden sills were recently whitewashed, clean and unmarked.

"Which one?" Cedar asked.

Mr. Gregor stabbed one finger in the air. "Attic."

Cedar craned his neck, then took a few steps back to get

a look at the second-story window. Narrower than the two windows below, it was built in the same manner: strong wooden casing, double-hung sash, no broken panes.

"Boy's four, five?" Cedar asked.

"Four this winter."

"Ever opened the window on his own?"

"No. It stays locked and he is . . . was . . . too little to reach. But he's always been curious. Head in the clouds, stars in his eyes. Easy to wander. And such stories he'd tell . . ." He swallowed, his words too thin to carry the weight of his voice.

Cedar studied the lengths of dark clapboard above and below the window, looking for marks or scraping of ladder or rope. Even with his sharpened vision, nothing seemed disturbed.

He studied the ground a few strides away from the window, out where the boy would have landed if he took a fall. He knelt, fingered the hard soil. The blacksmith was right. There was no sign of blood or scuffle. He glanced back up at the window, reckoning the angle of fall. This was where Elbert would have landed and yet there was no sign of an impact.

"You sure he didn't wander out the door?"

The blacksmith shook his head, wild red hair jostling. "Lock's set up too high. I make sure it's in place every evening. Had to unlock the door before I went out looking for him in the morning."

Cedar stood, dusted his hands, and walked across the dried grass and patch of dirt toward the house again. Leaning in close to the wall, he stood between the lower windows and craned his neck to look up. From this perspective he could see the bottom of the sill. Two thumb-sized holes were burned into the wood.

Cedar pressed his hand against the wall to get a better angle.

A vibration tickled across his palm like sunlight over a cold limb. He held his breath. Within the space of three heartbeats, he heard music. Distant, sour, pipe and strings. Not music of this world. That vibration, that song, was the mark of the Strange.

The Strange had been here. Left a trace of music in the wood, though it was a faint mark that would soon fade. If Cedar hadn't just been bound by moonlight, he wouldn't have sensed it at all.

The child hadn't fallen out of the window. He'd been taken by the Strange.

The porch door opened and Mr. Gregor's wife stepped out. She was a tiny plump woman with dark curls in a storm around her head.

"Robert?" She caught sight of the two men, then walked across the yard to stand next to her husband. Her head reached only as high as the blacksmith's chest, and she held a dishrag in her hand as if she'd forgotten it was there. He could tell she'd been cooking, likely for the funeral. And crying.

"Good day, Mr. Hunt," she said, looking at the rag in her hand, and nothing else.

"Mrs. Gregor." He nodded.

"Will you be by for the service?"

"I don't believe I will, ma'am. I have business that, regretfully, will keep me."

"Yes," she said, as if she hadn't heard his reply. "I understand." She stepped closer to her husband, but did not look away from her hands.

"Now, Hannah," Mr. Gregor said, "Mr. Hunt's a tracker. He's going to do what he can for us."

She inhaled a quick breath, a spark of hope flushing her cheeks as she looked up at her husband.

"To find him. For the burial," the blacksmith said gently.

Mrs. Gregor made a soft sob, and clutched her husband's shirtsleeve. She tipped her head down again, hiding her tears.

"I'll do what I can," Cedar said. He planned to look for more than the boy's body. He planned to find him whole and breathing, and return him to his parents. He didn't tell them that the Strange were likely involved. He wasn't even sure these God-fearing folk believed in the Strange.

There was a chance, pale as it was, that the Strange had swept off with Elbert for folly designed to keep him alive, though he'd ask no odds on it.

"You have my word I'll do all I can."

Mrs. Gregor pressed her face into her husband's sleeve, weeping openly now. The blacksmith wrapped his arms around her like a bear with a cub. He turned his back on Cedar, protecting his wife's privacy.

"I'm obliged to you, Mr. Hunt. Now, if you'll excuse us." He walked with his wife, shushing her muffled sobs as he guided her back to the house.

Cedar knew better than to give either of them false hope when the Strange were involved. He had tangled with the Strange before. The curse the god harnessed him with meant he could sense them most times. Worse, they seemed to be drawn to him like a needle pointing north. And though the god had compelled him to hunt the Strange, at every full moon, Cedar fought that urge and chained himself down, denying the god's will.

He'd be no one's pawn, man or god, cursed or otherwise.

But now his sense of the Strange would aid in finding the boy, though he'd need more than a keen eye to track them in time. More than just his instincts and luck. He'd need tools. And if those tools were made of the metal beneath the ground on which the Strange walked, all the better.

Silver was best. Which was his first bit of luck. He happened to know three men who had silver at their disposal, and who might have a passing acquaintance with the ways of the Strange.

Cedar strode back around the building, unhitched his horse, and swung into the saddle. The water tower clacked, splashed, then gave out a three-tone pipe-organ whistle, like a chorus of steam angels hollering for all their might. Daylight was burning. He'd need to work quickly if he wanted to find the boy before night took his soul again, and still have time to ask the widow Lindson what she could do to break his curse.

He turned north and set Flint at a lope to the mountains and the Madder brothers' mine.

CHAPTER FIVE

Jeb Lindson had learned that night was better for walking, even though the dark made it hard to see. So he had walked through the night. One foot up, one foot down, forward, forward. No matter the dark. No matter the blood dripping from his fingertips, or the rattle of the dragonfly's wings shivering in his chest, working like a bellows to keep his heart beating.

He had a man to kill. A man who killed him three times. A man who intended to hurt his Mae. Jeb knew that monster, that Shard LeFel, was a devil in a coat of hair and bone.

So Jeb kept walking. Walking to find the devil. Walking to keep Mae safe.

Mae. His beautiful Mae. Jeb paused, closed his eyes for some time, though the wind blew cold, tugging on the tatters of his shirt, and the night shifted with hungry creatures catching the scent of him.

He worked hard to remember her face, her lips, her laughter. Finally pictured her, as on their wedding day, the scent of honeysuckle in her hair, the sweetness of strawberries upon her lips as they kissed beneath white lace in the morning light.

Mae. His love. His wife. Until death did them part. He'd made that vow. Given that kiss to seal his heart, life, and soul to her. Forever. And she had given him her heart, life, and soul. Forever.

He opened his eyes. "Forever." Jeb went on walking again, one foot, one foot, through the night, the hangman's noose still around his neck dragging on the ground behind him.

By and by, dawn pushed birdsong and watery light down from the hills. Daylight, even weak at dawn's break, was too strong, too hot, for him.

The light burned where it touched his flesh and smoke rose in soft, foglike wisps. Jeb moaned.

Burning was not good. No, not good at all. Burning only ate up what strength he had.

And he needed his strength. All the strength in his bones and soul.

He had a devil to kill.

He stood for a long while, smoke lifting from his skin, as he thought things through. Finally, it came to him. The light was hot, but shadows were cool. Shadows were slices of night stretching out across the day. He needed the night, so he needed the shadows. He looked around. He was still in the forest where plenty of shadows clung to trees and stone. He walked toward a shadow beneath a tree and sighed as the damp wing of night covered him.

His skin cooled, the smoke thinning until it was gone. He waited, because he knew he should. Long enough for his flesh to be as whole as it could be. Long enough for his brain to think out how to get to that next patch of shadow. Because there was more than a need to see Mae moving him on. There was hatred, hot and pounding. There was a killing to be done.

Jeb took a step, but noticed a bird perched on a branch just above his head. The bird clicked and warbled.

It was a pretty thing—copper head wide and round with bright emerald eyes and a brass beak. It cooed, owllike, and clattered its wings.

Jeb stared at it. It stared back.

That was no bird. No, not at all. Birds didn't have clamps for feet. Birds didn't tick. Birds didn't tock.

That was the devil's toy. Shard LeFel had devised it to look for him, spy on him.

Jeb licked his lips.

He caught up the owl with hands too fast for a dead man. Then squeezed. It was easy to see how the bird fit together—a mite easier to see how to bust it apart.

The bird scratched and bit, nipping flesh off the thick of his hand. He held tight. There was something inside the bird that kept it alive. Not steam like any other matic he'd ever seen—the bird wasn't hot enough, though there was a coal and a small portion of water running through it. Something more than springs, more than clockwork. Something strong. All his life he'd known the best way to figure out how something came together was to tear it apart.

Jeb squeezed the bird in one hand, keeping the wings tucked tight, the tiny tick in its breast growing faster. He ran his fingers over its head feeling for the seam. Easy as a thumbnail through an apple skin, he split the weld on its face. The bird's head hinged open.

Inside that metal skull was more metal, fine gears and cogs that would make a watchmaker drool. But it wasn't just a tightened spring that made the owl tick. He pried open the back of the bird.

The innards looked like a watch, tightly coiled and geared, layers of things that ticked, pumped, spun. But there in the center of the copper and brass was a glass vial. Filled with an unearthly green light. Glim.

This matic wasn't fueled by steam alone. Something more fired it—the rarest thing of all—glim. Not a good magic, sweet magic, earth-and-home magic like his Mae's magic, glim was something else altogether. They said it was harvested by airships from the top of the sky, filtered, and trapped in glass to be sold to only the richest men. Jeb had never seen it, and never in his life had enough money or land to sell for even an ounce of it.

But it was a wondrous discovery that the most scientific of minds had put to use. Glim enhanced all that it touched. Made a piece of coal burn twice as long, made a crop yield three times its fruit, and, it was rumored, could even give a man a long, long life.

This glim must have come from whatever dark hole Shard LeFel himself had crawled out of.

Jeb smiled. He was hungry for that. For the glim that fueled an undead thing. Powerful hungry.

This he understood. This he could destroy. So easy.

He tore the ticker apart and broke the vial with his teeth. He sucked up the glim, taking it down like corn whiskey, and licking his lips for more.

It tasted good, the glim in that matic's brain. It filled him. Warmed him. Made him stronger. Fueled him too, just like it fueled the undead owl.

He dropped the ticker, which fell in a clank of copper and brass amid the brush and pine needles. Then he started walking again. A little faster than before.

And for the first time since he died, Jeb Lindson laughed.

CHAPTER SIX

Shard LeFel enjoyed his luxuries. He saw no need to be in anything but the finest comfort at all times. His train carriage was adorned in gold and rare woods, precious jewels set in the rococo arched ceiling of the long, wide living car that dripped with crystal gas-lamp chandeliers, wall sconces, and tapestries. Mirrors, murals, and reliefs depicted scenes from a much older earth where creatures of myth feasted upon pleasures, and his kind—the Ele and the Strange—walked the land as gods.

LeFel was not mortal by choice. Banished by his brother, the king, to this mortal land, he had been trapped here for three hundred years. And though he was immortal in his land, here, in this savage place, time chewed upon his soul and flesh like a dog tearing through meat. He was dying, becoming more and more frail no matter what concoctions or devices he employed to slow time's cruel hammer.

The beat of his death drummed ever nearer. When the full moon waned in just two days, he would die. Unless he returned to the immortal realm.

But he had not spent his exile brooding over his circumstances. He had spent it investigating the ways of cheating his sentence, and, thusly, his death. His long life had been devoted to finding a way to return to his own lands, so he could live forever, and mete his revenge upon his brother.

That one clear goal had guided him through the decades with a hard desire, and had, in its own way, afforded him yet more pleasures.

He was well schooled in the kept knowledge of magic, and well versed in both the wild and gentle sciences.

And he, a highborn Ele, had befriended the lowly Strange.

A most unusual happenstance. And one he had used to his best advantage.

In trade for their knowledge he had given the Strange a promise: he would lay the dead iron down, cutting paths to guide the Strange across the land so they could slake their hunger on the nightmares and pain of mortals, and walk as men.

Through the ages, some Strange had found ways to hitch upon a nightmare, slink through a shadow, and pluck, howl, or frighten in this mortal world. But they were little more than wisps, ghosts, frights. He had given them Ele knowledge of blood and moonlight and earthly magic. All things the Strange needed to devise bodies of flesh, bone, and other odd bits and gears into the dark and delightful Strangework.

His knowledge opened the New World to their appetites. Their knowledge devised for him a doorway home. But even so, the door would swing closed too swiftly for him to walk through, and only the most nimble of Strange would be able to slip between lands before the door was sealed for good.

So the Strange had gathered up bits and pieces and created a device most clever to keep that door open—the Holder. And LeFel had spent the last fifty years keeping the Holder hidden from the king's guards—those few men who walked the land protecting mortals from the Strange and Strange devices.

LeFel lifted the Holder in his hand, tipping the sphere to catch the thin light of morning in all the hue and tone fine metal could offer.

The Holder was the size of a large apple. Seven intricate pieces fashioned from seven ancient metals locked and bound together to create it. Gold, silver, copper, tin, lead, native mercury, and iron bound the cogs, gears, pistons, cranks, and valves that held still and silent within and without the sphere, overlapping, arcing, flowing as if carved by wind and softened by hammer. Odd symbols further detailed the jewellike Holder, the cryptic language of the Strange binding forbidden spells into the metal. And at the heart of the sphere, glimpsed by the artful wedges through which the inner workings could be seen, was a glass vial of liquid mercury, suspended by copper strings.

Each piece glittered and glowed, in equal parts art, design, and device. Shard LeFel took delight in knowing that fitted together the Holder was a great weapon, and also that each piece, if left separate, was a wicked weapon of its own. But the Holder would serve for him one purpose: to hold open the door between the realm of the Ele and Strange and this mortal dirt.

This was even more valuable than the glim dragonfly caught in the cage. This was even more valuable than a king's vault full of gold and glim. With this one device, Shard LeFel would shuck his mortal sentence, and change the face of the land forever.

The matics up the rail let out a screech and thump, a chain breaking free with a load of wood. Shard drew his gaze away from the Holder, and rose to replace it within the protective dead iron chest set deep within the floor of the railcar.

"Lord LeFel." A murmur from the far end of the carriage. Mr. Shunt had been no more than a shadow lingering, but now he took a step into the lantern light. "You have a guest come to call."

LeFel leaned back from setting the lock on the chest,

dropping the key into his pocket and picking at the lace of his cuff. "Who?"

"The storekeeper's daughter, Rose Small."

LeFel frowned. He had not met the daughter, though he had dealings with her parents. Owners of the mercantile, the Smalls were rich and set to benefit most by the rail's completion. Still, they offered to sell him their land to drive the rail straight through town, straight through the mercantile, the mill, and the church. He had agreed to see their terms, though he would have taken their land whether they offered it or not.

He would have made them beg him for the honor. May have made them bleed their consent.

But now, with the waxing moon drawing so near, he knew he would not remain behind to finish the rail. His investors from back East and overseas would insist that the project was completed with or without him. If anyone balked, Mr. Shunt would dispose of their reluctance, and their bodies.

"The visitor, Lord LeFel?" Mr. Shunt said again.

Likely, the daughter was bringing papers for his perusal.

"Yes, yes," LeFel said, irritated. "I will receive her outside."

Mr. Shunt narrowed his eyes at LeFel's tone, but bowed, one spindly hand fastened to the brim of his black stovepipe hat. He turned and was gone, uncommonly quick.

LeFel rose and donned his long coat. He stretched out his fingers and curled them in fists before stretching them out again to ease the ache of age in his bones. These small, painful mortal annoyances fueled his hatred for his brother, and sharpened his need for a most brutal revenge. LeFel straightened his lapel, then took up his cane and stepped outside.

Mr. Shunt waited at the bottom of the stairs with a massive black umbrella unfurled against the sun and held so that LeFel could enter its shade.

The day was bright, morning's shadows swept away by sunlight. LeFel paused midway down the stairs and surveyed his work.

His three private train cars were settled on the spur of tracks he'd insisted be constructed for his comfort. The rail itself was several yards to the west, trees and brush cleared back from either side of the rail leaving stump and stone jutting up out of the earth like old bones exposed to the open sky. The track cut sword-straight, stabbing northwest.

Down the grade a bit, the great hulking matic worked. Long screwlike wheels shaped like bullet cartridges the size of small canoes were attached to either side of the device. The spinning of the screws propelled the matic, and allowed it to scramble up and across the roughest terrain even while dragging a ten-foot iron blade at its base that leveled the ground behind it.

Alongside the rail, two matics the size of draft horses with brass boiler bellies, continuous track wheels, and loads of wooden ties on their backs trundled over the leveled grade. They dropped hand-hewn ties like setting coffins in graves, straight rows so close together you couldn't roll one without hitting its neighbor.

Steam puffed white and gray plumes from the pipes in the matics' heads while heavy brass centrifugal governors spun tight circles of gold and steel, and iron pistons pumped and turned gears.

Not a spot of rust on LeFel's matics. Not a drop of oil out of place. These metal beasts were well and lovingly tended.

Behind the matics worked the men. A crew of thirty rawboned French, British, Scots, and Indians heaved the iron rail down upon the ties already dropped, and used pry bars, spike mauls, and shovels to dig, lift, and hammer the rails into place.

It was hard work and broke a man down slowly. Likely as

not, it killed him too. It was the kind of work, the kind of pain, LeFel enjoyed watching the men shoulder. He kept their rations low and their pay modest, always seasoned with a small promise of better times ahead.

The wind snatched at bits of their crude work song and threw it his way, a sorrowful chant longing for hot meals, hard drinks, and the women they'd left behind. He inhaled their sorrow, their pain, and swallowed it down like an elixir, savoring every note. The rail had brought him more pleasures than he'd imagined it could.

The rail was moving forward, pounding forward, steaming forward. And soon the Strange would follow it out of the pockets and crannies of the land to every shore.

"Good morning to you, Mr. LeFel," a cheerful voice called out. A young woman walked toward him, her dun horse plodding behind her.

She didn't look a thing like her mother or father. She wore a plain cobalt blue dress with a split riding skirt, the dress so tight across her narrow ribs and waist that it required no corset. Her hair was pulled back in a braid, and a silk bonnet covered her head. He half expected her to be barefoot, but instead sturdy boots that may have been her father's castoffs adorned her feet.

Her cheeks were tanned and freckled, giving her a bit of a wild look, but when she smiled, she took the light out of the sun.

There was something about her that set his blood on fire.

"Good morning, my dear lady," LeFel said, surprised at his rise of emotions. "I don't believe we've met. You are . . . ?"

"I'm sorry. Where are my manners?" She blushed and LeFel's heart tripped a beat. Why did this border ruffian stir him so? She was certainly not the first woman he'd laid eyes upon, nor the most beautiful or refined.

"My name is Rose Small. Pleased to make your acquaintance." She did not extend her hand, but instead gave him a small curtsy, her gaze boldly holding his just a moment too long. There was no hint of fear in her eyes. No, the only emotion he could pin to her was faint distrust and far too much curiosity than was healthy.

A sweet flower with an iron spine. What an interesting dish.

"It is my pleasure, alone," he said. LeFel stepped forward and caught up her hand, intending to kiss the back of it, to taste what she was made of. But something around her neck made him pause.

She wore an oval locket the size and color of a robin's egg. That charm should not be in her possession. The locket was gold and silver washed in blue, carved with protection spells no mortal should set eyes upon, much less wear as an adornment.

It was an object of the Strange realm and given to very few.

"What a lovely locket you're wearing," he whispered.

Rose leaned back as if his words were heat and fire. She pulled her hand away from his and drew a leather envelope out of the satchel she wore over one shoulder. "Thank you kindly, sir," she said. She held the envelope out for him to take. "My parents, Mr. and Mrs. Small, asked for me to bring this out to you."

LeFel took the envelope from her fingers, his eyes still on the locket. "And where did you come by such a bauble?" He did not open the ties that kept the envelope closed, but instead peered down into the woman's eyes, and held her with his gaze.

He smiled, knowing the power of his attention when turned upon the fairer sex.

She hesitated. Her weight shifted to the edges of her feet, perhaps to run, to flee.

"It's been mine since birth, I'm told." Her words tumbled a little too quickly. "Found on me when I was left at the Smalls' doorstep."

She swallowed and pushed tendrils of hair stirred by the wind back away from her face. A thimble left forgotten on her right ring finger glinted in the morning light, and he noticed the black smudge of coal at the edge of her hand.

She was blushing again, understandably embarrassed she'd admitted she'd been abandoned. "Just a trinket of brass and tin, a silly thing." She gave him that smile again and tucked the necklace beneath the collar of her dress.

LeFel held her gaze, letting some of his hunger play through his expression. "I consider it a lovely trinket, no matter its common beginnings. From such humble soil rare beauty has grown," he said smoothly.

"I don't know that its beauty is all that rare," she said.

"I wasn't speaking of the locket."

Her eyes widened as his words sank in. But instead of falling for his sweet words, she took a step backward, her hand falling to the pocket hidden in her skirt. He wondered what she kept there. From the beat of her heart, he'd assume it was a gun.

"That envelope has the papers I was asked to bring to you," she said with a nod. "I'm sure my mother and father are looking forward to your reply. I'd better be on my way. Good day, Mr. LeFel."

"Oh, come, now." LeFel smoothly caught her elbow before she could walk off, effectively keeping the gun out of her reach. "Won't you have a cup of tea with me before you go, Miss Small?"

"I don't believe—"

"Surely, your parents wouldn't think poorly of a few moments indulging my humble hospitality. I so rarely find time to socialize with the fine ladies of Hallelujah, what with all the work I must do to see that the rail is completed. We shall sit there"—he pointed at a distance toward the trees and away from the rail—"beneath the canopy my man Mr. Shunt has erected, and oversee this fine morning. Mr. Shunt, fetch our tea."

Mr. Shunt bowed, and slipped silently up the stairs to the train carriage.

Rose looked after Mr. Shunt, then back at LeFel. He could tell she was sorting her options, looking for a way out. Fear had taken the sun out of her smile and he savored the shadow of her distress.

"You are too generous, Mr. LeFel," she finally said. "I'd be happy to sit awhile. A cup of tea would be very welcome, thank you."

"This way, then, my dear." He stretched his arm, pointing toward the red silk canopy set at the edge of trees not far from his train carriage. Rose kept a tight hold on her horse's reins, her other hand tucked in the pocket of her dress. Bits of metal and wood jingled quietly at her touch. Perhaps she did not carry a gun.

They made their way across the dirt and grass, her horse following quietly behind her.

"I was unaware you were orphaned," LeFel began, probing for her pain. "Did the Smalls know your parents?"

"No one knew my parents," she said steadily, as if she'd been repeating this statement all her life. "It's assumed my father was likely killed in the war. And my mother couldn't care for me. Plenty of speculation as to why that was."

"Yes," he said softly. "Such a tragic state of things, the war." They had reached the silk canopy, where two red and gold tapestried chairs sat beside a marble and wrought iron table.

Rose led her horse over to the nearest tree and wrapped the reins over a low branch. LeFel pulled a chair out for her and waited.

Rose walked back to him and paused beside the chair. He could see the fear in her, could see the hard line of her back as she fought not to run. That fear tasted sweeter to him than any rare wine. What was it about this woman that burned so bright within? It was more than the locket. There was something about her. Something Strange.

Sit, my little bird, he thought. *Drink at my table so I can better see your delicate bones.*

A gunshot rang out. Loud. Close. Two more followed.

LeFel and the men working the rail looked toward the sound, toward the other side of the rail track. The crew boss, a one-eyed Norwegian who was as wide as he was tall and as merciless as LeFel himself, rode the tinder cart, keeping a high watch over the workers and matics. He turned and swung his shotgun toward the thick undergrowth beyond the rail.

The three Madder brothers stumbled out of the brush, rifles in their hands. All three men were so drunk they couldn't walk a straight line if their feet were tied to it.

A hare was flushed out of the brush in front of them. It dashed to cover while the brothers hollered. One of them took another wild shot at the animal and hit the side of a pony-sized matic hauling a cart of water, the bullet ricocheting like a snapped piano string.

Rose's horse spooked and reared, tangling bridle and reins in the tree. "I'm sorry, Mr. LeFel," she said as she hurried away to her horse. "I do think I'd best be heading home. Perhaps I can stay for tea another time?"

She didn't wait for his answer. Just swung up into the saddle and turned her horse east, away from him, the rail, and the Madder brothers as quickly as she could.

LeFel snarled in irritation. He had barely had a taste of

her. Rose Small was a question he wanted answers to. Especially since the Madders seemed to have gone out of their way to show up just as he was sitting down with her. Perhaps, he thought, she was connected to the brothers. Wouldn't that be interesting?

The brothers had been a thorn in his side for years. He didn't know what their drunken game was today, but he knew they would not come out here, to the rail, to his place of power, on a whim.

They wanted the Holder and they suspected he had it. But they did not know where he kept it hidden, nor that he had devised a door for it to fit upon. It was particularly satisfying that it was here, right beneath their noses, and yet they could not see it nor do him harm without fear of letting the device loose in the world. For if it was freed, the Strange-worked metals would bring about destruction to the land, and the people who stumbled upon it. Worked within each metal was a curse. Depending upon where the metal lodged, plague would spread, the undead would rise, and insanity would claim the minds of reasonable men. Left alone in the world, the Holder was sure poison, and would bring about bloodshed, blight, and war.

He had his finger on the trigger of a gun that could do more than kill a man—it could demolish this new land. Such a sweet dilemma the Madders found themselves in: unable to call his bluff for fear of destroying the very land and people they protected.

The crew boss yelled at the men to get back to their shovels and irons, then strode over to the Madders and yelled at them to take their guns and leave before he dragged them back to town behind a wagon.

The Madders laughed, patted one another on the back, and seemed to finally get it through their thick, drunken skulls that they were outnumbered.

Mr. Shunt arrived at LeFel's elbow, a shadow sliding upon shadow, the silver tray and tea balanced on his fingertips.

"Tea, Lord LeFel?" Mr. Shunt asked.

"Yes, Mr. Shunt. Tea." LeFel settled onto one of the chairs and watched the brothers stumble back into the dirt and brush, singing a tawdry song.

Mr. Shunt poured tea from a kettle made of gold, the aroma of flowers and honey filling the air.

"They can hunt their hare. They can play the fools," LeFel murmured. He brought the tea to his lips, and glanced back the way Rose Small had gone. "They can snoop, they can pry, but they'll never find the treasure I have beneath lock and key. This game is still mine. And before two days are out, I will drown them in their own blood."

CHAPTER SEVEN

Rose eased her horse down out of a trot as soon as she was over the hill and well out of Mr. LeFel's sight.

The voices whispered to her as they always did. Trees saying they were trees, growing upward and digging deep, settling in for the season's turn. Plants underfoot calling out a breathy little song of root and wind and long days burning short.

Rose turned them a deaf ear insomuch as she could. She'd always been able to hear the thinking of living things. Over the years, she'd tried to make it stop. Not much seemed to help. The living world had a hundred and a half things it thought needed to be said, though most of it was just the babble of growing and dying.

Wearing the locket helped quiet the ruckus some. So did keeping her hands busy making and devising.

She knew it was crazy to say she could hear things. She'd told her father about it once when she was just about six. He'd beaten her soundly, then kept her on her knees for three and a half days, praying for a saved soul.

Though it pained her, she'd lied to him straight to his face and said all that praying had done the trick, and the voices were gone. He'd told her to tend to her chores that had languished while she was atoning for her sin. And then he'd never smiled at her again.

Somehow, Mrs. Dunken caught wind of what she'd been on her knees for—likely Mrs. Small had told her. Then the whole town knew it. Knew she was crazy.

No one had looked at her the same since, no matter how hard she'd tried to hide her strangeness.

Too wild, they said. Touched in the head. A pity she'd never amount to anything. A pity she hadn't died young. No wonder her mama left her on a doorstep.

Now, at the ripe age of seventeen, it was clear she was unmarriageable.

Rose tipped her face up and blew out the breath she'd been holding, trying to push some of the old pain away. Yes, she'd wanted a husband and children. Once. But that life wasn't ever coming her way.

She'd lost it the day she told her daddy she wasn't like other children.

It was the blacksmith, Mr. Gregor, who had taken her in. Let her sit at his bench and watch him work metal over fire so hot, it took her breath away.

She didn't hear the metal like she heard living things. But she seemed to understand it better, the way it could be dug up, melted, hammered, and molded. She would sometimes stop still in whatever she was doing, caught by the realization of how a brace could change the power a matic could muster, or how an extra wheel, a shorter chain, or bits never put together before could make something different. Something new. Something worthwhile and good.

Some women were clever with thread and cloth. Some with cooking and gardens. Rose was clever with metal, spring, and cog.

Next spring, she planned on leaving. She'd take what money she'd tucked back for herself, and she'd ride until she found a place in this wide world where she could make things, turn things, devise things, no matter that she was a woman.

Maybe she'd come up with a medical device, something that helped the lame walk again. Maybe she'd find a way to catch the light of a star and stick it in a jar for the kitchen table. Maybe she'd devise an airship powered by nothing but a song.

One thing was for sure: she refused to die out her days here, pitied, scorned, and alone. She even had a hope, though it was small and wan, that she might stumble across kin. That there was family out there somewhere, who knew the color of her mother's eyes, and had once heard her father's laughter. That there was family who knew her real name.

The matics puffed again, a loud thump of air pounding down. Rose wished she'd thought of bringing a coat or shawl. Even though there was still heat in the day, that Mr. LeFel sucked all the warmth out of a person.

He was clever; that was clear. He was charming and breathtakingly handsome. But he had the feel about him of a snake hidden in reeds. The strangest thing was that all the trees and plants and growing things went dead silent around him.

She'd never seen that happen before. Not once in all her years with all the folk who had stopped through her parents' shop. Living things didn't stop living just because a man walked by.

Unless that man was Mr. Shard LeFel.

Rose rubbed at her arms to take the chill out of her skin. Whatever sort of man he was, she wanted nothing more than to be away from him. She'd done her part and delivered the papers. If luck was with her, she wouldn't need to be anywhere near that man for a long, long while.

CHAPTER EIGHT

Mae didn't have much time. By the new moon, she'd be headed back to the coven, whether she wanted to or not. She'd vowed her life to Jeb, and those vows bound them together stronger than anything else on this earth. But now that he was dead, other vows, older vows, were tightening down on her, digging in like a thousand small fingers, and dragging her home.

She paced the floor of her cottage, restless, already feeling the need to turn east. Cedar Hunt had refused to help her. Unless he changed his mind, she would have to find her husband's killer on her own. And soon.

It wasn't just the vows that would force her home. It was the coven's magic.

Mae picked up a bowl of water that had sat in the moonlight, and walked with it to the hearth. Most magic could not be used for curse, for darkness, for pain. But in her hands, magic always followed a darker path.

The sisters refused to believe magic could be used for evil things. Mae wanted to believe that too. But when she called upon magic, it changed in her hands. And pain was always the way of it.

She'd done her level best to use it for good. Dark spells to speed the death of an animal who suffered. Dark spells to curse vermin so they wouldn't enter the garden. With time and practice she had found a way she could use magic as a binding between two things. Health to a bone, ease to a soul. Love to a heart. These were all good things, healing things. But it didn't take much for a binding, even the kindest of them, to become a curse.

And so she'd learned how to break bindings, untie vows, end curses, and stop magic from answering a prayer. It was not an easy thing to do. But she had practiced and learned.

The sisters were frightened of her and how magic bloomed dark in her hands. Though they never said it, she saw it in their eyes.

They had insisted she bind herself to the soil beneath the coven before she was even thirteen. And she'd done it, used her blood, and the blood of the strongest witch among them, to make it a binding that even she could not break. That binding was a rope around her foot, and if ever there was too much hate in her heart, or if ever she used magic for too dark an end, she would have no choice but to return to that soil so that the sisters could cleanse her of the darkness in her soul.

No matter what was in her way.

No matter her grief.

No matter if she wanted to stay in the home she and her husband had built, stay in the land where her love had died.

She had to return.

Mae absently wiped away the tear caught on the edge of her cheekbone. She knelt and placed the bowl in front of the heart of her home, the heart of the life she and Jeb had built together.

A small, bright fire crackled there, flames from the hickory burning clean and sweet.

To find him, she'd need a direction. Jeb had asked for work with the rail man, but he had turned him down—Mae had been there and seen firsthand how poorly Mr. Shard

LeFel treated her husband. It had made her angry, but Jeb bore it like it was no matter. But when Jeb heard a rancher out in Idaho was looking for hands to drive cattle across to Oregon City, he'd gone to see if the rancher would take him on.

He should have been home more than a month ago.

She drew a strand of wool out of her pocket, twined with a thread of her hair. At the base of the string was her wedding ring.

She had been sixteen when Jeb Lindson came walking through town on his way out west. She'd fallen in love with him from the first time she set eyes on him, heard his warm laughter, his kind words. She became his lover that winter, and his wife that spring.

And those vows, to love him and keep him, until death did them part, were the strongest and truest she had ever spoken. Those vows had overtaken even her ties to the coven's soil.

Jeb and she headed west to Oregon, with hopes of a quiet farming life on fertile ground beneath the shelter of the mountains.

It was a good life for seven years. Then something changed. Darkness crept across the land like a shadow cast by the railroad.

In that shadow, as mile after mile of iron was laid down, something Strange grew stronger and stronger.

And now her husband was dead. Fallen under that creeping shadow.

Mae drew the back of her hand across her cheek, wiping the last of her tears away. Crying would do her no good.

She could not see the future, but there were always hints, like scents in the wind that could send her down the right path to see that her husband's killer was dead and buried.

She let her wedding ring dangle from the string. The weight of the ring guided the wool in a lazy swing. Nothing yet decided, no direction for her to follow. She concentrated on her question. Should she search north or south?

The wool continued to circle.

Wooden trinkets on the shelves around the room clicked and cooed, as wind from the window propped open on the back of a wooden rabbit swirled into the house, stirring and stroking the devices lovingly carved by Jeb. One little carving set with copper springs and wooden cogs was a pipe of sorts, fashioned in the shape of two squat miners standing in a wooden river. The wind slipped in through the pipe's mouth hole, strong enough to push the miners up, giving out a bird-like warble as they rose and fell. That in turn shifted the cog, moving slots of the river slowly up and down, changing the tune like a slide whistle.

Mae glanced up at the toy. A much more delicate reed chime hung next to the whistle, yet the wind had not stirred the chime, choosing instead to make the miners dance.

Was that her direction? Miners? The Madder brothers mined the mountains to the north.

Should she go to the brothers and seek their help?

The wool across her fingertips shifted, and swung a new arc. North and south.

North. To the Madders.

She held her ring still against her heart for a breath or two. She had another question to ask. Would Mr. Hunt agree to her offer and come to her before nightfall?

She released the ring, and it settled into a counterclockwise spin.

The answer was no.

Mae closed her eyes. She had hoped he would agree to her offer. Had hoped his hunting skills would make finding the killer quick.

She had seen the curse that lay coiled within him, but

could not tell the exact nature of it unless he allowed her to use magic on him. He was a chained man, an angry man. But had refused to take the key she'd offered to put in his hand, and she did not know why.

Mae opened her eyes. She didn't need the hunter. She would find her husband's killer on her own and deal with him on her own. No matter how long that took.

The Madder brothers were said to be devisers, though no one in town had seen their contraptions. Likely they had weapons and tools suited for hunting.

She stood and dusted her skirt, then placed her ring back on her finger. A gust of wind, cold as winter's heart, rushed into the room. She gasped as it bit through the homespun of her dress and flew into the hearth, toppling the bowl over and tearing the flame apart so quickly, it smothered out. So thoroughly was the wood snuffed, not even smoke rose up the flue.

Mae stared at the hearth and the overturned bowl. It was a dark sign, an omen of death, of Strange things.

Mae shut the window. So be it. She aimed to see Jeb's murderer dead and buried. No matter how shadowed the path that would lead her down. She'd walk through death and more to make the killer pay.

She pulled her shawl off the hook, and tied her bonnet beneath her chin. Wooden clicks and clatter from wings and windmills and chimes hung about the house, stirred in the still air. If Jeb had carved words into those trinkets, they'd be whispering warnings to her.

"I mean to find his killer," she said quietly to the small bits of wood and metal, to the memory of Jeb within them. "And there is nothing that will stand in my way."

But all her anger wouldn't kill a man. She'd need a weapon. The omen warned it might be more than a man she hunted. It might be the Strange.

Mae paused at the door, then turned back to her sewing basket. She took up the delicate double-moon tatting shuttle Jeb had given her on a chain as a courting gift. It was a good-luck token, carved by his hand and inlaid with thin silver vines and gold leaves. It was the most valuable thing she owned. She didn't want to offer it up in trade to the Madders, but she would if she had to.

The knot of grief in her chest spread out and dug hard into her ribs. She took a deep breath and refused to cry a single tear more. Jeb was gone. His love, his warmth, ended. Now she had rage to keep her warm.

She folded the shuttle carefully within a bit of silk stitched at each corner with thread she'd spun in starlight, then soaked in rosemary. It wasn't much, certainly not a weapon that could be used against the killer. But it was valuable. She hoped, if necessary, it would be a good item to trade for the Madder brothers' help. If not, then she had coin in her bank safety box they might find fitting barter for a device that could kill a man or monster.

Her home was silent, not a click or whir from any corner. No longer filled with the sound of her spinning wheel and Jeb's singing set to the tick of his carving knife over wood, or the hot iron and crimps as he bent metal. It was silent as the grave. Dead as her heart.

She pulled the anger and rage closer. If death was her only life now, she would embrace it. She strode out into the morning light, pulling the door hard behind her.

CHAPTER NINE

Cedar made good time over the flats past town, then around Powder Keg Bluff. The wind was at his back, and what clouds came up with dawn burned away as the day went on. He'd been by the brothers' mine before, but not too close. The Madders made no secret of the trips and alarms they'd put in place to remind anyone who wandered their way of just how valuable they held their privacy. Rumors said they had gun-wielding matics that could take a man down at a hundred yards without a single finger touching a trigger.

Cedar didn't know whether that was true, and hadn't found a need strong enough to test the fate of a person arriving unannounced at the Madders' mine.

Until now.

He pulled up a good half mile from the mine, swung down out of the saddle, and swigged a mouthful of water from his canteen before pulling his crystal-sighted Walker out of his saddle holster. He drew his goggles up from around his neck. The enhanced-distance lens might do him some good. He stayed on the ground, less of a target out here with scant tree cover, and pulled his goggles over his eyes, tipping the brim of his hat to angle a bit of shade over his vision. With a roll of his finger over the brass gear at the side of the goggles, he adjusted his vision to high magnification. He could also slip down a thin slice of ruby, which gave a man an edge on seeing in the night, or shutter the goggles with slit brass, which made sight in the glare of sun on snow more bearable.

He'd purchased these from a watch deviser outside Chicago—the same man he'd bought his brother's watch from.

Animal trails led up the mountain, but the mine entrance and the area around it was covered by scrub. He paid particular attention to the stones stacked up in a tumble from where the mountain had shaken them loose. Looked for the telltale glint of metal among the rocks, searching for guns or tickers.

Not a flash of brass, not a copper glow. If the Madder brothers had guns or matics guarding the mine, they weren't visible from this angle.

Of course, if he was wanting to keep an entryway undisturbed, he'd keep his guns hidden too.

Cedar swung back up into the saddle and headed toward the mine. He pushed the goggles up on his forehead, the cut beneath his kerchief healed to an itchy ache. If the brothers were so set to keep folk out, they'd likely known he was there a mile ago, and closing in.

The raw call of a red-tailed hawk filled the air and beetles chirred like cogs rattling against a tin cup. The only other sounds were the steady clomp of hooves beneath him and the creak of the saddle.

The terrain started into an upward slope, loose shale deep enough that Flint was buried fetlock-deep into the rocks, each step akin to a slog through water. The shale tumbled and chattered like broken pottery down the slope, kicking up enough dust that Cedar could taste it at the back of his throat.

Nothing strange about dust at the end of summer. But the shale loosened a whirlwind, two small dust devils one-toeing ahead of him, picking up bits of leaves, twigs, and carrying them along.

Nothing strange about whirlwinds either. Except these whirlwinds didn't die out as they should. The wind went flat, but the whirlwinds danced on ahead of him, toe-to-toe and out again, a waltz of dirt and air. With no wind to drive them, they sailed against the natural world, and tottered up the road, right up the slope, right up, he reckoned, to the door of the Madder brothers themselves.

The dust devils folded in half, a bow; then the spinning wind and bits of leaves stretched out to point off toward the mountainside ahead, looking so much like two gentlemen lifting a welcoming palm toward an entrance to some kind of fancy hotel. They held like that a tick, then busted apart, leaves and dust flying off in every direction, whatever force that had kept the devils together gone now.

If there was a natural explanation for dust devils spinning when there was no wind, Cedar didn't know it.

He didn't cock his gun. Shooting at the wind would do him no good. He did rest the barrel across the saddle horn, ready if he needed it.

He clicked his tongue and urged Flint up the rise in the path, steeper than it looked, and lined with mountain mahogany and brush with thorns as long as his thumb.

At the top of the rise, the air grew damp and cool. The green scent of a stream running nearby mixed with the taste of stone and dust in his throat.

Huh. He didn't recall a year-round stream out this way. Didn't recall the Madders sluicing for gold. He wondered if they'd diverted a creek, wondered how they'd gotten it to run against its way, if that was so.

No other sign of the Strange here—no dust devils waiting to escort him on. No matics, small or large, at least none that he could see. The trail died off, leaving him surrounded on two sides by brush. To his right stood gunmetal gray stones that looked as if they'd plunged from the top of the mountain and buried themselves into the ground. Behind him was the shale and dust path.

He scanned the ground. No boot prints, no broken branches, no sign of anyone moving this way. Looked like no one traveled past this point, even though this was the only path that he'd known the Madders to take up to their mine. He'd seen them bring their wagon this way, loaded down with supplies. Not that he'd seen them bring out rail carts of stone. The brothers just brought out pockets full of silver.

It was looking like he'd followed a false trail.

Cedar cursed under his breath and checked the sky. Nearly noon now. He'd wasted half the day heading to a hole full of devisers that wasn't even where it was supposed to be.

And all that time, there was a boy out in the elements, caught up by such Strange as walked the land.

"Afternoon," he called out. "If the Madder brothers are here, I'd be obliged to a little of your time." He dug in his saddlebag and threw a purse full of coins onto the ground. It fell with a fat clink.

Funny how the sound of coins falling caught the ear louder than a man could yell.

The eldest brother, Alun Madder, pushed through the brush, looking to all the world as if he were out on a stroll, a long-stemmed corn pipe caught between his teeth, his overalls dirty and grease stained beneath a duster too heavy for the heat in the day. He had a red kerchief tied tight over his head, and sweat darkened it over his brow.

"Morning, Mr. Hunt. Bring us that striker?" he asked. He didn't so much as glance down at the bag of money between them.

Cedar pulled the striker from his saddlebag and tossed it to him.

Alun Madder caught it quick and nodded once before tucking it away in his coat.

"I'm looking for a device someone of your caliber might be willing to sell me," Cedar said.

Alun's dark bushy eyebrows notched up and he took a puff off the pipe, exhaling smoke that smelled like cherry-wood. "What sort of device, Mr. Hunt?"

"Something to track the Strange."

"Oh, now, you don't believe in those old fairy tales, do you? The Strange? Elfsies and faeimps, and creatures that lurk beneath a bed?" He grinned wider and pulled his pipe out to point at Cedar with it. "I thought you a level-minded man."

"A tuning fork of pure silver."

Alun's head snapped up. His smile was gone, his gaze sharp with a hangman's delight. "Now, isn't that a pretty thought? Forks of silver, spoons of moonlight. What do you suppose your knives should be made of, Mr. Hunt? Tears?"

Cedar cocked the hammer back on the Walker and aimed it at Alun's head. "Don't know about my knives, but my gun's made of pain."

Alun replaced the pipe in his mouth, slowly clamped down on it, watching Cedar's eyes. Finally, he laughed. "Can't help a man if I'm dead."

"Then it might be to both our favor for you to give me a straight answer. Do you have a silver tuning fork I can buy with that bag of money?"

"First you tell me exactly what you'd use such a thing for, Mr. Hunt. Silver from this mine doesn't just drop into any man's hand."

"I'm hunting the Gregors' boy."

Alun frowned, a fold crinkling between his brows. "The blacksmith's boy? Wee thing?"

"That's him."

"Lost?"

"Gone missing in the night."

"Just missing, you say?"

"Taken in the night is what I reckon. And the only trail left to find him is the music in his windowsill."

Alun smiled again, but this time it was a look of respect.

"Come on this way," he said. "Any man with an ear to hear it must have reasons to follow it. Who am I to stop a fool on his quest?" He bent and snatched up the bag of coins, stuffing it away in some inner pocket of his coat. Then he turned to his left, and strode toward the solid stone of the mountainside. "Leave your horse out here. He'll come to no harm."

Cedar dismounted, caught up his canteen and gun. By the time he'd shouldered his gear, Alun Madder had disappeared, taking a jag behind a standing stone that looked solid, but was really two stones so cleverly fit one in front of the other that the eye skittered right past the shadow of the doorway between them.

Cedar glanced back at Flint, who was already drowsing. No one seemed to be watching. Cedar's ears, sharpened as they were with the beast so close beneath his skin, could not pick up any other movement around them. Alun Madder had two brothers. It wasn't much of a stretch to imagine them waiting in ambush.

He hesitated.

"You're a cautious man for someone who uses a gun to end his sentences," Alun called over his shoulder, his voice echoing as if he was already surrounded by stone. "Come in, Mr. Hunt, before I close the door behind me."

Cedar adjusted his hat and stepped between the stones. Alun stood a good way behind the doorway in what looked to be a torchlit cave entrance. Cedar stepped into the cooler air of the cave and Alun spun a brass captain's wheel on the wall, guiding the heavy slab of stone to slide on rails silently until daylight was shut away.

"Now, then, Mr. Hunt, let's see what your money will buy you." Alun twisted another smaller valve and gas lamps flickered to life along the highest edge of the chamber, sending out a soft blue light over the furnishings and walls.

It was a chamber indeed. Three times as large as his one-room cabin, with walls that were smooth and slick, burnished to a soft glow, like ice under firelight. They were bare, except for a few wooden shelves with food and tools hooked and hanging. The only thing that caught the light was the pipes that stretched from ceiling to floor against one wall, and lined the room about knee-high. The ceiling was lost to the darkness above, where things Cedar could not see delicately scratched and skittered against the stone.

The floor of the room was dry packed dirt and there were three closed wooden doors, one to each side, and one to the back. All three doors were sealed tight as a miser's heart by locks as thick as Cedar's arms. If he had to guess, he'd say at least one of the doors led down into the silver vein, and likely hid the carts, narrow-gauge tracks, and other implements the brothers used to pull silver from the stones.

From the slight heat coming from the right of him, Cedar supposed the brothers' forge or smelting room lay behind that door.

Alun didn't seem to care that Cedar had not budged a single step since walking into the room. Once the lights caught full, he waved at a chair—stones cleverly cut in the shapes of a table, benches, and footstools farther back in the room. "Sit and be comfortable while I check and see what I may have. Pure silver." He shook his head. "Steel will give a truer tone. Where does a man like you get such ideas?"

"Books."

Alun plucked a lantern off the wall hook. "Must be an odd book, that." He stomped off toward the door at the back of the room and opened it. The light of his lantern did little to reveal more than a glint, a quick cascade of shine off an array of metals, from one wall to the next, as he stepped through the doorway and closed it.

It had been an odd book. Wil had found it, dropped in the street by a girl in a town Cedar couldn't recall. The first few months they traveled were a blur to him. What with his mind so focused on blotting out Catherine's and the baby's deaths, he'd near blocked out the world entirely.

Even so, he remembered that Wil chased the girl down to give the book back to her. But she'd slipped quick as the dickens through some door or another and Wil lost track of her.

Wil had brought the book back and spent the next several days reading bits of it out loud. Cedar recalled the leather-bound volume was slim and square, and Wil was always sniffing at the pages, saying they smelled of meadow flowers.

And he remembered Wil reading about tuning forks. Made of brass, made of copper. Steel was best. But silver— that alone could cause harm to the Strange and keep safe the wearer.

He didn't know that it would work. The book had been lost with all their belongings when the Pawnee gods leveled their curse. But Cedar would rather go against the Strange with the chance of a weapon and protection than just meet them on mortal terms.

Cedar paced, his own bootheels and spurs sounding like they'd been wrapped in sheepskin, oddly muffled against the dirt. He walked to the table, but did not sit. The chairs he'd first thought were made of crude stone were actually carved from marble and shaped to encourage a man to lean back, arms taking a slope downward like a ringlet curl. The table was likewise finely crafted, three sided instead of four, carved with a sure hand. A script framed the edge of it, lines that looked like lightning bolts, arrows, triangles, and slashes, reaching off to one end where the shape of an anvil held the corner, then off to a symbol that looked to be fire, and finally to the corner with a carving of a hammer crossed with the wavy lines of water.

He'd seen these same symbols on the Madder brothers' buckles and buttons, though not the language, if it was indeed a language that trimmed the table.

Cedar leaned closer. He'd guess the language old. Not Latin or Hebrew. This seemed tribal, but not from any of the natives of this land. Perhaps from the brothers' homeland, Wales.

He dragged a thumb over one of the lines in the table, the mark like an arrow. As he drew his thumb away, the symbol glowed blue, like moonlight on fog, and left a faint ringing of bells in his ears.

Music. Strange music.

"Might be you should sit down, Mr. Hunt," a voice said behind him.

Cedar hadn't heard a man walk up, hadn't heard a door open. Sound was lost inside this cavern like a scream behind a gag.

He turned. And saw the youngest Madder, Cadoc, pointing a gun at him.

CHAPTER TEN

I f the day could match Mae Lindson's mood, it would be raining ice and the sun would be cold as stone. She walked to the barn, her skirt catching in the knee-high grasses, the honey warmth of summer rising on the air.

Her gaze lingered the longest on the eastern horizon and she paused, feeling the tug of the call to return to the coven's soil at the soles of her shoes.

Not yet. She couldn't go home until she found Jeb's killer. She gathered up saddle, blanket, and bridle, and leaned it all against a fence post while she shook a bit of grain to call her mule, Prudence, to come round. Once Prudence had eaten the handful of corn, she saddled and bridled her, then swung up, taking nothing more than herself, her shawl, and the shuttle tucked safely in her pocket.

Mae turned northwest toward town, riding the shortest route to Hallelujah.

It was not yet noon when she came down Main Street. The town seemed quiet, even though the clatter of horses, wagons filled with crops and material for the rail, and men and women going about their errands lent to the busyness of the place. It wasn't until she stopped outside the Smalls' mercantile that she realized what sound was missing—the ring and beat from the blacksmith's shop that pounded out from dawn to dark ever since the rail's approach.

The rail depended on the smith to keep them in nails and bolts and repairs of the matics. All the farmers, ranchers, and millers in the area kept the blacksmith and his apprentices plenty busy. She couldn't imagine what would bring all that work to a day's halt.

She was sure Mrs. Horace Small would be happy to pass on that information and every other scrap of gossip if she asked. Mrs. Small didn't like Mae much, but she was more than happy to buy and sell the fine lace Mae tatted, and had never turned away a single sturdy wool blanket Mae wove.

Mae had been saving up the bit of money she made from cloth and lace for years, adding it to any extra Jeb brought in. They weren't rich, and she had never supposed they would be. But they had money set aside.

She eased down off her mule and tied her to the hitching post below the porch. A rise of men's voices, laughter mostly, rolled through the air along with the clank of the piano from the saloon down the street. Plenty of people hoping for better days. And it seemed some of them were more than happy to celebrate early.

Mae walked up the front steps and then along the white-washed railing to the open shop door. She didn't like entering the mercantile. Not because it was always dark, filled from floorboard to rafter with things folk needed to live a civilized life, some items like the dishes from China or the fine glass lamps shipped all the way from the old country. There was something about the clutter of the place, of so many things from so many lands all crowded together, that made her restless and wanting for the simplicity and quiet of her home.

Mae walked into the shop, the cooler air scented with the straw and dust of newly delivered goods. Mrs. Horace Small must be out for the day. Rose Small stood behind the counter in the dim-lit room, minding the till.

She looked over and a smile lit her up.

"Afternoon, Mrs. Lindson," Rose said.

"Good afternoon, Miss Small." Mae walked across the room. "I hope all is well with you."

Rose nodded, though a cloud passed over her eyes. "I'm good as glim. And yourself? Come into town with a few blankets before the weather turns?"

Mae shook her head. She should have thought of that. Should have brought in the blankets she'd finished over the long summer nights. But ever since she had felt Jeb's death, she'd been thinking of no other thing than revenge.

She wasn't even sure if she had eaten this morning.

"No blankets today."

"Lace, then? Mrs. Haverty was discussing her daughter's wedding dress and hoping we'd have a lace collar on hand. The shipments from back East didn't make it this far out. I reckon someone in Carson City must have a hankering for fine lace."

"No, no lace." Mae stopped at the counter where the coffee grinder sat next to candy in glass jars. She tugged off her leather gloves, one finger at a time. "I've come to withdraw from my safety-deposit box. I don't suppose your father is in?"

"He's gone to meet with some of the out-of-towners who came in early today. Investors and businessmen looking to set up business now that the rail's going to tie us to the oceans on both sides. We'll have all the news from the world at our fingertips and plenty of new people passing through. Might even get a telegraph office. Looks like Hallelujah's going to put itself on the map."

"Looks like it is," Mae said. "But about your folks. Is your mother round?"

"She's just down the road a ways. At church seeing about the wedding. These things take time and plenty of effort from all the able women." Rose looked down at the counter, and pulled a cloth from her pocket to rub at the wood. "Seeing as how it's the banker's daughter and the timberman's son, it will be a wedding of some importance."

"All weddings are important," Mae said. "Even for the most humble groom and bride."

"I reckon that's true."

Rose went back to wiping down the counter, though Mae thought there wasn't a spot of dirt left to rub. The thimble she wore on the top of her ring finger winked nickel gray in the wan light coming in from the shop's two windows.

Mae took a moment to really look at Rose. She was no longer the young girl she'd found running a kite in her fields back when she and Jeb had built their home seven years ago. Rose must be eighteen or so by now. And unmarried.

No wonder she wasn't lending a hand at the wedding preparations. The womenfolk had probably deemed her unfit for such things.

"You'll be a wife someday," Mae said gently. "There's still plenty of time for that."

Rose looked back up at Mae, and for a flash, there was hope in her eyes. Then she set her mouth and all Mae could see in her expression was clear resolve. "You're more than kind to say so." She put the cloth back in her pocket, ending the conversation.

"Now, about your business today," she said, digging up one of her sunlight smiles. "Can I help you in any way? Maybe go fetch my mother or father for you?"

"Oh, that won't be necessary. If you have the keys to the safe boxes, we won't need to trouble your parents."

"I know just where they're kept." Rose opened a drawer behind her and pulled out a set of master keys. She turned a glance over her shoulder. "I haven't seen Mr. Lindson in a long while. He working the rail?"

"No. He's dead."

Rose stopped, still as a deer under the eyes of a wolf. And the sorrow that crossed her face was heart-deep, bringing tears at the bottoms of her eyes. "I am so sorry," she whispered. She didn't say any more, didn't ask how he'd died, didn't ask if she was planning a burial, a funeral, a service with black lace.

Mae nodded, and Rose got herself busy with the locked drawer that held the keys to the safety boxes.

"Did you hear the Gregors' boy, little Elbert, has gone missing?" Rose asked softly, as if there was more than rumor resting on her words.

"I hadn't heard." Mae tried to remember how old the Gregors' boy was now. Maybe three? Four? She was glad for something different to think upon, even if it was bad news. "Did he wander off?"

Rose walked out from behind the counter, things in her apron pockets clacking quietly. "No one knows. He disappeared in the night. Right through the closed window and the locked door." She paused between one step and the next. "Is that something you'd have a way of knowing about?"

Mae looked down at her shoes. She'd never told Rose she was a witch, but Rose had a way of knowing about people almost like she could hear the truth of them without them even speaking. It hadn't been said, but Rose knew Mae was conversant with herb and magic. And unlike any of the other folk in town, who were suspicious of her, Rose had been her first and her only friend in Hallelujah.

"I don't know that I can be of help," Mae said. "Even if there were something I could do, there isn't much in me but grief." She paused, then added, "And that . . . clouds things. I don't suppose that will change for a long while."

Rose's hand gently cupped Mae's shoulder and Mae realized Rose was an inch or so taller than her. Her hand was warm and strong. Her fingers squeezed just a little. "There isn't anything more natural you should be doing but grieving, Mrs. Lindson. It takes a heart long days to heal."

Mae looked into her eyes. Rose had seen pain in her life, but Mae knew she'd never lost everything in the world worth breathing for. "The pain of loving someone never heals."

Rose pulled her hand away, flinching like she expected a switch to her back. Mrs. Small had obviously never learned to curb her temper before using the switch.

"I don't mean to overstep—," Rose said.

"And you haven't." Mae forced a smile. "I do appreciate your concern."

Rose nodded, and started off toward the back of the room. "If you'd wait out here, Mrs. Lindson," she began.

"Mae," she said. "I'd think by now you'd be calling me by my given name. As a good friend ought."

Rose tossed a smile over her shoulder and Mae marveled at the joy in it. There was something alive and glowing to her. She was the kind of woman folk should be drawn to, men should be drawn to. A strong charisma. But she'd learned to hide that light under a bushel. Mae figured she rarely showed anyone her true self. No wonder she wasn't married.

"If you'd wait a tick . . . Mae," she said, "I'll bring out your box."

Rose slipped through the doors at the corner of the shop. The mercantile wasn't a bank, but they had safe vaults made of cast iron. So heavy, it was said, each plate had needed a barge of its own and a full team of oxen to drag it to town. The Smalls had hired up the blacksmith to weld together the plates and set clever locks, so that anything within that vault needed a combination of keys to retrieve.

Fireproof, bulletproof, and heavy enough it was thief proof. People of town deposited money at Haverty's bank, but other valuables, jewels, rings, notes of property, and such, were often as not given to the Smalls for safekeeping.

Mr. Haverty wouldn't deposit money from a black man, but Jeb had done the odd job for Rose's father, Mr. Small. In return, Mr. Small tolerated keeping their money, so long as Mae gave them a blanket or length of lacework every season in payment for the safe box.

Rose once told Mae that Mrs. Small sent the blankets and lace down to her sister in Sacramento, where they fetched a high price from city folk.

Mae walked through the store, not much seeing the items for sale. Outside, the noise was starting to pick up as the men who worked LeFel's rail came into town for a midday meal, drink, or gamble.

"I think I have it all here." Rose pushed open the door, the box propped under her arm and hard against her hip. "One box?"

"That's right."

Rose carried the box to the countertop and set it down. "I forgot to ask if you have the key. My father keeps the box keys in another location I'm not privy to."

Mae withdrew the key from her pocket. "I have it here." She walked over to the counter, then set the key in the lock and gave it a turn. The internal gears snicked, and the lock sprang open.

The light in the shop grew darker as one of the railmen shadowed the door, stomping his boots of dust before removing his hat and stepping into the store.

"Afternoon, sir," Rose said, moving out away from the counter. "Can I help you find something?"

"You the owner?"

"No, sir. Owner's daughter, so I know my way around the shop. Maybe you're looking for the doctor, though?"

Mae glanced over at the man. He was rawboned, tall,

looked like he drank far more than he ate. His left hand was wrapped with a dirty cloth, stained with blood. Like all the railmen, he carried a gun at his hip.

"If I was looking for a doctor, I'd of found one," he said. "You got any of the fireproof gloves for sell? Those damn matics boil the meat off a man."

Rose gave him a smile that would sweeten honey, but still had a bit of sting to it.

"We sure do. Right back there on the shelf to the right, below the washboards. Cowhide suede with wool felt inside. Come in special from Chicago just last month."

He headed down that way, and Mae was very aware that Rose did not turn her back on him, but instead put her hand in the pocket of her apron. Mae wasn't certain what she carried in those pockets, but from the set of Rose's jaw, she'd guess it wasn't a Bible.

Mae opened the lid of the box and picked up the canvas bag. She pulled at the cords and glanced inside. This purse held more silver than copper, and no gold. She hesitated. It was enough to buy a horse, or a small matic to sort or thresh the crops, or plow the field. Maybe enough to set her right for the long winter ahead. She'd been saving it in hopes she and Jeb would one day need to put a room on the house for a child, or to send that child to a good school down in California, or back East.

No hope of that now. That tomorrow was gone. All the good this money would do now was buy her a man's death. She tucked the purse into her other pocket and closed the lid on the empty box.

Rose came back around the counter, dusting again, her gaze never leaving the rail worker for long.

Mae glanced over at the man. He slid looks their way, nervous, as if waiting for something. He did not seem to harbor intentions of the neighborly sort.

That was the downfall of having the rail push through. Too many men and women who followed the great landway were desperate folk who had supped on hard luck too much of their lives. Robberies, shootings, and more followed in the wake of the rail.

Hallelujah might be putting itself on the map, but that mark would be made in blood, as well as iron.

Mae locked the box and took back her key. "Thank you, Miss Small."

Rose nodded and put the box at her feet behind the counter, out of the man's sight.

"Is that all for you today?" Rose asked.

"I've a mind to wander the store a bit until your father arrives," Mae said. "I have a pertinent question for him. He'll be back any moment now, isn't that right?"

Rose shot her a look of thanks for the lie. "Why, I suppose he will. Said it wouldn't take him but a shake to finish his business with the sheriff. Said Sheriff Wilke might even come back to check the new rifles we got in yesterday."

At that, the man in the back stopped dawdling and came up to the counter to pay. Mae stepped aside and found herself interested in a collection of fragile glass globes with thin copper wires threading them set in a straw-filled bucket not far away. The man paid, took his gloves without a word, and left just as the tiny bird on the windowsill chirped the hour.

Outside, the water clock tower whistled out the noon bell, a melodious, lonely chord.

"I'm obliged to you," Rose said. "Never know what those sorts of men have in their mind. Mr. LeFel works them like demons. Come in wild-eyed and mean, near often as not." She made it sound matter-of-fact, but Mae could see the slight tremble in her hand as she brushed her hair back from her face. Rose might be too old to marry conventionally, but she was very pretty. Too often a man took that kind of beauty to be his right to spoil.

"You keep a gun in your pocket?" Mae asked.

Rose gave her a level gaze. "A proper woman wouldn't," she said. "But don't suppose I'm so proper as some."

Mae nodded. "That's well and wise of you."

Rose's smile was sunshine and summer breezes again. "Such talk! If my mother heard me, I'd be left scrubbing floors for the remainder of my God-given years. Is there anything else you'll be needing today? I cooked up a rhubarb pie this morning. I'd be happy to bring it out to your place this evening, and maybe sit for a bit of tea?"

"No," Mae said, "don't bother yourself."

Rose looked disappointed. Mae realized she wasn't asking to give the pie out of pity, but out of a need for friendship.

"I'm just not in the conversing mood, Rose. I'll come by again soon. To bring those blankets I've finished. And the lace, of course. When again is Mrs. Haverty's daughter being wed?"

"Not for three weeks, if a minute," Rose said. "Though they're going on about it as if Becky and John are going to burst out into vows any minute now." She'd picked up a small spindle from the shelf and she was rolling it between her hands, the wood clicking against the thimble on her finger.

Rose never held still, her fingers always flying from one thing to another as if all the world were something that needed touching, changing.

"I'll bring the lace before then. Will you tell Mrs. Haverty that for me, if you see her?"

"I'd be more than happy to."

Mae started for the door.

"I don't suppose you're looking for the Madder brothers?" Rose asked.

Mae turned in her tracks and gave Rose a long look. She

still held the spindle, but was no longer rolling it between her palms.

"Why would you think such a thing?" Mae asked, deeply curious. Rose might be winsomely clever, but she didn't seem to have a knack for reading thoughts. Mae was certain she hadn't mentioned the brothers to her.

Rose shrugged but didn't look away from the spindle and string.

"Just a guess is all. If my husband had gone to his death suddenly, I suppose I'd be looking for a gun, in the least. Maybe other contraptions in the most. The Madders have a way with contraptions that's better than the best in the old states, I've heard whispered."

She shrugged again and looked up at Mae. "It's known they devise, though no one talks about it in the cold light of day. Only by candlelight when they think there aren't ears around to hear."

"Do you know where the brothers are?" Mae asked.

"They haven't come into town today. I'd guess they're up at the mine. You aren't going out there alone, are you?"

"I won't be unarmed," Mae said. "I'm not near proper as some either."

Rose nodded. "That's well and wise of you."

The door opened again. This time a handful of women just come back from church sashayed in. They chattered like scrub jays before spotting Mae. One look at the golden-haired weaver and their perky demeanor snuffed right out, taking on the high-chin stilted manners of a trial, instead of an afternoon's chance meeting.

"Mrs. Lindson," said Mrs. Dunken dismissively. The baker's wife had a face that looked like it'd been pressed out of dough. Her eyes were deep set and nut brown, her nose a knot, and her cheeks round. She'd piled her hair up so high, it threatened to push her blue taffeta spoon bonnet right off her head, roses, lace, feathers, apples, and all. Mrs. Dunken had her nose in everyone's business, though she didn't lift a finger to keep her children—some of them, like her Henry, older even than Rose—out of making such trouble that the sheriff had a nightly seat reserved at their supper table. "Have you finally brought a scrap of lace today?"

"Good afternoon, Mrs. Dunken," Mae said. "No, I'm afraid not. I'll be bringing it to town next I come, though."

"I heard your man is gone looking for work," Mrs. Dunken went on. "Pity the rail man wouldn't take his kind. Employs all sorts. Even the savages. At more than a fair dollar. I can't imagine how you'll survive until spring."

Mae's shoulders drew back straight and hard. She'd heard worse, been through worse than four women's scathing stares and bitter barbs. She'd likely endure more before the day ended, what with the death she was contemplating. "We'll manage, thank you kindly," Mae said. "And thank you, Miss Small, for your time," she said to Rose.

"Been a pleasure," Rose said. "I'll let Mrs. Haverty know we'll have that lace in plenty of time before the wedding."

As soon as the word "wedding" left Rose's mouth, the women started up again like a flock of hens tattling over scraps of seed.

"We'll settle this nonsense for good," Mrs. Dunken said to one of her hangers-on—the long-faced, sad-eyed Mrs. Bristle. "Rose, fetch us the newspapers immediately."

The women bustled into the store, taking themselves back a ways toward the pharmaceutical counter, where glass bottles and waxes cluttered the shelves.

And before Mae could step out the door, a man was blocking her way. Tall, and wearing the newest style from New York, Henry Dunken, the baker's son, took his hat off his head and stepped inside. His eyes were green as river rocks, his jaw square as a sawed-off railroad tie, the rest of his features just as rough-hewn. He'd always had a meanness about him, and today was no different. He ignored Mae's presence and scanned the store like a surveyor judging the yield of his claim.

He pushed past Mae without a decent pardon-me and leaned an elbow on the counter. Then he helped himself to a handful of candy out of the jar and stared at his mother and her women, obviously waiting for something.

Rose came from the back of the room with a booklet of papers. "Here's all we have from the last year or so, Mrs. Dunken." She looked up and caught sight of Henry. Her eyes narrowed and her mouth took on a stubborn line.

"Where are your manners, Miss Small?" Mrs. Dunken snatched the papers from her. "You have a fine gentleman waiting for you. See to your customer." She waved a hand at Henry, and in the same motion dismissed Rose from her service.

Mae caught Rose's gaze, and Rose gave her a bored look. She didn't seem concerned about Henry. She stomped across the wood floor and stood behind the counter.

"Good day, Mr. Dunken." No honey in those words. Luckily, Henry's mother was too busy arguing about sleeve lengths to hear her tone.

Rose pulled out a ledger book and flipped through the pages. "I'll add that candy to your father's tab. Is there anything else your father will be buying for you today?"

"Now, now, Rose," Henry said. "Once I'm mayor of this town, a bit of free candy every once in a while might sugar my feelings toward your interests." He glanced down at her bosom, then gave her a wide smile.

"Miss Small," Rose said coolly. "I'd be obliged if you used my proper name, Mr. Dunken." She leaned a little closer to Henry and lowered her voice. "But I think you may want to reconsider your offer."

"Oh? Why's that?" he asked, warming to her presence.

"Because my interests all require you to cross lots off the short end of the earth."

Henry stood up tall and glowered down at her. Rose met his gaze with a bland expression. He glanced over at his mother, but she had heard none of it, then scowled at Rose again.

"And I'd be obliged if you treated me with the respect due my station," Henry said.

Rose put her hand over her mouth and coughed to cover her laughter. "Of course, Mr. Dunken. Anything more I can get for you? We have a fresh batch of pride carted in from the East, if yours has gone and gotten bruised."

Mae hid an approving smile and walked outside. Rose could take care of herself. And it'd take more of a man than the troublemaker Henry to match her.

After the warmth of the shop, the cool air felt like she had plunged into clean water. Her mule stood, head lowered, dozing in the afternoon sun.

The wind stirred, bringing with it the voices of the coven sisters calling her home.

East. She needed to be walking, needed to be packing, needed to be riding east. Mae could hear their voices as clear as the rattle and thump of the matic on the rail, as clear as the clatter and jingle of horses and gear making their way between the shops of the town, as clear as the laughter rising up from somewhere off by the butcher's shop. A pain in her chest flared out as the bind between her and the coven tightened like a string being pulled.

No. She swallowed hard and held tight to the porch rail until her mind cleared and the sisters' call eased.

She knew the sisters' call would only grow stronger. And each day she held off returning to her own soil, the more time and effort it would take for her to resist.

Mae took a few deep breaths, then rubbed Prudence's nose to wake her. She untied the reins and hitched back up into the saddle.

She looked up the street. More people walked between the wagons that were loading and unloading crates and barrels and bushels, people scurrying from wagon to storehouse. Winter was coming. The whole town knew it. Like ants desperate to get the last bit of food beneath the ground before the frost hit, the folk of Hallelujah were working to stock up against the coming storms. But farther off north, cool as the heart of a sapphire, stood the Blue Mountains. And at their feet was the Madder brothers' mine.

The sun shifted from behind a cloud, a dark shadow skittering down the street as the wind on high blew the clouds across the fields, tearing them apart until they were gone.

Sunlight poured down, strong as summer ever was, lighting the way north. As good an omen as she'd likely receive. With the sunlight on her back, Mae headed down the road toward the shadow of the mountains.

CHAPTER ELEVEN

Shard LeFel knew Mr. Shunt lingered, a dark shadow among shadows, inside the doorway at the far end of the railroad car that served as LeFel's living room. LeFel was always aware of the Strange, as one is aware of a draft that lets in the frigid breeze.

But it was not the Strange that held his interest most today. It was the two other creatures in the room—one a wolf and the other a boy.

The wolf was a mottle of black and gray, its underbelly and legs white, the tips of its ears and the top of its head pure black. It was chained and shackled, its neck caught so high and tight in the collar that it panted to breathe. Even so, it strained to reach LeFel, hungry for his blood, and would likely break its bonds if not for the brass collar with clockwork gears that let out a pitch only the beast could hear and clouded its mind.

The boy lay upon a simple cot, wrapped in a striped wool blanket as if tucked tight against a fever. His eyes were glossy; his red hair stuck up in unruly curls that were darkened by the sweat on his brow. He was staring at LeFel as if he could see right through him.

It took no collar or geis to keep the child quiet. No, LeFel had found that all it took to keep the boy complacent was the correct mixture of drugs.

"Mr. Shunt," LeFel said, more to get rid of the Strange than out of any sense of compassion, "bring the beast a crust of bread and water, and for the whelp, a bit of porridge."

Mr. Shunt bowed, one spindly hand rigored against the brim of his stovepipe hat. He turned, his long coat whispering at his ankles as he exited to the kitchen car.

The rail matics outside huffed low and steady like lumbermen heaving a two-man saw through a sequoia. Off rhythm at first, the spike mauls hit rails, drove spikes, dropped wooden sleepers to carry the track, creating a second and third rhythm—the beating pulse of LeFel's conquest of this land, and his promise to the Strange.

Still, it would take more than the Strange's door and the Holder to buy LeFel's escape from this mortal flesh. It would take a key. And that key was made of three things: the lifeblood of a dreaming mortal, the life of a man cursed by the gods, and the life filled with the magic of this earth.

Of all the devices he had commissioned over hundreds of years, of all the jewels and precious metals that had been broken down to dust to make way for this ticker or that, the most elusive thing of all had been finding each part of the key: three lives to sacrifice to open the door to the Strange realm.

He had never once concerned himself with finding a mortal dreamer—children often still saw the world through dreaming eyes, even through the most difficult of circumstances. No, finding a child to kill was easy.

But a man who was truly cursed by gods was a more difficult rat to corner. He had investigated hundreds of claims of mortals stricken by curse, and all were fakers, charlatans, or simply unfortunate beings living unfortunate lives. He had nearly despaired of finding a single man cursed by the gods.

Until he saw the wolf. Uncanny human intelligence in

those old copper eyes. LeFel had been curious enough he'd told Mr. Shunt to catch him up so he could better see him.

And when the moon went dark, the wolf revealed himself to be a man. A very cursed man indeed.

It had taken until just a few months ago for LeFel to find the last life—that filled with magic—that had so eluded him. To his surprise, he had found that magic lying heavy as a perfume on the colored man when he had come asking to work the rail. And he had tracked it back to the colored man's wife, the witch Mae Lindson.

But the dark man had stood in his way. LeFel had been unable to steal her away, kept as she was, safe under the colored man's devices and protections. Killing the man, three final times, should have finally broken his protections, and the ties of magic between the pair.

Now all that was left was to pluck the witch, like a ripe plum, and bleed her life away.

"On the waning moon, the door will be opened, and blood shall oil its gears," LeFel murmured.

The wolf flattened his ears and growled.

"You, dog," LeFel said, "have been more useful than I hoped. Tracking the witch, the child, the Strange. But in the end, it is only your death that interests me."

LeFel stood with the grace of a dancer, despite the catch in his knees, and crossed the car, the sound of his bootheels smothered by the layers of Oriental carpets. He paused in front of the glass and iron corner cabinet that shone in the candlelight like melted diamonds. Within the beveled depths was an assortment of treasures and oddities.

He drew a golden key from within his vest and let the chain fall over his high lace collar.

LeFel slid the key to the lock and opened the door to the cabinet. He brushed fingertips across the jewels, books, gears, springs, charms, boxes, and talismans that clicked and chirped and shivered beneath his touch.

He settled upon a finely made hourglass as thick as his thumb and long as his palm. Within one bulb of the hourglass were tiny golden gears, and hanging down the neck between the bulbs was a thin wire pendulum with a blue sapphire at its end. He folded his fingers around the tiny matic and closed the glass cabinet, locking it again.

He turned to the wolf, hourglass pinched between thumb and finger.

The wolf growled so low, the sound was lost to the huff and thump of the rail work outside.

"Ah, you do remember what this small trinket can do." LeFel turned the hourglass on end, tipped it back again, winding the spring. Three times. The tiny gears ticked, and the pendulum made its narrow swing, clicking softly against the glass.

The wolf growled again.

LeFel paced to the high-backed chair. Made of fine leather, goose down, and rare woods, the chair suited more than a railroad tycoon. It suited a king.

"This small matic holds very special properties," he said. "With the correct word, it is quite a remarkable device, tuned as it is to the collar you wear." He folded down into the chair.

"Shall I give you a taste of what you once were?" LeFel drew the hourglass tight against his palm. He leaned his lips in close and spoke a single word against his thumb.

The wolf growled, howled, and twisted shoulders and haunches, trying to break free of its shackles. The howls were not anger but pain. Pure sweet agony.

LeFel smiled. "Such a difficult change from one flesh to another without the aid of the moon. The gods of this land have given you their favor, and pain is your only song of praise. What cruel gods walk your mortal world."

The wolf whined, growled, and then its howls were replaced by a man's scream.

LeFel sat back, tipping his head down to watch as the beast became the man. It was a fascinating process, a curse, viewed scientifically, that should destroy human flesh. And yet, here before his eyes, the wolf stretched, spasmed, and melted into the form of a man. That aspect of the curse alone, the ability to shift forms, made the wolf worth keeping, worth experimenting on, and experimenting with. But for the passage it would pay him, the beast was invaluable.

Naked, sweating, and breathing hard, the man curled into himself, knees tucked up against his muscular chest, arms draped around them. He rested his head on his knees, brown hair catching at the beard across his jaw, and falling in a tangle to his shoulders. When his breathing quieted, he looked up at LeFel. His eyes were brown, the color of old copper.

"Let me free." The words were short, as if the shape of them was unfamiliar to his mouth, his tongue.

LeFel laughed. "You demand? I have nursed you from your wounds, fed you, kept you. Even now, you speak with the words of a man, think with the mind of a man—because of my favor. Without me, you are a mindless animal. I *am* your freedom."

The man glared at LeFel as if contemplating his murder.

Mortals never ceased to intrigue LeFel. Foolish, clumsy creatures, yes, certainly. Yet they carried a fire within them, living as if they were immortal, fighting for their short, meaningless lives, as if each day was precious as rain.

Even though he was more wolf than man, the mortal still carried pride and anger. A fire burned in him. LeFel enjoyed seeing that fire had not been broken. Yet.

"Can you feel your death approaching?" LeFel asked conversationally. "Every day spent as an animal steals from you a little more of your human intellect. Do you remember your name?"

The man's eyes narrowed. Finally, "Wil. Wiliam Hunt."

"Yes, Mr. Hunt. And do you remember why you are here?"

"To search." He frowned. Lifted a hand and rubbed his face, fingers digging at his forehead. "You told me you would cure me if I would hunt. Help you hunt. A woman?"

"Yes, a woman. The witch. And the child." LeFel pointed toward the boy.

Wil dropped his hand, and looked over, the chain and collar hampering his movement. He frowned.

LeFel waited. Waited as Wil Hunt realized he had helped LeFel imprison a slip of a child. LeFel had pulled the man out of wolf form more than once in the last three years. Not too often. No, that would blunt the blade of the game. But every time he had brought Wil Hunt respite from his wolf form, and shown him what he had done—the dead, the broken, and, of course, now the child—it had left the man raging and reminded him of his power.

LeFel never tired of it.

This time was different. Disturbingly so. The man clenched his jaw and fist, pulling his heavy shoulders back as if accepting a weight. He turned a smoldering glare on LeFel.

"Let the boy go."

"You think you can issue me orders?" LeFel threw the hourglass into the air.

Wil's eyes widened, then narrowed, his body instinctively bunching and reaching to catch the fragile clockwork glass.

"No!" Wil pushed against his shackles, arms snapping chains to their length, far short of reaching LeFel or the hourglass.

LeFel snatched the hourglass out of the air and smiled at Wil's fear, his anger, his desperation. "Never forget, cur," LeFel said through bared teeth. "I *am* your master. If you speak to me in such a manner again, I will kill that boy and feed him to you."

The French door clacked open and Mr. Shunt filled the gap. He tapped one needle-pointed nail against the silver tray he carried, announcing his presence, then ducked the doorway.

"Lord LeFel?" he murmured.

LeFel placed the hourglass on the arm of the chair, where it tipped precariously to one side. A tremble, a breath, and it would fall to the floor again.

Wil Hunt leaned his head against the wall, staring at the hourglass as if his gaze alone could hold it steady.

The shackle at his neck shifted, biting against his collarbone, but he did not shrug away from the pain, did not say any more, did not glance at the boy.

Much better.

Mr. Shunt glided into the room, looking neither left nor right at the man or boy. His overly long, strangely jointed fingers wrapped thumb and forefinger over the edges of the tray, the rest of his fingers splayed like skeletal wings. His eyes glowed yellow beneath the brim of his stovepipe hat, though the rest of his features were lost in the lacy shadows and scarves piled high around his neck.

LeFel glanced at the tray the Strange carried. "That will do. Feed them."

"Yes, lord." Mr. Shunt smiled, his teeth a row of points beneath the shadow of hat and scarves.

He moved to stand next to the man, offering him a tin cup that sloshed with water. Wil took the cup and waited. Mr. Shunt pulled a fistful of bread that smelled of oats and rye from the pocket of his coat and offered it on a flat hand like a treat to an animal. Wil took the bread without comment or question but did not eat or drink.

Mr. Shunt glanced back at LeFel, who nodded once.

Mr. Shunt pivoted toward the boy, his approach slower, more careful, as if he were stalking skittish prey. He shifted so he did not stand in Mr. LeFel's line of sight to him, then held a wooden bowl of cooked oats with a spoon stuck inside it out to the child.

The boy did not look away from LeFel, but his breathing hitched up faster the closer Mr. Shunt folded down nearer his side.

"Eat," LeFel cooed. "I am sure you are hungry."

But the boy did not move, not even to blink his eyes. The buttery aroma of oats filled the air, soured just slightly by the drugs that laced the meal.

"If you eat, I will let you go home," LeFel murmured.

"He lies," Wil Hunt whispered. "Ain't nothing to him but lies."

LeFel chuckled. "No. This man doesn't understand. You would have fallen from your window that night. We caught you, Mr. Shunt and I, and brought you here safe with us. And we'll be taking you home today. After you eat your food."

The boy pressed his lips together, his cheeks coal red against his pale face.

"Don't eat it," Wil whispered.

LeFel clucked his tongue. "Now, now. Every growing boy needs to eat. You do want to grow up to be big and strong like your papa, don't you?"

And those words, the mention of his father, finally broke the boy's thrall. A single tear ran down his cheek. He shifted his eyes, meeting, finally, LeFel's gaze. The boy nodded once.

"Good, then, good," LeFel said. "Mr. Shunt, help the boy eat."

"No," Wil said. "It's poison, boy. Don't eat it."

But Mr. Shunt had already scooped up a spoonful of the mush and shoveled it into the boy's mouth, like a bird stuffing a chick. The boy chewed, swallowed, and opened his mouth again.

Wil Hunt shifted, his heavy chains clanking. "Leave the boy alone. Do what you want to me—I'll take on whatever debt that child owes to you. Let him go, or so help me, I will tear out your throat."

LeFel rolled his head against the back of the chair. "You, cur, are less than a gnat to me. And a bothersome gnat at that. I tire of you." He picked up the hourglass and dropped it on the floor at his feet. He lifted his foot and smashed the hourglass with the heel of his boot.

Wil Hunt yelled out, in pain, in rage.

LeFel watched as he twisted, stretched, molded back into the form of an animal, a mindless beast. He lay there, whimpering in pain.

LeFel turned his heel upon the glass and gears, assuring it was crushed to dust.

"You are no matter to me now. Mr. Shunt," he said. "I believe it is time to invite the witch to join us. Bring her to me."

"Alive?" Mr. Shunt breathed, the empty spoon balanced in the air by just his thumb and pointer finger, the rest of his fingers flared out.

"Yes," LeFel said, "alive. For now."

Mr. Shunt scooped one last mound of oats into the boy's mouth. He tipped his fingers to the brim of his hat, and then ducked back through the doorway, dissolving into the darkness.

LeFel closed his eyes, letting the sound of the wolf's pain

and the boy's quiet sobbing fill him as no other nourishment could.

The crash and thrum of the steam matics outside the carriage was interrupted by a knocking at the door. He walked to the window, wondering who among his workers would dare bother him without invitation. He pushed aside the brocade curtains and squinted against the afternoon light.

There, on the steps of the carriage, was a small matic. Its portly copper body was balanced on spindly spider legs covered in dirt and dew and pine needles. The dual springs on the top of the device pumped puffs of steam out the side vents. It had been running all night, the fire within it nearly gone.

"No."

LeFel opened the door, and the little matic rattled in, coming to a rest at his feet, its spindly legs tucked beneath it.

Using his handkerchief, LeFel lifted the matic to study the alarm trip.

This was clearly the ticker he had left at Jeb Lindson's graveside. And it was also very clear that Jeb Lindson was no longer dead.

LeFel yelled, his fury cursed in a language that could blister the sun. He hurled the ticker at the wall, shattering it like a glass bell, pieces bursting apart on the floor, the embers that once drove it gone to ash beneath the heat of his words.

The wolf pushed onto its feet, head low, ears back, teeth bared. The boy, fallen once again under the effects of the drugs, did not stir.

"You will not stand in my way, dead man," LeFel said. "Not between me and the witch's powers. If death will not take you, I will tear you apart myself."

LeFel took up his curved cane and strode across the broken bits of metal to the boy. It was time he be of use. It was time to introduce the boy to the creatures LeFel kept locked away in the adjoining carriage.

LeFel paused above the cot the boy lay upon, then bent close to his ear. "Come, little dreamer," he whispered. "Time to bleed."

CHAPTER TWELVE

Cedar Hunt gauged just how quickly he could draw his own gun against Cadoc Madder, and judged it to be a losing proposition.

"Have a seat, Mr. Hunt," Cadoc said again.

"I'll stand, if it's just the same," Cedar said.

Cadoc pointedly looked down at the table where the arrow Cedar had touched still glowed faintly, then back up at Cedar. "Stones say you're hunting," he said, slow, as if each word were sorted out from among too many others.

"Stones are right."

Cadoc tilted his head, looking Cedar up from boots to hat. "You plan on killing what you're looking for?"

"I plan on taking back that which has been stolen. If it means violence, I'll not shy from it."

Cadoc nodded. "Stones say that's true."

Alun tromped out from the other room. "He's a guest of mine, brother Cadoc," he said. "You can put that blunderbuss away."

If Alun was surprised by his brother's sudden appearance, he didn't show it. Alun carried a thin wood and leather box held together with brass tacks. The wood between the tacks was dark with age, as if the box had been weathered by salt air or worn down by ten thousand fingers and a thousand hands.

"One of these should suit your need, Mr. Hunt," Alun

said. He placed the box on the center of the table, flicked the brass locks, and lifted the hinged lid.

The box was lined with black velvet that caught shadow and light like the night sky drinking down starlight. Three clean slashes of silver filled the box. Three tuning forks, each smaller than the next, nestled in the darkness there.

"And which one is for sale?" he asked.

"All of them. For the right price," Alun said. "We've other things to keep our hands busy than tuning forks, don't you say, Cadoc?"

Cadoc, still standing behind Cedar, *hmm*ed in agreement.

Cedar knew the longer he stayed in the cavern, the more daylight, and Elbert's chance of survival, slipped away. He drew just one finger along the tines and down to the handle of the first fork. It was finely wrought, but something about it didn't seem right. He'd learned long ago to trust his gut when it came to such things. So he touched the second fork, this one scrolled with a billowing etching along the handle that reached almost up to the tines.

He lifted his finger and finally rested fingertips on the smallest of the forks. Darker than the others, it was carved so that the tips of the tines flared out, sharp as an arrowhead. It looked more of a weapon than a tuning fork. He lifted it out of the box and struck it on the edge of his wrist, then set the handle against the wooden box. A clear tone rang out, louder than such a small instrument should be capable of.

Suddenly the walls, the stone, the pipes—the chamber itself—resonated with the bell tone and added to it the sound of pipe, drum, and harp, a rising, rushing tide of music not from this land. It was a call to battle, a shout, a joyous reel. Not at all the dark, sour song left behind in the boy's windowsill, this song stirred his blood and made him want to shout, to dance, to weep.

Heavy hands pressed down on his shoulder, guiding him

into a chair. As soon as the tuning fork was taken off the wood and out of his fingers, the music died, not even an echo of it left in his ears or thoughts.

He blinked. How long had he sat there, transfixed? Long enough that his eyes and mouth were both dry. The brothers were staring at him, curious smiles hidden in their beards.

"Aren't you an interesting man?" Alun murmured.

Cedar glared at the tuning fork lying silent on the tabletop. "I can't use something that strikes me dumb every time it sings a note."

The brothers exchanged a look; then Alun puffed his pipe and locked the lid of the box back down. "These forks are tuned to catch the trail of the thing you hunt. Most men only hear the old song faintly. You, Mr. Hunt, are apparently not a common sort of man." He pulled a thin length of leather braid from one of his many coat pockets. He threaded it through the eye hole in the fork's handle, then knotted it into a loop. "Maybe you shouldn't listen quite so hard."

He held the leather braid out on the crook of his thumb. "Give it a try."

Cedar took the fork again. No music. He struck it, this time against his sleeve. He pressed the handle to the wooden box. Just one sweet tone rang out—a perfectly tuned A. The song, if it had been there, was faint as reeds in a distant wind.

"Press it against anything the Strange have touched, and you'll know which way that Strange has gone," Alun Madder said. "The fork will be of little help with what you do when you find them."

Cedar pulled the fork away from the box. "Then we're settled?"

Alun chuckled. "We are most unsettled. That fork is a rarity. It cups a proper price, not just a palm of coin."

"How proper?" Cedar asked.

Alun stared at the ceiling as if chasing math through the shadows. "The coins you tossed at my feet are a little lean for such a fine instrument. You'll find no other to match it." He looked back down at Cedar. "No other in this world."

"Name your price, Madder," Cedar said. "Before the day burns down."

"The coins and a favor."

Cedar shook his head. "I won't be holding to you for two favors. The coins alone."

Alun snatched the tuning fork out of his hand, fast as a thief. "Then our discussion is done."

"And what do you think will keep me from killing you here and now?" Cedar raised the gun, aimed it at Alun's head.

Cadoc rambled over to stand shoulder to shoulder with his brother. He tipped his head at Cedar like he was waiting for the joke.

Alun puffed on his pipe. "What will keep you from killing me is that you have come to us today, out of all the days and years you've been in this town. You need this fork. And likely you'll need other devices at our disposal to deal with the Strange. You are not a stupid man, Mr. Hunt. There's that about you that makes me curious. I'd judge you for university learning. There's not a man of this town who'd take the time to nod at your grave, yet you are going to great lengths to find a wee boy of no relation to you. Don't reckon such a man kills another in cold blood, standing on the stones of his hearth."

Cedar lowered his gun. "Might not in broad daylight. Night might be a different matter." He rolled his shoulder. His temper was strung too tight across his nerves. Being in the Madders' presence, in the presence of things like the tuning fork, got his hackles up and made it hard to think straight this close to the moon. "I came for the fork."

"Yours. For coin. And a favor—on the same terms as the last favor: nothing that would harm the weak, women, or children."

"To be collected within the year," Cedar added.

Alun nodded. "I'll agree to that term for this favor only."

Arguing with the mountain itself would have taken less time. "Done." Cedar held out his hand.

Alun and Cadoc Madder leaned forward and once again shook his hand simultaneously. When Cedar pulled his hand away, the tuning fork was in his grasp.

"It can hang at your neck," Cadoc said as Alun turned to one of the line of cupboards along the wall of the room, pulling out a brown bottle, a wedge of cheese, and a loaf of bread. "Nearer your heart, the better and the truer it will lead you to the Strange."

Cedar removed his hat and slipped the fork over his neck. He tucked it down beneath his coat, on the outside of his undershirt. The Madders might think it would be best against his skin, but he wouldn't wear a device that near his bones.

"You do believe in the Strange, then?" he asked quietly, putting his hat back on.

Cadoc shrugged one heavy shoulder. "Wish that I couldn't." He paused, looked at Cedar like he was peering right through him. "You'll wish you didn't one of these days too, Mr. Hunt."

Alun set the food on the table, and handed Cadoc and Cedar a cup.

"A toast," he said. "To the finding, the killing, and the keeping. Luck to you in your search for the blacksmith's boy. May strong gods favor you."

"Strong gods," Cadoc echoed.

The brothers drank. Both watched him from over the tops of their cups. Cedar sniffed his drink. Moonshine. He swigged it back in one shot. It plowed a hot path down between his ribs to his stomach, and left the taste of pine sap in his mouth.

"I've had enough of gods, strong and Strange," Cedar said. "But I thank you anyway. Afternoon, Madders." He stood from the table and started across the chamber. "If you'd open the door, I'll be on my way."

Just as the words left his mouth, the door to the chamber opened. Cedar glanced back at the brothers to see if they had somehow devised a way to trip the lock from a distance.

"Ho, there, those within," Bryn, the middle brother, called out. "Is there room for two more?"

Cedar did not want to involve himself any more than he had to with the Madders' business. Seemed that each time he crossed paths with them, it cost him more than he wanted to give. Meetings with the Madder brothers were best done two ways: quickly and infrequently.

He did not expect to see Mrs. Jeb Lindson walking out of the shine of day into the deeper lamplight of the room.

She wore the same dress as this morning, but had put on a silk bonnet that made her brown eyes wide and warm, and cast her lips in a soft shade of pink. She'd been riding, that was clear, and the wind had tugged some of her fine blond hair out from under her bonnet, so that it fell in a gold curl against her cheek. He found himself entertaining the thought of what her hair would look like unbound, spilling around her bare shoulders—yellow as sunlight and soft as silk. Then wondering if her skin, white as moonlight, would be softer still, beneath his hands.

Mrs. Lindson folded her fingers over the bag on her wrist and gave him a calm look. He glanced away while adjusting his hat, buying up time to brush off the thoughts and heat that she stirred up in him.

She was lovely; that was plain sure. And every time he

set eyes on her, he was reminded of feelings he never thought he'd own again. Feelings he'd only ever known with his wife.

"Hello, Mr. Hunt," she said. That calm greeting of hers held a dark fury, a desperation.

"Ma'am." Cedar stopped fiddling with his hat and schooled his features. The brim had brushed against the goggles still fitted on his head and made his forehead itch.

"Have you reconsidered my offer?" she asked. Her words caught deep in her throat, as if wedging between sorrows before finding their way out.

Cedar said nothing. He'd given her his answer. It wouldn't change. He couldn't entertain so much as the idea of looking for her man's killer until he gave the lost boy a chance to be found alive first. "I'm sorry. No, ma'am."

Mae Lindson dropped her gaze. "I see." When she looked back up at him, he could tell the woman had made a decision. There was death in her eyes. "Then I wish you the best, Mr. Hunt."

Sounded like she wished him the best grave, or the best hanging rope.

"Didn't know this was going to be a proper social," Alun said, "or I would have washed up a few more cups."

"I'll be on my way," Cedar said.

"Now, now, we wouldn't think of it, Mr. Hunt," Alun said. "Come sit with us a spell longer. I'm sure Mrs. Lindson would enjoy the company."

Mae didn't look to him, but Cedar suddenly realized the situation from her angle. She was alone, possibly unarmed, and in the home of three men who had locks that could seal a person away in the mountain until the world wound down.

And even though the day burned on, and little Elbert's time grew shorter and shorter, he wasn't possessed of the kind of morals to leave a woman alone with the miners.

He tugged Wil's watch out of his waistcoat and glanced at the time. There was still a good seven hours of daylight ahead of him. He'd be able to cover a fair bit of ground before the moon came up. And if the silver fork led him lucky, he might yet find the boy.

He tucked the watch back into his vest pocket.

The Madder brothers had gone awful quiet. Alun and Cadoc stared at him like he'd just turned into a rattlesnake.

The brothers took a step toward him and Mae Lindson. Bryn Madder, still standing at the mouth of the chamber, spun the big brass captain's wheel and sent the door rolling on its hidden tracks.

"Tell us, Mrs. Lindson," Alun began, mild as church tea. "How is it we can assist you today?"

"I am looking to buy a weapon to kill a man."

"What sort of man?" Alun asked.

That, Cedar thought, was an interesting question. Most people would ask what sort of weapon she wanted.

"A monster. A murderer. The man who killed my husband."

"You had your eyes on his killer?" Bryn asked as he sauntered over from the door. "Know his height, build, manners?"

"No."

Bryn sucked on his teeth, disapproving.

"Is there a weapon you prefer to kill men with, Mrs. Lindson?" Alun asked.

"Something," she said, "that will make sure even his soul can't be found."

Alun laughed and so did Bryn. Cadoc Madder stared at Mae like a drift of snow had fallen out of a summer sky and landed right here in the middle of their dining room.

"A gun, I'm thinking, will do enough damage to unbreathe a man," Alun said. "Strong enough to break bone, stop a heart, unhinge the soul." He gave her a tight smile. "And not so powerful that a lady will feel the weight of its burden."

"It will be no burden in my hands." Mae stepped forward and touched Alun's arm.

His eyebrows shot up, but he did not pull away. Looked for all the world like he had suddenly been frozen in ice.

"You will find me the weapon that will destroy my husband's killer. The cost will be bartered between us. There are promises I can make you that are worth more than any coin."

Cedar took a step back. There was something in her words, a push, a power. It reminded him too much of the Pawnee god, and the curse the god had invoked. Fear, instinct, a good head for danger, made Cedar lift his gun, barrel tipping just up from the floor. He took a breath, ready to level the gun at her if need be.

Mae Lindson let go of Alun's arm. He exhaled like he was coming up from underwater. His face flushed red as a hot coal. "Keep your hands to yourself, witch. Our kind have no quarrel with you. But I'm not unwilling to reconsider my stance." He turned on his heel and barked at his brother. "Bring the gun she wants, Bryn. I want her out of here."

Bryn scurried across the room and through the same door into the room Alun had entered to retrieve the tuning forks.

Mae looked after him. Unconcerned. Calm, except for her fingers that tapped against the purse she held in one hand. At that motion, the clink of coins rubbed like spurs inside the purse. Between Cedar's and Mae's offerings, the Madders would be making a grand wage today.

"Will the coin cover your price, Mr. Madder, or will other agreements be necessary?" Mae asked.

"Agreements," he muttered. "Curses, more like. And you of the white magic. What would your sisters say if they saw you bargaining for a gun?"

"My sisters are not here, Mr. Madder, and I would thank you to keep them, and any mention of them, out of our business."

Alun opened his mouth, but Mae spoke first.

"Please, Mr. Madder. Some mercy."

He paused, then clamped his mouth shut with an audible click, and stomped to the table. He filled the cup again and drank the moonshine like it was water, shifting his glower between Mae and Cedar.

"You, Mrs. Lindson, are too quick to offer up such things that are in your power. And you, Mr. Hunt, are too reluctant to do the same. But when you both come to my mountain asking my favor, on the same bright morning after the full moon, it is I who sets the price."

He rolled the cup between his palms as if kneading his temper down to a soft lump. When he spoke again, his voice was even, controlled. Weary. "These times about us," he said. "They can't be escaped. There are dark things walking the soil, burrowing into the heart and marrow of the earth, and of the living. You have a part in this, Mrs. Lindson. I didn't think so, but now, seeing you here . . ." He nodded. "You have a part to play."

He set his shoulders in a hard line, pulling his chin up. He somehow looked more noble, more regal, than a dirty miner who banged around inside rock crevasses, scraping for a nugget and spark. He looked like the sort of man who had not only fought in wars but had also led men into battle and on to victory.

Cedar always knew there was something odd about the brothers, and now he had suspicions that they might be very closely tied to the dark things that burrowed in bones and walked this land. The Strange.

"If I've a part to play in anything, it is for my own benefit," Mae said. "And no other."

Alun pressed his lips together, something like sadness crossing his eyes. "I'd think two times before taking the weapon you asked for from this hill. If you want a life with joy left to it, leave the gun here and walk away from any involvement with myself and my brothers."

"There is no joy left for me, Mr. Madder. There is only death."

Bryn walked into the room, short-barreled shotgun held low in one hand, a box of bullets in the other.

"Pity, that. Then this gun will bring you what you ask for." Alun poured more moonshine, slugged it back, washing away the steely resolve of a commander and becoming once again a miner and mad deviser.

Bryn held the gun out for her, butt first. It was the color of wet stones, gray and black steel, stock and butt, as if it had been hammered out of one piece of metal. But the glint of brass cogs, worked in a clockwork fashion all along the forestock, and the copper tubes that created a cage around the trigger with room for a hand and finger—much like the hand guard of a swashbuckler's cutlass—gave the steel some relief. It was the copper tubes that most caught Cedar's eye as he tried to reckon their use. Each tube lifted up from the hand guard, like the head of a snake, right behind the bolt handle. And atop each tube was a thumb-sized glass vial.

"There is only one gun of this devising," Bryn said. "Chamber the shot, and this lever will lock these gears into action." He pointed at the gears. "A very small vial of oil within the gun will heat with the friction of the gears, fill the tubes, and send a gas into these vials, which is released on squeezing the trigger.

"It will take some time for a full charge, but as soon as you can no longer hear it whining, and you see the needle of that gauge there on the stock holding on the red, you can blow a hole straight through the great divide.

"These," Bryn added, "are the shells." He opened the wooden box and withdrew a cylinder as long as his hand, balancing it between two fingers. "A blend of mineral only we brothers know. There are only five bullets. That's all we've made, and all we'll ever make."

"All we'll ever make," the other two brothers echoed quietly as if it was a vow that needed repeating.

"This shot," Alun picked up now that Bryn had gone silent, "this gun, will kill any man, woman, child. It might even kill things that walk this land dark and hungry, so long as the gun is fully charged. Might kill the things that had a hand in the killing of your husband."

Mae took the weapon without hesitating. She looked natural to the heft of the gun, determination setting her jaw as she pivoted and lifted the butt to her shoulder, sighting right between the center gap in the copper tubes. She lowered the barrel to the floor and inspected the box of shot. She nodded.

"This is worth more than the purse I brought."

"That's true," Alun said. "The purse and a favor."

"I don't think I'll be here long enough to settle a favor," she said.

"Coin. And the favor, to be repaid whenever our paths should meet," Alun countered.

She considered it. "Done."

Cedar thought she might have agreed to almost any terms to keep hold of that gun.

She held out the purse, and Bryn exchanged the box of bullets for it. He loosened the strings and looked inside. "Done," he said.

"Done," Cadoc, to one side, echoed.

"Done," Alun pronounced. "Cadoc, see her out."

Cadoc gestured toward the door with the slightest bow. Mae looked askance at Cedar. If she was offering him to follow, or looking for him to challenge her on her fool quest for vengeance, he didn't have the right to act on either request.

"Good-bye, Mr. Hunt."

"Ma'am," Cedar said.

Mae walked with Cadoc toward the door. Cedar started off after them.

"Mr. Hunt," Alun said. "One last thing."

Cedar glanced over. "I think our business is done, Mr. Madder."

"All except one question that lingers with me." He poured two cups of moonshine, holding one out in invitation.

"There's a boy gone lost, Mr. Madder. Your curiosity will have to carry on without me." The door swung open behind him. He could tell the door opened only because a wash of air filtered into the room. The door itself, a slab of stone that ten men couldn't shoulder closed, moved silently on those well-oiled rails.

Mae stepped through the doors and Cadoc closed them quickly behind her. The youngest Madder moved over to stand in front of the door, fists on top of his hips pulling back his duster just enough to let Cedar see the guns holstered there.

"Tell me, Mr. Hunt," Alun said. "How did you repair the watch?"

The question was unexpected.

The Madders had said they'd tried to fix it and couldn't. And now, just a day in his keeping, the watch was running again. It appeared the Madder brothers didn't take kindly to being out-tinkered.

"Dropped it."

"That so?" Alun said.

Bryn, who stood near Alun, cleared his throat and held both hands up to show no weapons were within them. "Might I could see it, Mr. Hunt? Timepiece deviled me for weeks. Won't go so far as to open it up, but it'd be a pleasure to see it working as it should."

"That door behind me going to open up if I show you the watch?"

Alun chuckled. "The watch. Now, Mr. Hunt."

The brothers were spread about the chamber. He'd be lucky to get off three clean shots, luckier if they did enough damage to keep the Madders from pulling their own weapons. He gritted his teeth, swallowing back a growl. Easier to give them what they wanted and walk out of here than to waste daylight digging their graves.

He reached in his pocket and withdrew the watch, letting it dangle off his knuckles.

Bryn walked nearer, his hands still held upward. When he was an arm's length away, he tucked two fingers into his vest pocket and withdrew a pair of brass spectacles. He perched those on his nose, folded his hands behind his back, and leaned in, squinting at the watch face.

He breathed a word, not English, then craned his neck to meet Cedar's gaze.

"How?" he asked, honestly perplexed. "It was broken. More than broken. Irreparable. If any hands could fix it, it would have been mine." He stretched out the fastidiously clean fingers of one hand, waited for Cedar's assent.

Cedar nodded. Bryn gently placed his fingers at the back of the watch and tipped it to catch the light.

He frowned, then ran a thumb over the crystal face, running his nail at the seam.

"Blood," Bryn said. "Yours?"

"Don't see that it matters. This watch is none of your concern." He pulled the watch away. But Bryn was just as fast as his brother. He snatched the watch out of Cedar's hand, breaking the chain in two.

"Think it might yet be ours," Bryn said. "And our concern to boot."

"I've had enough," Cedar said. "There's deals been made and word been given. I'm as good as my word to settle my debt. Give the watch back."

Bryn took a step away, shaking his head. "You've done something to it we couldn't. Way I see it, the neighborly thing is to let us take it apart, see what moves it."

"Way I see it," Cedar said low, "is you'll give me back what's mine, or I'll break your jaw."

That did it. The brothers, grinning and always hankering for a fight, were on him. His gun was knocked out of his hand, as fists meant for breaking stone slammed into his head, his ribs, his stomach. Their laughter filled the chamber.

Cedar swung, connected. Swung again. Pulled his hunting knife from his belt, sliced through air, snagged the edge of cloth, hit flesh. A flash of light filled the cavern as one of the brothers set off a charge. Cedar blinked, trying to clear his vision.

A hand caught his wrist, twisted. Yanked his wrist up behind his back.

Cedar yelled. Another fist, then too many to count, rained down. A boot slammed into his chest. He fell back. He could just make out Alun's face as he dropped on him, a knee pushing all the air out of his lungs.

The brothers gave one hard cheer, Bryn and Cadoc holding down his arms and legs and utilizing rope they must have stashed in their coats to bind his boots and wrists.

"Didn't realize you wanted to get in a scuffle with us, Mr. Hunt," Alun said. "Not over something as small as a watch. Brother Bryn was just ribbing you. The watch is yours. We Madders are true to our word too. But now I'm hard curious as to why you'd be willing to come to blows over it, and why, exactly, your blood seems to have fixed it up, when all our skills did it no good."

Alun Madder grinned big enough to split his head in half. "I believe we're inviting you to extend your stay with us awhile." He wiped the blood off his mouth with his sleeve, then gave Cedar a mostly somber look. "With my apologies." He pounded a fist across Cedar's jaw.

The blow hit so hard, sparks filled Cedar's vision as the brothers' laughter filled his ears.

He tasted blood even before his head snapped back and hit the stone floor. His ears rang, and blood ran down the back of his neck mixing with the dirt.

Cedar struggled to stay conscious. He didn't know what would happen if he passed out. Didn't know if the beast that lingered just beneath his skin would break free, moonlight or no moonlight, to tear the brothers apart, or if he would simply fall unconscious.

The Madders finished binding his feet, legs, arms, then picked him up as if he were no more than a suckling pig trussed up on a pole. They dropped him into a chair.

"Now." Alun licked blood from his split lip and rolled up his sleeves. "Let's see what, exactly, you're made of, Mr. Hunt."

CHAPTER THIRTEEN

Shard LeFel carried a lantern hooked on the end of his dark, curved cane. The blacksmith's boy stumbled along beside him, holding the hem of LeFel's coat as they walked the enclosed split between the two train carriages to the boiler car. The boy was slow-eyed, dreaming on his feet, caught in the drugs LeFel had forced upon him, unable to think or speak. Not that it mattered for what LeFel intended to do to him.

He pulled open the door, which he never locked. The only man who had ever tried to steal from this carriage left the rails in a meat bag. His blood still stained the wooden stairs.

At night the shuffling, clicks, and huffs of steam from the windowless carriage rattled out beyond the walls as the things he kept inside stirred, restless. Pipes from this car ran to the other two cars set here on the rail spur, and the steam in those pipes kept LeFel's living quarters and private bath heated.

LeFel and the boy stepped inside. Even though the sun was in the sky, the interior of the boiler car was dark as a grave. He raised the lantern, but shadows hung heavy and thick, unmoved by the sweep of light.

"Wake, my sweet. Wake, my beasts. Wake and do your king's bidding." LeFel walked deeper into the room, placing the lantern on a small table to the right of the door. The boy followed.

LeFel pressed down on the boy's shoulder. "You will sit here, child. And dream." The boy dragged one hand down the wall as he folded upon the floor, curling up like an infant, his thumb tucked in his mouth.

So fragile, these human young, LeFel mused. So unable to defend themselves.

He walked away from the child and over to a heavy handle that jutted up to shoulder height from the floor. Made of black iron and brass, the contraption looked like a pump for water except for the gears and woven pulleys that ran from its joints up to the walls, wrapping among the pipes and valves and yet more gears and pulleys that flowed over the entire inside of the carriage like a fishing net made of metal.

LeFel drew his black silk gloves from his pocket and slipped them on. He detested manual labor, but waking his menagerie gave its own reward. He pumped the handle at a steady pace, allowing the complicated system of pulleys and gears to warm. Bellows pushed air through pipes down into the burner in the underbelly of the train car, fanning the coals there, and setting water to boil, then steam to push through smaller pipes—steam that pushed levers and spun wheels.

The lantern on the table reflected glints of brass, silver, ruby, diamond from the shadows.

Creatures stirred in that darkness. Creatures shifted and creaked and moaned, filling the carriage with their hot, wet exhales.

Metal creatures. Gears and steam. Matics. From all corners of the world, created by all manner of men's hands to do his bidding.

Pipes fastened to the walls of the carriage groaned and

clicked. It didn't take long before that power was pumped into the matics, giving the tick to the shuffling beasts' hearts.

When the moaning and stirring was replaced by the huffing chug and tapping metrics of matics under full power, Shard LeFel flipped the wall toggle on the gas lanterns, bathing the entire space in light.

Metal creatures pivoted toward him. They had no eyes with which to see, but they each contained a drop of glim mixed with a handful of powdered chemicals—a mix LeFel had stumbled across years ago. The mix of chemicals and glim gave the creatures a curious sort of awareness—not intelligence, but just enough rudimentary thinking skills to imprint upon them their single function: to kill.

They were not quite alive, and he preferred them that way. Killing machines with no room for remorse or reluctance were very useful to a man of his ambitions.

The matics had been constructed over the last two hundred years. Built by men he rewarded richly by giving them a quick death at Mr. Shunt's discretion. Mr. Shunt did not always kill immediately. Some of the men had lived for years before Mr. Shunt found them and paid them a most final visit. Still, LeFel had been assured their deaths were swift, if not entirely painless.

Looking upon his servants set fire to LeFel's pride. This collection, this zoo, this army, suited a king, a conqueror.

One creature was made of metals and riches from the Celestial Empire, ivory and gold, inset with jade and rubies and the jewels of an ancient emperor's crown. Another beast was pieced together with thick welds, hard steel torn from the narrow veins of the distant mountains of Germany and forged by the fire of volcanoes.

Hulking monstrosities creaked at every joint, wielding

hammers and pistons for arms, threshers for hands. Delicate tickers sculpted to resemble animals and birds, some so detailed to the natural world, they would be accepted by the creatures they imitated. Warped, twisted globs of metal, misshapen heads and gears, leather-accordioned bellows, potbelly burners, and great hinged chest-plate furnaces— they were matics, tickers, horrors made of steel.

And all of them, from the largest bent half over, to the smallest the size of a rat, waited for his command. He would need only half of them this night, free only half of them on this task.

"The dead man has risen from his grave. He walks again, our Mr. Jeb Lindson. You will find him. You will tear him apart into so many pieces there won't be two bones left to go walking."

He strode back to the boy and pulled him by the scruff of his shirt up onto his feet. "Are you awake, whelp? Are you enjoying your dreams?" He drew a thin knife from his coat and sliced the thick of the boy's thumb. The child whimpered, his eyes pupil-dark and wide with shock. LeFel caught up the drops of blood in a small glass vial. The matics would need mortal blood to understand the hunt. This child's would have to do.

The matics sensed the blood. They drew closer, tugging on their chains.

LeFel clamped his hand around the boy's wrist to steady him. If the boy fell to the floor now, the beasts would destroy him and carve out his bones. LeFel lifted his dark curved cane and caught it up in the ropes that hung in loops across the ceiling.

"This is the blood of a mortal. This blood is upon the dragonfly that drives the wings of one man's heart. Find the dead man with the dragonfly in his chest and kill him." The boy's blood dripped upon the wooden slats of the floor, and the matics lifted heads, snouts, mandibles, vents, to absorb the scent of it carried by the steam.

"Find this blood. Do not return to me until you have ground the dead man's body to mulch. But bring me his head. Whole." He yanked the ceiling ropes with the cane, loosening the pilot knot, then thunked the base of the cane into the floor at his boot. The knots untied, clamps released, and bindings—some metal, some magnetic, some fiber—unbound, fell away in shushing coils upon the wooden floor. A dozen matics, just half of his menagerie, large and small, were free.

Hungry, lumbering, slick and quick, the matics could fill their steam bellies with blood just as easily as with water—and they had done so over the years. Evidence of that could be seen in the blackened blood rust staining the joints of neck and chest and jaws.

They circled the boy, brushing against him to smell, to record, to savor the blood of the child who helped bind metal to a dead man's flesh. The rest of the matics, still trapped by chain and steel along the walls, moaned softly and shifted against their shackles.

LeFel released the boy, who swayed on his feet but did not fall, eyes lost in the middle of a nightmare, tears streaming his face, as the free matics touched and stroked and sniffed and plucked, scenting, tasting, recording him.

LeFel strode to the center of the carriage and opened the trapdoor in the floor. "Now," he commanded. "Hunt the dead man."

The army of cogs, jointed limbs, razor jaws, and glittering gears dragged away from the boy, then skulked past LeFel. They slipped through the trapdoor in one step, or skittered down the iron ladder to the ground, then away, out from beneath the carriage, unseen by the rail workers, silent as ghosts.

The stink of steam and oil and coal hitting the cooler air of the afternoon lifted up through the trapdoor and filled the carriage. LeFel pulled the lever, closing the trapdoor. The other matics cooed, moaned, reached toward the lever. Hungry for blood. They waited, huffing, clacking. Waited to kill for him.

"Today is not your day to serve. I am loath to waste two centuries of my collection on one dead man. But your day to feast will come. Soon."

He strolled back to the boy and looked down at him, silent a moment. He wondered how much longer the boy would last. Wondered when the horrors would finally break his mind. "Does your hand hurt, my child?"

The boy did not answer. He stood, shaking, as if chilled, or perhaps in shock. LeFel needed the boy to endure only a day more. Just until the waning moon.

LeFel placed his fingertips on the child's back. "Sleep will solve all your ills, little maker. Sleep will make this world fade away and bring to you the soothing world of dreams."

The boy finally blinked and took a deep, stuttering breath. He closed his eyes and leaned against LeFel's coat, his fist caught tight in his sleeve.

"Follow me," LeFel murmured, "follow me to dreaming." LeFel placed his hand between the boy's shoulders and propelled him along with him.

Before they left the carriage, he snatched up the lantern with the crook of his cane, leaving his creations hunkered in darkness again.

Outside, LeFel paused. It was difficult to see the movement in the dappled shadow and light of the forest, but he had a keen eye. He smiled as his tickers, his slaves, his children of destruction, ran smooth and quick, faster than living beasts, faster than steam and metal should move, spreading like a plague, hunting for a dead man—hunting for the only thing that stood between him and the witch.

"And when they are done with you, Mr. Jeb Lindson, not even the witch will recognize your bones."

CHAPTER FOURTEEN

Mae Lindson rode down the mountain, her mule, Prudence, slow and surefooted through the loose shale path. She glanced over her shoulder again, scanning the ridge for Cedar Hunt. She had thought he was leaving and had hoped to ride with him awhile. Not to convince him to help her—she'd given up on that. He'd made up his mind, and told her no twice. She was sure there wasn't anything she could do to change that.

But Cedar Hunt ranged the mountains and hills tracking cougar, wolf, bear. She intended to ask if he'd seen any sign of her husband. But since he wasn't riding out, she'd just have to find the killer her own way.

Her mule settled into a plodding pace, head down. It would take more than a few hours to reach her cottage. And by the time she provisioned, it'd be too late in the day to set out to hunt the killer. It would have to be tomorrow, then. Tonight, she would pack supplies, tend the goats, and cast a scrying spell to lead her in the right direction.

Tomorrow would be soon enough to start her journey.

She thought about riding through town again and buying supplies, but she had all she needed at home. Still, Rose's smile and the promise of the rhubarb pie almost made her head into town for no other excuse. It had been a sure comfort to see a friendly face. But instinct told her the night would come on too quickly, and she had best be tucked up tight in her home before it fell.

Even though the day was still warm, she shivered. The Madder brothers had some strangeness about them. She was sure of that. It wasn't witchcraft. When she put her fingers on Alun Madder's arm, she had felt like she was touching the deep roots of the mountains themselves. And then, when she had offered her skills to him, she had felt a power in his presence, an authority about him.

Finding Cedar Hunt mixed up with the brothers was a surprise. Mr. Hunt kept to himself almost as much as she and Jeb did. She'd never thought him to have dealings with the brothers who were known for brawling, drinking, and driving hard bargains. What, she wondered, would send Cedar up the mountains today, asking the brothers' favor?

Perhaps she and he both had problems that required the brothers' particular abilities.

Even though she hadn't let on back in the mine, the shotgun was a magnificent piece of genius. If it worked half as well as it appeared to be built, it was a very powerful weapon indeed. But she didn't dare fire it to get accustomed to how it performed. Five bullets meant she would have no more than five chances to end the killer's life.

She had bundled the gun in a blanket and lashed it to the back of her saddle. The shells were safely tucked in her saddle pack. But even though the shotgun was safely behind her, she wasn't unarmed. A woman traveling alone, even near town, or perhaps especially, was most likely to draw trouble. Therefore, Mae kept a Colt in the saddle holster near her knee.

By the time Mae reached the outskirts of town, the day was burning down to evening. She decided to take the route through the fields outside town, rather than navigating the roads that would be traveled by the rail workers coming into town to gamble and drink.

Prudence seemed to walk slower each mile they covered and it was closing in on dusk by the time she had put Hallelujah far behind her. Mae pulled her shawl closer about her shoulders, feeling more than darkness closing down with the ebbing light.

The field and hill were interrupted ahead by a wallow, where a dense stand of fir stood between Hallelujah and her home.

Mae guided her mule into the forest, where dusk had already taken claim, stretching the shadows, cooling the air. As she rode through the trees, Mae felt something else, felt something following her. She shifted in the saddle and looked all around, but could not catch more than a slide of movement at the edges of her vision. No ground nesters rustling, the birds, the animals in the forest were strangely silent, as if they too knew something dangerous moved between the trees.

A cool stroke like a finger against bone sent a shiver down her spine.

"Witch." The word was breathed and seemed to come from all around her.

Mae's heart jumped.

The shotgun might be tied behind her, but her Colt was in the saddle holster near her knee. She pulled the handgun and put her heels to Prudence, urging her to break into a trot.

The mule jolted through a few steps, then settled back into her numbing plod. No matter how Mae wanted to hurry, the mule would not.

"Witch."

Not her sisters. No, their call was dulcet tones. This voice hissed, scratched, scrabbled through the air.

Whatever that was, the voice, the follower, was danger. She scanned the ground, the underbrush, the shadows of the trees around her, ahead and behind. With every slow step closer to her cottage, the forest was swallowed deeper and deeper into darkness.

A rattling behind her, a scattering of leaves. She turned. Nothing but shadows.

Then one of the shadows behind her moved. The shadow was a man standing, watching her, his long, thin hands folded. Tall, he was stretched taller by the stovepipe hat upon his head. His black coat brushed the ground, the large collar hiding his neck and face, so that all she could see of his features were his eyes. And his eyes burned red.

"Who—," Mae started, but the man was gone.

She clicked her tongue and urged Prudence faster. "Get on now," she said. "Get on up."

This time the mule worked up to a jarring trot, then stumbled into a lope. The tree line was just ahead. Beyond that was a sky with more light than the forest, a field, and the safety of her home.

Mae leaned forward, keeping her heels to the mule. "Get up, Prudence, get up." She guided Prudence through the brush and trees, hooves churning the soft needles and loam, the mule's breath coming out in snorts. Mae's pulse ran faster than the mule's hoofbeats, pounding in fear.

That man hadn't walked away, nor had he hid himself. He had simply disappeared as if he were made of nothing but shadows.

She had seen spirits, and she had seen the things magic could do, but she had never seen such a Strange thing here, in this world, walking in the last light of day. Whoever he was, he had not come calling with gentle intentions.

The edge of the forest and pale evening light were just a few strides away. Light might not stop the man, but escaping the shadows of the forest would make him easier to see.

There. There—she was almost through the trees.

A hand grabbed for her reins, cold as stone and sharp as knives. Mae lifted her gun and fired, just as Prudence reared back.

The wind lifted, a hard breeze that shoved branches aside, letting a stream of light into the trees. Mae watched, horrified, as the man sidestepped the bullet as if it were a feather driven by a lazy wind. Then he was on her, long arms reaching up to her elbows, oily fingers catching at her shawl and skirt and skin, scratching, hooking, dragging.

Mae held her seat and fired point-blank at his face.

The man recoiled, knocked back, bent back, but still on his feet as if his boots were glued to the earth, long fingers of one hand securing his hat to his head. And then, as Mae raised her gun to fire again, he fell apart.

Like grain emptying a silo, or water from a tower, it was as if the pin had been removed from the undercarriage of his skeleton, and he crumpled, first from his boots, then dissolving downward in a rush that clattered and clanked like old chains. His hat was the last thing to hit the ground, falling into a dark smudge of shadow where just a moment ago flesh and bones had stood.

Mae swore and put her heel to the mule.

That man, that thing, was dead. It had to be dead. But that did not stop her flight.

Prudence jumped into a gallop through the trees, out of the forest, and into air fresh and clean with light. Her cottage was not far. The mule did not slow, headed toward the corral. They made quick work across the field. Mae glanced over her shoulder again and again, scanning the shadows, her gun at the ready, wind pricking tears from her eyes. Nothing followed, no man, no beast, no shade, no Strange.

She guided Prudence to the small corral and dismounted with the gun in her left hand. She unlatched the gate and led the mule inside the split-wood fence. Her hands shook as she removed the saddle and bridle, fingers slippery with fear that made even old Prudence tremble.

She soothed her, patting her neck before taking the bridle off over her head. Hooking bridle over the saddle, she hurried into the small shed with Prudence's tack propped against her right hip. It might be dead, but she didn't know if more of its kind were upon the land. She wanted the safety of her home, her hearth.

"Witch." The whisper scratched against the shed's roof and scattered on the wind.

Mae untied the shotgun from the saddle and pulled the box of shells out of the pouch. Keeping her Colt within reach, she loaded the gun, levering open the chamber and sliding in the shells, slick, heavy, and cold, with trembling fingers.

"Yes," she said to the empty shed, to the empty air. "And who do I have the pleasure"—she levered in another bullet—"of addressing?"

No answer, other than the wind creaking through the shed.

"Oh, now, don't be shy." Mae fit the last bullet and raised the gun hip high. "If you have some business with me, let's have it done now."

Nothing, not even the wind, moved. The only sound was her own blood pounding in her chest, thrumming in her ears. She had never felt a creature as dark as that man in the forest. The Madders had said the shotgun would kill any man, woman, or child. And they said it might kill any other Strange creature in this land.

Might be time to find out just how true their word was.

She thumbed the lever that snapped hard against brass, setting the gears in motion. The gun emitted a low thrum. While the mechanism warmed, she picked up her Colt. Ordinary bullets didn't need any preparation.

There were scant magical protections on the shed, blessings

to ease the snow and gentle the wind. The strongest protections against the Strange were within her cottage. Across the open yard, where she'd be exposed to whatever was out there.

Mae took a deep breath and said a prayer. Then she walked out of the shed, the revolver cocked and ready.

She strained to hear any stray sound, strained to catch movements, shadows. Not even a mouse shifted in the straw.

She hurried, her gaze on the front of her house, still a distance ahead. No porch or railing—Jeb had laid a wooden walk beneath the threshold of the door to stomp the mud from his boots before he entered their home.

Mae ran for those boards, ran for her door, ran for her home.

A rumble of thunder rolled beneath her feet. It was not an earthquake. Something beneath the ground paced her, scraping its back against the sod and pushing soil and grasses up to trip her feet.

She didn't slow, didn't pause. She ran, lurching over the uneven ground. Just a few more feet, a few more steps. Thunder rolled, lifting the soil like an ocean wave and crashing dirt and rock and grass into the front of her home like a swell breaking against stone cliffs.

Mae flung her arms wide. The wooden walk caught her, and held steady beneath her feet as she stretched out for the door and yanked it open. She stumbled into the room backward, Colt aimed at the field and forest.

The same man, same creature, filled the doorway, his long, long arm catching at the door, his long, long fingers clicking on the doorjamb.

He should be dead. She'd seen him fall into pieces. And yet he stood before her, put back together again.

Mae took no time to question. She fired the Colt.

The man shattered into pieces outside her door. Just as he had in the forest.

Then he rebuilt himself. She caught a glimpse of too many hands beneath his coat, fingers, arms, and oily mandibles clicking into place with the flash of gears, piston rods, and ropy tendons strung tight between pulleys, until he once again stood before her in the shape of a man.

Nightmare. Ghoul. Bogeyman. The Strange.

"You may not enter my home." Mae fired the Colt again, aiming for his chest this time. The creature staggered back one step, but he did not fall apart.

There was no blood on his coat. There was just a bullet hole and a shine of bent brass where his heart should be.

He sucked his teeth, making a *tsk*, *tsk* sound, and then pulled on the door so hard it snapped the bottom hinges, sending splinters of wood flying.

Mae stepped back and lifted the shotgun to her shoulder, sighting between the copper tubes and the glass vials that had now begun to glow an odd green light.

Only five bullets. All the bullets in the world. It was likely she'd need all five to kill the man who killed her Jeb. But it was also likely she needed to practice her aim on this creature first.

She aimed for his head. The hum of the gun was so high only a dog could hear it, but she wasn't sure if the needle showed a full charge. No time to wait. She took a breath, braced for the recoil. Before she could fire, the creature put one foot across her threshold and screamed, pulling his foot away.

The wooden trinkets in the room echoed the creature's shouts, as if his scream triggered them to life.

Jeb's gifts to her held their own kind of protection. She had always known that. Mae could feel their protection falling like a spiderweb down the edges of the room, digging deep into the wooden floor, holding her safe inside, and holding that creature, that Strange, outside.

The man pulled away from the threshold and tipped his

head down, his eyes burning red as stoked coals from beneath his hat. He folded his arms across his chest and tapped razor-tipped fingers against the cloth of his coat, snagging small holes.

"You will come with me," he rasped.

"I will not. Leave my land. Leave my home." Mae shouldered the gun again, but she must have done something to unhitch the gears. The vials were no longer glowing and the clockwork was still. She thumbed the lever setting the gears into motion once more.

Then she took a deep breath and began chanting the words of blessing, protection for her home, for herself, and for all things nurtured by the light. The wooden devices around the room hummed, picking up on the song like strings resonating to a bow.

And the web of protection grew stronger.

The man paced, his fingers tapping, tapping, glaring at Mae, at her house, looking for a way in, waiting for her to pause for too long a breath.

Mae was afraid to shoot him again, afraid the shotgun would break the fragile web of magic and song that held him out. She did not step any farther away from the door, though. She sang, chanted, prayed, the wooden notions humming along with her, strengthening her song. And she held the gun at the ready.

She realized she'd seen this man in town when she was trading a blanket for nails from the blacksmith. He'd been standing in the shadow of the shop, watching, silent. The forge and fire sent heat rolling out of the shop, but when she'd passed this man by, she had felt the dead of winter.

The man stopped pacing. He strode to the left of the door out of her sight. Mae sang softly, hoping to catch the sounds of his footsteps. But he was too quiet.

The shutters across the wall behind her rattled, first the

one above her spinning wheel, then the other near the hearth. The shutters were strong, carved by Jeb's hands, and rubbed down with linseed infused with Saint-John's-wort for safety and strength.

Mae swallowed down the taste of dust and fear and kept on singing.

The shutters each rattled again, then lay still. A moment passed in silence. Then a knocking stuttered across the chimney; the pounding of fists—too many fists—pummeled the back door. The man walked the perimeter of her house, pounding, prying, plucking. But her house, her song, held strong.

There was nothing she could drag to the broken door to close it, no way to stop him from stepping in, except her magic. If the magic didn't hold, she would sacrifice a bullet and use the shotgun.

He strolled around the front of the house again, standing in her broken doorway. He smiled and bowed low, rolling his hat off between his long fingers with a grand flourish. He paused at the lowest point of the bow, and Mae heard something metal hit the wooden planks.

She glanced down. It was a brass button. And as the man stood again, he was missing a button from his coat.

"Begone," she whispered in the pause of her song. But the man smiled and said a guttural word.

The brass button at his feet sprang open and flipped over. A hundred wriggling legs tucked beneath its armored body. The head was a drill with long mandibles and no eyes. It quickly tipped its snout to the wood plank at the man's feet, and burrowed into it, sawdust and soil pushed up and out of the tunnel by its back legs as it headed toward her doorway.

"Easy as threading the eye of a needle," the man hissed. "Spy the hole, pierce the hole, stab the weave."

Mae swallowed, glanced down. She could not see the

burrowing creature, but knew the man was right. If it could dig past her protections, if it could dig up inside the circle of magic that held her safe, it would break her barrier and the Strange man would be able to cross into her home, easy as thread pulled by a needle.

What could she do? Shooting him didn't kill him. The shotgun was still humming, warming slower this time, the needle on the gauge not even at half charge. There were no spells that would make a man drop dead in his tracks. She could curse him, but if she stopped singing, the wooden devices would fall quiet and the web of protection around the house would end.

What did she have that could stop him? She glanced around the room, still singing, her mouth going dry, her heart pounding too hard, too fast. Herbs and wool and tinctures. Healing things, loving things, living things. Cooking pots, frying pans, her woven blankets stacked in a willow basket.

None of these things would do him harm.

Then she remembered the tatting shuttle in her pocket. It was a token of Jeb's love to her, made of hawthorn, silver, and gold, given to her as a courting gift. She slid her fingers into her pocket and caught hold of the slim oval. It warmed at her touch, the edge of it sharp against her skin.

Sharp enough to draw blood. Heavy enough to be used as a weapon.

The drilling beetle dug and dug. She could see the scar it chewed into the threshold, a hump of wrinkled wood trailing its progress. Any second it would be drilling up and up, and then the man would have a hole small enough, large enough, to thread his way through and into her home.

No time to wait for the gun to charge. No time to reload the Colt. No time left at all. She threw the shuttle at the man. It flew as if it had wings. The shuttle slashed across the man's cheek, drawing a deep red line through his flesh. Blood gushed from that wound, pouring black as liquid coal.

The man screamed, an unearthly screech, his spindled fingers fluttering up to his face, tapping and tapping. Black thread, thin as silk, appeared between the man's restless fingers that wriggled as if he were weaving a net.

No, not a net. He was stitching the wound in his face.

He pulled his fingers away, the bloody thread spooling out from his finger that ended in a long, thin brass needle. He pulled the bloody threaded finger to his lips and bit the thread in two with serrated teeth.

Even stitched, the wound kept bleeding, black liquid pouring down into the scarf around his throat like ticks gone crawling.

Mae raised the shotgun, aimed. Charged or not, she was going to fire the thing. The shotgun whirred, and the wooden trinkets lining the wall picked up the hum. The man's eyes narrowed.

Mae pulled the trigger.

This time, he did not step aside of the bullet.

This time, the shot struck flesh and gear and all else he was made of.

The man stumbled backward. Threaded fingers plucked at his coat, as if trying to pat out a burning flame. A globe of gold light surrounded him.

This time, the shot exploded.

And so did the man. Bits and pieces of him flew apart, scattering over the field.

Mae waited a moment, two, for the Strange to rebuild the bits of himself. There was no movement. Not even a shift of shadow.

Mae rushed over to the door, the gun still in one hand, and pulled her skinning knife. The brass bug had dug its way up through her threshold. It poked its head out of the hole, then wriggled free. She stabbed it with the knife. The bug writhed, tucked all its legs up, and popped off the edge of her blade, once again nothing more than a brass button, cold and still as a button should be.

Mae glanced out at where the man had been standing. Not a single scrap of him near her door, and nothing in the grass stirring.

The wind picked up again. One lone meadowlark sang a few unsteady notes. Another answered.

Dusk settled gently over the horizon, bringing the cool scent of rain and the voice of crickets.

Mae trembled. She had never faced anything as foul as that man. The shotgun was silent in her hand, the gears locked. With one last look out into the night, she picked up her tatting shuttle, which lay just outside the door, and made herself busy. Even shook, her feet wanted to run east, away from here, back to the soil that held her owing, back to the sisters who would wash her clean of the killing need for revenge.

Not yet. She couldn't run yet.

She used the fire tongs to pluck up the button and drop it in a thick glass jar with a glass lid. Then she found the hammer and nails it would take to repair the hinges on her door, and hurried to do so. Before night closed in. Before the moon rose. Before other Strange creatures came calling for her blood.

CHAPTER FIFTEEN

Cedar could not move. His hands were bound behind him, numb. His legs were strapped to the chair, and his chest and neck were similarly cinched down tight.

Alun Madder plunked a chair down in front of Cedar and sat astraddle it, his thick arms crossed over the back of the chair.

"You are an interesting problem, Mr. Hunt." He pursed his lips and sucked the blood off his teeth. He spit into an oily kerchief and wiped his mouth and beard.

"Been a while since the boys and I found a puzzle we couldn't solve. We thought we had the way of you—a man running from his past and pain. That's a common story for a common enough man. Then you go on and show you're learned in old ways, Strange ways, and also foolhearted enough to lend a hand where you shouldn't, putting your nose into business that's none of your concern to save a boy who's not your own. Seems you're not that common a common man after all. Thing I wonder is how it took us so long to see the way of you."

Cedar said nothing. They hadn't gagged him, but he doubted there was much he could do to talk them into untying him.

If they held him until the full moon rose, he'd be happy to

show them his uncommon way up close, and personalized. Then he'd tear their throats out.

Bryn brought another chair over and sat rightwise upon it. He had on a pair of goggles with a star spray of lenses fanned off his bad right eye, giving that cloud-shot eye a golden sheen. He'd taken off his coat and wore his sleeves caught in a band at the elbow, hands clean as a christening bowl. His vest seemed constructed entirely of pockets, and in those pockets were bits of chain, cotton, wicks, scissors, and blades.

"So," Alun continued, "now you're here, in our home, with a watch that wouldn't take to fixin'. Not even for Bryn." Alun shook his head, and Bryn fingered one of the lenses down over his right eye: snick, his eye was orange. Then another: amber. Another: gold. Snick, snick, snick, until his eye peered bloodred through the lens.

"You come asking favors," Alun said. "And for our help in hunting Strange things. Even know the specific tools for tracking: silver and song. Things a common man should not know. Why do you suppose that is, brother Cadoc?"

Cadoc stepped out of the shadows behind his brothers, and into the lantern light. His hands were tucked in the pockets of his overcoat. He was silent for such a long time, staring at Cedar, that Cedar thought the youngest Madder had lost his wits. But his brothers waited. And so did Cedar.

Far off, Cedar thought he heard rocks falling, a deep-earth mumble, as if the stones had rolled in their resting place and spoken of their dreams.

"He carries a curse," Cadoc finally said. "Not the old ways. Not our ways. But some way. Some way of this land has cursed him."

"Do you see the mark of the Strange on him?" Alun asked.

Cadoc stared, silent again. Finally, "No. Not so much as."

Alun nodded and rubbed his chin whiskers, giving Cedar a measuring look. "You know about this curse, Mr. Uncommon Hunt?"

"Untie me."

"Do you know the manner of this curse?" Alun asked, like a man calling bluff on a bet.

"I know my own business. And how to keep it," Cedar said.

"Then I reckon you know when keeping your own business won't put your boots on the road. I am powerful curious about that curse, Mr. Hunt. It's a curiosity that you could snuff with a word or two. Tell me, what do you know about your curse?"

Cedar could feel the beast pushing from within him. He was sure he'd blacked out for a bit after the brothers had dropped him in the chair. He didn't know what time it was. Since they were asking him about the curse, the moon must not have pulled up into the sky. It must still be the day he'd come here, maybe even still daylight.

Changing into the wolf would assure he'd get free of these ropes, maybe even free of this hill, so long as the brothers weren't too fast on the draw. But there was no mind of a man left to him when he fell on all fours. There was nothing but hunt, kill, feed.

If he became a beast, he'd not be able to operate the wheels to open the doors.

Still, the idea of letting the beast take over his mind and end this situation was sore tempting.

Cedar took a deep breath, trying to push away the killing thoughts. He was still a man. Best solve this before that was no longer true.

"There is a boy out there who might be alive," he said calmly. "But he's on short time seeing as how he's been gone more than a night. I have the tools to hunt for him, and I have paid the price you asked for those tools. That is my business. And that is all. Untie me."

Bryn was still clicking lenses into place, staring at him through his right eye that had gone from gold to red to emerald and was now drenched in indigo.

"Moon," Bryn said. "And blood." He leaned forward and his brothers mimicked him, leaning in as if they too could see through the lenses over his eye.

"*Blaidd gwaed,*" Cadoc whispered.

"Blood wolf," Alun agreed.

They all leaned back, as if pulled by the same string.

Alun scratched at his beard. "Shape-shifter, eh? Do you remember much the day after the change?"

Cedar blinked. He didn't know what to say. Anger, fear, or disbelief he expected, not casual curiosity.

"It's only for a night, I reckon? Or say a few nights around the full moon?" Alun pressed.

"Three," Cedar said. "Three nights. Beginning with the waxing full moon."

"Your sudden need to be rushing out of here makes a mite more sense." Alun stared up at the ceiling while Bryn pulled a pair of scissors that looked like a tiny brass heron, and a small leather satchel, out of a pocket.

He ambled over next to Cedar and snipped off a bit of his hair.

Cedar jerked and glared at Bryn. "Keep your hands to yourself, or I will break them joint by joint."

Bryn grinned, and waggled his fingers at him as Cedar flexed his arms, pulling against the straps that held strong.

"Do you remember, Mr. Hunt?" Alun asked again.

"About?" Cedar glared at Bryn, who wisely backed away and sat back down.

"Being a man, being a wolf." The eldest brother pulled

his gaze off the ceiling. "Do you carry the thoughts from one skin to the other?"

"No."

The far-off rumbling of stones rattled a trickle of dust down one wall.

Cadoc, who still stood behind the brothers, exhaled a breath he'd been holding far too long.

"Well then, might be we could do you a favor, Mr. Hunt," Alun said, the gleam of negotiation back in his clever, dark eyes.

Cedar pushed against the ropes, but they did not loosen.

"We'll return your coin, return the favor owed for the silver tuning fork, if you'd do a job for us."

"What job?"

"Hunt for us."

Cedar laughed. "Are your ears full of wool? I told you, I'm hunting the boy. Until I find him, living or dead, I will hunt nothing else. For anyone."

Alun looked over at Bryn, who shrugged and smiled.

"Say we give you something to make it worth your while," Alun said.

"Say we give you something to cage the wolf," Bryn said.

"Say we give you something to keep the man's mind in the wolf's clothing," Cadoc said.

"Say you untie me, boys, and let's be done with this," Cedar said.

Bryn chuckled and walked off into the shadows behind his brother Cadoc. He passed through the door where both Mae's gun and the tuning forks had been kept. Cadoc took Bryn's seat and stared at Cedar.

"We have a need for you," Cadoc said careful and slow. "Otherways, we'd not ask it of you. Not ask it of any man."

"That's truth, Mr. Hunt," Alun said. "Our word on it."

"But," Cadoc said, "a man who can hear the Strange, a

man with the wolf in his bones and his eyes in all the worlds . . . well, that's the sort of thing that might suit our needs. Something we will pay handsomely for. No price too high to pay if you'll find our Holder."

"The Holder," Alun explained, "is a device that's been taken, piece by piece, from many a land. A device we have spent all these long years searching for. We believe the Holder is here, in these hills, maybe even in this town." He leaned forward, thick arms crossed over his chest. "We want you to find the Holder for us, Mr. Hunt."

Bryn walked back into the light, carrying a short length of chain. It was black, the links thin as a stalk of wheat. The links were worked loop through loop and a spiral of thin silver snaked through it. At the join point was a clasp shaped in a crescent moon, and on the opposite side, a small brass arrow that would pierce the moon and hold the chain together.

"Don't know the ways to keep the moon from calling you," Bryn said as he walked over to stand behind Cedar. "Don't know the ways to keep the wolf away. But this should break the thrall so you'll have a clear mind. Even after you've gone beast."

"Think of it," Alun said. "You will have all the instincts and keen senses of the wolf, so too your reasoning. Finding the boy, if he can be found, will be swift. After that task is put to fallow, you will look for our Holder."

Cedar's stomach tightened, his chest hot with anger. The whiskey-heavy heat of the moon was stirring him even through a mountain of stone. The moon must be near its rise. He could feel it in his bones, calling, calling. His thoughts were already slipping, shifting, his ears filling with the rush of his own blood pumping hard. His hands opened and closed. He needed the heavy chain around his neck—not this collar the Madders offered, but the links that would hold him trapped against the stones of his hearth. Links that would keep him from killing the very child he intended to hunt.

"What do you say, Mr. Hunt?" Alun asked. "Care to take the gamble?"

Cedar hankered to say no. All he wanted was a chance to find the lost boy. But saying as much was beyond him now, his reason slipping quickly. The alcoholic haze of the moon-rise licked through him, the heavy weight bringing his body taut with a need, a hunger, bloodlust.

He pushed against the ropes. This time, they creaked. Snapped. Cedar grinned at the spice of fear rising from Alun's skin. He pushed harder.

Something cold and heavy looped around his neck, clicked into place.

And then the world slowed.

Cedar was aware of every second of the change, his bones and muscles stretching, curving, compacting. Luxurious pleasure flooded his senses. He pushed again against the ropes, which fell in a pile at his feet as if someone had released the knots. He needed free of these clothes, and stood, dreamlike, pulling each piece away from his skin, and folding it carefully upon the chair where he had sat. Coat, vest, shirt. His hand paused at the tuning fork and chain, both of which he left hanging against his heart. Belt, boots, pants, and drawers, all stacked neatly in the pile.

With every inhalation, a heady rush of heat pushed through him. He was alive, nerves burning, filled with the need for the air, the sky, the ground beneath his claws, and blood in his mouth. His eyesight sharpened, clarified, colors draining down to only the necessary few. His hearing cleared of the blood and thrum, and smells became infinite.

He fell down upon four feet, his mind sliding at last into the final haze of unthinking—blood hungry and needing to kill. An icy shock radiated out from the chain at his neck, clearing away the haze.

Cedar wanted to hunt, to tear and rend and mutilate. And the Madders would be the first to fall.

Coolness washed his mind again.

"You've your senses, Mr. Hunt," Alun said. "If you use them."

Cedar realized he was in possession of his thoughts, the man in him nearly as strong as the killing instincts of the beast.

Kill, the beast in him said.

Cedar pulled against the blood hunger, like hauling back on reins. The need for blood eased.

He looked up at the three brothers, who did not seem one bit surprised at his state.

"Do we have a deal, then, Mr. Hunt?" Alun asked. "The silver tuning fork is yours. This money is yours." He bent and dropped the bag of coins on the floor between them. "The favor between us is absolved. If, in return, you will find our Holder."

Cadoc reached into a pocket inside his vest and pulled out a small, clothbound book. Inside the book was a single dried flower. He carefully turned a page so that the flower was covered, and then tore the next page out from the spine of the book.

The internal binding on the book showed bare stitches and ragged bits where too many other pages had been removed.

Cadoc closed the book and then tore the page in half.

The air filled with a fragrance Cedar had smelled only once before—from the book Wil had found. Sweet as honey, it carried the promise of music, wine, joy, and warm summer nights that never ended. It carried a promise of something just beyond reach, just beyond taste. Something powerful.

"That is the scent of the Holder," Alun said. "Find the blacksmith's boy. Then find the Holder. Do we have a deal?"

Cedar opened his mouth to agree, but only a breathy *woof* came out. He might have the mind of a man, but he did not have the words. Fine. He picked up the bag of money and placed it on top of his clothing.

The brothers laughed. "As sound a yes as we need. Good hunting to you," Alun said, "and luck besides. Bryn, the door."

Bryn was already headed to the wall where he worked the lock, then the wheel to set the door rolling smoothly on its hidden track.

A rush of night air pushed into the cavern, bringing with it a thousand different smells of forest and creature and sky. Too many scents for a man's mind to sort. Cedar knew what every smell belonged to, not by name, but by the texture of the scent.

It was a powerful knowledge to break the world apart into so many pieces. It made it easy to find the Strange, easy to find his prey.

No, Cedar thought, first he'd find the piece of the world that belonged to the Gregors' boy, then the Holder, then whatever else he hungered for.

He walked to the door, sniffed the air, sorting the possibilities riding the wind. Life throbbed out there, animals and humans and Strange, filled with blood and bone. A haze of red covered his vision.

Kill.

The scent of the boy was faint, shuttered by too many other scents, too many other things he needed to tear apart, destroy. Cedar raised his voice and howled with want, with need. His hold on the beast slipped, and he fell, his thoughts buried, his control lost in the need to hunt. To kill.

He ran into the night, inhaling scent and odor, searching for blood, for bone, for flesh.

A horse nearby, hot from a long day's ride. His horse. So easy to bite, first the hamstring, then the neck, then blood would fill his belly. He stalked off that way.

Something skittered in the brush to his right and ran.

Jackrabbit. Fast, hot. Terrified.

Cedar tore across the scree after it, weaving through the brush, faster than any other animal, gaining on the kill, savoring the chase, closing in, fast. He clamped his jaws down on the rabbit's head.

Blood, sweet, warm, and salty with the slick of brains burst through his mouth. He chewed and chewed, licking the fluid off his muzzle before tearing the heart out of the chest. That he swallowed without chewing.

The need for blood eased as he made quick work of the rest of the hare.

A thought lifted through the heat of the kill. A boy. He was supposed to find a boy.

Cedar followed that thought, and rose up out of the beast's needs like a man breathing free of a deep dive. He reined in the beast once more and sniffed the wind, catching the boy's scent.

A cool wash poured over his mind as he loped toward the town.

Find the boy, not kill the boy, he reasoned.

The beast within him growled.

Find the boy, find the Strange, find the Holder, Cedar thought. Each word was a rope around the beast's neck, building a harness that pulled it back into his control.

But the need for blood pushed at him. The beast would stay calm so long as its hunger was slaked. And he had not let the beast eat for many, many months. Soon, he would need to kill again.

He must go by the boy's house and pick up his trail

quickly. Before the beast, before his need to kill, overtook him again.

Cedar ran, faster than any other creature in this world, wild and alive, the tuning fork singing one sweet note against his heart as the hunt began.

CHAPTER SIXTEEN

Jeb Lindson had been working his way from shadow to shadow all the day. Some shadows were so far apart, sunlight had plenty of time to pour over his skin and burn down deep, leaving his flesh weeping. But that didn't stop him from walking. On and on. Into the next shadow. Through the light and into the shadow again. For Mae. For his beautiful wife.

The sun had taken its time to roll across the sky and down behind the hills, but it was nearly gone now. Shadows hooked the edges of night and pulled darkness like a quilt back over the ground again.

Jeb liked the night. He could move faster in the night. That meant he could find Shard LeFel faster in the night. And then he could kill him.

Other things moved along with him in the night. Animals going about their hunting and scratching. Some pausing to watch as he shambled by. They didn't come too close, so Jeb paid them no never mind.

Pretty soon he heard something more than animals moving. Pretty soon he heard the hiss, the pump, and the clatter of matics. Matics coming closer. Coming toward him. He stopped and listened while the wind hushed itself up high in the trees. Could be the matics were set out in the night to work the land. Maybe for a farmer. Maybe for a logger. Maybe for a rancher.

He'd seen matics, seemed a long stretch of time ago. Matics working something more than fields. Iron. Laying down dead iron for the steam engines. A rail. They'd been building a rail. He could not recall which way that rail had fallen. He thought and thought, but no memory filled that hole.

Jeb looked to the sky, the hangman's rope around his neck shifting across his back. He squinted to make out the stars through the juniper branches. He could not remember which star set the sky north. Could not remember much about the land he walked across, or the sky he labored under.

He was not much of a man left.

But the dragonfly wings fluttering against the silver box somehow dug deep down into his heart reminded him of one thing. He was set upon finding Shard LeFel. And once he did so, he was going to tear him apart.

The huff and hiss of steam escaping through metal vents filled the night. Might be the matics that worked for Shard LeFel laying down that rail.

Jeb cocked his head toward the sound. To his left. That was where the sound came from. That was the way he'd go.

A flash of brass out in the scrub brought his attention back down from the spangled sky.

A matic tromped out from behind a bush. Big as a horse and black as coal, it had spindle legs, four sets of two that all seemed to work independent of the others to keep it upright. The water tank hung down from the back of the long boiler body of the thing, and the chimney at the front had been worked into a horselike head with no eyes. Steam poured out of its gaping mouth. Brass pipes and valves and a ruby red whirring centrifugal governor stuck up out of the beast's riveted back like a porcupine's quills. And all across the side of it were six piston-driven arms, each ending in a thresher blade. Looked like a thing made to stomp a man to death, then mince his bones for bread.

It paused, huffing, six arms clacking, six blades clicking. The wind shifted, pushing at Jeb's back, and taking his scent right as you please to the matic.

The matic swiveled its misshapen head and stared straight at him—if it'd had eyes. Then it screamed—the sound of metal on metal—and a plume of thick white steam poured out of its mouth to swirl around its head. It took straight aim and charged him.

Jeb grabbed hold of a thick bough and tore it from the tree. Splinters sprayed over the dry ground. He'd been a strong man in life, and dying, each time he'd done it, had made him stronger. He hefted the branch across his shoulder like a baseball bat. The legs, he thought. First the legs, then the pressure valve there at the neck. Arms next, if he had to, then head.

The matic was almost on him. The heat from it stung Jeb's nostrils. The huff and clamor clogged up the strangely silent air.

Jeb stood his ground, no fear in his heart. He'd come back from death so many times, fear didn't have a hold in him no more. But hate . . . Well, hate he'd give all the room it needed.

Jeb swung high to block the blades and arms, then low and hard, taking out the first two legs. The matic's momentum sent it tumbling to the ground. Three sets of legs scrambled to lift it back up, while three sets of arms sliced at Jeb.

A blade cut his shoulder, drawing blood.

Jeb roared and swung again. The pressure valve just behind the thing's head popped. Steam screeched in a wild, blasting stream, but the valve didn't fly off.

Before the thing could fully right itself, Jeb took one more swing, this time at the head.

The branch broke; the head dented. The matic pushed up on its legs and threw Jeb to one side.

Jeb stumbled to catch his balance on his broken ankle, even though the rope around his neck dragged at him and slapped his boots.

The ticker paused, the steam still screaming out of it as it worked to balance without a set of legs to stand on. It didn't pause for long.

Jeb had to take it down and keep it down this time. He opened and closed his hands, wishing he had some kind of weapon to beat it with.

Maybe he could get to the tree and pull off another branch. He took a step and the rope around his neck struck against his boot again, near enough to trip him.

Jeb stopped. The rope. He had himself a weapon all along.

The matic wasn't moving quickly yet. In a tick, it'd be within stomping range; it'd be within mincing range, all six arms aimed to take Jeb's head off.

Jeb tugged at the rope at his neck. His fingers were thick and slow to work the knot, forcing it to loosen as he stumbled toward the tree.

The matic found speed in its footing and lunged.

Jeb tugged the knot free. He ducked the first slice and pulled the rope off over his head. The matic reared up, threshers slicing down, one after the other, tight and close in mechanical precision. Jeb scrabbled back and threw the rope up round the matic's arms, pinning them tightly together.

The matic jerked back, tightening the knot set in the rope. Jeb slung the rope over the meat of his shoulder and heaved to.

The metal beast dug back against the pull. Without its front legs it was heavy, unbalanced. The matic's back legs slipped in the loose soil. Jeb heaved again. It toppled, boiler gouging ruts into the hard ground as Jeb yelled out his rage, dragging the monstrous device a dozen paces, before dropping the rope and turning.

Jeb threw himself on the beast and grabbed at a valve with his left hand. He didn't care that it was so hot metal burned the flesh off his palm. He squeezed and tore it apart.

Steam released in a gout of wet heat. Jeb jerked away, out of the way of the steam, out of the way of the matic that thrashed like a fish tossed ashore, trying to right itself. He scooped up the rope, and took hold of the lowest arm at the joint. Then he leaned back with all his weight. Metal twisted and screamed as the ball popped free of the socket.

Just like ripping legs off a crawdad. Jeb plucked off the next arm, rods and gears twisting, snapping. Then he ripped off another.

The matic clacked and shook, running out of steam, running out of fire, legs driving like pistons, digging deeper into the soil.

Jeb dropped the rope and the thresher arms and reached for what was left of the head. There was glim in there, he could smell it, could taste it. More of it in that head than in the whole little owl ticker he'd ate.

Insatiable hunger washed over him. He didn't care if he had to walk into a storm of bullets or an army of knives to get at that glim. He would do anything to drink it down.

He got both hands around the head and twisted. Metal buckled under the strain, but the welds held. He squeezed harder, set his good foot against the boiler, and heaved backward, wrenching the head clean off.

He stumbled and fell flat on his back. If he'd been alive, it would have taken him a minute to get his lungs working again. But he didn't need for air, as such, anymore. Shard LeFel had seen to that. He sat and ran his fingers over the rivets and along the seams that held the head together. Then he pulled the head apart, his fingers strong, stronger than any living man's.

Suspended by wires and balanced among cogs was a glass vial filled with the same sort of green light he'd found inside the owl.

That glim would fuel him. Make him stronger.

Jeb pulled the vial out of the metal shell surrounding it, and shoved it into his mouth. He bit down hard, molars breaking glass.

The vial shattered. Not quite liquid, not quite gas, the glim filled his mouth with a hot, sweet juice. The burn warmed him all the way down his gullet, and set the dragonfly in his chest fluttering faster. He felt stronger. Much stronger. And the glim did some good to power the dragonfly too.

The devil's devices might be tough to crack, but the sweet inside was worth the trouble. Without the vial, the matic rattled like an unbalanced flywheel, the clatter inside it slowing, the steam cooling, until it lay still, a lump of useless metal, cold unto dying.

Jeb brushed the bits of glass off his tongue and smacked his lips. He stared at the matic a while or two. He had to get moving, had to get walking again. Where there was one matic, there would likely be more. Enough to slake his hunger. A dead man didn't need food to fill his belly. He needed glim to fuel his brain.

He pushed back up on his feet. His hand wasn't working as well and his shoulder seemed out of joint. Fighting the matic did him harm, but that would not stop him from finding LeFel. Would not stop him from returning to Mae. He took a few steps more—then a thought came to him. He should take himself a weapon.

The rope was a good weapon, so he took the rope. The matic's arms were strong and long and sharp like a scythe, so he took two of those too, hooking them over his shoulders.

Satisfied, he started walking. Toward the rail. Toward the end of Shard LeFel's life. Toward his Mae.

He made it quite a ways. Up off the scrabble of stone. Up onto a path through scrub that reached as high as his chest. Far enough his shoulder found its way back into the socket. Far enough the thin forest gave way to rolling hills with very few trees. He took the easiest path—along a tumble of boulders to one side that became a sheer rock wall on the other. The rail was out there. And he aimed to find it.

By and by, as he worked his way slowly through the dark, he heard them.

Matics. Clattering over the ground, thumping, skittering over the stones. They were coming. Coming for him. More than one. More than two.

He looked out far as he could see. There, through the scrub, cresting over the hill and pouring down toward him. Matics. He counted up to four, but more kept coming. So he stopped counting. Jeb found himself a stone to put at his back with plenty of room in front of him for swinging. He tugged the thresher arms off from over his shoulders and stood his ground.

Two of the matics spotted him. He licked his lips, already hungry for the sweetness in their heads.

The matics rushed.

Jeb Lindson smiled.

Then he started killing.

CHAPTER SEVENTEEN

Shard LeFel rarely slept. He had found no use for nights spent dreaming of death.

But tonight he was more restless than most. He waited outside the rail carriage, pacing the length of the observation platform, waiting for the return of the tickers he had sent to bring him Jeb Lindson's head.

The night was calm, a summer breeze mewling through the treetops. LeFel could feel his life ticking away like water through his hands. It was terrifying, this slow descent into death. If his brother only knew what he had cursed him to suffer.

Three hundred years of dying.

He'd torture him slowly for that, over months, at the least. Years, if he could.

The waning moon was tomorrow. It would be his last day alive, his last waning moon whose light would guide his return home. After three hundred years of searching, devising, making, and breaking, it came down to a mere twenty-four hours. If he didn't open the door before dawn, he would succumb to the sleep eternal.

The last component necessary to open the door out of this mortal world was the witch. And she was just moments away from being his. And now, knowing she was close, her magic nearly in his hands, LeFel could not hold still. Instead, he paced, the thunk of his heel and the tap of his cane metronome to his urgency, his need.

With his curse broken, the door open, the rails hammered down, he could fulfill his promise to the Strange and set them free from their pockets and nooks and nightmares. He would be their king, giving to them bolts and wire and steam to make whole their bodies. He would set them free to travel the iron rails laid down from shore to shore. Free to feed on mortal fear, blood, and marrow.

His brother had done all he could to stop the Strange from entering the mortal world, from supping on the humans here. But Shard would give the dark ones their desire. The mortals would die, Strange sicknesses, Strange blights, plagues, and madness, until the humans were erased from the land.

Shard would watch the fattening of the Strange with glee. He knew what it was to be a despised shadow. He knew what it was to be feared, hated, imprisoned. He understood hunger so very, very well now. That knowledge was a gift his brother had unknowingly given to him.

It was time for the Strange to hunger no more.

It was time for his death to end.

It was time to use the witch for his own desires.

The hulking frames of his rail matics, devices that pounded, ripped, hauled, and hammered, rested like slumbering metal giants along the edge of the forest. Shadowed except for where the rising moonlight rubbed iron and steel to a mercury shine.

The men who worked the rail were either in town drinking and carousing or else sleeping in the tent town up the rail nearly a mile or so.

He had seen nothing of the Madder brothers since earlier in the day, which suited him fine.

The brothers were part of the king's guard—he was sure of it. They hunted the Holder, and had stayed only a step behind him all these years, traveling faster through their underground tunnels and mines than he could on iron and wheel. They might suspect he had the Holder kept safely under lock and key, but they could not know that he had all parts of it assembled, could not know that he had it here, in his keeping, nor that he intended to use it this waning moon.

He was certain they did not know what else he possessed in the other two railcars: his menagerie of matics, and the door forged between worlds.

LeFel chuckled. It had been a game well played. He had trumped their moves, one for one, always a step ahead. Three hundred years among mortals had taught him nuances of deceit that had kept the king's best hunters, best devisers, best guards, stumbling behind his trail like blind fools.

The air suddenly washed cold, carrying ice and fogging LeFel's exhaled breath.

LeFel looked down into the darkness.

Mr. Shunt stood at the step at the bottom of the train-car platform, his face tipped up, lost in shadows even though the moon poured full upon him. The strong stink of oil and blood and burned flesh hung about him like a pall. He had been undone again. Mr. Shunt's uncanny ability to stitch himself up, no matter how much he was taken apart, was one of his more useful attributes.

"Why have you returned to me, Mr. Shunt?" LeFel asked. "Do you carry the witch in the corners of your cap?"

"No, Lord LeFel," Mr. Shunt whispered, his voice rusty. "The witch is in her house, at her hearth. Beyond my reach."

"It. Is. One. Small. Thing," LeFel said, biting off each word as if it were poison. "One small mortal!" He inhaled, exhaled, but still anger shook him. "A frail woman. Are you so weak that you cannot reach in and take her?"

"The dead man." Mr. Shunt's voice was just above a growl. "The tie between them—the magic—still holds her safe."

LeFel held very still though rage tore at his reason like a storm.

"Perhaps aligning my interests with you was a mistake, bogeyman."

Mr. Shunt jerked as if the words struck him flat across the face. But he wisely held his tongue, and narrowed his eyes as he watched LeFel pace.

Finally, LeFel came upon a second plan. "Since your arm is too short to reach her, we shall dig her out with a twig. Come," LeFel ordered.

He turned and opened the door, striding into a dark interior striped by moonlight. He knew the Strange would follow. He had all the things Mr. Shunt most craved—the door, the Holder, the key, and power.

The boy slept on a cot to the left of the train car. Even asleep, he held his breath until Shard LeFel and Mr. Shunt passed him by.

Through the inner door, and into the largest section of the carriage, Mr. Shunt trailed Shard LeFel, a silent shadow. Here the wolf was kept. A creature of night, it stared at LeFel, copper eyes glowing. There was too much intelligence in those eyes, too much hatred.

LeFel struck the wolf with the cane as he walked by and the beast snarled. But it was not the beast that he needed. No. He needed something of dirt, of earth, of stone. Something of cog and wire and bone. Not here. Not in this carriage.

Only Strangework would do.

He stormed through the outer door and into the boiler car, where his remaining half-dozen matics hunkered, chained and waiting. Even though the steam had long ago cooled, the matics shifted as he entered, the spark of glim in each of them powering muzzles and heads to rise, ready to do his bidding.

LeFel paused and considered each metal creature. Which should he destroy to power his needs? Not the strongest, a hulking man-shaped creature half-bent to fit within the car, piston hammers for arms. Not the swiftest, two beasts the size of dogs constructed of steel pounded so thin, you could see the shadow of the gears slowly ticking behind their curved ribs and knife-filled jaws. Not the deadliest, a heavily armored tractor with two self-loading, pivoted *mitrailleuse* barrels holding enough loaded cartridges to fire more than two thousand shots in under fifteen minutes.

No, it would need to be either the rabbit-sized ticker suited for scouting or the whiskey-barreled self-propelled battle mace.

"Mr. Shunt, disembowel the small ticker, and take from it what you need."

"Yes, Lord LeFel." Mr. Shunt swiftly caught up the rabbit-sized ticker in his hands, and put to use his wickedly sharp fingers.

LeFel did not stop to watch. He strode straight down the center of the carriage, not looking right or left at the metal creatures that shifted closer to the shadows, then were as still as gravestones. He opened the outer door and crossed to the final car coupled to his train.

One witch, one human, one dead man, would not stand in the way of his immortality, his revenge.

He pulled a key from a chain in his waistcoat and unlocked the door. He threw the door open. There were no windows in this carriage. There was just the one door. No other cracks for anything large or small to enter or exit.

Shard LeFel stepped into the room and Mr. Shunt scuttled in, latching the door tight behind him and throwing the room into complete darkness.

"Light, Mr. Shunt," LeFel barked.

Mr. Shunt snapped his fingers, steel scraping flint, and

caught fire to an oil-drenched wick of a lantern he plucked from the wall.

Mr. Shunt held that lantern high, the golden light washing over the room like a silken veil.

The room was spartan, shockingly so when compared with the other two carriages. Walls were lined with worktables, benches, drawers, crates, and shelves of iron and wood. Tools glittered, hung above the workbenches, tools that could pry, vise, weld, rivet. No curved edges, no rich trappings, no comforts here. This room was a place of extrapolation, of bending metal to the fevered dreams of the mind. A place of devising in a way most uncommon.

In each of three corners of the room stood a creature of bolt and gear and bone. Similar to Mr. Shunt, the creatures wore long woolen coats, layers of gray lace, tatters, and high collars and hats that covered their faces. They seemed nothing more than beggars hung to rot, but they were more. Much more.

They were Strange come into the Strangework bodies Shard LeFel and Mr. Shunt had devised for them. Fueled by blood and glim, they did not move, did not breathe, did not make a sound as LeFel and Mr. Shunt moved about the room. They were still as death itself. Only their eyes betrayed their true state, burning through the darkness and following LeFel's and Mr. Shunt's every move.

The Strangework had sworn to stand guard to the one precious thing in the room.

In the exact center of the floor was a platform. And upon that platform lay a closed black door the size of a coffin. That door did not lead to the ground outside the train car. That door, when pried by a blood key and moonlight, would take him home, and remain open, a hidden opening to this world, rolling on the dead iron tracks across the land.

LeFel strode to the wall and hooked the crook of his cane

into one of the lower cupboard doors, pulling it open. Just enough lamplight fell upon the contents to make out the shape. A wooden coffin. No larger than a small child. Just the size that would fit the blacksmith's boy within.

LeFel rested his cane against the open cupboard door and drew the coffin out with both hands. He carried it a short ways to a worktable and placed it on top.

Mr. Shunt craned his long neck to better see over LeFel's shoulder. Even the Strangework guards in the corners stirred in anticipation.

LeFel thumbed the latches and pushed open the lid.

Inside the coffin was a swaddled form, the size of a small child. LeFel removed the swaddling cloth away from the figure. Within the blanket was a gnarled, twisted piece of wood. The bark was papery as madrone, showing just peeks of pale wood beneath the peeling exterior. Three bones, perhaps each a joint of a human pinkie, were placed upon the wood, and all around it were gears, springs, levers, and wheels.

Once the blanket had been removed, LeFel spoke. "This, I will leave to you, Mr. Shunt. Prove to me again your worth."

Mr. Shunt drifted forward to stand next to LeFel. "The pleasure will be mine." He extended one long arm, spindly fingers wrapping around the chunk of wood.

LeFel smiled while Mr. Shunt worked a matter of devising he'd seen only the Strange attempt. By and by under Mr. Shunt's quick fingers, the bark shed away from the heart of the wood. Leaving behind something soft, something malleable.

It took no time for Mr. Shunt to carve the wood into the likeness he wanted. Eyes, nose, mouth, curve of cheek, and hollow of neck. Arms, body, legs. It was fine work and LeFel savored the mastery of each slice, gouge, and cut.

Then when the carving was done, when it was clear even in the watery lamplight that a child lay within that coffin,

Mr. Shunt dug in his pockets, and leaned forward to open several small drawers, withdrawing more gears, springs, and bolts, more bone, tendon, and bits of flesh floating in liquid-filled jars.

These he plied to the wood, hooking with steel, sewing with copper threads, running pulleys of sinew for joints, and bits of bone hammered in place like nails. For the Strange to walk this land heavy enough to leave footprints behind, they needed more than a doorway. They needed gears, blood, and flesh. Strangework.

"Blood?" LeFel asked as he watched Mr. Shunt's devising.

Mr. Shunt turned his head to stare at LeFel, eyes wide and red. "Yours, perhaps?" he whispered.

LeFel scowled at Mr. Shunt's naked desire. "You forget yourself, Strange," he said. "My blood is not in our contract."

"Yes, lord," Mr. Shunt said. "Of course, lord." He bowed, but his eyes did not lower. "What blood pleases you?"

"The dreamer's will do." He withdrew the small vial of the boy's blood he had taken earlier.

Mr. Shunt smiled, his teeth a ragged line of ivory blades. He took the vial, twisted the cork free with his teeth, and dripped the blood over the gears and flesh and heart of the wooden child, liquid splattering like a dark stain.

Then Mr. Shunt pulled a tiny vial of glim from his cuff pocket. The glim glowed like a green star upon his palm. This, he placed delicately into the slit in the child's chest, resting it carefully among copper wires and springs. He unstitched a thread from his own face, and sewed the glim up tight. He spoke a litany of words, old words, snake soft, clucking and catching in rhythm as each stitch joined flesh and fiber and cog.

When Mr. Shunt was done, he bit the string in two, setting the glim-fed gears into motion.

At the snap of thread, the creature in the coffin shuddered, then opened its eyes.

The Strangework in the corners of the room inhaled, and that smallest movement shifted the tubes that bound them at ankles and wrists to the doorway itself.

The stock, the changeling, the Strange, looked exactly like the blacksmith's boy, looked just like the little dreamer. Except when it smiled. Then its eyes were as old as the gravewood and flesh of which it was made.

LeFel picked up his cane. "To catch the witch, we must catch her heart." He considered the changeling with a critical eye. "The boy should show some hardships, wandering for days in the wilds; don't you agree, Mr. Shunt?"

"Indeed," Mr. Shunt breathed. He dragged thumbs across the boy's cheek, leaving behind a bruising welt.

The Strangework laughed. "More," it said.

Mr. Shunt tugged at its hair, nicked its ear, tore the shirt it appeared to be wearing—a shirt that looked exactly like the shirt the blacksmith's boy wore. The more Mr. Shunt nipped and scraped, cut and clipped, the more the changeling laughed.

"Enough," LeFel finally said. Then, to the boy, "You will lure the witch from her home."

The changeling nodded, somber as an undertaker.

"Bring the witch to where Mr. Shunt waits for her."

The changeling nodded again, then hopped out of the coffin, landing spryly on his feet.

That was no child standing in the middle of the floor. Even though it was the perfect image of the boy, from tousled hair to scuffed feet.

"See that she thinks you the lost child. Weep for her, laugh for her. Fear for her," LeFel said. "And do not fail me."

LeFel turned to Mr. Shunt. "You will take the dog with

you to catch up the witch. I will not have this night end without the witch at my feet."

Mr. Shunt bowed again and clicked his tongue. The changeling skipped up beside him. Mr. Shunt glided toward the door, the changeling at his heels, tearing holes in its shirtsleeves, pinching its own arms while it hummed a soft song to itself.

And then the Strange and the flesh-and-gear boy were out the door and gone.

Shard LeFel carefully placed all the shavings that had fallen from the making of the boy, all the splinters of bone, wood, and metal, into the swaddling, then tied it in a tight knot. This dark devising was best not to be left where even a stray breeze could stir it. He closed the coffin, set the latches, and returned the whole thing to the cupboard.

Shard LeFel walked over to the black coffin door in the center of the room. He dared run a single finger over the edge of the door, constructed by the Strange, bathed in the blood of a hundred sacrifices. He dared dream again of the moment he had waited three hundred years for. Death of the wolf, the boy, and the witch would open this door beneath the waning moon, and the Holder would see that his passage was clear.

He would be home.

Soon. So soon he could taste the need for it on the back of his throat.

He lifted his finger away from the door and instead pulled a silk kerchief out of his cuff. He wiped the kerchief over his lips, again and again, trying to blot up the hunger, the need.

"Soon," he breathed. He turned and hooked the lantern with his cane, then slipped out of the carriage, locking the door, and his only way home, behind him.

CHAPTER EIGHTEEN

Cedar ran. The night coursed by him, through him. His claws punctured dirt, tearing, rending the earth with each stride. The mountain thrummed with life, with movement, with living things that should be dying things. The need to kill rolled over him in a hot wave.

No. He had to find the boy. Cedar pulled against the beast, against instinct that leaned a hand over his throat.

The beast whispered: *Track. Kill. Devour.*

Cedar focused on the boy. Clung to that one goal to drown out the blood need. Repeated it like he was repenting a sin. *Track the boy. Hunt the boy. Find the boy.*

The beast twisted against his hold. Snarled at his thoughts, his litany. It was all Cedar could do to think through the hunger, to remember a need that was not bent by fang and claw.

Save the boy.

He followed jagged jackrabbit trails through the brush across the fields. The boy was not here. Not on this mountain. Not in these hills, nowhere near enough for the wind to bring him his scent.

Town. The tuning fork slapped against his chest as he ran, a single pure tone humming in beat with his footfalls, music only his keen ears could hear. The Strange were here.

Not near, but close enough the tuning fork whispered of their presence.

Kill.

Cedar stumbled as the blood need pressed against his hold.

No, he thought, taking back control. He would find the boy.

The wind rose as night deepened, dragging cold fingers through his thick fur and prickling against his skin. He shivered at the invitation, the freedom, the rightness of the night around him. No chains to hold him down. No locks to keep him caged. He could run forever and belong only to the night.

The boy, Cedar thought.

He was at the edge of the town now, and slowed. The press of humans living too near one another wove a thick blanket of odors. Softly, carefully, through patches of shadow and moonlight, he crept into town.

The blacksmith's shop beneath the water clock tower was dark and stank of coal. He didn't like coming so near the shop and tower. The slosh of water, ratchet and clatter of gears, stink of oil and grime, were too much. There were too many smells, too many noises to hide the sound of killing things, of footsteps, of bullets slid into chambers, of breath caught before a finger squeezed a trigger.

This was no place to hunt. This was a place to be killed.

Cedar stopped, fighting his dual nature.

Instinct said run.

Reason held strong to one thing only: *Find the boy.*

Cedar reined in his fear and made his way along the edge of a split-wood fence, then the side of the street to the Gregors' shop. The stink of ash and metal and grease stung his nose and fouled all other scents. He took two cautious sniffs, then crept around the back of the shop.

He could smell the sweat and booze of the blacksmith here, the second sugary scent of his wife, and other people he needn't name. His mouth watered. The overwhelming need for blood washed through his veins, took over his thoughts.

Cedar held against it, though he knew he could not hold for long. He sniffed the ground, working his way closer to the house. The beast was gaining strength the longer he denied the hunger. Quickly. He needed to find Elbert's trail quickly.

The boy's scent was strongest here, though still faint. The child had been gone too long, his scent rubbed away by other living things.

Cedar stood on his back legs, paws on the lower window-sill, nose at the wall.

The silver tuning fork swung forward and rapped the wood.

The single sweet note soured with the song of the Strange, too loud in the night, too loud in his ears, twisting in harmonies that made him want to growl.

The song was thick in the air. The Strange had been here. He sniffed for the Strange's scent and found it, an oily earthiness and rot, and beneath that, the faintest scent of the boy.

The Strange had taken the boy, covered the boy's scent, carried the boy. And he knew which way they had gone.

Cedar dropped back to all fours and turned, muscles bunched to run, to howl, to hunt. To kill.

A figure across the street paused. "Mr. Hunt?" a voice called softly.

Cedar froze. Man and beast warred. Man won.

"Mr. Hunt?" The figure across the street came closer.

He knew that voice. Knew that figure. Miss Rose Small.

But how did she know it was him? Maybe she was tetched in the head, and thought all wild animals were people from the town. Even if that were so, what would be the chance that she would call him by name? What was the chance she would know he was behind the wolf's eyes?

Rose had a handful of bolts and wires and washers. As she stepped into a pool of moonlight, the hunger pushed over him again, dragging against his reasonable mind.

Kill.

She sucked in a quick breath, her hand flying up to touch the locket around her neck, the cogs and gears and wires chiming to the ground. "Are you quite well?"

Sweet blood, sweet bones, flesh to tear, heart to pierce.

Cedar pulled against the beast's need, struggling to keep control.

Rose Small did not look like Rose Small.

To his man's eyes, she was the woman he had seen just yesterday. But through the wolf's eyes and the veil of the curse that brought both minds together, Miss Small was a woman filled with a glim light. It was as if she contained sunshine and summer, and all the stars glinting in the sky.

There was something of the Strange about her. Even the tuning fork hummed softly, not the sour song of the Strange in the windowsill, but a song much like he had heard back in the Madders' mine.

Miss Rose Small was not wholly human, a condition he reckoned she had not yet discovered.

She stepped out of the moonlight, and took to looking like herself again. She was bundled up in a long coat, but her bonnet was pushed back off her head. She'd obviously been out in the night, strolling the streets, ducking beneath limbs and crevasses to collect up nails and bits of wire. He wondered what she did with those bits and bobs, wondered if she devised matic and tickers and other such trinkets.

"Do you need assistance, Mr. Hunt? A doctor, perhaps?" She didn't come any closer, though she wasn't far enough away to be safe from him.

He inhaled the scent of her. His hold slipped slightly, and the beast within him whispered, *Kill.*

Cedar pushed against the beast.

She did not smell like the Holder the Madders wanted him to find. She did not smell like the Strange who had taken the boy, and she did not smell like the boy. Standing here was doing nothing more than wasting moonlight.

Find the boy. Cedar took a step backward, two. Three.

Miss Small nodded, just that easily accepting him as a wolf. "I see that you have things to do and a need to be doing them. I don't want to keep you, Mr. Hunt. Good night to you."

Kill, the beast in him whispered again.

Cedar silenced the voice with one word: *Hunt.* Before the moon set and dawn burned the beast out of his bones.

He ran, out into the fields. Not following the boy's trail yet, looking instead for blood and meat to sate the beast's hunger and give him back his reasoning mind. And he found it, in a calf who had staggered away from its mother, too frightened to cry out before Cedar lost control over the beast, and tore out the animal's heart.

CHAPTER NINETEEN

M ae Lindson heard a child sobbing outside her door, but did not want to unlock the shutter to see if her ears were telling her true. There was as much of a chance the Strange was outside her door, tricking her to think a child was outside. And equal odds that the Strange wanted to lure her into the night away from the protections of her cottage.

The door latch shook, rattled by feeble hands. The crying was right on the other side of her door, close as lips to the keyhole.

No words. Just sobbing.

Mae hesitated. She had spent the last few hours working spells on the bullets and shells, working protections on the Colt and the shotgun. She didn't know if a magic blessing would do any good on bullets. Didn't know if it would work against the Strange.

She held the Colt in one hand, the shotgun—not yet charged—in the other, one more precious shell set in its chamber. She fingered the switch on the stock of the shot-gun, and the weapon hummed. When the humming reached the inaudible tone, and the needle on the gauge pressed tight to the right, indicating the weapon was fully charged, she unlatched the door. She did not break the threshold, but stood there, shotgun at her shoulder, ready to fire.

On her doorstep stood a child, dirty, bloody, and bruised.

His nightshirt was torn, and his feet were bare. But his hair was wild and red—just like his father's—and he had brown eyes wide with tears that tracked a line through the dirt and welts on his cheeks.

The wooden trinkets and toys along the walls stirred. The breeze brushed through them, their song soft and uncertain.

"Elbert?" she said.

The boy swayed on his feet, obviously exhausted. He held out his hands like a baby reaching up for his mama.

Mae looked out past him. Nothing moved in the night. No sign of the man, or anything else chasing the child.

She quickly bent and picked up the poor little thing and brought him safely into her home, closing the door behind them and setting the lock.

Elbert clung to her like a burr, his head on her shoulder, arms wrapped tightly around her neck. He took a shaking, sniffling breath. He was cold as the night itself. Too cold. She needed to get him wrapped and warm, before he took to his death from exposure.

Mae rested the gun against her table, releasing the lever and stopping the motion of the gears. The hard green light in the vials drained away. She carried Elbert over to the hearth and eased him down into a chair.

"There, now," she said, working to get his arms off from around her neck. "You're going to be just fine now. Where have you been, little one? Your mama and pa have been looking high and low for you."

He let go of her neck, but didn't speak, just shivered and shook as he tried to wipe away his tears with the back of his dirty hand.

She pulled a thick, soft blanket out of the basket at the foot of her loom and wrapped it around his slight shoulders, tucking it tight beneath his chin.

"Do you want some water? Some milk?"

He sniffed and nodded.

Mae walked over to the cupboard, and drew out a jug of milk. She poured half the jug into a cup.

"Some nice milk will make you feel better," she said. "Drink it up and then we'll see if we can clean some of the grime off you so you can sleep. When morning comes round, I'll take you home to your folks."

She handed him the cup of milk, which he took in both hands and drank greedily. He licked his lips, and held the cup out for more.

She poured more milk, and again, until the jug was empty.

"Are you still hungry?"

The boy nodded.

Mae fetched him some bread and the last of the cheese. He ate both down quick as if he'd never eaten in all his days.

He held out his palms, fingers clutching air, begging for more food. Poor thing had been frightened dumb. She'd heard of children who never regained their voice after a hard scare. She hoped the boy was young enough to forget all this, and to grow up strong.

Mae dug through the cupboards, pulling out two apples. She gave one to the boy. He gnawed on it from the top down, core and all.

"Your mama and daddy will be so happy to see you in the morning. Let's wash your face and get you in a clean shirt." She walked off to the bedroom—really not much more than a bed tucked behind the privacy of the wall. The bed she had shared with Jeb. The bed that would always be too cold now.

She took a breath to steel herself. One of Jeb's shirts would be a good bit cleaner and warmer than that tattered thing Elbert was wearing. She opened the chest of drawers, and drew out a cotton shirt. She'd not cry. She'd not let her thoughts linger on her sorrow, on her heart keening with the knowledge that she'd never touch her husband again, never kiss him again, never say good-bye.

She shook the shirt, trying to dislodge the melancholy and hold tight to her anger. At least there was strength in anger.

The child started crying again, his snivel rising into a lusty wail.

"Hush, now, hush," she said, walking out into the room.

But the boy stood at the door on tiptoe, his fingers turning the latch.

"No, Elbert. Don't open that door." She ran across the room to stop him. But he was uncannily quick. He threw open the door, the hinges she'd repaired squalling at the force behind the swing.

Elbert glanced over his shoulder, eyes wide with fear and tears. Then he bolted out into the night.

Mae paused on her doorstep, every nerve of her body telling her not to go into the darkness. "Elbert!" she called. "Come back! Elbert!"

He was still crying, his plaintive voice carrying on the cold air to her. And just as likely carrying for any beast or Strange creature tripping the dark. She scanned the night for him. There—just the slightest blur of his white shirt in the darkness, like a dim lantern bobbing off across the field toward the forest. The forest where the Strange man had first appeared.

Mae grabbed up her shawl, her holster and Colt, and the Madders' gun. The child would be eaten alive, torn apart by Strange like that man, if she didn't catch him in time.

Loath to leave the safety of her cottage, she could not abide by letting the boy run to his death. She whispered a prayer, and ran out into the night. "Elbert," she called, loud enough surely the child could hear her. "Come on back now, Elbert. It's not safe out here in the dark."

From the sound of his crying, he was ahead of her, a bit to the left, and running fast to the forest.

He should be too tired to run so fast, should be too scared to do much more than curl up and hide. But the boy had gone senseless. Fear was probably the only thing that had kept him alive these two nights on his own. And it looked like it was going to be the thing that got him killed.

Mae could catch him faster on the mule, but if she took the time to run to Prudence, the boy would be lost for good. Again.

She wouldn't let that happen.

Something stirred ahead, toward the forest, then was silent. Mae recited a spell of protection, kept the shotgun high, and hurried that way.

She found Elbert just inside the forest. He was lying face-down in the sparse grass. Not so much hiding as just lying very, very still. She knelt beside him and gently touched his back.

"Elbert," she whispered. "We need to go now."

The boy did not move. He was so still, so stiff, it was as if he were carved from wood. She didn't know if he was breathing. Had he fallen? Had he hurt himself?

Moonlight slipped loose from the clouds, revealing a dark red stain matting the hair on the back of his head.

"No," she said. Mae brushed her hand over his head. He was bleeding. He was also still breathing, shallow and hitching, but enough. He still lived. But this wound would be more than she could tend on her own. He needed the doctor in town. Quickly.

She set the shotgun down to pick up the child.

"Witch," the wind whispered.

A hard chill ran down her spine. The voice sounded like the Strange. The same Strange she had shot. The same Strange she thought she had killed.

"I am the one who killed your man," the voice said. "And now I will kill you."

A beast growled from between the trees. Mae saw a flash of fang and claw in the moonlight. A wolf! She scrabbled for the gun and fired, sending one more precious bullet and an orb of gold light that bent the trees with a hurricane force.

In the split-second aftermath of the shot, the Strange screamed and a wolf snarled in pain as if that single shot had struck both creatures.

Mae did not wait for her eyes, half-blind from the gun-shot, to clear. She snatched up the boy and the gun and ran.

No time to reload. No hands to reload now that both were full of boy. Her heart pounded hard, fast. Her house was just ahead. If she could make the house, she could set the boy down, load the gun, fire the Colt.

The boy whimpered and grew even heavier in her arms.

Mae bent under the sudden increase in weight and nearly lost her balance. She scrambled to keep hold of the gun, hold of the boy, and hold of her feet beneath her. The child cried out, even though he was fainted away. Mae caught herself on one hand and one knee, then shifted the shotgun for a better hold to lay tight across the boy's back.

The child startled away from the touch of the Madders' gun, yelling for all his worth, his voice a shot of pain burst-ing up through the night.

And beyond his voice, she heard a wolf growl.

If she turned, the wolf would be on her, would strike her, hitting the child in her arms first, killing him. Then her.

Run, run, run. Faster. The door was just a few yards, a few feet, a few steps.

The boy stopped struggling, most likely fainted again from his wounds, boneless and heavy as an ox. Mae's blouse was wet with blood, her arms aching and shaking. The gun slipped from palm to curve of finger to fingertips in her sweaty hands. She was losing her grip on it.

The wind picked up, the Strange voice riding the air. "Glory be. The witch is free. Now I shall take what I see."

Steam blasted across her back as a hand slammed her into the door, nearly crushing the child, and knocking the wind out of her. Mae gasped to get air in her lungs, her ears ringing from the blow.

Hands, fingers, hard and cold and sharp as blades, tore the back of her dress, tore her flesh, tugging at the gun, her hair, the child.

Mae yelled and yelled and somehow pushed into the house. She lost hold of the gun, but kept the child safe in her arms. She ran to the bedroom, unminding the open door. She lowered the boy quickly onto the bed, groaning at the pain across her back. He woke and clung to her, holding her down by the neck like a rock on a rope, a pain-rigor smile on his face, his eyes wide and glossy, bloody spittle on his lips.

"Let go," Mae said. "Elbert, let go. I'll be back. You're safe. You're safe now."

It took some force to pry the boy's hands from around her neck. He was holding tight. Too tight. She was sure she left bruises on his little wrists, but she finally unlatched his grip, though his fingernails scratched a necklace of blood around her neck.

She turned, dizzy with pain and fear. She had to get the boy to a doctor. He was wailing in agony even now. But she had to kill that Strange first, and the wolf. Mae drew her fully loaded Colt and crossed to the door.

No Strange in the doorway. No wolf.

She was sure it was the same Strange as before, even though she knew that could not be possible. What sort of living thing put itself back together when it had been blown to bits?

She stood a yard or so away from the doorway. The Madders' gun was out there, beyond the wooden step. Jeb's trinkets along the wall hummed, perhaps lending what protection they could. Such a small hope against the hulking weight of the night that breathed and shifted, a living, brooding thing just beyond her door. Creatures waited for her out there. For the taste of her blood.

Mae whispered a spell, a protection, a blessing of magic and light to surround her home and all within it. The child's wail grew louder.

She kicked a stool in front of the door so it couldn't slam shut behind her; then Mae Lindson fired her Colt into the shadows beyond the door, and rushed forward. She bent, and grabbed for the shotgun.

From the screaming in the night, she reckoned the bullets had found a target.

She moved the stool and slammed the door. Mae threw the lock and reloaded both guns, her hands shaking, blood streaming down her back and neck. The Strange pounded the door, hinges she had just repaired already groaning under the assault.

The Madders' gun was charging, but its gears worked slower than last time.

The house wouldn't stand long. No, if she was to get the child to a doctor, to his family, she'd have to run now, before the roof came down and buried them both.

Mae rushed to Elbert, who was still as death, his eyes glossy red and staring at the rafters. Gone out of his head with fear.

Something slammed onto the roof and rolled like a boulder down the shingles. The windows rattled, and claws scraped against glass and pane.

"We need to go, Elbert." She wrapped him up in the blanket, tucking it tight around him as if he were a babe instead of a small boy. "I'm going to take you home to your mama and pa now."

He stirred to that, blinked, and started crying again.

"There, now, bear up just a bit longer." Mae gathered useful things into her satchel and pockets. Her tatting shuttle, an extra blanket, water, flint, and steel. Around her waist she strapped one of Jeb's work belts, buckled with pockets of leather that held tools. She slid her skinning knife onto that, then fastened her bonnet tight under her chin. She took a kerchief and folded it over the child's head, trying to stanch the bleeding.

His head wound was grim. Over the kerchief, she tied a woolen hat she had knit. It was too big for the boy, but it would help absorb the blood and keep his head warm from the night.

The wind and the Strange pushed, rested, then shoved at the house so hard, she threw her arms out to the side as the foundation shifted.

Mae scooped up the boy, and, thank the heavens, he wrapped his arms around her neck and held on. The shotgun was ready, no longer humming, the needle on the gauge cocked hard to the right. Mae opened the back door, quiet as could be. The Strange was still out front, rattling the shutters. Mae ran to where Prudence was sheltered beneath the eave of the shed, eyes rolling with fear.

Mae set the boy on the shed floor, took up the saddle, and geared Prudence as quickly as her shaking hands could manage. She ran back to the boy, Prudence in tow, and hoisted Elbert up onto the mule, swinging up behind him. She tucked him tight against her, one arm over his chest to hold him close, and still let her reach rein and stirrup. Mae rested the rifle across the saddle horn.

She pressed her heels to old Prudence's side. "Get up now."

Prudence didn't need urging. From round the back of the

shed, Mae set her off at a gallop toward town, up the rise in the hill, then down the drop of the tree-filled gully. Once through that edge of forest, she'd go straightway to Hallelujah.

She didn't want to enter that forest again, but the boy didn't have any time to spare. He was fever hot, as if coals lay beneath his skin.

Prudence shied at the edge of the forest.

"Go on, get," Mae said, putting her heels to her again.

Prudence locked her legs and refused to take even a step forward into the shifting shadows.

The boy whimpered, squirmed with pain.

Mae turned Prudence in a circle, and the mule, thinking she was headed back to the shed, finally lifted her feet. Then Mae dug her heels in again, spurring Prudence into a trot, straight into the forest.

The wind howled, wailed. She heard the crack of a tree-top breaking high above her. Old Prudence ran as if ghosts and goblins were on her heels. It was all that Mae could do to keep her on the trail to the town.

Trees flew by as Prudence galloped. Mae held tight to the boy, sparing a glance down at him just once.

He smiled, his small white teeth sharp and feral, his eyes too wide, too dark, too hungry in a face that was no longer sweet.

Then he attacked.

Mae screamed as he sprang up and bit her shoulder. She shoved at him, but he clung tight, fingers digging at her eyes, tearing her hair. He kicked the gun off the saddle and laughed. Even with all her strength, Mae Lindson could not hold him off as he sank his teeth deep into her neck.

CHAPTER TWENTY

Jeb Lindson knew how to fight. He had lived by wits first and fists second for most all his life. He knew how to tamp his temper too, when a fight weren't never going to go his way. And he knew when the odds were against a man, sometimes that was when the mettle of a man was made.

Jeb wasn't the sort of man to give up easily. Jeb wasn't the sort of man to give up at all.

But even an undead man with inhuman strength could see when he was outnumbered.

The tickers had surrounded him. Instead of attacking all at once like he thought they'd do, they'd taken their turns, deciding which monstrous metal beast would strike him. The small, fast matics had done him the most damage.

Matics, tickers, did not have the brains or reasoning of a man. But these tickers, these devil toys, carried vials of glim in their heads. Glim gave things power and unholy strength. And Jeb was sure it was that which made these matics clever.

They wanted him dead—he knew the truth of that. But they seemed to have put some consideration into how to kill him. Near as Jeb could figure, they wanted to kill him slowly, wear him down, then chop him up for good.

He still had the boulder at his back. The ground round in front of him was littered with scrap metal.

Jeb swung the scythelike arm of the first matic he'd taken

down. The blade was strong and sharp. Strong enough and sharp enough to cleave through six metal torsos of six metal monsters. Strong enough and sharp enough to smash through skull casings and pop rivets, so Jeb could suck out the sweet glim in their brains.

But they had done damage to him; that was plain sure. Jeb didn't so much hurt, even though he had cuts and gouges and hunks of missing flesh. He was wearing down, picked apart, broke apart. Soon he wouldn't be much left but a bag of bones.

A new ticker faced off in front of him. It was near the size of a man, body and head made of mahogany casing over brass and iron. Water filled what looked like a wooden keg on its back, and brass pipes fitted around from that pack into its belly. From the smell of it, it was powered by wood, not coal. Its four legs were all piston and spring. When it bent, it launched up and bounced from boulder top to boulder top, grappling hold with two retractable clamps at the ends of arms.

Jeb watched it bounce back and forth between the rocks, puzzling out how it might be strung so he'd know how to unstring it. It finally landed in front of him with the strangled-siren sound of pistons thunking and pumping.

Every ticker that had come at him had a way to be unmade, a weakness. There was a pile of twisted, dead matics behind him. He'd figured the jugular of every one of them. Cut through pipes, torn off valves, jammed vents, and ripped appendages and torsos apart. Didn't matter to him how to take one apart, just so much as he got it done.

This one, with the springs where legs and joints should be, was the hardest yet. Quick and wicked, it was near enough height to Jeb, but when it landed on its feet, rocks crushed to dust.

Heavy, then. Like a steam hammer.

Jeb watched it squat, the cow-sized head swiveling up to

pour green light in his face. He didn't know how many more tickers waited to attack back in the scrub. Maybe two. Maybe two dozen. There was still steam in the night, rising in wisps of clouds like thin lines of campfires, stovepipes, chimneys, rising in a wide half circle in front of him. Were there less tickers now? Were there less glowing green eyes, burning orange furnaces, glints of copper, silver, and steel in the night?

Hard to tell. Made no never mind. One at a time, by and by, he'd break them down, drink their glim, and leave nothing but metal bones and cold ash to show for it.

Spring feet clattered, like a chain somewhere inside it was pulling gears, winding tighter, tighter.

Jeb shifted his grip on the ticker arm he kept tight by his side, the length of which tucked between his arm and rib. He'd lost the other matic's arm he had also used as a weapon. But he still had the hanging rope, and held it by the end, letting the weighted noose dangle from his fingertips.

He tipped his chin to his chest, set his feet wide, and waited for the matic to attack.

The chain rattled louder, then paused, as if the ticker in front of him was holding a breath. The matic leaped.

Jeb swung the rope. The matic was up so high, it was as if it had wings.

The rope missed. But the matic did not. It landed against Jeb, long arms wrapped around him, pincers snapping for his neck.

Jeb roared as the heat from the matic burned through his clothes. His arms were strapped down tight. And the ticker squeezed tighter.

Jeb worked to think this through. Drawing a thought up through the fog in his head was hard as pulling roots out of parched soil. He had to break the matic's hold. Had to break it before it burned him up and cut his head off.

Jeb took a deep breath, then exhaled all of a sudden and

dropped the weapon out from between his arm and ribs. It was a sliver of room, the smallest space. But the matic's arms were ratcheted as tight as the workings inside it would allow. Jeb had a thought the matic hadn't been built for holding a man. It was just built for killing a man.

That small stretch of space was enough for him to pull his arm down. He twisted. Pulled one arm free as the ticker huffed and mandibles sharp as saw blades snicked and snacked at his face.

Jeb got cut, more than once, but he didn't care how much he bled so long as there was freedom at the end of it. With his free hand he grabbed hold of the matic's arm and wrenched it out of the socket.

The matic squealed. Steam and heat burst out of the hole in its side. A hole that revealed pipes and gears. The matic rolled its hand, trying to catch at Jeb's clothes, his flesh, and draw him in close.

Jeb beat the thing with its own arm, clanking away like a man pounding down a railroad spike. It squealed and squalled, bit and tore.

Jeb kept beating. Nothing but anger driving his arm that fell again and again like a pile driver. Nothing but anger driving him to keep going, keep killing, keep living so he could find his Mae. So he could kill LeFel.

Didn't matter how much the matic tore into him. Didn't matter the burns, didn't matter the chunk of ear lying on the ground, the three fingers he was now missing. Anger mattered. And anger got the job done.

It took a while, maybe a full five or ten minutes, before Jeb realized the matic had stopped moving. By and by he came to realize he'd been pounding away on the ticker, pulverizing it into a shredded pile of metal and wood. Water dribbled out over the mess of it, water dark with ash and oil.

All of it going cold.

Jeb raised the arm one last time, but the ticker was undone, unstrung. He straightened and felt the ground beneath his feet sway. He was tired. Sore tired. But there were more tickers in the shadows waiting to crush his bones.

He looked up, through the water and blood and bits of flesh that hung wrong-ways on his face. He looked up to see how many enemies he had left to kill.

The shadows were quiet. Silent. The wind was quiet. He didn't see any smoke rising. He didn't see any white plumes in the night, no glow of eye, no glitter of iron.

But he did not drop his weapons. Did not drop the rope that he still clutched in one hand.

The dragonfly wings in his chest beat hard, scraping against the silver bars of its cage.

And then the shadows were pierced by two red eyes, each as big around as Jeb's head. Jeb held very still, waiting for this new death.

The eyes disappeared, opened again, closer this time, disappeared again.

Dying made it hard on his reasoning faculties. But Jeb finally caught on to it. They weren't eyes of one beast coming to get him. Moonlight scuffed over the iron hulls of two huge round balls, each the size of a horse, but twice as wide. They dragged thick links of chains behind them.

And just as Jeb got his arms up to hit them, fight them, destroy them, the chains whipped out and chomped shackles down round his wrists, metal cuffs with teeth that bit straight through his bones. The matic balls whipped past him, yanking to one side of the boulder at his back, near enough to try to rip his arms clean out of their sockets. Jeb dug in his heels and yelled, leaning forward with all his weight, with all his anger, on one bad leg and a broken ankle. The matics rolled to a stop behind him, knocking together like uncoupled rail-cars hitting head-on.

Jeb held fast, stretched so far forward he was near flat above the ground, as he strained to keep his arms in his sockets.

The matics whirred, clanked. Two heavy hisses of steam dampened the air. They weren't pulling nearly as hard, and Jeb pushed his feet until he was standing straight again. He refused to step back toward them, but he did look over his shoulder.

The tickers had opened up at the bottom, and pushed out sets of wheels that were wrapped in a continuous track linked together and looped around like a belt.

Jeb pulled on the shackles, trying to break the chain between him and the matics. He was uncommonly strong. But the chains held fast.

A clank and puff of steam, and the tracks were rolling. Backward.

Jeb's feet dug in tight, then slipped. He leaned against the pull, but the tickers rolled slowly, inexorably around the boulder he had kept at his back, and backward still. Dragging him, inch by inch, to his death.

There was a cliff just a short ways back. And that was where the tickers were aiming.

Jeb pushed harder, the dragonfly wings in his chest buzzing at the strain. He lifted one foot, paused to keep his balance as ground gave way beneath his other foot, then took a single step forward. His left arm slipped its socket and he yelled again.

The matics strained against him, like to take his arm off. But Jeb lifted his other foot, and took another step. The matics didn't stop. They dragged him backward, tracks pulling harder, faster than he could outwalk them. Then a sharp tug yanked on his arms and he couldn't hear the tickers grinding dirt no more.

For good reason. Jeb Lindson felt the ground give way as he was pulled by the tickers over the cliff's edge, and down to his death.

CHAPTER TWENTY-ONE

Cedar Hunt paused on the leeward side of the ridge. The wind stirred, an unnatural gust in the otherwise still night. He crouched low, offering no silhouette against the darkness, his ears flat against his skull. He had lost control of the beast and left at least one cow dead before he had regained his hold over his need to kill. Now he followed the scent of the Strange and the boy. It had led him beyond town to this forest in a gully near the witch's house.

Something Strange pushed the wind, pulled the wind. Something unnatural rode the night.

He sorted the scents. Oil, death. Something more. Blood, flesh gone to rot, and the hot, burning stink of green wood scorched by fire.

And the boy. Somewhere in those scents was the boy. The boy's blood.

Cedar's heart beat faster. That was what he had gone out into the night for. He tightened his hold on the beast, even as the blood hunger rose up his throat.

He had found the boy. And now he would save him.

Cedar ran, taking the quiet ways, the hidden ways, the ways of predator and prey. It didn't take long for the wild rising wind to bring him more scents. Mr. Shunt, the rail man's creature, was out in this night.

And Wil.

Cedar stopped, pulling his head back and up. The hunger surged, blinding his senses with the painful need for blood—Strange blood.

No. He pushed against the beast, pushed against the hunger, and inhaled the scents again. Could he believe, could he trust, what his nose told him was true? He sniffed the wind, catching the telltale scent of his brother, the texture of the living Wil.

Wil, who had always been laughing.

Wil, who had always been trusting.

Wil, who had died at the beast's fang and claw, his fang and claw.

Cedar stuck his nose as high in the air as he could. Too many scents in that wind. Too many glints and hints of creatures, both living and dead. Wil. The bit of the world, the scent, that was uniquely Wil was there; he was certain of it. And it was not an old trail.

Wil was near the scent of the boy's blood. They might be somewhere near each other. Not that it would have mattered. Cedar ran. Not for the boy he had promised to save. Not for the Holder he had promised to hunt. Not for the Strange the gods had cursed him to kill.

Cedar ran to find the brother who had been dead all these long years.

He was wild with that thought, that fear, that hope. Wil. Alive. Wil. Here. Wil. In this land, on this soil. Wil.

Instinct whispered *trap* and *caution* and *death,* but Cedar was getting better at silencing the voice, smothering it. He would find Wil, find this scent of him and follow it into the fires of hell if need be. He would find his brother.

Brush rushed past, limbs whipped and lashed, the sharp fear of prey, large and small, lifted on the wind, carried by pounding heart, hoof, and paw, as Cedar ran through field, hill, and valley, even his great speed too slow for his racing thoughts.

And then the wind shifted, bringing with it the heavy stink of the Strange. Of old blood and dark metals. Of broken things strung with pain.

Of Mae Lindson. The witch. The beautiful golden-haired widow who stirred his heart in ways he could not admit even to himself. Her scents, her terror, and, more than that, her pain thick on the air, stronger than the boy's scent, stronger than the scent of his brother.

Cedar slowed, instinct finally winning over desperation. He'd go carefully into this place of death, tread softly, and kill swiftly.

Kill, the beast echoed.

The widow Lindson's house was near enough he could smell the fire from her hearth and the sweet spice from her herb garden. He peered through the night. Should he cross the field to her house?

No, the scent of Mae, of the boy, of his brother, came from the stand of trees.

Cedar slipped beneath the sheltering boughs, immersing in the deeper darkness.

Ahead, he heard a mule bray and a woman scream. Ahead, he heard the growl of a wolf. A male—his brother.

Wil.

Cedar ran to the edge of a small clearing in the trees, and saw with his own eyes a vision out of hell.

The widow clung to her mule as the animal bucked and reared. Something the size of a child crawled at odd angles over the beast, clinging like a spider to a wall, biting Mae, scratching, pulling, slapping.

And near a tall tree, not much more than a shadow himself, stood that Strange, Mr. Shunt. Too tall, too cold, fingers made of needles and blades and hooks, fingers tapping impatiently over the leather leash held in one hand.

At the end of that leash hunkered a wolf, ears flattened in fear, in hunger, eyes the brown of old copper. His brother, Wil.

It felt as if the whole world spun itself into the wind that battered at the treetops. Too many images, too many memories, warred through his mind. Wil's blood spread across stone and grass. Wil's mangled corpse. The taste of blood and flesh in his mouth. He had thought it was Wil, had known it had to be Wil. He had seen Wil change, twist beneath the curse just as he had changed. But then the blood hunger, the dark beast's need, had cast its thrall.

And he had lost all control.

Cedar was a learned man. He had not considered it before, too wild in his grief, but there was a chance, narrow, slight, that he had been so crazy from pain, from the change, from the cursed blood hunger, that he had not recognized his own brother. There was a chance that the wolf he had killed that first night he'd become the beast was simply that— a wolf.

He'd not stayed to bury it. Caught in the clutches of a high fever, he'd wandered incoherent for days.

A heartbeat, a breath, was all it took for those thoughts to rush through Cedar's mind.

And then the hot urge to kill the Strange gripped him again.

For the first time, Cedar agreed.

Mae Lindson fell from the mule, a yell of anger and pain filling the night. She scrabbled for a weapon—the gun turned by the Madders' ingenious hands—but the creature, the boy that was not a boy, caught it up first.

Mr. Shunt let loose the leash on the wolf. "Punish her, or I shall punish you," he hissed.

The wolf growled again, baring his teeth, his eyes

shifting from Mae and the boy to where Cedar crouched, hidden in shadow.

"Now." Mr. Shunt flicked his fingers, and the wolf snarled as if fire had sparked beneath his skin.

Cedar could smell the pain. Every nerve in Cedar's body told him to stay away from the Strange. Stay away from the collar snapped around his brother's neck. Stay away from the boy who was not a boy, who held the shotgun high and humming at Mae's chest. The boy who laughed while she bled.

But Cedar was not about to run.

Kill.

He rushed out of the sheltering brush, launched himself at the boy who was not a boy.

He caught the Strange boy and chomped down on his head, jaws pumping to crack it open.

The Strange boy screamed, yowled, beat at him with hands that were stronger than any grown man's. Cedar bit harder.

There was no crack of bone. No burst of blood. Nothing soft and savory beneath the Strange boy's hard exterior. The boy tasted of old flesh and copper coil and burned wood. Cedar growled. He shook the Strange by the head, and snapped its neck.

It was still laughing, plucking at Cedar's eyes, fingers sharp and stabbing.

What did it take to kill a thing like this?

Something struck Cedar from behind, throwing him to the ground in a tangle of fangs and claw. Wil.

Cedar pushed away and stared straight into his brother's eyes, at the madness of pain caught there.

He had a second, a breath, to rejoice. Wil was alive!

Then Wil launched at his throat, jaws catching his fur as Cedar twisted away.

Kill.

No. This was his brother. He would not harm him. Cedar snarled, hackles raised, head low in warning.

Wil lowered his ears, teeth bared in challenge.

There was no reason of a man in those eyes. There was only hunger, kill, and pain.

Blood hunger pushed at Cedar, but he would not attack his brother. Cedar growled in warning. Mr. Shunt snapped his fingers, the sound of flint against steel. Wil yelped, the stink of pain heavy on him.

Mr. Shunt had more than a leash keeping Wil kowtowed. He was using the collar to cause him pain.

Wil worked a slow circle to Cedar's left. Cedar glanced at the boy that was not a boy. Most of its face was gone, stripped away as if bark from a tree, leaving a fish belly–smooth surface where eyes and nose should be. A crack ran straight through the head, behind which peeked glints and spikes and spokes of gears and cogs. A rotted-flesh stink radiated out of the crack in its head, and the slash where its mouth should be was now an open maw where small black bugs skittered and oil seeped.

The witch, bloody and bruised, her hair free as spun gold in the moonlight, picked up the shotgun and snapped it to life.

At the sight of that gun, Cedar knew it meant his death. Knew it meant his brother's death.

Run, Cedar thought, *run, run, run*.

Wil rushed him, biting deep into his flesh.

Cedar howled in pain and fought his brother, no longer thinking of the collar, of the gun, of anything but being free of this attacker.

Kill.

He fought back, tearing at the wolf, as the wolf tore at him. Fangs, claws, jaws. Blood over muzzles, clogging nostrils. There would be an end to this fight, and that end would be death.

An orb of pure gold light shattered the night and stole Cedar's sight.

He scrambled away from the fight, dodging back to the safety of cover, his ears, his eyes, slowly sinking back to correct levels.

"Come out of the shadows, Strange," the witch said, her voice rough with anger. "And fight me on your own." She held the shotgun toward the shadows where Mr. Shunt had stood, but the gun was not yet recharged, the hum too low, the light too faint.

The boy that was not a boy was nothing but a pile of splinters now, smoking from the impact of the shotgun, metal springs and bits of bone sticking up like gristle in a stew.

Wil had backed away into cover just as Cedar had.

And for a moment, Wil's eyes were clear, sane. He looked at Mae, at the broken boy, and over at the shadows where Mr. Shunt had been. And then he looked at Cedar. There was a spark of recognition between them. Wil knew it was Cedar in wolf form just as Cedar knew it was Wil.

Cedar could see his laughing brother, his trusting brother, in the wolf's eyes. They held gazes for a moment; then Wil threw himself across the clearing, fangs bared. Launching himself at Cedar.

Cedar heard the snap of a twig behind him and spun.

Mr. Shunt was behind him, a long, hooked prod in his hand. His teeth glinted bloody red as he jammed the stick into Cedar's side.

Cedar twisted, but not fast enough. The stick punched through his skin and scraped bone. An explosion of pain shuddered through him, like lightning from the sky had just fused him to the ground. He howled and snarled, but no voice was big enough to contain the heart-stopping pain.

The world was agony. Agony that burned him alive, agony that ate away his bones and flesh and mind.

He could not move. Not even his eyes.

He felt the weight of his brother hitting Mr. Shunt in the chest. And that impact broke the stick off in his wound.

Cedar heard Mae cock another gun—a revolver—but she did not fire, likely could not get a clean shot at Wil or Mr. Shunt with Cedar in the way. He wondered where the Madders' shotgun was, but knew, by the low humming, that it had not charged enough for the next shot.

Cedar braced against the pain, rolled his eyes, and pushed his feet. He could not move them. His muscles strained, but he could not feel them.

And then he heard, very clearly, Wil howl in pain. He smelled the thick stink of fur and muscle and bone burning away.

The prod.

Wil howled and howled.

Cedar pushed against the pain, moved a foot, struggled to lift himself, but only his front legs responded. He pushed up.

In time to see Mr. Shunt, one arm full of the bloody, broken bits of the boy who was not a boy, his other hand stabbing Wil again and again with the jagged pike.

Killing Wil, killing his brother, when he'd barely discovered he still breathed.

Cedar snarled and dragged himself toward Mr. Shunt.

Mr. Shunt glared at him, then shifted his gaze to Mae.

Shotgun at her shoulder, there was no more humming. The glass vials fanned out like a half-dozen lanterns, throwing her face in blue light and grim shadow. The shotgun was charged. Ready to fire.

Cedar smelled the fear roll off Mr. Shunt as he stared down the barrel of that gun.

But before Mae could squeeze the trigger, Mr. Shunt turned and ran—not like a man runs, but on all fours, new hands sliding out of his coat to hold Wil and the bits of the boy who was not a boy tight against his chest. More hands, feet, limbs, sliding out from where his legs should be. And all those limbs, hands, feet, and gears made him fluid and as fast as rainwater rushing down a pipe.

In less than a blink, Mr. Shunt was gone.

Cedar dragged himself toward the spot where his brother had been. Alive. Cursed, but breathing. He could still smell his brother's blood, his brother's pain.

Cedar tipped his head to the sky and keened out his sorrow. He had lost him, lost him so soon to finding him.

And he didn't know if Wil would live through the night. Didn't know where the Strange had taken him.

Branches snapped again, the sound of footsteps coming near. He snarled in warning, though that was all he could do.

"Is there the mind of the man still left to you, Cedar Hunt?" Mae asked from close by. "It's the moon that ties you to the wolf, and the moon will be setting soon. But I won't stay out in this dark for a moment more."

Cedar was panting. He understood half the words she was saying, his mind falling into an exhausted fog. The pain still rolled through him, as if the pike had been covered in coals that bit and chewed, trying to burn a way out from under his skin. The wound Mr. Shunt had given him felt like it was getting worse fast.

The witch stepped nearer.

She pointed the shotgun at him. "I'll tend you best I can, but the mule's gone and run home, and I can't carry you. Can you walk, Mr. Hunt?"

Cedar understood "tend" and "walk." More, he sensed in her a willingness to soothe, to mend and comfort.

He wanted to run, to hunt and tear the flesh off the Strange who held his brother captive. To kill. But the urge to follow her was stronger, even though breathing was a chore and the only blood he could taste was his own.

He pulled his feet beneath him and pushed up. His bones felt like they were stitched together with fire. But he could move. And he did. Following behind the beautiful widow, Mae Lindson, who carried the charging rifle in one hand and her revolver in the other.

He didn't know how long it took; it felt like miles, it felt like years. But they were finally at her doorstep.

"Come into my home, Mr. Hunt, and welcome here. May these walls give ease to your pain."

Mae pushed open the back door and stepped inside.

Instinct whispered: *Run.* But he was too exhausted. Thirsty. There was water in the house, clean water. And the walls would hold out the Strange as good as any hollow he could curl up into.

Even now the moon was sliding down the edge of night, and the change would strike him. He would wear a man's skin. The need to find shelter and safety before that happened was overwhelming. Stronger even than the wolf's instinct to kill.

Cedar stepped into the house and let the witch help him to a bed of blankets spread out by the fire, and water poured into a bowl. He rested his bones and drank his fill, then fell into a hard, unbroken sleep.

CHAPTER TWENTY-TWO

Rose Small stood and stared long after the wolf had turned and run. She knew it was the bounty hunter, Cedar Hunt. Could tell from his eyes, could tell from the living things, trees and such, whispering to her that he was not the animal he seemed to be. That he was a man hidden in plain sight.

She'd never seen anything like it, and didn't deny it rattled her to her bones. She knew she should go home, sneak back into her room beneath the notice of her pa and ma, as she had so many restless nights in the past. They ought to be asleep by now. Rose turned and took no more than three steps down the street when she saw a group of six men, rowdy and drunk, rambling her way.

And at the head of them all, swigging off a bottle of whiskey he'd likely annexed, was Henry Dunken.

Rose slipped into the shadows, pressing her back against the blacksmith's shop. The smell of ash and metal calmed her, the feel of the familiar shop soothing. She carefully, quietly dropped into her apron the bits of metal—springs, nails, bolts—she'd been gathering. Rose Small put her hand around her gun instead.

The men were yelling now—arguing. Rose winced at their language. They were arguing over which woman who worked the brothel did her job the best.

Rose held her breath as they drew nearer. If she was

quiet, they might just walk past her. But something, maybe just plain bad luck, turned Henry Dunken's gaze her way. He stopped cold in the middle of the street, then started over toward her, his pack of friends following behind him.

"Well, well, well," he said, each word slurring into the other. "Look who's out wandering the night without an escort. Little Rose Small."

Rose pushed off the wall and started walking. The gun had one shot only. She couldn't take them all down. The kind of men Henry Dunken ran with wouldn't let one gunshot stop them. From doing most anything.

Rose went through her options methodically, but with amazing speed. Fear did that to her—slowed down the outside world, and gave her plenty of time to sort options, discard, and choose. Not the blacksmith's shop. Even though she could turn herself around and get in there before they caught her, and even though almost every inch of the shop was covered in something that would make a good weapon, it was still one against six. They'd pin her, beat her, and then they'd do things she'd only heard whispered in the lowest tones, by people like Sheriff Wilke.

Yelling for help wouldn't do anything. The sheriff and any other decent souls wouldn't hear her, tucked up in houses, far off on farms.

Not running. It was too far to run to her house—or the mercantile. They'd outpace her. She had no horse. No chance reasoning with them.

That meant she'd have to bluff.

Rose turned quick on her heel and headed for the blacksmith's back door. She knew it was locked. Knew Mr. and Mrs. Gregor must be sleeping. But she doubted either of them was sleeping deeply since the disappearance of Elbert. There was a chance they might hear her.

The men behind her laughed and picked up their pace,

boots thumping the hard-packed dirt like a ragged army on the march, aiming to run her down.

Rose's hands shook and her pulse quickened. She reached the blacksmith's door and knocked and knocked. She was already doubting her decision. Tucked up this tight against the house, Henry Dunken would hold her down and do anything he could think of to her.

She'd grown up with him. She knew what kind of mean he got when drunk.

Well, she knew where she'd be aiming her gun first. She turned.

"I'll say good night to you now, Henry Dunken," she said firmly, with no hint of fear in her voice. "And you and your friends will be on your way."

"Oh, I don't think so, Rosie, posie, crazy Rosie." His voice was singsong sweet. "I think you and I are going to dance off the night."

Rose pulled the derringer out of her apron and pointed it straight at his head. "You think wrong."

One thing she could say about the men. Even drunk, they recognized a gun when it was pointed at them.

"That little pepperbox ain't gonna do you no good, little Rosie," Henry Dunken said. "Only got yourself one bullet there. And there's six of us."

"Then I suppose I'll need to prioritize who, exactly, I despise the most." Rose held the gun level with Henry Dunken's head. "Why, I do believe that is you, Mr. Dunken. And once this shot goes off, Mr. Gregor will be out here faster than your boys can run."

"Think that old mule can get here faster than the boys can shoot?" Henry asked.

The door behind Rose clacked with the heavy slide of a bolt being unfastened and a key turning.

"Don't think we need to find that out, now, do we?" she said.

The door opened and the big form of Mr. Gregor loomed up behind her.

"What's all the racket about?" Mr. Gregor stepped forward. Rose moved to one side to let the big man pass her. Mr. Gregor's hair was stuck up at odd angles. He had on his trousers over his long johns, suspenders snapped in place, and his boots untied, but no shirt or coat. They must have gotten him out of bed.

Mr. Gregor carried a shotgun. He quickly assessed the situation, noting with a grimace the gun that Rose hastily stowed back in her apron.

"Henry Dunken," Mr. Gregor said. "I don't care what fire you're full of tonight, but you and your boys will take your shenanigans away from my doorstep and my property, or I will bring Sheriff Wilke into this."

"Why, of course, Mr. Gregor," Henry said with a smile. "Didn't mean to rouse you. I was just seeing Miss Small back to her home, like her folks told me to. Miss Small?"

"No, thank you, Mr. Dunken," Rose said to his outright lie. "I'll find my own way home."

"Can't have a lady like you out wandering." Henry Dunken gave Mr. Gregor a tolerant look. "You know how she gets sometimes." He tapped his forehead. "Poor thing."

Rose clenched her teeth to keep from telling Henry Dunken just what he could do with his false pity. But Mr. Gregor saw right through Henry's words.

"Go on your way," Mr. Gregor said. "I'll see that Miss Small gets home."

Henry's smile disappeared. He looked from Mr. Gregor to Rose Small, back to Mr. Gregor. Rose kept her hand on her gun, and her chin high.

One of Henry's boys slapped him on the shoulder, breaking the tension. "Come on, now, Henry. She's gonna be fine."

Henry wiped his face with one hand and positioned his

smile back into place. "I reckon that's true, now, isn't it? Good night, Mr. Gregor. Good night, Miss Small."

He turned about and sauntered off, the ruffians crowding around him like dogs in a pack. Rose forced her fingers to let go of the gun, her knuckles stiff and sore from holding on to it so tightly.

"Mr. Gregor, I'm so sorry," she began.

"Rose Small," he rumbled. "If I were your daddy, I'd give you a proper talking-to. What in the devil got into you to be out on the street this late at night?"

Rose normally wouldn't stand that kind of talk from anyone. But she reckoned Mr. Gregor was more of a father to her than her own father had been. So she told him the truth. "I was restless. Needed some fresh air. I went to stand on the porch, is all. Then I noticed a bit of metal in the street." She dug in her apron for the proof of it, fished out a nail. "I didn't want to leave it to waste."

Mr. Gregor took a deep enough breath, his chest rose up a good six inches. When he let it out, his words were worn down, soft. "I don't know what gets into that head of yours, Rose." He started walking and Rose followed along.

"You're old enough to be a man's wife now, and yet you still do these things." He shook his head. "Just because people in this town think you're wild, doesn't mean you should give them more reason to talk."

"But—"

"Listen to me, Rose Small. You're too old for this now. It's time you pull your eyes down out of the stars and start thinking about getting married, raising a family of your own. And it's time you stop walking out at night alone. These streets aren't safe. Not for a lady. Not for anyone." He glanced down to see if she understood.

"What if I don't want to raise a family? Don't want to be married?"

They were halfway to her house now, the moon slipping behind clouds, darkness growing thicker.

"What else would a woman want for?"

"To make things. Devise things. Maybe fly an airship to China and back." She paused, then, "I have *dreams*, Mr. Gregor. Of making a difference in this world. I can't think of living any other way."

Mr. Gregor was silent for the rest of the walk. Rose didn't know what he was thinking, and didn't have the courage to ask.

Once they made it to her doorstep, he finally spoke. "Dreams can be dangerous things, Rose Small."

"Reckon the whole world is filled with dangerous things, Mr. Gregor," she replied. "Can't imagine dreams should be any different. But thank you for your kind words. They haven't fallen on deaf ears."

He nodded and nodded, looking relieved she'd admitted as much.

Then Rose Small let herself into her parents' home, locking the door, and the night, behind her.

CHAPTER TWENTY-THREE

Shard LeFel gazed down at his floor at the pile of wood and bones and gears that had just hours before been a creature most strange and divine. Mr. Shunt lingered in the shadow of LeFel's living quarters, but held just inside the railroad car's exit, LeFel noted.

"You have failed me, Mr. Shunt. Twice," LeFel said to the skeletal shadow of a man. "What a pity you are. I shall not offer you another chance to bring the witch to me."

He picked up his cane and prodded the pile of flesh and wires with it. Nothing in there, not a spark of living left to give the Strange another chance to occupy that body, to walk whole and solid in this world.

It was a waste of gears, a waste of gravewood, a waste of blood, bone, and steam.

And it had all been a waste of time. The witch's life, and her magic, were no closer to his possession.

He had gears, he had matics, and he had steam. But he did not have time left to waste.

"If you cannot secure me the witch, then I shall call upon her own kind to place her in my hands. Mortals have their uses."

LeFel turned. The wolf, barely breathing and bleeding heavily from Mr. Shunt's disciplinary administrations, didn't even have enough air to whimper. It would be dead soon, but not before the moon rose to open the doorway home. LeFel would make sure it lived that long. One day. And no longer.

LeFel picked up the bits of wood, bone, and metal, heavy in his hands, and warm even through the black leather gloves that he wore.

He threw the mess at Mr. Shunt, who did not flinch as limbs and coils struck his coat and slid to the floor at his feet, leaving a slime of oil and blood behind.

"Stitch that back into breathing. Set a tick in its heart. And be sure that it exactly resembles the blacksmith's child. Exactly."

Mr. Shunt did not smile. His gaze was hard and dead as iron.

"And do it before the sun burns to noon."

Still Mr. Shunt did not move.

The Strange was showing far too much of its own resolve. Any other day in his near three hundred years on this land, he would have reminded the Strange exactly of its place. And who, exactly, was its lord. But so long as Mr. Shunt did as he was told for one day longer, LeFel didn't care what notions or hard hungers the Strange hid from him.

"Leave me, Mr. Shunt, and see that you do as I bid," LeFel commanded.

Mr. Shunt bent, just so much as a degree, his gaze locked on LeFel. He swept out his arm, and his coat followed, the hem lifting and brushing over the pile of bones and bits, wiping the expensive rug clean of the shattered creature.

And then he was gone, through the door that let a breath of air into the room, stirring the lace and silk curtains, with the clean, fae light of stars promising a new day rising.

The door latched tight and the shadows of the room returned.

The mortal boy, the true blacksmith's child, shifted in

restless dreams on his cot. "Not much longer, my child," LeFel cooed. "Before the next dawn, I will slough off this world as nothing more than a bad dream, and all your pain, your fear, your dreams, will be gone, forever."

The child did not open his eyes, but LeFel knew he was listening, knew his dreams were filled tight with his words.

"There can be no steam without fire," he said as he pulled his gloves off one finger at a time, then poured fine brandy from a crystal decanter. "Just as there can be no justice without bloodshed."

He drank from the glass, and drew the curtain aside, waiting patiently to watch his last sunrise break over this mortal world.

CHAPTER TWENTY-FOUR

Mae Lindson pumped a bucket of water in the sink and first washed her hands and arms. She was scratched and torn even though she'd been wearing gloves and long sleeves. Her neck stung with sweat; so did her chest and face. Her back hurt whenever she moved her shoulders too quickly. Every inch of her felt hot and stiff.

Elbert . . . no, not Elbert. That Strange, that changeling child, had turned on her like a wildcat.

She splashed water over her face and held her hands there, cold and shaking. That changeling child had tried to kill her. It had tried to tear her apart.

Ever since the rails, ever since the dead iron had stretched out like poison in a vein across this land, the Strange had become stronger, hungrier. She'd never known a Strange to be more than a spirit, a nightmare, a wisp. At the most, they could slap, bruise, tangle a knot, and lead astray.

But this thing, this Strange child, had seemed alive as any mortal man, so much so, she had thought it really was Elbert and held it and soothed it as if it were a babe. Mae exhaled through her palms and pulled another handful of cold water to her face, then down to her neck.

The Strange were spreading like a blight across the land, as quickly as the rail was laying down. And for no reason she could understand, they were becoming bolder, stronger.

Mr. Shunt, a Strange if ever she saw one, had said he killed Jeb. She did not doubt that he spoke true, especially since she had seen just how vile he could be. And in so showing himself, he gave her the face and nature of the killer she hunted.

She pulled a cloth from the wall peg and wiped it over her face, the back of her neck, then her arms.

She took stock of her wounds. Her gloves had done good to keep her hands whole, but she'd need to bind the deep gouge on her upper arm and tend a hundred other scratches that already felt as if they had gone rank.

Mae took her time to do that right, then applied tinctures to her cuts and bruises. It was not lost on her that she had brought a wolf into her home. Bleeding in front of it was foolish. But the wolf that covered the man inside was so still upon the blankets by the fire, she would think it were dead except for the infrequent rise and fall of its ribs.

If Cedar Hunt was going to survive those wounds—much more grievous than her own—he'd need care, likely bones to be set, and whatever blade was buried in his side removed.

She didn't know that she had the will to tend a beast that could turn on her and kill her. Didn't want to tend a beast holding a gun to his head.

But he had fought the Strange for her, and stood between her and the other wolf. He had protected her. Likely as much saved her.

Mae tugged tight the binding around her arm, using her teeth to set the knot. She looked over at the wolf. She had thought she could break his curse, and she wondered now, looking at it clear in front of her, if she was strong enough to do so.

She might be able to ease the curse, to give him some respite. But she was too exhausted and too shaken to so much as try to now.

Best she could do for him would be to tend him. Her hands were still shaking, and all she wanted was to curl up in her bed, in the bed she and Jeb used to share. But if she didn't do something to help the beast, Cedar Hunt might not make it to the rise of morning.

Mae set herself to the task. She knew how to mend a bone, tend a wound. She had a deft hand with herbs and tincture and the blessing of magic to encourage health and strength.

She put a pot of water over the hook in the hearth and then made herself busy collecting what she would need. Fresh water for him to drink if he came conscious, her Colt, loaded, in the likelihood he wouldn't listen to sense. She also gathered a basket of rags and tinctures and her cotton sewing thread.

She first put the bucket of water down by his head where the bowl had been.

"That's water for you, Mr. Hunt," Mae said. "It'd do you good to drink your fill."

The wolf opened his eyes, but just as soon closed them again. He hadn't moved.

"I'm going to wash your wounds, what I can, at least," she continued. "I'll thank you not to struggle, but if you do, I'm not afraid to use my gun." She knelt with the basket on one hip and the gun in the other hand.

Still, Cedar did not move. "I'll be talking so you remember it's me here doing what I can to ease your pain. Do not bite, do not scratch, and do not fight me, Mr. Hunt. Neither of us wants to see the other dead this night, I'd presume."

Mae placed one hand on the beast's side. He did not move, did not twitch. Whatever the Strange and wolf had done to him, it had wounded him deeply. Deep enough that even the wolf instincts could not make him fight her.

His fur was long and bristled on top, but beneath that, it was thick and warm. She smiled despite the weary weight of the night on her shoulders. She had never touched a wolf before, never felt a living heat, a pulse, beneath such fur.

Though she found herself wanting to savor the sensation, she didn't let her fingers linger long. Instead, she began ascertaining his wounds.

The puncture between his ribs was deep and wide. It looked as if a torch had been thrust into his bones. The fur was burned and matted with blood, his flesh curled back and blackened. There seemed to be an oil of some sort on the edges of the puncture, and blood and other fluid welled from it.

Deep, that was sure.

"This isn't so bad," she said, keeping her voice calm. "First I'll wash it out. The water will be cold." She tucked a towel against his stomach and rested her gun over her knee where she could catch it up quick if she needed it. Then she poured a cup of water over the wound, holding it open with her fingers as she did so.

He whimpered, a faint hurt sound in the back of his throat, but did not move.

The water welled out of it, bringing up with it a skittering of black bugs that swiftly died and liquefied into oil.

Mae rose up quickly and traded the water for a jug of whiskey. Whatever Mr. Shunt had broken off in Cedar, it had turned into creatures that crawled, and likely bit and bred inside his flesh. If she didn't kill them quick, and clean the wound thoroughly, they might just nest inside him and eat him from the inside out.

Mae kept talking. "That's good, Mr. Hunt. I know it's a deep wound and it hurts, but I'll be able to ease some of the pain and burn. First, though, you'll feel fire."

She knelt again and opened the wound with her fingers, pouring the alcohol into the wound. Cedar whimpered and growled, but still didn't move, as if even that much sound exhausted him.

She soaked a strip of rag in the whiskey and tamped it as deep as she could into the wound, then pulled it out. It was covered in dead black bugs that smeared into an oily mess.

Mae threw that cloth in the fire, and poured more whiskey into the wound. She repeated the process a dozen times until the last cloth came out bloody but mostly clean. Then she packed the wound with herbs that would soothe and draw out infection.

Cedar had long ago gone unconscious.

Mae still talked to him, her voice as much soothing her nerves as his. "What manner of curse do you bear? I've never seen such magic used on a man to change him. The old lore speaks of beast and man exchanging skin, but I've never seen a curse thrown so heavily, so bone deep."

She paused, letting her hands rest gently upon his side, well away from the wound. Magic came best with herb and earth and song. A curse was like a spider's web—silken and difficult to see, but strong and clinging, knotted tight. And this curse was more powerful than she'd ever seen. If she had the right herbs, if she had enough time, and perhaps a circle of sisters to support her work, she might be able to break his curse.

But she had no time, herbs, or sisters' helping hands tonight.

"I'm going to touch your legs and see if there is blood any-place else," she said, giving up for the moment on the magi-cal, and tending to the practical. She ran her hands quickly down his legs, over his back and hindquarters, then drew them up to his head.

He was scratched and bitten on his muzzle and by his eye, and one ear was torn and bleeding. There was a puncture at the top of his head too, and all the scratches and wounds seeped. But there was nothing like the wound in his side, and no other oily black bugs.

"I'll clean your head next. Mind you, keep your teeth to yourself." Foolish to bathe a wolf on her hearthstones, but

Mae had given up being afraid of him. Oh, she should be, but either the events of the night had dulled her good sense, or the look of intelligence in the beast's eyes before he had fallen asleep had won her over.

She gathered cup and cloth and did what she could to clean and dress his other wounds.

After an hour or so, exhaustion near stole her breath, but she wasn't yet done with his scrapes. She reckoned the shallower cuts could wait until morning.

"That's enough for now," she said. "There's still a bucket of water if you want it, Mr. Hunt." Mae pushed up onto her feet, and locked her teeth against a moan. Pain stitched down her back, her hips, her arms. Not only had that creature torn her up, but she'd also taken a fall from the mule.

She longed to crawl into bed, to curl up and sleep away this nightmare her days had become. But she couldn't bring herself to lie again in the bed she had shared with Jeb. The rocking chair would have to do. That way she could be on her feet if Mr. Hunt woke.

Mae kept the gun with her and stepped back to the bedroom and pulled off her dress, boots, and stockings. Standing in nothing but her underdress, she pulled the heavy wool blanket around her shoulders and walked out to the living room. The wolf was still sleeping.

She picked up the shotgun where she had left it on the kitchen table, and took it and her Colt with her across the room. She sat in the rocking chair, nearer her spinning wheel than the hearth, and turned so she could keep an eye on Mr. Hunt. She propped the shotgun across her lap, and kept the revolver tucked inside the blanket with her.

She closed her eyes and slept.

The sound of water sloshing woke her.

Mae opened her eyes.

Cedar Hunt—a man and not a scrap of animal left—sat on his knees, the blanket he had been lying on now wrapped about his legs and waist, leaving his wide, scarred chest bare. He scooped water out of the bucket and drank handful after handful.

His hair was wet—he must have poured some of the water over his head—and lines of water trickled down his neck, shoulders, back, and chest, falling along the chain and tuning fork he wore, to drip upon the blanket.

It had been a long, long while since Mae had seen a bare-chested man, and Mr. Hunt was so much lighter skinned than her Jeb, she caught herself staring.

The thin light of dawn pushed in through the shutters, scattering splinters of light over his bowed head and the thick muscles of his arms and shoulders and back. With the sunlight glinting off the crescent moon and arrow clasp of his chain, he almost looked like a man knelt to pray, or repent.

Cedar pressed a palm of water over his face, wincing as he sat back a bit.

He held one arm tighter over the wound in his side.

"Good morning, Mr. Hunt," Mae said quietly, not knowing quite what else to say.

He turned his head, hung still so that his hair brushed over his eyebrows and dropped water into his hazel eyes. The scratches on his face were nothing more than thin red lines that went pink and healed to new white skin even as she watched.

Must be the wolf in him that healed him so quickly, the wolf in him that looked out at her with such heat, such hunger in his eyes.

"Could I offer you breakfast?" she asked, hoping to spur the man behind those eyes to come forward. "I've a bit of bacon and cornmeal, and coffee too."

He closed his eyes, swallowed, his Adam's apple sliding along his throat. He needed a shave.

"Did I kill?" Raspy, but the words were clear.

"You did. That creature . . ." She paused, wondering what the boy had been. "That nightmare that looked like Elbert. You saved me from it. And I'm obliged to you. Let me begin to show my thanks with breakfast."

Mae stood. "It will be difficult to cook with a gun in each hand. I'd appreciate it if you gave me your word I don't need to worry about your company, Mr. Hunt."

He nodded once, swallowed again. "You have my word, Mrs. Lindson," he whispered, still not enough voice to the words. "And my thanks." He tried to stand, got his feet under him, but his knees wouldn't hold. He folded back down. He panted, his color white as lye, one arm braced on the floor all that held him upright.

"Let me see the wound," Mae said.

She didn't know if he heard her, so she touched his shoulder. He twitched, but did not tell her no.

She pulled the cloth away from the puncture in his side. It was bloody. And pus yellow. Infection.

"I think it best you come to the bed, Mr. Hunt," Mae said. "You'll need a bit of rest yet, and someplace better to heal than the hard floor."

"Fine," he whispered. "I'm fine."

Mae raised her eyebrows but said nothing. She knew when a man said things out of stubborn pride. She'd been married for nine years.

And she knew better than to ask his permission. "Up now. Take a deep breath. On three. One, two, three." She wrapped her arm around his waist and pulled him up onto his feet. He leaned heavily on her, breathing hard, but somehow managed to get his feet moving. With her help, he limped across the room to the bed.

Laying him down was easy, and she rolled him on his side so that she could see to the wound. Pus, blood, and the glisten of the black oil. It wasn't as clean as she'd thought.

Mae pulled the comforter from the foot of the bed over him, then took herself to the other room, and stoked the fire. She'd need the water to boil, and she'd need to lace it with herbs. Mae pulled the jars she needed from her herb shelf, and finally noticed she was doing it all with the Colt still clutched in her hand.

She glanced toward the bedroom. Mr. Hunt had not stirred. So she set the gun on the table and busied herself steeping herbs and pulling out a length of clean cotton linen for a compress.

When the water was tea brown and the house smelled of the good clean green of herbs, she picked up the kettle and walked back to the bedroom.

"I can't," Cedar Hunt whispered as Mae brought in the kettle and poured some of the water out into the washbasin to let it cool before she put the kettle on the floor.

"Can't what?" she asked quietly.

"Stay. My brother. Wil. The boy. I have to find . . ."

And then his words were gone, replaced by the labored breathing of a fever.

"Rest easy, Mr. Hunt," Mae said, hoping he was of a high enough constitution to endure this and recover. She didn't want another man dying so soon. She'd had enough of dying. "May healing come to you quickly and ease your pain." She blessed the herbs, the compress, soaked the linen in water, and repacked his wound once again.

She would need to get his fever down, and with little else of medical supplies on hand, and certainly no ice, the surest way she knew to lower a body's temperature was magic.

Magic always leaned toward curses in her hand, so she would curse the fever and give healing more room to take root. She set about the house gathering the herbs, stones, fire, and water she would need for the spell.

Once she had what she needed, Mae stood again next to the bed. Mr. Hunt was shivering, the blankets pulled up to his chin.

"You'll hear my voice, Mr. Hunt," Mae said softly. "You'll hear me singing a bit, whispering prayers and spells. But don't worry, and don't wake. I'm going to do what I can to help you heal. And all you need to do is rest."

Mae set out each item on the bed around Cedar, surrounding him with a piece of each element. Magic was a gentle art, drawn from the earth, sky, streams, and hearth. Mae took her place at the foot of the bed, and held her tatting shuttle, the precious gift Jeb had given her, in her hands. It wasn't so much necessary for the spell as it was a comfort and strength in her hands.

Mae spoke a word and her chest caught with pain. She pressed her hand against her chest and breathed until the pain passed. She spoke a word again, beginning the spell, and pain once again rattled through her.

It took her a moment before she realized the cause. The binding between her and the coven soil was tightening down. The sisters, and magic, were calling her home. The time she would be able to endure being away from the coven was running out.

Mae took a steadying breath and held the shuttle tight to her heart. She still hadn't killed the man—the Strange—who killed Jeb. She still hadn't finished her work here. And she was not going to turn east and leave a man dying in her bed.

Mae began the spell again, continuing on through the pain. There was still living and dying left to see to. The sisters would have to wait.

CHAPTER TWENTY-FIVE

Shard LeFel's crew boss had the men up before sunrise. The constant clang and chug of workers setting the rail, punctuated by an occasional blast or ground-shaking thump from the matics pounding the land into shape, was music to Shard LeFel's ears.

This would be his final day in this land. Tonight, beneath the power of the waning moon, before another dawn could rise, he would open the door and stroll back to the land where he rightfully belonged.

He was so close to his goal, he could taste it like heavy wine on his tongue, could feel the burn of it beneath his skin, stirring his hunger in ways he had all but forgotten over the centuries.

Death. All he needed to complete his crossing was the three mortals' deaths.

Shard LeFel sat within his train car, a fine breakfast spread out before him. Caviar, cheeses, fruits, and meat from the far lands, all set upon solid gold plates thin as rose petals and fine lace.

A silk napkin lay upon his knee, but LeFel had touched none of the food, had taken not even one drink. He was content to look out the window and down upon the rail, the iron that lay like prison bars upon the land. But they were not prison bars—they were roads of freedom. Freedom for the Strange.

Before the last iron was laid down, before the last spike was hammered into the earth, LeFel would have the witch— the last death he needed to open the doorway. Then he would have his way home and his revenge.

When his gaze finally wandered from the rail, he looked upon the beautiful Holder, set as it was, glowing like seven shards of seven precious gems fused together as one, upon a gilt pedestal in the corner of the room. After three hundred years of finding each piece, the remarkable metal ingenuity was his now and would be triggered to its best use.

He did not know how long Mr. Shunt had been standing inside the arched doorway that separated this car from the others. But finally, LeFel noticed he was there.

And standing next to him, holding on to the cuff of his coat as if not quite steady on his feet, was the changeling.

"Are you finished, then, Mr. Shunt?" LeFel asked.

"As you demanded," Mr. Shunt whispered through a serrated smile.

"Good. Ready my carriage. And wait for me outside."

Mr. Shunt bowed and exited the room, leaving the changeling behind.

"Come to me, Strange," LeFel commanded. "Show me the child you pretend to be."

The creature shuffled across the floor, one leg dragging a bit, its eyes wide and blank, no smile on its sweet, pink lips.

No skipping or laughing this time. Whatever it had taken to make this thing whole again had also dulled it, changed it. But that was no matter. So long as it lasted through the day, it would have outlived LeFel's use.

But to the Strange he said, "You have done well to sink back into this broken body, this flesh. Does it pain you?"

The Strange focused glossy eyes on LeFel and nodded.

"Not much longer," LeFel said. "I will reward you richly. Give you a new body to plant yourself within." He leaned forward just a bit. "Give you the boy's body."

The Strange's eyes lit with an unholy hunger. It glanced over at the blacksmith's son, who lay in drugged sleep, curled upon the wide seat of a chair.

"Would you like that?" LeFel asked. "A young, firm, fresh body to walk this world? To grow in, to breathe in, to taste all the flavors of pain and fear and joy a mortal has to offer?"

The Strange nodded again, and this time it mustered a smile.

"Turn around and show me your back." Shard waited as the Strange obeyed him. Then, with the tip of the diamond-encrusted dinner knife, he carved a symbol into the creature's flesh. It wriggled and whimpered but did not cry out.

The clock tower whistled the noon hour, and the hammers and matics slowed and silenced while the laborers took their midday meal.

Shard LeFel sat back, inspecting his work on the Strange. A star burned there. Five points with the horns up at the creature's shoulders, flames already dying, tendrils of smoke that smelled of charred wood rising in the still air of the car.

"Yes. This will do."

Pleased, LeFel lifted the silk napkin and rubbed it over his lips, then placed it back upon his knee. "Go, rest in the shadows, Strange. The time is near. When you help me snag up the witch, your hunger will be sated."

He turned to the table in front of him, picked up the gold fork, and cut a deep bloody chunk of meat off the plate. Then Mr. Shard LeFel savored, slowly, his last mortal meal.

CHAPTER TWENTY-SIX

Mae woke with a start. She hadn't planned to sleep, but only to rest in the living room chair. From the slant of light coming through the window, it was noon, or later.

She held her breath a moment, waiting to hear what had woken her. It was the creak of the bed frame. Mr. Hunt was moving.

Mae stood and smoothed her dress. She had taken the time to tend her own wounds again, to wash, and pull on a dress that was not torn and dirty.

"Are you up, Mr. Hunt?" she called out as she walked toward the bedroom. "I'm coming in."

Cedar was standing next to the bed, the blanket wrapped haphazardly around him, his hair stuck up and tousled. But his eyes narrowed a little when he filled his lungs for a deep breath.

"Afternoon," he said. "I'd be in your debt if you have something I could eat."

Relief washed over Mae. She hadn't known if he would make it through the night. "So I see the fever's broke. You do heal quickly, Mr. Hunt. Are your wounds bothering you?"

"They will mend." He took a step and placed one hand on the back of a chair beside the bed. He was moving slowly, not limping, but guarding a pain. "Food, though . . . if you have it."

"I'll see to changing your dressings after I put some

coffee on to boil," Mae said. "You'll find some clothes in the drawers. They'll fit you with room to spare."

Cedar looked up at her, his hazel eyes clear. "I want . . ." Whatever he had intended to say he thought better of. "Thank you, Mrs. Lindson. For your kindness."

Mae nodded and walked off to the larder. She heard him open the chest of drawers, and then the jangle of belt and suspenders.

Mae stoked the fire, added wood, and got the coffee on. She set bacon to cook in a pan, and mixed water and corn-meal together for jonny cakes. By the time the jonny cakes were in the pan sopping up the bacon grease, Mr. Hunt was done dressing and had walked out into the room.

"Could you reach down the honey from that shelf?" Mae asked.

Cedar did so, his bare feet making little sound against the boards.

"This here?" he asked.

Mae set the empty bowl down on the table and glanced over at him. It was an odd thing seeing a man in her husband's clothes. He had on Jeb's work breeches, belted around his narrower waist, and the blue flannel shirt tucked in tight to show the width of his shoulders. No undershirt, no shoes. Looked like he was at home, comfortable in a state of undress around a woman. But he kept his left arm near his side, still holding the compress there, she'd wager.

He was pointing to the top shelf with his other hand, his hazel gaze watching her with an expression she could not quite place.

"That's the one," Mae said, taking her eyes off the man and off the clothes he wore. She swallowed back a lump of pain. Wouldn't do for nothing to cry. Wouldn't make Jeb come back alive, or bring justice down on his killer. No, that was in her hands alone now.

Cedar Hunt put the honey on the table, found two plates, and set them out also, then stood there uncertain while Mae flipped the jonny cakes and turned the bacon.

"Have a seat, Mr. Hunt. It will be done in a moment or two."

Cedar pulled a chair away from the table and sat.

"How did you know," Cedar began, more of a voice in his words again, "last night—how did you know it was me?"

"I told you—I can see your curse. Though there's more to it than I thought. You've angered someone in a terrible manner. Someone very powerful. What did you do, Mr. Hunt?"

"Survived."

"Don't think whoever cursed you did it just because you're breathing. You're certain you did nothing to anger them?" She pulled the pan off the rack and turned toward him. She slid one jonny cake and a bit of bacon onto her own plate, then filled Cedar's plate near heaping with the rest of the breakfast.

He eyed the food, and Mae could tell it took everything he had not to dig in and start eating. She wondered what held him back, then realized it was manners. He picked up the fork and waited for her.

"I walked on the wrong land," he said, while she poured coffee for them both and took her seat. "Pawnee land. I did no harm other than to be under the wrong god's scrutiny." He glanced over at her, his knuckles white around the fork, holding back a hunger she could almost feel from across the table.

She picked up her cup and took a sip, nodding at him slightly. "Eat your fill, Mr. Hunt."

Cedar fell to the meal in front of him with vigor and made short work of the food. She wondered if the change to wolf made him ferociously hungry or if it was because of his wounds.

Mae ate more slowly. "A lot of men have crossed the gods, I'd imagine, and not been turned into a wolf for it. Have you any idea why the Pawnee gods would curse you so?"

Cedar swallowed coffee, even though it was hot enough to scald. "Told me there were Strange rising in the land. Told me I was to hunt them. Kill them."

"Have you?" Mae asked.

Cedar paused, the cup not yet tipped to his mouth. "Yes, ma'am, I have."

"And that hasn't broken the curse," Mae mused. "Have you tried any other things to break the curse?"

"By the time I came to my senses, I was walking west." He took another drink. "I've stopped in any town that had books, but there aren't many universities out this way. Any book I've found that mentions curses is a conflagration of legend and myth with very little scientific thinking to support the theories. . . ."

He took down another forkful of food and chewed thoughtfully. "There's no logical, tested remedy that I could find; that much I can say."

Mae took another sip of her coffee to cover her surprise. The man who sat across the table from her right that moment was more than a hunter, a loner, a mountain man. He was thoughtful, educated. She had never suspected he might have been university bound before he wandered out this way.

"Maybe in the books back East? The library in Philadelphia?" Mae finally said.

Cedar nodded. "It's crossed my mind." He spent some time and attention on the food again. "Haven't had a lot of desire to head back that way. More people, more chances I could harm more than just the Strange."

"How often does it strike you?" Mae asked.

"Every full moon. And I come out of it hungry as if I've been a week into a fast." He drained his cup, then poured himself another, and looked up, the pot still in his hand, offering to pour for her.

Mae held her cup out, enjoying his company and the meal despite the circumstance for it. "And when you're beneath the thrall of the wolf, can you reason things out? Remember what you do?"

"Not before the Madders gave me this chain." He poured the coffee. "Last night is the first of my recollections as a wolf."

"Is that why you went out to their mine?"

"No. Went out asking for something to help me find the Gregor boy." Mae was silent at that.

Cedar waited a bit, then finally asked, "Did you find that man you were hunting for?"

Mae met his eyes, hazel with flecks of copper thick at the center, and more green at the ring. There was a kindness behind them, a compassion. It surprised her.

"I know who killed him. What killed him. That Mr. Shunt. And I cannot bear to think what he must have done to turn that child into such a beast. . . ."

"Wasn't a child. It was a Strange too, come out of the pocket of Shunt."

"He looked so much like Elbert. Warm, soft. He even cried like a child."

"It wasn't a child," Cedar said again. "Had the smell of the boy upon it, though. The blood of him."

Mae took another drink of coffee. "I've never seen such a Strange," she said. "So . . . alive and solid."

"They're more than storybook tales and wisps of light," Cedar said. "They've always been around, been more alive than God-fearing folk want to believe. I've yet to see any good follow in their path. Pain, madness, blight—seems to be all the Strange leave behind them. Maybe the Pawnee god wanted them killed before they became a force."

Mae finished her food, and placed her fork on her plate. "Dark words, Mr. Hunt. Do you think the Strange are here to kill?"

"I haven't seen proof otherwise." He looked away from his coffee cup and up at her. "Have you?"

Mae could not hold that gaze. She pulled the shawl tighter around her shoulders.

"I should thank you, Mr. Hunt, for coming to my aid in the forest last night. I don't know how I would have come out of that unscathed. What can I do to repay you?"

Cedar rested the cup between his palms. He took a long bit before he answered, seeming to be thinking through many things, and discarding them one by one. Finally, "Other than a fine hot meal?"

Mae smiled at that, and he smiled back, then grew serious. "You can see my curse. Can you break it?"

"I can do some good for you," Mae said. "But I am not sure if I can break such a powerful thing on my own. It would be best done at the time of your change, when body and soul are tugged by the moon. I will need some things. Some herbs. Maybe . . . maybe my sisters."

"Think it will take some time?"

"To break a god's curse? Yes. A night, I'd say. Maybe a day too. And we will both need to be strong. Certainly stronger than I'm feeling now."

Cedar nodded. "Then it will wait."

"Perhaps I'll be strong enough tonight." Mae stood and gathered the plates.

"Not so sure I want to be free of the curse tonight," he murmured.

"Have you seen that other wolf before?" Mae asked.

"No."

The tone of his voice, more breath than word, made her turn.

"But you know of it?"

Cedar drained his cup. He weighed something, decided something. She walked back around to the fire, and did a bit of tidying there, waiting for whatever thought had taken him to bring him back.

"Do you suppose you could break a curse, a curse like mine, for another?" he finally asked.

"I'd have to see this other before I could say."

Cedar was silent so long, Mae wondered if he'd gone to sleep sitting there with his eyes open, staring at the wall.

"It's my brother." Soft, those words, as if they had never been said before. "The wolf was—is—my brother. Wil. Wiliam."

Mae gave him some time longer. Waited for him to ask her fully, the favor he wanted.

He cleared his throat and seemed to come back from a long distance, breathing deep and rubbing a hand over his face.

When he turned and looked at her again, he was composed. "I still have the boy to find—Elbert. But once that's set aside, I'll help you find that killer," he said. "If you'll break the curse my brother carries. Provided he's still alive."

Mae searched his face, his eyes filled with the pain of losing a loved one. She understood that pain. "I'll do what I can, certainly," she said. "Do you know where to find him?"

Cedar thought a moment, as if trying to drag memories out of a thick mud. "Mr. Shunt was there last night. In the forest. He took him. I'd say he'll be where Mr. Shunt is. If Mr. Shunt is who killed your husband, then our intentions are in agreement. We both want Shunt dead. But I should tell you, I've two other promises to keep."

"You've told me as such, though last I asked, it was only one promise you were beholden to. I suppose if we're going to be hunting and killing together, we may as well tell each other full what we're beholden to."

"Don't recall saying we'd be hunting or killing together," Cedar said.

"That shotgun was given to me, Mr. Hunt. I'll be the one who pulls the trigger." She held Cedar's gaze until he nodded.

"First, I'll want my boots." Cedar stood, and hissed, bending to one side, his elbow tucked tight into his ribs.

"First," Mae said, "I'll tend that wound of yours."

"It'll heal," he muttered through clenched teeth.

"It will heal faster and far better after I dress it. Remove your shirt, Mr. Hunt," she ordered.

Cedar's eyebrow hitched upward at her tone. For the briefest moment, a smile curved his mouth. Then his lips flattened as he carefully kept his face neutral. "Yes, ma'am."

"That's better," Mae said archly, though her cheeks flushed with color. There was something about him that she found pleasant, though she shouldn't. The man turned into a killing beast at the full moon—not much pleasant about that.

Still, there was a sorrow in him, a familiar pain.

She gathered up fresh cloth, the steeped water, and the last bottle of alcohol she had. She rinsed out her herb pot, a pretty little copper pot she'd bought three years ago from a man traveling from the East, and pumped fresh water into it. She placed the pot on the hook over the fire.

"I'll wash it out first, then soak another compress." Mae dropped comfrey into the water and prodded the fire to rise up and bring the water close to a boil.

She turned around. Cedar Hunt stood there, bare to his waist, holding her husband's shirt in one hand. She glanced up to look into his eyes, which were soft, apologetic, and a little curious. She had a feeling he hadn't stood half-naked in front of a woman for some time. She had a feeling he didn't mind it so much.

Mae looked away from his eyes, and studied his chest. Wide claw marks scarred from collarbone to hip, but otherwise, he was strong, lean, the muscles of his body hard from a lifetime of work.

"Would it be easier if I sat?" he asked.

Mae nodded. "It's just the wound at your side that's still hurting?"

"Mostly." He sat on the edge of the chair, turned so that his injured side was facing her.

"Let me remove the compress." Mae stepped over and touched his elbow gently.

Cedar moved his arm, propping his palm on his knee, his elbow straight. She pulled the compress off. The wound was red and raw and about as big around as her cupped palm. Fluid and blood oozed from the depth out over the burned edges of skin. It didn't carry an odor, thank goodness, and didn't seem to have any more black oil in it.

"Feels like I have a hole all the way to my spine," Cedar said.

"Does the open air pain it?" Mae asked.

"Yes." He craned his head, and shifted his shoulders, trying to get a good look at the wound. "Stitches, you think?"

"No. Not enough skin to sew together. I think it needs another cleaning, a better cleaning, and then some time to drain. Hold still, now. You're just making it bleed more." She pressed the cloth back over the hole. "Just hold that there, while I brew up a new compress and get something to clean it with. It won't take long."

Mae pulled over a bowl and put some of the warm water from the copper pot into it, then dropped a cloth into the pot to let it soak. She poured a little more cool water in with the water in the bowl and brought that to the table, dipping a handkerchief into it and, without squeezing it out, traded its place with the compress on the wound. She placed a dry towel at his waist to catch the water cleaning the wound, then squeezed the wet handkerchief into the puncture.

Cedar narrowed his eyes at the pain.

"So where are you from, originally?" Mae asked, hoping conversation would help ease his mind away from the discomfort.

"Boston."

"Pretty city, or so I've heard." She dipped the handkerchief back into the water and squeezed it against his side again.

"It can be," he said on a held exhalation.

"Not much need for a bounty hunter in a city," she said. "Did you come out west for the land or for the work?" She removed the handkerchief, filled it with water, and pressed it against his side again.

"Neither."

"Family? Your brother?" she guessed.

"West just meant more land between me and a life I'd never have again."

He might mean the war. Might mean property or family he lost because of it. Mae figured it wasn't her place to pry into matters that private.

"And yourself, Mrs. Lindson?" he asked, filling the silence before she could. "What drew you so far west?"

"The land." She soaked the cloth again, pressed it into his side. He wasn't wincing every time she touched him. She hoped the willow in the water was numbing the pain a little.

"Good rich land here in the Oregon Territory. Plenty of it. Thought we'd follow the river all the way to the sea. But when Jeb saw this valley tucked against the mountains, he said he'd never seen a more beautiful corner of God's earth. So we set to farming here, living here. It's been a good life. . . ."

She realized she'd stopped working and was instead just kneeling there, thinking of a life she also could never return to.

Cedar Hunt caught her gaze. There was sympathy there. Understanding. Maybe something more she couldn't quite describe. A kindness and warmth. In that moment she knew he too had suffered death. But instead of giving her gentle words that would do no good for her pain, he simply nodded once. "Your pot's boiling."

Mae was grateful that he didn't ask her any more. She stood and walked to the kettle, pulling it with a poker away from the fire. Outside the wind lifted on the day, pulling birdsong through the air.

She had known she'd never have Jeb again, but had pushed the reality of it away as often as she could, using anger to keep her mind on her task. But seeing Mr. Hunt here, a man who had left a life behind, who had suffered death and never returned to the life he had once lived, made her realize she was alone. Truly alone. And would have to find a way to carry on, build a new life with no one beside her.

"Mae?" Cedar stood beside her and gently pressed his fingertips onto her arm.

How long had she been standing there, the copper pot hanging from one hand, the wind stirring and nosing between the wooden trinkets on the shelf?

"I'm fine, just fine," she said. "Have a seat. This will be hot, but we'll wrap it tight to keep the injury clean."

Cedar hesitated a moment. He glanced out the cracks in the shutters, and held his breath. Listening, she realized. Listening for whatever thing had distracted her.

"Suppose you didn't get much sleep last night," he said as she brought the pot over to the table and used a clean knife to draw up the soaked cloth.

"Not so much as I prefer, but enough." She opened the cloth with her fingertips, and scooped out the leaves and bark and seeds.

"That Strange, the one that looked like little Elbert," she said, "you said it smelled of his blood. Do you think the boy, the real Elbert, is still alive?" She folded the cloth around the herbs like an envelope, then wrapped it up in a long strip of cheesecloth she would tie around his ribs.

"The blood was fresh," Cedar said. "And it was Elbert's."

Mae pressed the compress against his skin. "Hold this." Cedar held it in place with his right hand. "So there's a chance the boy's still alive?"

"I've seen Strange, Mrs. Lindson, but none that uses gear and bone and blood like a child plays with sticks and mud. These are something more. Stronger. Wicked."

Mae walked across the room and pulled down extra strips of cloth and brought those over. "Mr. Shunt. Do you think he somehow devised that Strange boy?"

"Yes." Cedar grunted as she bound the cheesecloth, then the length of cloth, around his ribs. "But I don't know why he would want to. And I don't know why he would want such a fine woman as you, Mrs. Lindson."

Mae swallowed at those words and kept her eyes and attention on laying the cloth down smooth and wrapping it evenly. She didn't want that compress to slip.

"He has killed my husband. The one true love I vowed my life unto. I don't know what he wants with me. Now that Jeb is dead, there's not much of me left to hurt. Maybe the Strange don't approve of our marriage vows. A colored man and a white woman."

She stood and handed him Jeb's shirt.

Cedar paused before putting it on. "Don't think the Strange much care about the color of a person's skin. Don't think love much cares either."

Mae held her breath at those words. They were likely the kindest thing she'd ever been told in her life.

"Thank you," she breathed.

Cedar shrugged his good shoulder and buttoned the shirt, not meeting her eyes. "You suppose the Strange want you for the spells at your disposal?"

"Spells?"

"You are a witch, aren't you, Mrs. Lindson?" Cedar tipped his eyes up and caught her gaze. He was not afraid of her—no, she'd be surprised if he were afraid of anything or anyone. He wasn't encouraging nor demanding. And yet, she felt a need to answer him, to tell him what so many had gossiped, what so many had feared.

And putting this truth in his hands could mean her life. The townsfolk did not like her, were afraid of the simplest blends of herbs she made for healing. What would they do if Cedar told them she was indeed the ungodly thing they feared?

And what would they do if they found out the hunter they trusted with their herds, with finding their children, was a cursed and killing beast?

It seemed they both had equal to lose, and to gain. That made up her mind.

"Yes, Mr. Hunt, I am a witch. And I trust my secret is as safe with you as yours is with me?"

"Yes, Mrs. Lindson, it is." Cedar smiled, and it did his face good. She found herself smiling too.

"I'd wager," he said, "that particular skill is why the Strange are looking for you."

"Well, I can't undo what I am. It's not so much a choice, Mr. Hunt, as a way you're born. I'd follow the ways of magic whether I knew to call myself a witch or not."

"Wasn't saying anything needed undoing. Are there others of your sort around these parts? Your . . . sisters?" he added.

"I don't really know. I'm from a small coven—a community. And I was seventeen when I came this way with Jeb. Hallelujah is tucked off of the trails. Well, until the rail finishes, that is."

"If there were a witch nearabouts, do you think they'd contact you?" he asked.

"Perhaps."

"Could be just that you are the only witch in a hundred miles, and that's why the Strange are looking for you. Or it could be that you have something particular that they want. Something particular Mr. Shunt wants."

"All that I have you are looking at now. Do you see anything worth killing me for?"

"Never know what whets the interest of the Strange. Sometimes it's a bit of metal, a bob of glass. Sometimes it's a song or a dream, or a rare skill. Is there something you specialize in?"

"Weaving and lace, though I imagine there are those better than I at it. And vows, bindings, and curses," she added quietly.

"What?"

"It's not something that's spoken."

"Maybe not. But I think it's something that needs to be heard."

Mae walked over to her spinning wheel and dragged her hands over the blankets in the basket. She didn't want to give this secret words to cling to. Didn't want to give it shape to fill. Even words—no, especially words—carried magic.

"I am particularly gifted to using magic with vows, bindings, and curses. It's not approved. It is not even the correct way to guide magic. But it is the way of me."

"Must be that," Cedar said as if talking about magic in this civilized world were commonplace. "Though I still don't know why Mr. Shunt would want to harm you. Maybe he's doing Shard LeFel's bidding. Maybe it's Mr. LeFel who wants what you have."

"I don't see as how that can be. I don't think I've seen Mr. LeFel but once since he's come to town."

"Once is enough when a man sees what he wants." Cedar said it slowly, softly, his gaze holding her. He hesitated, as if he would say more, then cleared his throat and changed the subject. "I don't suppose you have a pair of boots I could borrow?"

"I should." Mae oddly found it a little difficult to breathe. There was something about Mr. Hunt. Being near him caught her up in most confusing ways. "Let me go fetch them. Then will you be leaving?"

"I'll follow the trail of the boy's blood. See if I can find Wil. See if I can find Elbert."

"I'm coming with you," she said over her shoulder.

Nothing but silence filled the room. Mae found Jeb's old boots near the bed. They had holes in the sides, and might be too big for Cedar's feet, but she had spare socks he could use to take up the difference.

As soon as she stepped back out into the main room, he stopped pacing and slanted a look at her. "No, you most certainly will not." It was a commanding voice. A stern, lecturing voice.

Mae ignored it. "If I didn't know better, I'd say you were a lawyer, Mr. Hunt. Declaring your opinions as if they were fact." She held out the old boots and socks for him.

He scowled. "A teacher," he said.

Mae smiled. "I'll be going with you. That shotgun is the only thing I've seen that can stop Mr. Shunt in his tracks. Not that it kills him—no, he snaps and pulls and stitches himself back together again as easily as he falls apart." She swallowed hard at the memory of him. "He's not made of the natural world."

"Not this natural world, at least," Cedar said. "Which is all the more reason you should stay here where it's safe."

"There is no safe place for me." Mae didn't mean it to come out quite so plainly, but there it was. So long as she was a witch in this God-fearing land, with Strange things that crept through pockets of shadow and cozied up to nightmares, she would be pointed to as different, and killed for her ways.

"Mrs. Lindson," Cedar tried, then, "Mae."

She looked up at her name, surprised.

"Listen to me. To reason. I know you can stand on your own. You've proved you have a strong spine. But first I'll be headed back to the Madders to reclaim my weapons and clothes. There's no need for both of us to deal with the three brothers. Their doors too easily turn to walls. I owe them favors I'd never promise another man. If you hold tight here, with the gun at hand, then when I return, well before night-fall, we can set out together to track the boy and the Strange that killed your man."

Mae had had enough of men promising her they would take care of things a man should, and then return for her as a man should. She'd had enough of men going away and not coming home.

"I'll be back for you soon," Cedar said. "I give you my word."

Mae looked him straight in the eye. "That's what my husband told me, Mr. Hunt. And now he's dead."

Cedar took a breath, and let it out slowly. He walked over to the door and opened it wide, letting in the clean promise of daylight. He paused there, one foot in her home, the other out in the afternoon light, his eyes scanning the horizon before he turned back toward her.

"That may be true," he said gently, "but I am not your husband, Mrs. Lindson." He moved to close the door.

Mae spoke up. "Take the mule. She's out back. You can just point her toward my house when you're done. She, I'm certain of, will find her way home."

Cedar nodded, just the quirk of a smile at the corner of his mouth. "Thank you, Mrs. Lindson. I'll do just that." Then he stepped outside and closed the door behind him.

CHAPTER TWENTY-SEVEN

Rose Small rubbed the soft cloth over the top of the pew, the honey smell of wax filling the still air of the empty church. Cleaning every scrap of wood in the building wasn't her idea of a way to spend an evening as nice as this one, the dusk still clinging to the warmth of sunlight before autumn shook the heat and leaves off the land.

But her folks had heard about her walk last night. Likely from Henry Dunken's gossipy mother. So Rose was here in the church, as she would be every night this week, contemplating her inexcusable behavior beneath God's watchful eyes. Offering up to Him elbow-grease tithing for her sins.

At least here in the church she was left in peace to think her own thoughts away from her mother's angry tirades, away from the women who shook their heads in pity at her, and the men who thought she didn't notice how they looked at her like she was a broken thing they could use if they wanted.

Oh, she'd seen the letters her folks had written up, asking about eligible men in the nearby towns. She'd more than seen them—she'd volunteered to put them in the mail, and thrown them down the privy hole instead.

The thought of tying herself down to this little town and only ever seeing the sun pull up over the same horizon for the rest of her life near about gave her hives.

She wanted to explore the world, wanted to see what

amazing gadgets and tickers and inventions chugged along between the high buildings in the old states, or pressed wide, round backs against the sky, steering the winds across the ocean to far-off lands, or harvesting the rare glim. She wanted to touch those things, make those things.

She wanted to fly. And wanted to do so much more.

When Rose was six, she'd insisted she wanted to be a blacksmith and a deviser when she grew up. She'd heard her father make the blacksmith, Mr. Gregor, promise he'd never put a hammer in Rose's hand.

And he hadn't. Though he'd let her pump the bellows and mind the coals and fetch his tools, all the while talking to her of what he was doing and why. Rose figured she knew more about metal and the making of it than a whole university of books and thinkers.

She'd done her devising in secret, hidden in her pockets, hidden beneath her bed where no one ever looked. Little trinkets, little tickers. When her mother had discovered the thimble bird Rose had made when she was nine, she'd demanded to know if Rose had been devising, doing the work allowed only to men.

Rose had told her Mr. Gregor made it. Told her it was a gift to the family and that she'd kept it in her room because she liked it so.

She hadn't counted on her mother marching her by the arm down to the blacksmith's shop. Hadn't counted on her demanding the truth of the story from Mr. Gregor.

And she sure enough hadn't counted on Mr. Gregor telling her mother, without a bat of a lash, that Rose's story was true and that he had indeed devised the bird and given it as a gift.

But whatever thin warmth she had felt from her mother froze away over the next few years. Rose knew her mother wanted her married off so that she was no longer a problem to hide or to mind.

Some days she thought the only reason she hadn't left this town was because of Mr. Gregor. Just thinking about poor little Elbert wandered off into the wild made her heart catch.

She hoped that Mr. Hunt—in whatever skin he was wearing—would be able to find the little child.

Her thoughts lingered on Mr. Hunt. She'd heard stories from travelers passing through that there were men who could change into wolves. Native stories of men turning into all sorts of animals.

But she'd never thought to see such a thing here, with her own eyes, in the little town of Hallelujah.

It might be the wolf in him that kept him private. Or at least she assumed.

There was something behind the closed-off pain in his eyes. A way to his words that spoke of knowledge she didn't have and wished he'd share.

Rose walked across the aisle to polish the next pew. She supposed she should just be grateful that he believed in the Strange, or at least seemed to. When she'd mentioned the bogeyman to him, and Elbert gone missing, she'd seen the recognition in his eyes.

Rose had always known the Strange were real. The land grew thick with them. Something about the gears and metals drew them, she thought. Something about matics and contraptions called to them. It was one of the reasons she combed the shadows at night, looking for castaway bits and gathering them up before the Strange could come find them.

The door to the church opened, letting in the early-evening air and a liquid wave of dying sunlight.

The shush of petticoats and bustles swept in by the slow chattering of voices, gossipy as birds.

Rose didn't have to glance their way to know it was Mrs. Haverty, Mrs. Dunken, and the others come to go through the church yet again for wedding plans.

So much for her peace and quiet. They'd likely have her fetching them tea and cookies and things down from the attic for the rest of the night.

As soon as they caught sight of her, they fell silent like birds ducking a wing that had just covered the sunlight.

"Rose Small?" Mrs. Haverty, the banker's wife, had the sort of bearing Rose had always imagined a queen would hold. Never a hair out of place, never a wrinkle in her skirts, she looked like she'd stepped right off the pages of a fancy catalogue. "I did not expect to find you in the church this evening," she said. "Did your mother send you to lend us a hand with the wedding planning?"

Rose did not stop wiping down the woodwork, but did glance over at the women, eight at least, all clucking about, with plump and pushy Mrs. Dunken giving her a smug look she'd never seen on her face before.

"No, ma'am," Rose said. "My mother promised the pastor I'd dust down the pews. So everything is ready for service tomorrow."

Sad-faced Mrs. Bristle spoke up. "Are you saying you don't care about Mrs. Haverty's daughter Becky's impending nuptials? Even a . . . castoff like you should show some respect."

Rose squared her shoulders and kept the backs of her teeth together so no words could slip out. She was taught to respect her elders, but words would fall through her lips too quickly if she didn't keep her mind on them. Then they'd all know exactly what this "castoff" thought about them and their judging ways.

"Now, don't be so cruel to the girl, Mabel," Mrs. Dunken said. "I'm sure Miss Small will settle down and behave properly soon enough. She just needs a man with a strong hand to rein her in. A man like my boy Henry."

Rose rolled her eyes and went back to dusting. Henry thought he was the strongest, prettiest man in town because that was what his mama was always telling him. Even though his parents had sent him off to school in New York more to be rid of him than to get him some real learning, he'd come back only a year later, saying he'd decided politics were his future. He'd set his eyes on taking the mayor's place.

"That's kind of you to think so," Rose said to Mrs. Dunken. "But I'm sure Henry has his sights set on a girl of much higher standing than I, what with his political aspirations and all."

"Don't sell yourself short, dear," Mrs. Haverty said.

Rose stopped dusting out of shock. She'd never heard the banker's wife say a kind thing to her in all her days.

"You may be of low standing," Mrs. Haverty continued, "but you do have land to your name. A good parcel of land can make even the most plain of girls pretty enough to marry."

A slow, creeping dread came along with those words. Mrs. Haverty sounded like she was certain about that. Rose glanced over at Mrs. Dunken. Still the same smug look.

Oh no. They'd done something, made some plans to marry her off.

A shadow crossed the doorway and Rose knew who it was before she even glanced that way. Henry Dunken.

"Good evening, ladies," he said, striding into the room and taking up too much space. "I understand you need a hand with the wedding preparations?"

Rose tucked the cloth away in one of the pockets of her apron and picked up the tin of wax. She crossed the room to take it back to the storage cupboard, and to get herself out from beneath their notice.

"Henry, yes, I'm so glad you're here," Mrs. Haverty said. "You can help Rose fetch down the candleholders from the attic."

Rose froze halfway across the room. She most certainly would not go into the attic with that man. She'd known him nearly all her life. He was mean when they were young and was meaner now. His smiles and polite manners fit him like a bad suit, and fooled no one, least of all her.

"I'll have to beg your apologies," Rose said. "I promised my mother I'd help her close down the shop. And it's already late."

"Nonsense," Mrs. Haverty said. "I was just at the shop, and your mother said she's coming this way any minute now. I'm sure the store is already closed."

Rose's mind tumbled and spun, looking for a new escape route. "I have chores at home, waiting for me."

Mrs. Dunken swished her way over and took Rose's arm. Firmly. She tugged her off toward the stairs to the attic in the back corner of the room. "My old knees just won't do those stair steps any longer. Be a dear, for us, Miss Small. I'm sure your mother is in full agreement with you minding as you're told."

She gave Rose a shove, and Rose took the first two steps, just to keep from falling.

And then Henry Dunken was right behind her, smelling of booze and blocking her retreat. He leaned in far too close for a man who should know his place and his manners in front of his mother and other women of the town.

Rose took another step, just to fit some air between her and him, and the candle he carried in one hand.

"Go on up, Miss Small," he said quiet and nice. "Won't take long to bring the women their fancy candles; then I'll be on my way."

She didn't believe him. But unless she wanted to shove him down the stairs and stir the wrath of all the old biddies, it'd be best to get this done and over with.

Rose clomped up the stairs, Henry just a step behind her, breathing hard enough she could smell the alcohol on each exhalation.

The attic was dark, the posts and beams and rafters

dancing side to side in the light thrown by Henry's candle. The window at the end of the attic was dark too, the moon not yet off the horizon.

"If I recall, the candlesticks are back there near the window." Rose pointed. She had no intention of going into the dark corner with Henry in the room. She was staying at the top of the stairs, where she could retreat, if needed.

"I'll need a hand gathering them," he said, still too quiet and still too nice. "I'd be right obliged if you held the candle for me, Miss Small."

He stepped up close to her, too close, and offered her the candle he held. He smelled of booze and smoke and sweat. She didn't know where he'd spent his day, but she'd guess it was in the saloon.

Rose took the candleholder, but Henry did not let go. He smiled, and nice Henry, quiet Henry, melted away, leaving that cruel boy she'd known all her life.

"You grew up real pretty, Rose. Got yourself curves that keep a man awake at night. If it weren't for that smart mouth of yours, and all those wild contraptions you busy yourself with, you'd be married off, softened up, and have six babies tugging at your skirts by now."

Rose tucked her left hand in her apron pocket, but did not let go of the candle that Henry still held.

"Henry Dunken, if you don't have the decency to treat me like a lady, I will leave this attic and tell your mother what a hog you are."

That got a smile out of him. Not a nice smile. "You're gonna run and tell my mama? That didn't work when you were ten. That ain't gonna work today." He stepped tight up into her. "And there ain't no Mr. Gregor to run to here."

Rose got her fingers around the gun she kept in her pocket. She jabbed the barrel of it below Henry's belt. His eyes went wide.

"You feel that, Mr. Dunken? That's one of those wild contraptions I busy myself with. It shoots a man clean through. Then the powder and oil I devised eats away at flesh and bone until there's a hole left behind wide enough to stick two fists through."

Rose smiled. She reckoned it was not a nice smile either. "You step away from me, Henry Dunken, or I'm going to blow your manhood to kingdom come."

Henry's eyes narrowed, and a bead of sweat trickled down his temple to catch in his sideburns and beard. She could tell he didn't believe her. Maybe didn't believe she had made such a thing. Maybe didn't believe she would use such a thing.

But she had. And she would.

Rose cocked the hammer, and the click of gears sounded like knuckles breaking.

Henry Dunken let go of the candle and took a step back. His hands were in fists. Rose remembered how much those fists had hurt when she was nine. She vowed then she'd never let a man hurt her so again.

"You're a hell-spawn woman. Made of the devil's rib. No wonder your mama squatted you out in the dirt on the Smalls' doorstep. You're nothing but evil."

Rose nodded. "So it appears I am, Mr. Dunken. And now that we agree to my nature, I'd say it's best to your advantage to gather up those candlesticks and carry them down these stairs."

"Man doesn't turn his back on a rattlesnake," he said.

"Might be he should, if the snake's pointing a gun." Just to make sure he believed her, Rose took the gun out of her apron pocket. Plenty enough candlelight to show the bulky weapon—not the little derringer she carried. This was a modified Remington revolver. Warmed her heart to see the shock in his eyes.

"Candlesticks," she said.

Henry got busy piling up the carved, polished candlesticks like rough kindling into his arms. When he walked across the room again, he glared at her. "I'll be mayor of this town, Rose Small. And I will make your life more miserable than even your mad mind can imagine. If you live that long. After all, I know where you walk at night. And where you sleep."

He stormed down the stairs, bootheels hard and heavy with his anger.

Rose stayed at the top of the stairs for a few moments. Her heart was beating so hard, she could feel it in her throat, hear it in her ears. That man meant to kill her for his bruised pride. And if he caught her alone again, he'd do just that.

She tucked the gun back in her apron, but kept one hand on it. She didn't want to shoot a man in front of his mother, but if he tried to hurt her, she wasn't above it either.

Rose was halfway down the stairs when the steam clock whistled. Three short blasts and one long. There was an emergency. Something was wrong. That whistle would call all the townsfolk from miles around to the church, to find out what the trouble was and what they needed to do about it.

Rose stayed on the stairs a minute or so more, waiting to see where, exactly, Henry Dunken would position himself in this emergency.

He dropped the fancy candlesticks in a pile along the wall and rushed outside, the women aflutter behind him. If Rose wanted to leave the building, now was her chance, out the back door. Easy to slip out unnoticed when an emergency was rising. Course she might just run off into the very emergency the town was rallying against if she wasn't careful. But if choosing between an unknown danger and Henry Dunken, she'd take the unknown.

She blew out the candle, ready to leave

Then it struck her. Maybe it was little Elbert. Maybe Mr. Hunt had found the child alive and brought him home.

Maybe he had discovered the bogeyman that took him and all the town was being gathered up to go hunt it down.

Rose moved up the steps just enough that the shadows from the attic hid her from a casual glance. She wanted to know what the trouble was, but didn't want to be volunteered just yet in the fixing of it.

"Bring him in here, Mr. LeFel." Sheriff Wilke's voice filled the hall. "Mr. and Mrs. Gregor will be here any minute now."

Sheriff Wilke strode into the room; then Mr. Shard LeFel, resplendent in his velvet long coat and silk ruffles, strolled in behind him. He held an unconscious child in his arms. Little Elbert Gregor.

The rest of the people, and there was a crowd of them gathered behind him, stayed well back from Mr. LeFel and his man Mr. Shunt, who followed, as he always did, on Mr. LeFel's heels. Mr. LeFel walked across that floor like a king, his head high, his eyes filled with a sorrow Rose did not believe. He placed the child gently upon a pew at the front of the room, and Doc Hatcher went to one knee, his hands on the child's stomach, chest, then face, where he gently drew back the child's eyelids.

The sheriff had taken the stage behind the pulpit. Mr. LeFel and Mr. Shunt stood to the sides and behind him.

"Come in and have a seat, everyone," Sheriff Wilke called out. The whole town, and then some, seemed to be trying to wedge themselves into the building.

"Mr. LeFel has some information we all should know," he continued. "First, though, I'll tell you the Gregor boy is breathing." He looked over at the doctor.

"He's in bad shape," Doc Hatcher said, and if Rose hadn't been looking right at his face, she wouldn't have heard him over the chatter of the crowd. "He needs rest."

"Sit down," Sheriff Wilke hollered over the crowd. "Take a seat. Make room for your neighbor."

"Out of the way," Mr. Gregor bellowed from the door. Rose knew the blacksmith's voice, though she had never heard that mix of anger and panic in his tone. And just like snowmelt before the fire, the crowd receded, leaving a clear path between the pews for Mr. Gregor and his wife. Little Mrs. Gregor bobbed down that aisle, one hand pressed over her mouth, holding back the sound of her sobs, the other clutching up the hem of her skirt to keep from tripping.

Mr. Gregor stormed down the aisle behind her, his hands curled as if he wished the weight of a hammer and vise lay within them.

"Where is my son?" he demanded.

"He's here, right here." Sheriff Wilke pointed to the pew. Mrs. Gregor was already pulling Elbert up into her arms and sobbing over him.

Elbert fussed and then cried softly, clinging to the fabric of his mother's dress.

Mr. Gregor glared at the men on the stage, the sheriff, the rich dandy, and his servant, Mr. Shunt. "Who found him? Who had him? Where was he?"

Shard LeFel stepped forward and it was like every candle in the room leaned his way, every eye locked on him, every head bowed to hear his words.

"I found him, Mr. Gregor." Shard LeFel's voice was like hot wine, and there were folk in the pews who sighed at the sound of it. "And not a moment too soon."

"What do you mean?" he asked.

"He'll be telling us all now, Mr. Gregor," the sheriff said. "Take your family home, if you want—get that poor boy in bed. We'll take care of matters here on out."

"I'll stand and stay," Mr. Gregor said.

The blacksmith glanced down at his son, who looked up at him with tearful eyes before burying his face once again in the crook of his mother's neck. Mr. Gregor placed his hand gently on his child's head, and the boy turned his face away. Elbert's eyes were dazed, and Rose shook her head, her heart catching when she thought of what he must have been through.

Then the little boy looked at her. Saw her there, in the shadows. And smiled.

Rose pressed her hand over her chest, as if the boy's eyes had shot an arrow. A cold and fearful sensation crawled over her skin. That little boy was not Elbert. He might look like Elbert; he might cry like Elbert. But that boy had more of the Strange to him than Rose had ever seen in a child.

She pressed herself up against the stairwell wall, wishing there were more than just shadows between them.

The sheriff took a few steps away from Mr. Gregor so he could catch everyone's attention. "Listen up, folks. Mr. LeFel has something to tell us all."

The townspeople had filled the church to the brim, every pew taken, and every wall with people standing along it, right up to stuffing up the aisles. Rose saw more people gathered than she'd seen at the last county fair. Must be nearly three hundred tucked up tight in the room that wasn't built to hold more than a hundred, most.

"Mr. LeFel?" Sheriff Wilke gave the rail man the floor.

LeFel glided up to take his place behind the podium. When he smiled, it looked like an apology.

"Good people of Hallelujah, I bring you most distressing news."

Before he could continue, the church doors opened, and a fresh breeze sliced through the thick air, drawing the candle flames straight up on their wicks again.

"Hear there's been a ruckus," Alun Madder said as he sauntered in, his brothers, Bryn and Cadoc, shoulder to shoulder with him.

They all clapped their gloved hands together and rubbed them like they were scrubbing warmth up out of a campfire.

"What seems to be the trouble?" Alun asked.

Everyone in the church turned at the brothers' entrance. Except Rose. She watched LeFel's face screw into a dark visage of hatred. The kind of hatred that made a man carve another man's heart out and spit in the hole left behind.

Rose unconsciously clutched the locket beneath the thin cloth of her dress.

At that small movement, Mr. LeFel looked up away from the Madders, his eyes searching the shadows where she stood until he spotted her there. He was startled to find her watching him; that was clear. And the smile he gave her was no comfort. It was a warning.

"Settle in, and quiet down, Mr. Madder," Sheriff Wilke said. "All of you. Mr. LeFel has the podium."

Alun's eyebrows rose. "Didn't see you there, Mr. LeFel," he said without a hint of apology in his voice. "Must be the rising moonlight so bright it struck me blind. Carry on. Carry on. And *do* take your time." He and his brothers folded thick arms over their wide chests and simultaneously leaned against the church doors, blocking the way out.

Mr. LeFel licked his lips and glared at them. "As I was saying, I have dire news for us all."

He glanced out over the people gathered. There was that aristocratic air about him. It hooked up each and every eye and mind, and not a soul seemed able to lean away. When he flicked that gaze at Rose, she put her hand back on the gun in her pocket and glared at him.

He scowled, looked back at the Madders, then once again looked at her. But this time there was surprise, and some kind of new understanding, in his expression.

"Mr. LeFel?" the sheriff prompted.

LeFel finally turned his attention back to his breathless audience.

Rose's heart thumped hard. In LeFel's look was the same

cold creeping she'd sensed in the boy. But she felt the sure pressure of someone else looking at her. She glanced down the stairs. Alun Madder was indeed watching her. He smiled . . . and nodded.

She didn't know that it should, but it seemed a reassuring gesture. She didn't know if he saw the hatred in Shard LeFel. She didn't know if he saw the Strangeness of him and his man. But all the same, she was glad to see there was at least one—no, three other people in the room who weren't caught under Mr. LeFel's thrall.

"I was out," Shard LeFel crooned, "taking an evening constitutional, and by and by I wandered past the widow Lindson's property. I heard a terrible crying—a child wailing—and beyond that, I heard a woman singing. But not any church song. It was a witch's tune." He paused a moment, letting his words steep.

"I didn't want to believe it myself." He shook his head, and more than one head shook along with him. "But when I stepped up close to look in the window, I saw Mrs. Jeb Lindson, working her magic—the devil's magic—on this poor boy."

He nodded again, and this time all the folk nodded with him.

"Nonsense." Alun's voice cut across the silence like a fire across the plain. "Do you have any proof at all? Anything that would cast that poor woman as a witch?"

Shard LeFel's head snapped up and Rose saw the devil himself behind those eyes. No, worse than the devil; she saw the Strange. "Of course," Shard LeFel growled. Then, regaining his composure, "Of course I have proof. Mrs. Gregor, if you would just pull up your son's shirt, you'll see the mark, the cursed spell, she left there on his back."

Rose couldn't see Mrs. Gregor's face from her place on the stairs, but she heard her gasp as she drew up Elbert's shirt.

Rose instead watched Sheriff Wilke's reaction, since he could easily see the boy's back. He frowned and shook his head.

"It's a pentagram." Mrs. Gregor stood up with Elbert in her arms. She turned toward Mr. Gregor. In doing so, she revealed the boy's back to the room.

Very clearly, the mark of a star standing on one point was scratched into his back.

"Mae Lindson has done harm to this boy," Shard LeFel said. "And that's all the proof needed. She is a witch."

"Witch," Mr. Shunt repeated from the shadows.

"Witch," the people in the church echoed, inhaled, exhaled, back and forth to one another, the word building and growing, breathing stronger at each repetition until it seemed as if the very walls vibrated with it.

Until another word was born in its place: "Burn. Burn her."

Rose couldn't believe her ears. In just as much as a heartbeat, the entire town had gone mad. Regardless of if Mrs. Lindson was a witch or not, this was a civilized age. People didn't go around burning people just because one man stood up and called them a witch.

Her heart was pounding and every instinct told her to run, to flee, to get away from these people before they turned on her and called her something worth burning.

But Mae was her friend. She had to do something. Anything to help her. To stop this. Which meant she had to stand up against Mr. Shard LeFel.

And an entire town of people with murder in their eyes.

Rose pulled her shoulders back and walked down the stairs, her boots making too much noise for such a quiet room. Her knees shook and her hands went slick with sweat.

"You're wrong," she said, blunt as that.

Mr. LeFel looked over at her, hatred twisting his face into

a mockery of a smile. He opened his mouth to speak, but Rose spoke first.

"Mae Lindson isn't a witch. She's a kind and helpful woman who hasn't done more than mind her own business and weave blankets for this town. She's a lace maker, a wife, and nothing more."

"Don't mind the girl," Sheriff Wilke said. "She doesn't understand these things."

"I understand you are all talking about killing an innocent woman," Rose said.

An angry murmur rose up in the room, and Rose caught more than one voice saying "mad," "wild," "crazy."

Shard LeFel waited a moment, letting the voices hush against the rafters. Then he spoke. "You have seen what this 'lace maker' has done to the boy, Miss Small. She has left him with the devil's mark, taken his blood. Would likely have killed him. She is a witch. And that is the proof."

"That," Rose said, "isn't the Gregors' boy. I don't know what gears and steam you have cobbled together, but that boy isn't Elbert. It's a monster."

A startled cry rose up from the women of the town and the men's deep grumbling rolled beneath it. This time it did not quiet, but instead grew.

"I swear to you," Rose said, "that it's some Strange thing left in Elbert's place. Some Strange matic."

"Rose!" her mother called out sharply. "This is no time for your fool mouth." She stood up from where she had been sitting near the front of the room and stormed toward Rose.

"It's the truth. That's not Elbert." Instead of retreating, Rose walked down the crowded outer aisle, getting more than one surreptitious prod and elbow. But she didn't care. She only needed to make one person believe her. She marched over to Mr. Gregor.

The sheriff stepped in her way, keeping her from coming any closer to Mr. Gregor, or the boy.

"You believe me, don't you, Mr. Gregor?" Rose asked. "I tell you true—that's not your boy. I'd know Elbert. I'd know him like my own brother."

Mr. Gregor shook his head, his expression a mix of shame and pity. "That's enough, Rose. Go on, now. Do as your mother says. You should go home."

"I'm not wrong." She searched his face, searched his expression, for the man who had always smiled at her curiosity and applauded her strong spirit. Looked for the man who had always believed in her. "I'm not crazy. I promise you so."

"Go on, Rose," he said tightly. "This business isn't for . . . people like you."

Rose felt like he had just dunked her in a trough of cold water. He didn't believe her. He thought she was insane. Wild. Foolish.

She might believe the whole town could be blinded by a stranger's words, but not Mr. Gregor. He had always been kind and helpful to her, and wasn't afraid to speak against a crowd with calm words and reason. But not today. Today she meant nothing to him.

Sheriff Wilke put his hand on her arm. "Mrs. Small," he said. "Please see your daughter home."

"Rose Small," her mother said. "Come here this instant."

Rose knew a losing fight when she saw one. There wasn't a single chance anyone else in this town would believe her. They were set on burning an innocent woman alive for a crime she didn't commit. Rose might not be able to change their minds, but that didn't mean she was going to stand aside and do nothing.

Rose shook off Sheriff Wilke's hand and started walking.

But not toward her mother. She was headed toward Mr. Shard LeFel. "I know what you're doing, Mr. LeFel." She was close enough she could smell the lavender and spice of his expensive perfume. "And I know what you are—what you and your man are. Strange. Come to blight this land."

LeFel's eyebrows raised again. And his man, Mr. Shunt, lowered his head, until his eyes burned from beneath deeper shadow.

"I am quite sure you are mistaken, Miss Small," LeFel murmured. "I am here with only the highest regard for this town and these people. I am bringing to Hallelujah all the riches and future the rail and steam can offer."

"You are a liar."

Mr. LeFel's hand shot out so fast, Rose didn't even see him move. He caught her wrist in his grip, and squeezed down tight.

The entire room seemed to go distant and fuzzy. No one moved. Seemed like no one breathed.

"Mind your tongue," Shard LeFel growled. "Lest you lose it altogether." He squeezed down so hard, she couldn't feel her fingers. She slipped her left hand into her apron, fumbling for her gun.

Still no one in the church spoke. Still no one moved.

Except the Madder brothers.

Rose could hear them push away from the door as if they were one man. She felt the vibration of their steps as they marched down the aisle, their boots heavy as the mountains falling from the heavens.

"Let go of the girl, LeFel," Alun said low and clear, coming closer and closer, "or we'll have ourselves a go at you."

The brothers were smiling, eyes mad and drunken bright. They each brandished weapons in their hands: hammer, ax, and gun.

Shard LeFel's gaze shifted between each of the brothers.

"Might be a good night for someone to die," Cadoc said. He pulled a pocket watch out of his vest and pressed the winding stem down, sending the watch ticking.

Shard LeFel eyed the pocket watch, then let go of her wrist. "You are a waste of my time, poor Rose," he said. "And so too your kind."

Kind? Rose looked back to the Madders. Their expressions were unreadable. Was she somehow like them?

But as soon as the watch had begun ticking, the townsfolk seemed to wake up out of their sleep and the room came back sharp again, though not a person appeared to notice they'd lost a minute or two.

The Madder brothers stood shoulder to shoulder in the center aisle. They moved apart just enough to make a place for Rose to stand between them. She hurried to do so and walked with them back to the doors of the church.

"Think he broke your wrist?" the second brother, Bryn, asked as they walked forward behind Alun. Cadoc walked backward, watching LeFel.

"No," Rose said as she rubbed at her hand to get the blood moving in it. "It's fine."

They were at the back pews now, and all the room was riled up again, mumbling and chattering, repeating the words "bewitched" and "deviser" and, most frightening of all, "burn her too."

Her mother stood behind the last pew, face stoked red as a baker's oven. She pointed at the door. "Get on home, Rose Small. Lock yourself in your room. You make me sorry I've ever called you my own. No wonder your mother left you to die."

Rose opened her mouth, closed it around nothing but air. She had no words, not apology or anger, though both raged a wild storm in her. A deep, silent sob of betrayal twisted at her heart.

"Get home before I throw you out for good," her mother said.

Alun Madder smiled at Rose's mother and tugged his beard. "Maybe the girl's old enough not to belong to anyone anymore, Mrs. Small."

"You have no place preaching to me, Mr. Madder," she said. "You and your dirty brothers don't belong in this town."

The Madders laughed, but Rose kept on walking, head up, arms straight at her sides, wooden as a doll. Her eyes burned with tears.

She pushed open the door and hit the fresh night air like she was running from a fire. She wasn't running home. No, she'd never go back to that house. Never go back to those people. She didn't belong there. She had never belonged there, and her mother had just put words to the truth they'd both been denying all her life.

There wasn't a lock or latch that could keep her in this town a moment longer.

And there wasn't anyone, or anything, that was going to keep her from helping her friend.

She ran straight down Main Street, the bits of metal and wood in her pockets jingling with each step. She had to get to Mae's farm. Had to get there in time to warn her. Had to get there faster than the townspeople's torches.

CHAPTER TWENTY-EIGHT

Cedar Hunt was halfway back to Mae Lindson's house, having made his way to the Madders' mine. He'd found the brothers gone, his clothes and guns wrapped up tidy as a parcel near their front door. Didn't know where his horse was, either somewhere in the brothers' mountain or maybe set loose. Didn't take the time to track it down.

He'd promised Mae Lindson they would face the Strange together, but more than once he'd found himself blacking out in the saddle on his way back to her house, the wound stealing his strength and his senses away. Now he was on foot, pacing, waiting for the curse, the change, to slip over him.

The deep-belly warmth of the wolf stirring in him eased the pain in his side some. Maybe, he thought as he unbuttoned his shirt and folded it atop the mule's saddle, the change would heal the wound. It would help; he was sure of that.

The moon, shaded to the waning, pushed up at the horizon's edge as Cedar pulled off his boots, pants, and belt. He secured his clothing alongside the borrowed clothes and weapons, then drank down the last of the water from the canteen and secured it too.

He rubbed the mule's muzzle, then pointed her in the direction of Mae's house, and sent her on her way.

Moonlight, silver and pure, burnished the dry golden

land. And Cedar Hunt's fingers found first the tuning fork, then the crescent moon and arrow chain still around his neck. He hoped the chain would help him keep his reason and wits one more time, so that he could find Elbert, find his brother, and hunt down Mr. Shunt.

He arched his back, bathing in the moonlight, no longer feeling the pain of his injury, no longer feeling any worries, any cares. If he couldn't kill Mr. Shunt as a man, he'd sure as hell find a way to kill him as a wolf.

Cedar gave in to the change, relished the warmth and the thick haze of sensation that stretched and remade him. And then he lost himself, drowned himself in the killing needs of the wolf. And ran, toward town, toward Mae Lindson.

Rose Small considered not returning to her home. But there were things stashed there she might need, things that might help her save Mae. She ran up the porch stairs and through the main room to the stairs that led up to her bedroom tucked against the rafters. As she ran, her mind sorted options.

She didn't have much time. If Mr. Shard LeFel had a few minutes more, she was sure the entire town would be marching out to burn Mae's house down. Speed was the best she could do. Reach Mae before the town reached her. Warn her to run.

But if that didn't work, they'd need weapons.

Rose pulled out a knapsack. The canvas was stiff, the buckles old, but strong. Into the bag she stuffed her spare dress, underthings, shoes, and sweater. She added the leather-wrapped tools Mr. Gregor had given her on the sly, and which she kept stashed beneath her bed, out of her parents' sight.

She hesitated over the bits of brass and gears in the box under her bed. She had gathered all of it over the years, things she used to make things, fix things, devise things.

She didn't want to leave so much behind, but didn't see how the weight of it, nor the bits themselves, would be of practical application tonight.

Instead, she packed bullets for her Remington and derringer.

Rose pulled on her overcoat. She'd added pockets on the inside of the coat, and into those she stashed bullets.

Rose found the messenger satchel, which she'd fashioned out of oiled leather. She tucked into it a sheaf of paper, pen and ink, her three books, and a thin but sturdy wool blanket.

Lastly, she drew her heartiest bonnet and a tool belt out from under her bed. She buckled the belt around her waist, holstering both guns into it, then put on the hat.

She took a moment to look around her room, at the only home she had known. Even though she wasn't wanted, she would miss it. But it was time to move on. She'd known it for years. And now there was no denying it anymore.

Just as she turned toward the door, she saw one last thing. A palm-sized china doll that had been wrapped up in the blanket with her when she'd been abandoned on the doorstep. Impractical to take along now. She'd need room in her packs for other things. Like food.

Rose picked up the doll and hugged her tight to her chest. She had whispered all her hopes and fears to that doll, had held her and pretended she was a gift from her real mother, an admission that her mother left her behind out of love, not hate or shame.

"No place for you now," Rose whispered to the doll. She placed her on the window, facing the street below and the horizon beyond, so she could look out at the world.

Then Rose left her room, her home. She closed the door behind her and did not look back.

The grumble and growl of the crowd spilling out from the church, the racket of horses and wagons being mounted, lined up, and loaded, pricked fear into her heart. Rose ran down the street, taking the shadows, taking the less-traveled ways. She might yet be able to steal a horse at the livery and ride hard out to Mae's. She might yet get there before the town had even started their hunt.

The edge of town was coming up quick. The livery just a few yards off. She could smell the wet straw and stink of the horses inside. Almost there now.

Hands grabbed her arms and waist, lifted her, and pressed her against the wall of the livery outbuilding.

Rose struggled, and worked to get at her gun in her pocket. "Let me go, Henry Dunken!"

"Hold on, now," a voice said. Not Henry.

Rose blinked, and realized it wasn't Henry who had hold of her wrists. It was the Madder brothers. All three of them, hair wild, eyes wilder, and their smiles looking half-crazed.

"We hope you'll excuse us our sudden detainment of you," Alun said, "but time is ticking down."

"Let me go," Rose demanded.

The brothers, Bryn and Cadoc, who held her on either side, let go of her. Rose hadn't expected that.

"This is a matter of grave importance, Rose Small," Alun said. "Otherways we would not have snatched you down in the middle of your flight."

"I have matters of my own to attend and no time for any other grave things, Mr. Madder," Rose said with her chin tipped up.

Alun's grin appeared in his beard. He nodded. "Aye. Then tell us this and we'll let you about your way. What did you see in that boy back at the church?"

"Why do you care?" Rose replied. "It may as well have been nothing for all the good it did."

"Enough of nothing that you're running, pockets full and foot-fast, out of the town you've been raised in," he noted.

"They won't believe me," Rose said. "I thank you for standing up to Mr. LeFel back there on my behalf. But that doesn't make us beholden to each other."

Alun glanced over at Bryn, who shrugged his heavy shoulders.

Cadoc, the youngest brother, spoke. "Please forgive our crude manners," he said. "We've been long, too long, unto these lands, and the heat of our concern tempers our actions." Here he gave Alun a look. Alun shook his head and stared up at the sky, shoving his hands in his pockets as if awaiting a late train.

"What we wonder, Miss Small," Cadoc continued, "is if you see the Strange."

Rose caught her breath. What should she say to these drunken miners? She'd barely spoken to them in the time they'd been in town, and she had no reason to trust them not to do her harm. Except for that they had stood up for her back in the church.

"I don't know that I understand your meaning," she hedged. "If you'll excuse me, I need to go now."

"Rose," Alun said softly in the tone she'd always thought best suited a father. "Miss Rose," he corrected. "We mean you no harm, lass. But if you can see the Strange, it would make a difference to us, and to what we can do to help you save your friend Mae Lindson."

Rose blinked and tried to swallow that all down. "Help me? Why?"

Alun grinned and it was a wicked thing. "If for no other reason than to make that whoreson LeFel squirm."

"I don't throw my lots in with strangers," Rose said.

"We give you our word." Alun extended his hand.

"Our word and honor," Bryn added, placing his hand alongside Alun's.

"Word, honor, and protection," Cadoc said, leaning in to

add his hand to the brothers', so that their hands were offered, palm to back to palm, toward her.

Rose supposed it wasn't a safe thing to accept the promise of men who were likely mad. But then, folk thought the same thing about her, and they were wrong. "You'll help me save Mrs. Lindson?" she asked.

"Aye, girl," Alun said. "That and more."

"And what will you expect me to pay?"

Alun nodded approvingly. "Your answer to our question. And a favor."

The sound of the town rising up and making ready made Rose glance over her shoulder. She half expected to see men riding with torches and guns. No more time to think this through. She had made her decision.

Rose shook their hands. "Done."

"Can you?" Cadoc asked.

"Can I what?" Rose said.

"See the Strange?"

Rose looked into his eyes. He was patient, waiting, as if he had all of time for her answer.

"Yes," she said in a rush. "I can. Mostly. But that doesn't matter now. I need to warn Mae Lindson."

"No horse, no mount, no wings," Bryn mused. "You'll not get there fast enough with those feet of yours." He gave her a sly look. "You weren't figuring to procure a horse from the livery, were you?"

Rose felt the blush fire her cheeks. "There's no other way I can get to her place fast enough."

"We've ways," Alun said. "Come this way, lass. We've a shortcut."

Alun rambled off into the dark, moonlight sliding over him and setting him to burnish as if he were made of steel. He waved his hand over his shoulder. "Now, girl. There's not much time."

Rose started off after Alun, his brothers following behind her. This was madness, following three crazy devisers into the brush, alone, in the night. "This shortcut will take us to Mae Lindson's house?" she asked.

"Yes," Alun's voice floated back to her through shadows cast by trees and the stretch of chimneys and walls of the town. "But first, we'll need weapons."

He stopped by a large boulder and Rose stopped behind him. They were on the edge of the town where scrub rolled up and away across the rocky hill. Alun looked over at her. "We trust you'll keep this secret minded," he said.

"Is that the favor I owe you?"

Alun's eyebrows shot up, and then he laughed, loud and belly-full. "You've got wit, for sure. No, that's not the favor proper. That favor we'll come to terms on after we take care of your friend. But I have your word?"

"Yes." Rose was about willing to promise anything if the brothers would hurry this up. She was losing far more time than she was gaining.

"Good." Alun pulled a lever, cleverly hidden at the base of the boulder, and the boulder itself rolled aside, clunking and grinding as if unused, dragged on pulleys beneath the ground.

Cadoc and Bryn struck flint and steel to candles they produced from within the voluminous pockets of their coats, and Alun did the same. In the wan candlelight, Rose could see a wooden ladder leading down deep into the earth.

Alun walked to the edge of the hole and started down. "Hurry on, girl. These tunnels will take us quickly to your friend's side."

Rose looked away from the fall of his candlelight sinking deeper and deeper, looked instead at the brothers Bryn and Cadoc.

Bryn said, "We have supplies hidden in the tunnels. And

have mapped a route that will take us to the Lindsons' farm. You'll see no harm at our hands, Miss Small." He gestured toward the mouth of the tunnel. "After you."

Rose took one last deep breath of clean air and nodded. Then she started down the stairs into the heart of the world.

CHAPTER TWENTY-NINE

Shard LeFel looked out upon the people who hung on his every word. They were hopeful, angry, vengeful. They wanted what he told them they wanted: revenge upon the witch who had hurt one of their young, who had damaged one of their innocents.

"In these modern times, we have laws and jails," Shard LeFel said to the people gathered by torchlight and lamplight outside the church. "But there is an older law, an older reckoning, that bids us to tend to our own. To protect our own. And to punish those who are wicked and vile even— no, especially—when they are among us."

A murmur rose up from the crowd.

"I would not presume to tell you good people what it is you must do. This is your town, your laws, your home. But justice must be done."

There was a pause. LeFel watched, calmly waiting to see who would strike the tinder he'd so carefully prepared, and set it ablaze.

"Burn her!" It came from the back of the crowd. From Mrs. Dunken's boy Henry. And his cry was picked up, carried by each voice, until it became a chant.

"Burn her!" the crowd cried. "Burn the witch!"

LeFel tugged at the lace at his cuff and then rested the tip of his jewel-encrusted cane upon the ground. Mr. Shunt sidled up beside him, silent as death's gaze.

"The wick is caught," LeFel said to the Strange while watching the sheriff and Henry Dunken make out their plans of surrounding the witch's cottage, and calling her out to stand trial.

"We'll approach her and give her the chance to turn herself in," Sheriff Wilke said. "I want you all to understand we're not going to raise a gallows tonight. There will be a trial. Justice will be served."

"But if she resists," Henry said above the rise of voices, "we'll burn her out. I won't stand idly by while she does her devil's magic. Nor shall she harm another man, woman, or child of this town!"

"And now," LeFel said quietly, "we shall watch the fire I've set in these mortals do that which even you failed me in, Mr. Shunt."

Mr. Shunt said nothing. He folded his bony fingers together, each one clacking against the other, metal upon metal, bone on bone, as if wishing for a neck to break between them. "Yes, Lord LeFel," he murmured.

The townsfolk assembled in the street, men gathering horses and wagons, guns, and torches while the women all rushed off with Mrs. Gregor to tend and fuss over her and the Strange Elbert.

Shard LeFel stood in the shadows, mostly forgotten, as he intended. He would let them ride forth and smoke the witch out. And he would be waiting, near enough that he could snatch her out of their hands. He would take her. And kill her for his own purposes—her and the wolf and the real little boy—to turn the tumbler and locks and open the door to his land.

And if the townsfolk turned their rage on him . . . well, he would simply let Mr. Shunt take care of that.

Cedar Hunt ignored the weeping pain of the wound in his side, ignored his hungry belly, ignored the night that called him toward the rail, called him to find Strange, any Strange, to kill.

He ran despite the limp it caused him, toward the witch's house, toward the wallow of trees in front of her property. There, he would find the dying scent of his brother. There he would find the scent of the Strange who had taken him, who may have killed him. There he would track the Strange who was going to fall beneath his fang and claw.

The wind brought him the scent of fire and wood and oil burning. He heard the rise of voices, felt the rumble of wagon wheels and horses coming from the town behind him. He stopped on a ridge that looked over the town. Orange and yellow globs of light marched down Hallelujah's main street. Torches. Heading out toward the witch's house. Heading out toward the stand of trees.

The beast in him twisted his hold. *Hunt. Kill.*

Cedar pushed against the urge. Why would the people of Hallelujah be out in the night, burning torches, riding through the darkness? Were they headed to the trees? Were they looking for the same Strange as he?

Muddled by the wolf's need to hunt Strange, Cedar could not think through why the town was rising in the night. But he knew they would destroy his brother's trail if they tromped through the forest before he got there.

Cedar started down the ridge, and ran, faster than the men, faster than the horses, faster than the torches of Hallelujah, to catch the scent of his brother's murderer.

Mae Lindson had waited the full day for Cedar Hunt to keep his word. But now it was well into night, and clear he wasn't coming back to her.

Just a short while ago, while she was outside pumping

water, her mule, Prudence, had plodded up and stopped at the corral gate, wanting to be let in for water and food. Bundled on the saddle were Jeb's clothes and a spare set that must belong to Mr. Hunt. Strangely, his canteen, goggles, and guns were also with the supplies. Or perhaps not strangely. Now that the moon was on the rise, she guessed his curse would be in bloom, and he was traveling the night as a wolf, not a man.

Which left the finding of Mr. Shunt and the killing of him in her hands alone.

"Do as you please, Mr. Hunt," Mae said as she tended Prudence, removing her saddle, and brushing her down. "I have a killer to find." Mae finished caring for the mule, keeping the Madders' shotgun in one hand, the Colt tucked in her belt, and an eye out for anything stirring in the shadows.

The night was full of natural noises—animals and insects skittering about in the underbrush. A restless wind tugged from the northwest, and for a brief moment, she thought she smelled smoke on the breeze, but otherwise the night was quiet.

Mae resaddled the mule and took Cedar Hunt's clothes and gear off the saddle. She had left her supplies for hunting Mr. Shunt back in her house, though she had already banked the fire and locked the cupboards tight. While it wasn't a common thing to head out on a hunt in the middle of the night, she knew her time was nearly up. The pull of the coven's voices stabbed at her like claws in her lungs, insistent now. She would have to be heading east, likely by tomorrow. If not, she'd fall too ill to make the return.

But before she left this pocket of the West, she would see Jeb's killer dead at her feet.

Mae patted Prudence's side. "Won't be a minute more, girl. I'll gather my things."

She strode back to the house, the moonlight doing some good to light her path. She would use the Madders' gun to kill Shunt, full charge. The other times she'd used it against him, it hadn't been ready. Which would mean she'd have to charge the gun before she spotted her target.

She paused at her back door. A chill pricked her skin, even through her heavy coat.

Not a breath of Mr. Shunt. Not a shift of a shadow, nor a glint of his coal-lit eyes. He was not here, but something in the night made her uneasy. Even Prudence snorted.

Mae tipped her head, listening, waiting for a hint of what was tickling at the back of her spine. But the night was silent.

Mae pulled together everything she could take with her without hitching the wagon. A satchel of food, herbs, clothes. She did not want to leave her spinning wheel behind and hoped once she had killed Shunt, she could return for it before heading east.

She buckled and tied the satchels closed and slung them over her shoulder. With one last look at her home, she hefted the shotgun and headed toward the door. Time to head off to the rail and see if that dandy Mr. Shard LeFel had his man Mr. Shunt nearby.

But before she could open the door, a sound drifted through the night—voices, horses, carts. It sounded like the entire town of Hallelujah was taking to the road, striking out into the night.

She risked a glance out her front shutter.

Torches, dozens, maybe near a hundred, came marching through the forest and the field, burning holes in the darkness. Horses, carts, and wagons rattled across the rocky field headed straight for her home, headed straight for her. And the huffing chug of an engine behind the mob filled the air with steam and heat.

Fear plucked her pulse. The wooden whimsies lining the room rattled and trembled even though her house was still as a tomb.

"Mrs. Jeb Lindson," a man's voice yelled out. She knew

that voice. It was Sheriff Wilke. "You're to come out of your house and stand trial for the harm you've done to the boy Elbert Gregor, and for the witchcraft you have practiced here in the town of Hallelujah."

Mae pressed her gloved fingertips against her lips. Through the crack in her shutter she could see all the men of town, men whom Jeb had worked for, men who had sold her goods, men whose wives had bought blankets and lace from her with a nod and a smile.

She might not live within the town, but she'd never once thought she had made an enemy of the people.

And then she caught the burnish of copper and brass, brightened by the orange torchlight, glinting hard in the pale moonlight.

A ticker—a matic made of iron, brass, bolts, and piston-driven wheels with smokestacks at its rounded carriage top coughing up plumes of white—rolled to a stop at the back of the crowd. And within that device, sitting as if on a throne, was Mr. Shard LeFel. Behind him, his man, Mr. Shunt.

Her heartbeat slammed in her chest and a high-pitched ring of panic filled her ears. The shotgun didn't have enough range to shoot him from here, and if it did—even if she got a shot off—the townsfolk would open fire on her. They'd carried their torches and hatred out this far. She knew they weren't going to go home until her blood was spilled.

Somehow she had to get to Mr. Shunt.

"We know you're in there, Mrs. Lindson," the sheriff yelled out again. "You'll spare yourself a lot of hardship if you just turn yourself over now."

They'd throw her in shackles, beat her unconscious. The fear of magic ran thick in the New World. Even the rumor of it had gotten more than one of the sisterhood hanged.

It would be suicide to walk out into that mob, no matter how much she'd like to put a bullet through Mr. Shunt's head.

She ran to the back door. Maybe they hadn't made it around the house yet. Maybe she could still get to Prudence and run, then follow Mr. Shunt at a safe distance until the opportunity to end his life presented itself.

She cracked open the door.

The door flew out of her hand. A man grabbed her wrist. She bit back a yell and swung the gun just as her captor ducked back.

"This way if you want to live," Alun Madder said. "And mind that you don't use that priceless shotgun as a cudgel, Mrs. Lindson." He didn't wait for her reply. Holding tight to her wrist, he jogged out across the back of the property between the house and the shed, then farther out yet.

"Stop," she said, "let go of me!"

"Keep your voice down. We have a way out of here that mob can't follow."

Three stones in her field suddenly stood up to become the other two Madder brothers and Rose Small.

At the sight of Rose, Mae didn't know if she should be relieved or terrified.

"We have to get you out of town," Rose Small said. "They mean to burn your house. They mean to kill you. Hang you."

"But I've done nothing. Nothing." One of the brothers, Bryn Madder, she thought, draped a rough blanket over her shoulders.

"Pull it into a hood over that sunlight hair of yours," he said as they all ran across the field. "It soaks in shadow and repels the moonlight."

"They'll overtake us," Mae said. "They have mounts that will travel the fields much faster than we run."

"We're not traveling the fields," Alun Madder said. He slowed from a run into a brisk walk. "The tunnel is just ahead."

Rose Small slipped up beside Mae. "Don't worry; we'll get you safe and away and on the road by sunrise."

"On the road?" Mae said. "No. I'm not leaving. I'm not done taking care of my own business with this town."

The crowd roared.

Mae glanced back over her shoulder. A low glow was rising, flames licking up the walls of her house, burning through the home she and Jeb had built with their own hands. Burning her life away.

They had taken it from her, the last of her life with her husband. All the things he had carved on long winter nights, the quilts she'd made for their bed, all their memories, all the time—their life—gone.

"Here we are," Alun Madder said. "Mind the ladder—it's a bit uneven."

Mae heard his boots tap out a muffled echo down wooden stairs as he descended into whatever tunnel they'd decided to dig. But she had no plans to run away. Her husband's murderer was on the other side of those flames. Her husband's murderer was in that matic that squatted and huffed like an iron buffalo on the other side of this field. And if this blanket could keep her hidden in the night, she planned on using it to get her close enough to put a bullet through his brain.

She took a step, but Rose Small caught her hand again. "You can't go back," Rose said. "Mrs. Lindson, Mae, come on with us now, please. We have to go. All of us, or we'll be dead."

A shadow ran low to the ground, fast, slick in the night, darting across the field toward the flames. For a moment, the light from the fire caught it in silhouette, a wolf with a silver chain around its neck.

Cedar Hunt. He was running toward the fire, toward the flame, toward the mob.

Mae took another step. Rose Small tugged her harder. "You can't go back." Her voice was high and harshed by fear. "Please."

And then the Madder brothers were there, Bryn and Cadoc, blocking her path. "You must trust us, Mrs. Lindson," Bryn Madder said. "If it's revenge you seek, you'd be better for it without walking through fire first."

"Now," Cadoc Madder said.

A cry rose up in the crowd. Gunshot exploded the still night air. And the matic, the great metal beast carrying Mr. Shard LeFel and his man, Mr. Shunt, turned toward the open field. Turned as if it could see Mae and Rose and the Madders. Then it huffed, steam punching the air like a percussion of thunder, and huffed again. Even at this distance, Mae could see it lurch forward and begin racing their way, a nightmare beast scenting a blood trail.

Mae turned and ran down the ladder, Rose, Bryn, and Cadoc behind her. At the base, holding the ladder steady, stood Alun Madder.

"Quick, now, quick," he said. As soon as the last in line, Cadoc, had lowered his head beneath ground level, Alun turned what looked like a valve wheel set on the wall—the same sort of wheel she had seen them use at the door to their mine. The roof of the tunnel above the ladder closed in, a stone piece set on rails rolling quickly into place.

Bryn and Cadoc Madder made fast work of folding the blankets they had been wearing and stuffing them into their satchels strapped across their chests and hanging at their waists. Then Bryn Madder lit a candle and Cadoc Madder lit two lanterns that were pegged on the wall, handing one lantern to Rose Small.

"Here." Rose gave the lantern to Mae. The lantern was a green glass globe caught all round in silver vines and leaves, so that it looked to be a glowing flower. Oil wick inside, it was a beautiful device, and made with a master metalsmith's fine hand. Not what she'd expect rough miners to stock in case of emergencies such as this.

The tunnel was tall and wide enough for two people to walk shoulder to shoulder. Here and there along the wall were crates and sacks covered with heavy canvas. Wooden cross-beams and bracers were set off down the tunnel at a steady distance, holding the earth above, while straight down the middle of the ceiling, supported by the wooden beams, rested a single rail.

She hadn't a clue what the rail was in place for and could not believe how many supplies the Madders had stashed away. A veritable storehouse this close to her home and she'd never once suspected the tunnel was here.

"You'll want a sling." Alun Madder pulled the canvas cover from the pile of gear by the ladder and started digging through the odds and bits.

"Sling?" Mae said.

"Sling." Alun pulled what looked like an unattached rope swing out of the pile. "Netted bottom here is the sling part. That you'll sit upon. These"—he strung out the two heavy ropes that looped together through an iron hook—"you'll attach to the eye loop there." He pointed upward.

Mae lifted the globe and could just make out several metal loops hanging from the iron rail above them.

"Why?"

Rose Small took the sling from Alun and handed it to Mae. "It's quite a lot of fun, if a little breezy."

"Fun?" Mae asked. "Swinging in a tunnel?"

"Not swinging," Alun Madder said. "Soaring." He produced a sling from the pack on his back, then hooked it into an eye loop. "Mind that you keep your feet tucked on the corners or you might break an ankle. Or worse." He stood in front of the sling, hands on the rope just as if he were a child ready to get a push on a swing. But as he walked backward to the ladder, the hook and eye above him clacked like a chain tightening a spring.

"I'll see you at the first junction. We'll have to switch lines there." He sat down in the sling, which lowered slightly under his weight, then lifted his feet. The spring device above shot him forward so fast, Mae sucked in a breath at the gush of wind that filled the tunnel.

The light from Alun Madder's lantern swung across the walls and ceiling of the tunnel, showing a good, long, straight shot, before suddenly the light whipped left and was swallowed by darkness.

"Quick," Rose Small said. "It's safe enough. I rode it most of the way from town." She took a sling out of her pack and shook it out, righting the ropes and seat. That she left on the ground and instead snatched up Mae's sling. "Just mind to keep your skirts tamped tight and tuck your feet on that corner." She hooked the eye loop, and held the seat of the sling out for Mae.

"Latch the lantern here." Rose used a leather thong sewn into the rope to secure the globe near Mae's shoulder. The lantern tossed up enough light to catch on the clever wheels and gears that were attached like a miniature cart above the rail, the eye loop hook directly below it.

"Where does the tunnel lead?"

Rose Small shrugged. "Don't know that it matters so long as it's away from that mob who want you burned. They think you did witchcraft on Elbert."

"They found Elbert?" Mae asked.

"That devil LeFel brought in a boy who looks like Elbert," Rose Small hedged.

"The Strange," Mae breathed.

"You know about them?" Rose Small's words came out in a tumble of relief.

"Yes, I do," Mae said. "Too well."

"Hurry up now, ladies," Bryn Madder said. "We need to be out from under their feet before they realize we've gone."

"I'll be right behind you," Rose said, holding up her own sling and smiling.

"Just walk backward toward me, Mrs. Lindson," Bryn Madder said. "When you lift your feet, you'll swing down the line and go it strong."

Mae held tight to the ropes and walked backward. It wasn't difficult to pull the rope back. She kept a good hold on the shotgun in her left hand, her heart pounding.

"That's good, now," Bryn Madder said. "Sit back and hold on to your bonnet."

Mae sat. Then she lifted her feet. The sling shot forward at a remarkable speed. She held tight to the ropes, surprised at how smoothly the wheel device above drove down the rails.

Other than the occasional crate or sack stacked along the wall, Mae had no good handle on distance, but knew she must have gone far enough that she heard the twang of another sling being shot behind her. She twisted to see who it was, but in the darkness and shadows thrown against the walls and ceiling, she couldn't make out much.

With no horizon, sun, or moon, she couldn't say which direction she was going, but knew the corner must be just ahead. She tucked her feet, just as the lantern slapped light across a wall dead ahead of her.

The sling rocked up to the right, sending Mae's feet precariously close to the wall before sliding down the left curve of the tunnel. Mae suddenly worried how she was supposed to stop the sling. She didn't see a brake line or any other slowing device.

Then the ground, the entire tunnel, shook. At first, just a tremble. She wondered if it was her imagination. Then the shaking grew stronger and stronger. Something huge, something heavy, moved above them.

"That's a matic," Alun Madder called from somewhere

down the tunnel ahead of her. "And Shard LeFel. Hurry. Hurry!"

Mae didn't know how she could hurry any more. The tunnel walls rushed past at a dizzying pace. It felt as if the track would never end.

Rocks pelted down in dusty plumes, battering her shoulders and legs. The ceiling shook rocks and clods of dirt like a rusted sieve. It was hard to see through all the dust kicked up. Hard to breathe. For a brief, wild moment, she wondered if she should jump.

And then the tunnel exploded. The force of the concussion knocked Mae off her sling and tumbled her to the ground. Rock and dirt collapsed and filled the tunnel ahead with rubble, cutting off their route.

A huge metal hand reached down into the hole that had been punched through the tunnel ceiling. No—not a hand. It was a steam hammer, five metal pistons pounding down like great metal fingers, each attached by rods and tubes and wheels to a hunk of metal—the matic's arm—somewhere above the ceiling.

"Back!" Alun Madder was on his feet. He threw off the sling and ran. "Turn around!"

Mae spun, a thick cloud of dirt and stone sucking all the air out of the tunnel. Rose, Cadoc, and Bryn had all been knocked out of their slings too. Bryn Madder and Rose were both running behind Alun Madder, but Cadoc stood there, calm as a prophet watching the doom come calling, while Mae ran past him.

"LeFel," he said.

"Run, run!" Rose Small pushed past Bryn, pushed past Alun.

The floor lifted, held there for what felt like an eternity, then fell. Hard.

Rose Small, ahead of them, lifted, fell. Mae was battered

to the ground. She landed on her hands and knees as all the world broke apart. A five-fingered wall of iron sheered the sky from the earth.

There was too much noise: the thunderous pounding of iron and steam, the pulverizing of rock and dirt, the Madder brothers cursing up a blue streak.

And Rose Small, screaming.

Mae scrabbled up out of the dirt that threatened to bury her, swimming free, digging free, up and up toward air. She broke out just as the Madder brothers pulled up through the hole where the ceiling had been.

"Rose, Rose!" Mae called. She blinked away the light—too much moonlight and firelight after the soft underground lanterns. And finally her vision fell to focus.

Rose Small stood in front of the giant matic that was nearly as tall as a house. The hammer contraption that had busted apart the tunnel was retracting slowly, folding like an elbow alongside the main body of the device.

High above, perched in the matic on his throne, was Mr. Shard LeFel, his gloved fingertips holding brass levers as if they were reins. Mr. Shunt, too tall, too thin, a shadow with bloody eyes, stood in front of the matic, pressing a knife to Rose Small's throat.

"Give me the witch," Shard LeFel said, his voice carrying over the chug and hiss of the matic's engine, "or Mr. Shunt will rip this girl apart."

CHAPTER THIRTY

Cedar fought instinct that told him to run, far from the flames, from the mob, from the matic that rumbled over the ground toward Mae Lindson's house.

But where there was a matic, Mr. Shard LeFel would not be far behind, and neither would Mr. Shunt.

Cedar intended to put a final end to that monster.

He paused in the stand of trees, watching the mob. There were too many people, too many guns, too many torches, between him and the matic. He growled, low and unheard over the heat of the fire, the heat of the men shouting. The tuning fork against his chest rang out with a single sour note even though he stood perfectly still. The Strange who had taken Elbert was near. Near enough to kill.

Inside that matic was his foe, his enemy, his prey. Two beating hearts waiting to be ripped free of the sinew that held them, two spines to break, two skulls to crush. Mr. Shunt and Mr. Shard LeFel.

Cedar crept low and growled softly again. The mob swarmed closer to the house, yelling. His ears pricked up. Faintly over the yelling of the crowd, he heard the back door slam shut.

Mae. Mae trying to run free. Mae trying to escape. His heart beat faster as the thoughts of a man overrode the beast's need to kill. Mae had been in that house. He'd told her to stay until he returned. They would trap her. Kill her.

A blaze of flame shot up the side of the house, wood catching fire beneath torches and quickly turning into an inferno.

Cedar Hunt rushed silently through the cover of underbrush, the cover of shadow, the tuning fork screaming a bitter song.

Mae couldn't die. He couldn't let her die. Couldn't bear her death. He ran a wide berth to get behind the house to the door he had heard slam. The wind heaved with smoke, fouling Cedar's sense of smell.

She couldn't survive that fire. He'd told her to stay. She would be burned alive.

Wolf instinct yelled: *Run*. Every nerve pumped hot with panic, powering his muscles to bunch and push. Faster. Faster.

Cedar pressed his ears down against his head and bared his teeth as he ran across the field. The wound in his side split open, poured with new pain. Almost there. Almost there to save Mae.

The heat from the fire grew stronger and stronger with every step he took. The light ruined his vision.

He leaped through the open back door and into a blistering hell.

Fire roared, chewing away the walls, snapping the wooden whimsies, burning them to ash, destroying the chairs, the floor, the walls, the ceiling, with white-hot liquid heat. Cedar crouched, eyes slit, and pushed into the living room. Searching for Mae.

Smoke burned his eyes; embers singed his fur. His skin charred. He could not find her. Could not find Mae.

There might be a nook or corner where she hid, but there was too much fire. He could not endure.

Run, run, run, the beast howled.

And Cedar Hunt could not hold against that instinct any longer.

He ran from the house. Out into the night. Ran until his lungs filled with air instead of smoke. Ran until the cool winds cleaned his eyes and soothed his flesh.

He had to believe Mae had found her way out. He had to believe she had left the house earlier in the day; had to believe she had tired of waiting for him and gone hunting. Had to believe that the door slamming was just a trick of the wind.

But he didn't. Not in these lands where nightmares spread roots and sucked away all hope, all life.

The mob broke up, chose which men would stay and see to it that the house burned to the ground. Just then the matic suddenly huffed louder, and rumbled away from the gathering, out into the field.

Cedar knew where the matic would go. Back to the rail.

And that was where he would kill.

Cedar Hunt raised his voice, sorrow and anger howling against the night sky.

He took a step, and the pain from the wound in his side bloomed hot through him. It was bleeding again, bleeding still, worse than it had been. He didn't care. There was no time to stop. No time to feel pain. He ran, first just a lope, then a ground-eating run. To the rail. To death.

Mae Lindson couldn't get to the shotgun on the ground next to her and charge it in time to shoot Mr. Shunt. Rose Small didn't look so much frightened in Mr. Shunt's grip as just angry. That Rose was keeping her head about her was one thing good to their advantage. Unfortunately, Mae couldn't think of many more.

"Your end is come, Shard LeFel," Alun Madder said, his

voice low, but commanding. "We have played this game to its finish. And just as you were banished to walk this land, you will die in this mortal land. Enough of your hollow threats. If we had the mind to, we'd shoot you now."

"And lose the Holder?" Shard LeFel smiled. "How would the order of the king's guard reward you when they find that you have let a weapon of that magnitude slip through your fingers?"

"You underestimate the guard's resources," Alun Madder said. "We'll find the Holder, whether or not you're breathing."

"Or you'll find pieces of it."

Alun's head jerked up.

Shard LeFel smiled. "If you kill me, the Holder will explode like glass under a hammer. And every piece will be loose in the land. Even one fragment of the Holder will destroy cities, kill hundreds, thousands, in most unusual and painful ways." He smiled again. "You will not shoot me. But I have no such qualms about this girl. Mr. Shunt, make her bleed."

Mr. Shunt raised the knife to her face.

"No!" Mae stepped forward. "Don't hurt her. I'll come with you. Let Rose go."

"Mrs. Lindson," Alun said, his voice tight, his eyes on Shard LeFel. "Don't do what this dog says. We'll find a way to save Miss Small."

"Not before he has that monster cut her apart," Mae said. "No, I'm going with him."

Alun Madder took a step forward and extended his hand to her. They shook and he said, "I only wish you'd take a minute when you need it the most. Think things through."

"I have thought this through," she said.

"Then that might just save us all. Good luck to you." Alun Madder searched her face, finding, she knew, her determination. Mr. LeFel might know she was a witch. But he most certainly did not know she was a witch like no other. Vows and curses came to her as easy as drawing a breath. And Mae didn't need any weapon greater than that.

Alun stepped away and Mae realized he had pressed a pocket watch into her palm. It was warm, as if an ember lay coiled within it. No, not an ember—glim. She had seen glim once, from a man who tried to sell just a drop of it to her when she and Jeb were traveling out this way. She would know the feel of it anywhere.

She had no idea how a pocketful of glim would do her any good, though it was said the glim could give strength to anything it was set upon. She tucked the watch away in her coat, and turned back to face Mr. Shard LeFel.

"Let Rose Small go." Mae took a few good-faith steps toward the matic, then stopped, waiting.

Mr. Shard LeFel worked the levers in the monstrous metal beast. "Yes, of course. Let us make good on our promise, Mr. Shunt. Let the girl go."

Mr. Shunt pushed Rose so hard she flew several feet before landing on the ground.

And just as quickly, Mr. Shunt suddenly appeared in front of Mae.

She sucked in a gasp. Before she could exhale, he had cut the straps of her satchels and packs. They dropped in a thump to the ground. He wrapped at least two arms around her, another clutched to the brim of his hat.

And then the world became a blur. Ground sped by, the side of the matic pulled up beneath her as Mr. Shunt scaled it nimbly as a spider climbing a wall.

Once over the edge of the cab, Mae was shoved, face-down, and pressed into the leather cushions behind Shard LeFel's throne. Mr. Shunt pressed his knee in her back with a punishing weight.

She couldn't move if she wanted to. Steam pounded the air and jolted the matic into action.

Facedown with Mr. Shunt's wide, hard hand clamped against the back of her head and his knee digging at her spine, Mae could still tell the matic moved faster than anything she'd ever known, faster than trains or ships.

And she had no idea where they were taking her.

Rose Small hurt from her bonnet to her boots. More than feeling bruised and scraped, she was angry. She pushed up and staggered to her feet, but it was too late. The matic thundered off over the field faster than a racehorse on Sunday.

"Stop!" she yelled, which did absolutely no good.

"They can't hear you," Alun Madder mused. "All those gears and steam deafen." He tapped at one ear for good measure.

Rose turned on the Madder brothers. She knew she shouldn't, but she had so much anger boiling up inside of her, she thought she'd about go insane from the noise of it. "You should have stopped him! How can you just let that, that Shard LeFel take Mae? He's going to kill her!"

Bryn Madder was down in the collapsed tunnel, handing up packs, gear, and a crate or two. Alun and Cadoc took each load from him, spreading the barrels and crates out, then digging in their packs. They were paying no attention to her.

"You promised me you'd help me save Mae," Rose said. "Help me get her out of town and out of harm's way. Have you always been liars, Mr. Madder, or were you saving it all up for today?"

Alun Madder, who was crouched next to a pack, sniffed and looked her way, his arms resting along his knees, his weight balanced on the toes of his boots. "We're so much as liars as we've always been, I suppose."

He turned back to the pack, digging away, just as his

brothers were digging through crates and boxes. "However," he said, "if Mr. LeFel had wanted to kill Mrs. Lindson, he would have simply had Shunt cut her heart out. He is more than happy to do such things." He pushed that pack aside, stood up to pry the lid off a crate, and began digging.

The brothers were spreading out a collection of metal and gears and plates of wood and copper and glass. They scattered them on the ground like a strange puzzle or game, occasionally glancing up at the sky as if gauging the distance, the stars, or the wind that pushed them.

"So we sit here and wait until he tires of her company and then kills her?" Rose looked around. "And build a . . . a barn? No. I'm going after him."

"Ah!" Alun said, and his brothers stopped rummaging through their packs to look over at him. "Here it is." He pulled out his pipe, dusted the dirt off it, and clamped it in his teeth with a satisfied grunt.

Rose made a frustrated sound. The brothers had gone completely mad. Fine, then. She would save Mae on her own.

She picked up Mae's tinkered shotgun and started walking. Got about a dozen steps away before Alun called out.

"By the way, Miss Small. We'll need that locket of yours," he said.

She turned, hands on her hips. And nearly lost her grip on the gun when she saw what the brothers had built.

In the short stomp she'd taken, they'd assembled the pieces of wood and metal into a perfectly square basket of some sort, large enough for six people to stand within it. Rising up at each corner was a lattice and attached to that were ropes. Spread out behind the basket was what looked like a huge blanket, white in the moonlight, and fine enough that the slight wind rippled the material.

Bryn Madder knelt beside the basket, using a ratchet to tighten a bolt on a fan or small windmill blade attached to the side of the basket. Cadoc Madder finished straightening the material over the ground and walked toward the basket, one finger up as if testing the air, a tuning fork pressed to his ear.

"What is that?" she asked.

Alun Madder held a lit wick to the bowl of his pipe, puffed several times, then exhaled smoke. "Just a little gadget we made."

"What does it do?"

"It takes us faster than feet can travel."

"How?"

"Steam and wind." He frowned over at the basket, where Bryn was feeding coal into a firebox set up high in the middle of it. He had sparked and turned the tinder uncommonly quickly into flame and poured water from his canteen into a small keg set atop the tinderbox. "Mostly," Alun added.

He grinned, clamping his teeth on his pipe. "Let's have the locket, girl."

"No."

Alun's bushy eyebrows shot up. "No?"

"You heard me."

"Means something to you, does it?"

"More than to you."

He gave her a considering gaze. "Well, then, let's have you use it. Come on. Time's a-wasting."

Cadoc Madder stopped pacing and was now pointing the tuning fork northwest like a compass needle. "The rail," he breathed. "They're headed to the rail."

"Nice of them to make it easy," Alun said. "Just a hop and a skip." He shrugged on his backpack, then pulled a sawed-off shotgun out of a crate and attached it by tubes and lines to his backpack before climbing into the basket.

Bryn Madder finished tinkering with the two windmill-blade contraptions on either side of the basket. He pulled a squat-bodied blunderbuss and a sledgehammer out of his pack before getting into the basket next to Alun. "Coming with us, Miss Small?" he asked.

"Where?" she asked. "How?"

"The rail, apparently," Alun Madder said around the stem of his pipe. "And as for the how, you're looking at it."

Rose glanced over her shoulder toward the way the matic had left. She couldn't catch it on foot. And even though the Madders were clearly not in their right minds, she wasn't sure what choice she had other than to run to town and get a horse. And she had no time for that either.

She gathered up her skirt and tucked the hem of it through her belt beneath the heavy coat she wore.

Alun Madder raised one eyebrow but didn't say anything as to her impropriety, and she wouldn't have cared if he did. Hitching up her skirt gave her a better stride, and the long coat hung nearly halfway to her boot tops, but was split front and back so she could run if needed. Even so, there was a good palm width of her stocking in clear view that would have scandalized her mother if she'd seen it. Rose climbed over the edge of the basket, where the heat from the boiler made it almost unbearably hot.

"Stand behind me, girl," Alun Madder said.

Rose stood beside him instead.

Alun laughed. "Well, then. Are you coming, brother Cadoc?"

Cadoc Madder took in a breath as if to say something, but instead drew a two-bladed ax out from his pack. He nodded thoughtfully, and lifted up the edge of the cloth on the ground, standing to one side to reveal a hole.

"What?" Rose started, but then she didn't need to finish.

Bryn pulled a hose that was coiled at the side of the burner and tossed it to Cadoc, who turned, caught the hose, and clamped it down tight to the hole in the fabric.

Bryn Madder worked the valves, and a blast of hot steam roared into the fabric.

Cadoc Madder waited until the fabric started taking on a round shape before he stepped into the basket with them. From the shape of it, Rose suspected there was a second fabric inside the first, filling with steam. Cadoc hauled on the ropes and pulleys and helped lift the fabric—the balloon—into the sky above the basket, then fastened a tube that was already wet with condensation down onto a drip hole in the water reserve.

Wonder caught at Rose's heart. "A balloon? We're going to fly?"

"No better way to travel," Alun said. "Be to it, Bryn. Quick, now. We wouldn't want to miss the party."

Bryn adjusted levers and turned valves on the burner, which clicked and rattled and shook in a most distressing manner. "If you'd step to me a moment, Miss Small," he said. "With your locket?"

Rose did so, and pulled the locket out from beneath her blouse, but did not take it off from over her head. She held it out on the chain for him. "I don't see as how this can help."

Bryn gently caught the gilded robin's egg with his clean fingertips. He pulled a chain out of his pocket, on the end of which was a collection of thin watchmaker's tools. He chose one tool and inserted it into a tiny hole at the base of the locket. The locket spun open like a flower blooming.

Delicate gears and spindles within it twisted and rolled, revealing a small glass vial couched in the center of the locket. The vial glowed a soft green light, but Rose could not tell if it was filled with liquid or gas or something else altogether.

"What is it?" She could not look away from the locket, and did not want to.

"Glim," Alun Madder said quietly. "And all we'll need is a drop or two, to set this ship in the air."

"Glim?" She could hardly believe it. She'd been wearing a fortune around her neck, and never once suspected it. "How can it help?"

"Not much glim can't help," Alun said.

Bryn nodded once, asking permission to pull the vial out from the tiny latches that held it in place.

"Yes," Rose said.

"Want an engine to run faster, add glim," Alun continued. "Want a fire to burn hotter, a coal to last longer, a wound to heal better, add glim."

"Does it really come from the sky?" Rose asked, watching Bryn break the wax seal on the vial with his thumbnail.

"Harvested by specially equipped airships," Alun said. "Not that the scientific minds can agree upon what, exactly, glim is made of, nor why exactly it works the way it does."

"Wait," Rose said, finally looking away from the glow in Bryn Madder's hand. "You don't know how it works?"

"Sometimes a man doesn't need to know how a thing works so long as he knows that it does work."

Bryn opened a small gearbox on the side of the burner, and tapped out exactly one drop of glim. The drop floated down into the gears.

The basket lurched and a whirring racket started up. Rose grabbed hold of the railing, her breath frozen in her chest as the balloon above them snapped taut and round.

And then the world seemed to take a step away.

The sturdy basket made it feel like she was standing on solid ground, but when she looked over the edge, the ground was growing farther and farther away. They were lifting up, soft as a sigh, now at about midheight of the trees, and still rising.

They were flying!

"Put this back in the locket." Alun took the vial from Bryn and handed it to her. She looked it over as carefully as she could in the moonlight. He, or maybe Bryn, had remelted the wax on the mouth of the vial, effectively sealing it. Rose placed the vial back in the locket. It snicked into place and then the locket spun closed all on its own, though she figured there was a spring set to trigger it to lock again. She tucked the locket back inside her dress.

When she looked up again, the bottom of the basket was above even the tallest trees. She grinned and put one hand over her mouth to hold back on a whoop of joy. She was flying!

Bryn Madder took hold of the levers, and with the assistance of the fans on each side of the craft, and some clever saillike rudders that Cadoc and Alun manipulated on the sides of the balloon, they were able to steer the craft off over the trees and the hills and the creeks, to the rail.

Rose had imagined this moment for years. How the trees and mountains and town would look. She had always known it would be beautiful. Breathtaking. But even so, she had underestimated the thrill of being above all the living world, had underestimated how small and pretty and quiltlike the earth rolled out beneath the moonlight. And she could not believe how far to the horizon she could see.

The boiler rattled so hard, it shook the basket. The whole craft lurched to one side, and Rose had to brace her feet not to go sliding across the floor.

"Whoa, now," Alun said. "Easy on us, brother Bryn."

They were beginning to descend, quickly, the ground growing larger and the black-shadowed tops of trees coming much, much closer.

"How much longer?" Alun asked, trying to correct their angle through the trees with the sails. Branches scraped the bottom of the basket, and a flurry of crows took off squawking.

"Almost out of steam," Bryn called over the boiler's thunderous noise.

Evergreen branches whipped against the sides of the basket and snagged up the lines tethering the balloon.

"Too many blasted trees!" Alun yanked on a sail line, dislodging a limb, and Bryn worked a lever to angle the fans and push the balloon out of the tree's reach. But they were still falling too fast, branches slapping, cracking, catching at the aircraft, grazing over the delicate balloon fabric.

"Give us a sign, brother Cadoc," Alun said.

The unmistakable rasp of material tearing sent a cold wave of fear down Rose's spine. The balloon was broken. They weren't going to land. They were going to crash.

"There!" Cadoc pointed to a clearing not far from the rail. They were just a ways, maybe half a mile, down from the building end of the track.

"Down," Alun yelled. "Put 'er down, quick, Bryn!"

The boiler stopped rattling, completely burned dry of water. Wind rushed by, cold and wet from the steam gouting out of the balloon above them.

Alun and Cadoc heaved on the lines, opening pockets in the fabric, trying to push the balloon toward the clearing.

They sped down. Fast and faster.

Rose clutched the rail of the basket and watched, transfixed, as the skeletal giants of moonlit trees slapped at them with silvery fingers.

The fans whirred like hornet hives as Bryn put all the steam, and likely all the glim that was left, into them. "Brace for it!" he yelled.

Rose sucked in a deep breath and said a prayer.

The basket rammed into something solid, then just as quick was whipped the other way. Rose lost hold of the edge of the basket and fell as the entire craft tipped. She caught a glimpse of sky, trees, basket, the wind rushing past her, and then was caught by strong hands around her waist.

"Hold on!" Alun yelled.

Rose, half in and half out of the basket, facedown to the ground, couldn't hold on to anything, but Alun Madder's hands were a vise around her ribs. The basket tumbled, bounced, and then even Alun Madder's strong hands couldn't keep ahold of her.

Rose spilled free of the basket and hit the ground so hard, all the air was knocked out of her lungs. It took her a full minute to get air back in her chest and wits back in her head. And when she did, she realized two things.

One, she was on the ground. Scuffed, bruised, and mussed, but by most parts whole and undamaged.

And two, the Madder brothers were all laughing their fool heads off.

She pushed up to sitting, and tried to get her bearings.

Somehow, they kept the basket from breaking apart. Somehow they brought the basket down, close enough, and, more important, slow enough, that when the basket finally struck the earth, they hadn't all perished falling out of the thing.

The balloon, however, was caught up in the tree branches, and torn open like a child's wayward kite.

"Fine a landing as ever, brother Bryn," Alun, who sat no more than a few feet away from Rose, said.

"Thank you, brother Alun." Bryn chuckled and heaved up to his feet. He swayed a little, then seemed to get his footing and stomped over to the tipped basket. He twisted a valve, and threw open the burner grate. There was not a coal, not a stitch of fuel, left. "Well, she won't burn the forest down."

"Looks like a one-way ticket," Cadoc said from where he was sprawled on the ground, staring up at the tattered balloon in the tree above him thoughtfully. "Pity. I do like air rides."

"We'll make you another balloon, Cadoc," Alun said. "And you can try your hand at flying it." He slapped at his shoulders and trousers, then stood. "Miss Small, are you in one piece?"

Rose took a deep breath to steady herself. She felt jostled and rattled as if she'd ridden a day in a horse-drawn carriage, as if every inch of the space they had traveled had rumbled beneath her as they passed over it. But that had been flight. Her first. And she had loved it.

She stood. "I'm fine enough, thank you, Mr. Madder."

"Good," he said, "that's good. Thought I might have lost you there at the end, what with you jumping ship."

"I assure you, I did not jump," Rose said.

The brothers all laughed again, and went about reclaiming their weapons and supplies.

Rose wanted to know how they had built the ship, wanted to know what the balloon and sails were made of and how the tubes and hoses and steam and glim had powered it, but there was no time.

The thump of steam exhausting a stack rolled through the air from up the track and a long hiss followed. The matic that Shard LeFel rode was somewhere up the rail ahead of them and coming closer, like as not headed to LeFel's railcars.

"Bring your weapons, lady and gents," Alun said, jumping free of the basket. "It's time we see to the end of Mr. Shard LeFel."

They gathered their gear, and Alun pressed a modified Winchester rifle into Rose's hands. "As a thank-you. For the use of the glim," he said.

She nodded and turned to one side to sight the gun.

"You'll want these." Bryn pulled a pair of glasses out of his pocket—well, more like modified goggles, thin brass out to the edges and wide round lenses, clear, set in permanently, with a tiny brass loupe over the right-hand corner of each lens. A spray of other colored lenses fanned off on one side.

Rose put the goggles on her forehead. "I don't know that I understand this gun," she said as they strode up the track. "Or these glasses."

"Each lens is for a different distance," Bryn said. "There's a small tube there by your left ear."

Rose reached up and touched the side of the goggle.

"There's a retractable clamp on the barrel. Connect the two, and the brass loupe will show you your target."

Rose slid the goggles over her eyes and connected the tubes. Nothing seemed to happen.

"It's powered by pumping in a round," Bryn said.

Rose stopped, and Bryn stopped with her, though Alun and Cadoc kept walking, their boots crunching in the gravel, their heads turned up to watch the moon more than their feet.

Bryn handed her a box of bullets from his pocket, and she loaded a single shell. The lever load snapped the bullet into place and the brass loupe on the goggles shifted to the lowest corner.

She raised the rifle to her shoulder and looked out along it. The brass loupe shifted smoothly like oil on water to show her exactly where her bullet would strike: rock, tree, leaf.

"Isn't that glimsweet?" Rose said. She lowered the gun and pulled the goggles back up to her forehead.

"Thank you."

"Wouldn't want you injured in this fight, Miss Small. You're a right special woman to survive traveling twixt-wise as we just did."

"Survive?" Rose asked, surprised. "Think that would have killed us?"

"There's not anything in this world without risk," he said. "Especially untested devices."

Rose shook her head. "I'm sure I agree with you there, Mr. Madder." She hefted the gun. "But I enjoyed every second of it."

A crashing squeal of metal on metal ground into the night behind them, coming up the tracks as if something huge was being dragged. If LeFel's matic was coming from ahead of them, Rose had no idea what sort of thing was coming up from behind.

"Don't dally," Alun yelled back to them, jumping to one side of the track, and still jogging while he navigated a way through the bushes. "Sounds like the fun's just beginning."

Bryn turned and jogged to catch up with his brothers, and after a moment's hesitation, and a moment's prayer, Rose did the same.

CHAPTER THIRTY-ONE

Cedar Hunt stalked the perimeter of the dozen or so tents and cook pits of the workers in Shard LeFel's employ. Unlike most railmen, who brought a crew of stragglers and ruffians to work the rail, LeFel had only a handful of men he brought along, and had hired up another handful or two of men from the town. For the rest of the rail work, he used his matics and tickers.

The men were sleeping, vulnerable, lying quiet and easy for the kill. The cook fires had gone to ash and smoke. No sentries watched over the rail. Even the matics were powered down, cold, silent, unmoving sculptures of iron and leather and oil made supple by moonlight.

It would be easy to kill the men. But it was not men Cedar hunted. It was the Strange. And the tuning fork that whispered against his heart said the Strange were close.

Cedar had to find Wil, dead or alive. Had to find the boy, Elbert, dead or alive. And he had to kill Mr. Shunt. He may not have been able to save Mae Lindson, a sorrow that made him want to keen, but he had made her promises, and he would see them through.

Mr. Shunt would likely return to the three railcars on the track, down a ways from the men's tents and matics. Cedar headed that way. He didn't know why a man like Shard LeFel needed three cars, but he had a suspicion. One car to live in, maybe one car to work in. And likely one car to hold his prisoners in.

Cedar slipped through the darkness to the railcars on the spur off the main rail, staying in shadow, silent as the moonlight.

He crept to the first car and sniffed at the underbody. Death and Strange. There were things, Strange things, in this car just waiting to be killed. But the tuning fork did not hum louder. There might be Strange within the car, but it was not the one Strange who had taken Elbert. And that Strange was the one he would kill. First.

It took everything he had not to give in to the beast's need to kill. He pulled against the urge, tamped it down, and sniffed at the car again. Something skittered in the three corners of the car, dragging long tails or ropes behind, and then was still. He could not find the boy or his brother's scent in the death and blood and oil above him.

There might be prisoners in this car, but they were not Elbert or Wil.

He moved on to the next car. It stank of oil and steam and burned metal. Faintly, he caught the scent of the boy's blood. Old. No other smell of him. And still no smell of his brother. The tuning fork remained quiet.

The last car was filled with scents. The heavy, moldy pall of Mr. Shunt filled his nose. Cedar stifled a growl and licked his muzzle. Mr. Shunt had been there, but he was not there now. He could not kill him, tear him apart, dig out the bits of him that made him tick. There was no movement, no talking, no signs that Mr. Shunt and Shard LeFel had returned to the car.

Other odors filled the air—Shard LeFel's rich cologne, meat, liquor, metals, old wood.

The smell of Elbert was in that car—the musky milk scent of a child deeply sleeping, strong and alive. Cedar's heart quickened with hope. If that was true, he had a chance to save Elbert, to bring the child back to his father alive.

All he had to do was find a way into the railcar. He sniffed along the edge of the car, looking for a trap, a latch, a door in. And then he caught the scent of his brother.

Wil. Here. Above him. Wounded. The rot of infection was already tainting the smell of his blood. But it was new blood. It was not the smell of death. Wil still breathed.

Cedar wanted to howl with joy, but that joy was short-lived. To save his brother, he had to get into the car. It was not flesh that stood in his way; it was wood and metal, latch and hinge, things that took a man's hands, a man's fingers.

All the claw in the world would do him no good.

The ground shook. The matic Shard LeFel and Mr. Shunt rode was coming closer. Cedar hunkered down beneath the edge of the car. Shard LeFel's matic huffed across the ground. It rolled up the ridge and would be at the rail any minute.

Cedar waited. Waited for Shard LeFel and Mr. Shunt to walk up the stairs and open the doors. And once they opened the doors, he would no longer need them, or their hands.

The steam-powered matic huffed nearer and nearer.

Over that noise, Cedar could just make out the sound of men shifting in their tents.

Easy kill. Heart. Throat. Brain.

No. Men would not slake his thirst. He wanted the Strange. He wanted the Strange who took Elbert and hurt Wil. He wanted Mr. Shunt. Dead.

No other creature moved. Not even those who were inside the carriage above him. It was as if the whole of the world held its breath.

The matic grew louder until Cedar's teeth rattled from the vibration of it. It stopped next to the tracks in front of the first car Cedar had investigated. A hiss of steam expelled in a roll of heat; then the huffing slowed and slowed, like a heart losing the will to beat.

Cedar waited for the footsteps. Waited for the stride. Waited for the hands to open the way to the boy, the way to his brother. Waited for Mr. Shunt.

A rattle of a hinge. The door on the matic swung open. Then bootheels scuffed down metal stairs. One set of boots was Shard LeFel's; another set of boots shushed and smooth, almost without noise, belonged to Mr. Shunt. And the third set of footsteps was smaller, lighter than Shard LeFel's. Who?

Cedar took a sniff, and caught the honey and flower scent of Mae Lindson. She was alive. But captured.

Rage pushed through him and the beast squirmed under his hold. *Kill.*

He bared his teeth, holding back a growl. They needed to be closer. They needed to open the door. Then they needed to die.

They said nothing as they hurried down the track, Shard LeFel's cane clacking like a second hand ticking seconds into minutes along the dead iron rail.

Cedar counted footsteps. Three people. Counted scents. LeFel, Shunt, Mae. Mae was not bleeding, but he could smell her anger. And her fear.

Cedar could not suppress the sudden, livid anger at the thought of Mae in that monster's hand. The beast inside twisted again with the rage of Mae's capture. He pulled his muscles tight, ready to lunge. They walked up the stairs, Shard LeFel in the front, Mr. Shunt in the back, Mae Lindson between them.

Wait, the part of him that was a man commanded. *Wait for the door to open.*

Shard LeFel pulled a chain of keys out of a fold of cloth and unlocked the bolt on the door, but did not open it.

"Hurry, Mr. Shunt," he said. "The moon will soon be at the end of its journey and I will have no time left."

Mae Lindson gasped and stumbled up the stairs, pushed or pulled by her captors.

This. Now. The door. Run.

Cedar's muscles pushed.

A flash of light burned against the southern sky, and the sound of something crashing through the trees rolled like thunder.

Shard LeFel paused at the door and swore in a language Cedar had never heard.

"The Madders," he breathed. "I will not have the king's dogs keep me from my passage. Go," he commanded. "Kill them. I want their flesh in bits, and their bones crushed so fine they won't fill a tobacco box."

"And the matics?" Mr. Shunt asked.

"Yes, yes. Release them. All of them. But keep your Strangeworks near. Kill the Madders, kill Miss Small if she is fool enough to be with them, and kill every man and woman in the town if that is what it takes to keep them from my threshold this night."

Rose Small?

Cedar growled so softly, it was almost too quiet for even his sharp ears to hear.

But Mr. Shunt paused, his boot soles scuffing the rocks and dirt. His body shifted with a subtle rub of fabric over metal and bone, oil and blood dripping into warm, soft folds of flesh and cloth as he bent to look under the railcar where Cedar crouched in shadow, eyes slit.

He had a prod in his hands. Just like the one that had wounded Cedar.

If Cedar leaped now, the door would remain closed. He would have no way to save Wil or Elbert.

If Cedar held still, Mr. Shunt walked free.

Both. He wanted the door open and Mr. Shunt dead.

Cedar held his breath and did not make a sound, though the tuning fork on his chest burned hot enough it felt like it was searing a hole through his fur. If he moved, he knew the fork would ring out. If he moved, he knew he would tear Mr. Shunt apart, lose all reason, and lose his chance to save Elbert and Wil.

Strange. The Strange who took the boy. Attack. Fight. Kill.

Cedar pushed back against that belly-deep need, his control of the beast slipping. He needed the door to the car open. Needed it as much as he needed Mr. Shunt's neck in his jaws.

The open door would save Wil. Save Elbert. The open door would save Mae.

"Kill them," Shard LeFel said. "Quickly, before the moon sets, or I will shatter the Holder, and the door for the Strange will remain closed forever."

Mr. Shunt straightened, the whisper of wool and silk stroking his leather boot tops. Cedar could smell the hatred on him. The ever-so-slight whir of a spring coiling and uncoiling beneath those folds of cloth where only bone and blood and heart should be filled Cedar's ears.

"Of course, Lord LeFel," Mr. Shunt whispered. Mr. Shunt took a step away.

Cedar strained to hear the carriage door open.

But instead, a great noise roared out into the night. It didn't sound quite human, but it was a voice, not quite a man's, raised in a yell of pain, of fury.

Behind that voice was the ungodly screeching of iron bending, straining, breaking. Something was coming down the rail. Something was tearing up the rail. And whatever that creature was, it was surely coming this way.

"Go!" Shard LeFel hissed as he finally opened the door.

Cedar leaped out from beneath the carriage and crashed into Mr. Shunt, knocking him to the ground. He snapped at

Shunt's face, but the Strange snarled and blocked his jaws with one hand.

Cedar clamped down on the hand and twisted it, jerking back. Mr. Shunt screamed as his arm dislocated with a grinding *pop*. Cedar pulled harder and tore it the rest of the way off. Severed from the Strange, the arm still ticked and twitched, the gears and bones forcing the hand to open and close.

But that did not stop Mr. Shunt. He dashed backward so quickly, Cedar could not track his movement. Mr. Shunt stood several feet away and lifted a gun from his pocket. He pointed it at Cedar.

"Killer," he hissed. "You will not stop us."

Cedar growled and lunged.

Mr. Shunt's lips split in a blackened grin filled with serrated teeth. He squeezed the trigger.

The impact threw Cedar backward. The bullet dug deep through his lung, taking the breath out of him and leaving behind pain. He landed hard, blacked out, and came to again, barely able to hold on to conscious thought. The bullet was still moving, digging through him like a beetle burrowing between his bones.

Cedar howled, anger and rage colliding in his mind and bringing him to his feet.

Mr. Shunt was gone. Shard LeFel and Mae were gone, locked up tight in the car.

He heard the middle train car door open. Water hissed over hot coals, and chains clattered from inside the car. Mr. Shunt must have been releasing the matics and tickers to protect the rail.

Cedar started toward the railcar, each step agony. He had to stop Mr. Shunt. He had to save Wil, Elbert, and Mae.

The night air punctured with the inhuman cry of rage and twisting metal that was coming up the track.

Cedar limped to the shadows near the train car, as half a

dozen metal beasts, some as large as a bison, others small as a fox, lumbered out of that car, puffing white and black plumes of steam into the air.

They were made of steel, iron, leather, wood, brass. They were made for pounding, tearing, cutting, stabbing, breaking. They were made to kill.

"Kill the Madders," Mr. Shunt commanded from where he stood on the platform by the car door. "And every living thing with them." The menagerie of matics ran, rolled, pounded down the rail, along the rail, running fast toward whatever bellowing creature was coming this way.

And then Mr. Shunt strode through the car to the last in line. Cedar pushed himself to follow, still clinging to the shadows. The bullet hadn't exited his body. It rubbed and dug with every movement, every breath. But pain meant nothing.

Kill, the beast within him urged. *Kill the Strange.*

Behind Cedar in the car that held his brother, the child, and Mae, something moved. If he took the time to hunt Mr. Shunt, Shard LeFel might kill Wil, Elbert, and the beautiful Mae Lindson.

Cedar Hunt was not a man who hesitated in making decisions. And yet he paused, torn between the choice of killing or saving, the mind of man and the urge of beast locked in stalemate.

A gunshot rang out, breaking through his thoughts. He glanced over at the rail where bullets pinged and sparked and rattled off the matics, peppering the metal monsters to no effect.

The Madder brothers' laughter filled the silence between the shots, their guns roaring like cannon blasts, each concussion illuminating the night and clouds of smoke from their guns with flashes of lightning and fire. Over all that, he heard Rose Small call his name.

"Cedar Hunt!"

Cedar saw her, amber hair stirring wild from beneath a bonnet, goggles over her eyes reflecting the spark and fire of the gun in her hands. A gun she fired at the matics, and the railmen who had roused out of their tents, and come running down the line to face the demons in the night.

"Find Mae!" Rose yelled, her aim taking three shots in a man's heart at seven hundred yards. "Save Mae Lindson!"

She was calm as a sharpshooter, taking careful aim at a matic's head. She shot out an eye, then reloaded and aimed at a valve line as the ground shook.

"Find Mae!" Rose Small shouted again.

Mae. Cedar knew where she was—in the train car. With Shard LeFel. With Wil and Elbert.

Mr. Shunt was nowhere to be seen.

But down the track, walking forward as if dragging a mountain behind him, was a man.

Big, dark, bloody, and charred, Jeb Lindson walked down the railway, two huge chains strapped to his wrists. On those chains were two round matics taller than the man himself, screeching and squealing as he dragged their dead metal husks over the rail. Every step loosened bolts, pried spikes and ties, and forced the rail to rise up like a giant, twisted snake behind him, broken free of the earth, broken free of the binds that held it down.

Smoke rose up from the rail. And the tick, tick of blood and sweat falling off the big man's fists sent a pockmark of plumes up off the metal like two tiny engines following behind his steps.

The wind shifted and brought Cedar new scents. And he knew that man, that creature, tearing apart the rails was not alive, nor was he dead. He did not know what could power a man to keep moving, keep walking, pounding forward.

Jeb yelled out, a single call of pain, anger, and longing wrapped around one word: "Mae!"

Cedar's heart beat painfully, his blood too hot, his wounds agony as he ran. To find Mae. To save Mae. To get to Mae before Jeb Lindson.

No, to save his brother. To save the child. Yes, and to save Mae.

Cedar leaped up onto the platform of the middle train car where the door hung open. He needed to get into the first car, and that door was shut.

The door slammed open.

Mr. Shunt stood in the threshold, oil pouring slick from his empty sleeve. Mr. Shard LeFel and Mae Lindson stood behind him.

Cedar snarled. He leaped.

Mr. Shunt raised his remaining hand from within his coat, and fired the gun again.

The world tipped sideways, filled with explosions and noise. And all Cedar could do was fight to breathe as waves of pain crashed through him.

CHAPTER THIRTY-TWO

Shard LeFel tightened his grip on the Holder he held tight to his chest as if it were a babe made of glass. In his other hand was a spiked chain looped around the witch's neck. The same chain noosed the necks of the wolf and the boy.

"Well done, Mr. Shunt," Shard LeFel said, watching the other wolf twitch and bleed at his feet.

Mr. Shunt bowed slightly, and then bent toward the wolf who struggled to breathe. He splayed his spiked fingers, itching to dig out the wolf's heart.

"Leave him," Shard LeFel said. "He will be dead soon. I'll not have this interruption stop my return."

Mr. Shunt hissed, then seemed to compose himself. He straightened. "Yes, Lord LeFel."

Shard LeFel handed the chain to Mr. Shunt and walked through the open door into the car his collection of matics had once filled. Empty now. But he could hear them out on the battlefield, the magnificent screech and hiss and thump of the devices killing the Madders. Music. Sweet and fitting for his last grand night in this mortal world. Fitting to send him back to his own lands and immortality.

An explosion rang out and then a ragged howl of a voice lifted above it: "Mae!"

Shard LeFel paused between one step and the next. "Could it be?" He glanced over his shoulder at the witch, whose eyes were wide in fear, her voice silenced by the leather gag in her mouth and the barbed-wire chain that left beads of blood around her throat every time she swallowed.

"I believe that is your husband, Mrs. Lindson, come back from the grave. Such a pity he is too late to save you."

He continued through that car and to the next. The door opened before him and one of the Strangework bowed, and stepped aside to allow his entrance.

Shard LeFel strolled over to the center of the room, where the door lay like a coffin on a pedestal.

"Three hundred years of exile," he said softly. "And now, finally, I shall cheat this death, cheat this mortal world, and mete my revenge upon my brother in the lands from whence I came."

He placed the Holder at the very top of the door's frame, pressing it down into a hollow carved perfectly for the device. The device pulsed, moonlight caught there in echo to a faintly beating heart. But Shard LeFel knew it would take more than moonlight to open this door.

It would take three lives.

The three Strange against the walls shifted, a slight moan escaping their lips as the Holder found its place in the door. Each of the Strange was attached to the door by wires and tubes that ran from its neck, wrists, and feet and fed into the door.

Shard LeFel meant to savor his moment. A decanter of three-hundred-year-old wine and a crystal goblet awaited his celebration.

"Mr. Shunt, see that our guests are comfortable," LeFel said. "Then open the sky for me."

Mr. Shunt gave the witch's chain to the first Strange who clung to the wall at his left. The wolf's chain he gave to the Strange at the far end of the car, and the boy's chain he gave to the final Strange standing nearest Mr. Shard LeFel.

Then Mr. Shunt walked across the floor to a crank set near the door. He turned the crank, and the ceiling of the train car drew aside like a curtain pushed back by a hand.

Shard LeFel uncorked the wine and poured it into the decanter. "And unto this world, I bid my most final farewell."

Moonlight streamed thick and blue-white into the room, striking the Holder and the door. Light from the Holder poured flame into the runes and glyphs and symbols the Strange had carved into the doorway.

And from outside the train car, bullets rattled the night.

"Beautiful," LeFel said. "And now all that is needed is the key." He glanced at the boy who slept curled and chained at the Strange's feet. He glanced at the wolf that panted in pain. He glanced at the witch who stood wide-eyed with fury, tears tracking her cheeks to wet the leather gag.

"Mr. Shunt, begin with the boy, then the wolf, then the witch."

Mr. Shunt bowed, his eyes bright, his teeth carving a sharp smile. He walked to the Strangework who stood above the boy, and inserted one of his bladed fingers, like a key, into the Strange's chest, where a heart should be. He twisted his hand, and the Strangework shuddered. Mr. Shunt withdrew his finger.

The Strange changed.

It spread its arms wide and the front of its body split open, revealing gears and sinew, pulleys, pistons, and bone that worked in dark concert to expose spikes and edges and blades lining every inch of it. A living, breathing iron maiden, remarkable in its ingenuity of both form and function.

Mr. Shunt picked up the sleeping boy and deposited him deep inside the gears and spikes, pressing him back, but not far enough to prick his skin. Not yet.

Then he moved to the wolf, who was too injured and too

drugged to fight. Mr. Shunt shoveled him inside the spiked guts of the Strangework there.

And lastly he walked to the witch.

"I will not miss this wretched land." LeFel sipped the wine, savoring the heat and flavor of ancient blooms across his tongue.

"Nor will I mourn its destruction." He sipped again, and pressed one of the jewels on the bent cane in his hand, releasing the pure silver blade cased within it. A blade that would carve out his brother's heart.

"Mr. Shunt," LeFel said. "It is time to spill the blood of our coin."

Rose Small watched as Cedar Hunt ran, limping hard, to the train car where Mae must be trapped. She ducked behind the thin stand of trees, put her back to a fir trunk, and pushed her goggles out of the way as she reloaded.

The Madders were still out there, standing in the open in front of the trees, firing off those blunderbusses and shotguns, shrouded in smoke and fire and moonlight, and laughing like wild jackals.

The matics were coming. Five of the most amazing devices that would each have struck her dumb with awe if they weren't so hell-bent on killing her and the Madders. Rose chambered the bullets, her hands trembling, her heart pounding, then glanced out from behind the tree.

The full moon set the devices into full contrast, even at a distance. She didn't know how, but the matics were working in conjunction with one another. Through the smoke and blasts from the Madders' guns she could see one of the doglike beasts was down and twitching, and the other stood stock-still, steam gushing up out of it like a geyser. But the others, the Goliath with steam-hammer arms, the battlewagon, and the huge, spiked wheel, were bearing down faster than the Madders could shoot them dead.

And if that weren't enough, the railmen from up a ways had come into the fight with more guns than an army. She like as not figured one of the train cars up the line had to be an arsenal of weapons.

Rose swallowed hard and tasted the oil and burn of spent black powder. She didn't reckon there was an easy way out of this alive.

She fitted the goggles back over her eyes and fired cover shots at the hulking Goliath that hammered an arm down so near the Madders, one of the brothers fell flat from the impact. The big beast reared back, screeching and clacking. It was recharging, ratcheting up its firing device to slam its arms down again.

Rose shot at the thing, aiming for what she prayed were vulnerabilities: tubes, connecting valves, and gauges.

But the matic did not slow. It rolled this way on strange tracked feet that chewed over the terrain as if it were riding on rails.

The Madders used her fire as a chance to run back behind the screen of trees with her.

"Do you have a plan, Mr. Madder?" she yelled to Alun as he skidded to a stop behind the tree to her right, both his brothers half a tick behind him, grinning and breathing hard.

Bullets zipped through the night air. Needles and dirt sprayed down around them.

Rose leaned out again and fired off the last of her shots at the railmen, who were holding ground behind the metal monsters.

"Plan to kill the matics and crack LeFel out of his fortress," Alun said. "Reload, Miss Small. The boys are going to need cover."

Rose was already reloading. She glanced up at the Madders. Bryn and Cadoc were gone.

Just then the rapid fire of what sounded like a hundred guns tore flashes of light through the night.

"That's the battlewagon," Alun yelled over the peppering recoil of bullets. "Figure it has a twenty-five- or thirty-shot cartridge." He reached into his pocket and pulled out his pipe, then sparked a wick with a tiny striker, and puffed until the tobacco caught.

Rose's heart beat harder than a hammer. She'd heard tales of the rapid-fire guns used in the war, but she had never seen such a device, and didn't want to become intimately acquainted with one now.

"That one's done," Alun yelled into the sudden pause of gunshot. "Fire, Miss Small." He clamped his teeth down on the pipe stem and leaned out from behind the cover of the tree. He sent off a volley of bullets. The battlewagon had extinguished its cartridge and must be reloading. But how much time would that take?

Rose Small shouldered her gun and aimed back at the field. The battlewagon was indeed reloading, but the hulking Goliath rumbled toward them on its tracks, hammer arms pulled back and ready to tear down the trees they stood behind. Rose took aim at the Goliath, but nothing seemed to stop it.

"Look low," Alun yelled.

Rose lowered her rifle.

Another matic, the huge spiked wheel, was rolling their way, rattling over dips and tree stumps, one hundred yards and closing fast.

Rose fired everything she had at it. So did Alun. But they didn't have nearly enough firepower to stop that thing.

Alun was no longer laughing. He was cussing up a lung. He pulled something from his pocket and lit the wick of it with his pipe, then lobbed it at the rolling matic.

A ground-shaking explosion rang out, but the wheel kept coming.

Rose was out of bullets. She pulled her handgun and stood her ground, setting off shot after shot at the spiked wheel. Bullets didn't stop it. Bullets didn't even slow it.

Fifty feet out. Thirty. Twenty.

Rose turned to run.

And in front of her rose a monster out of nightmare.

Mr. Jeb Lindson.

Rose froze and stared into the eyes of a dead man.

"Move!" Alun hollered.

Rose threw herself to the side.

Jeb yelled.

Just as the spiked wheel bashed through the trees. Limbs cracked and crashed to the ground with skull-splitting impact.

Rose tucked up tight behind a boulder and covered her head with her arms. She peeked out just in time to see the wheel come to a crashing stop in front of Jeb Lindson, the forward-most spike pulling back like a cannon ready to fire.

With inhuman strength, Jeb Lindson swung the huge round tickers attached to the chain around his wrists. He slammed them into the matic. Metal met metal, crashing and sparking. Steam gushed into the air as the wheel matic faltered under the blow. Jeb didn't wait for it to fall. He lifted the giant chain and ball and smashed it into the matic again, busting seams, popping rivets. The wheel matic exploded, hot scrap and ash raining down out of the air.

Then the big man went walking. Toward the rail. Toward Mr. Shard LeFel's train cars, where his wife, Mae Lindson, was held captive.

Rose smelled hair burning and patted at her shoulders. Her hair was on fire! She pulled at the base of her braid, dragging her hair forward over her shoulder. A very bad mistake. The fire licked up the side of her cheek. Rose yelled and slapped at the fire, blistering her palms. She snuffed it out just before it reached her ear, and sat there, for a second or two, trying to get back her breath and her courage.

The night filled with bullets again. The battlewagon was rolling closer, firing another deadly round off into the night.

Blinking back tears of pain, and swallowing down her fear, Rose scrambled for her gun and prayed she had enough bullets in her pockets to end this.

Mae Lindson had no weapon except her magic. It would take her voice to curse or bind, or draw upon magic of any kind. And she had no voice.

Jeb yelled out in agony. He was alive, trying to find her. Trying to save her. But that monster Shard LeFel was right. He was too late. There was no time left.

Time.

Alun Madder had given her a pocket watch. She knew it carried a speck of glim. Could she use it as a weapon?

As Mr. Shunt turned his back to stuff Elbert inside the gory clockwork of the Strange, Mae worked to get the pocket watch out of her coat. They had bound her hands together in front of her, but she could still move them.

The Strange that held the chain around her throat was hypnotized by Mr. Shunt's work. If it noticed what she was doing, one hard tug on her chain would crush her neck.

Mae fingered the watch into her hand, then slowly pulled it up to her mouth. She tugged at the leather gag, but it wouldn't move. Over the top of the pocket watch she whispered, more song than word, more breath than voice, calling on magic, begging magic to come to her, hoping the glim would work as an amplifier, a cupped hand, a bullhorn, to call the magic and make it stronger. She begged magic to not so much break a curse but interrupt it and hold it away for one single minute, for one single man: Cedar Hunt. And then she pressed down the watch stem, stopping the watch, and stopping Cedar Hunt's curse, for just one minute.

Cedar Hunt gasped for air and pushed himself up onto his knees. He didn't know how, but he was a man, even though moonlight filled the sky. He saw the gun on the platform beside him. The gun Mr. Shunt had shot him with. He picked it up and pushed onto his feet, nearly blacking out from the pain. He staggered through the train car toward the child, toward his brother, toward Mae.

Rose Small looked for Alun Madder. He was sprinting over the matic Jeb Lindson had reduced to a pile of rubble, and headed straight at the Goliath, an ax in each hand, his pipe cherry bright in his mouth. The battlewagon trundled over the terrain, headed right for him, reloading a cartridge as it picked up speed.

It was suicide. There was no cover, no way Alun would survive a rapid-fire round from the matic.

"This way!" Alun Madder yelled. "Quickly! The boys will take care of the men."

Boys? Rose heard Cadoc and Bryn let out a hoot from down the rail. The two younger Madder brothers had clambered up inside the big rail-matic scraper with bulletlike wheels that leveled the land. Somehow they'd powered the thing and were now riding it down over the bank of men, Bryn looking like some kind of bug as he worked the levers in the cab—his goggles reflecting moonlight and gunfire. Cadoc, wild-haired and laughing as he hung by one hand and one foot off the side of the beast, unloaded shot after shot into the rail workers' rank.

The railmen returned fire on the big ticker, but bullets pinged off the huge metal scraper. The rail matic powered forward relentlessly, smashing flat roots and stumps and anything else that got in its way, big screw wheels covering the ground with ease.

The rail workers were outgunned. Those that could turned tail and ran from the nightmare scene. The rest were crushed where they stood.

Alun was at the foot of the Goliath. Far too nimble for a man his size, Alun Madder ducked low and jammed both axes into the bottom links of the matic's wheel track, then followed that up with another lit bomb that he lobbed up into the beast's chassis.

"Run, Rose," Alun Madder yelled. "Run!"

The matic hammered down with a mighty *whump* and the earth itself bent beneath its blow.

She couldn't see Alun, didn't know if he had been injured or killed by the hammer. The other two Madder brothers were driving the rail matic up behind the battlewagon, on a clear collision course that would crush the mobile gun.

They were crazy, all of them. Plainly suicidally brained. But she didn't take the time to ponder further. She ran. Toward LeFel's train cars, toward Cedar Hunt and Mae Lindson. To save them if she could. Before it was too late.

Mae Lindson threw her hands up to ward off Mr. Shunt, but he slapped the watch out of her hands and then, for good measure, struck her hard across the face. Stars filled Mae's vision as the barbed-wire chain around her throat tightened and bit.

She couldn't breathe.

The hot, wet heat of the Strange surrounded her as Mr. Shunt shoved her into the clockwork monster behind her.

Spikes scratched, slashed, clamped. The heat and oil inside the Strange caused every open wound on her body to sting as if salt had been rubbed in it. She tried to scream, but had no air.

"Now, Mr. Shunt," Shard LeFel said. "The blood. Turn the key and open our door so that I may see to my brother's end."

Mr. Shunt spun so quickly, his coat billowed around him like dark wings. Then he was at the Strange door where Shard LeFel stood waiting, hunger twisting his hauntingly beautiful features.

Mr. Shunt triggered a switch. And the Strange that held the boy, Wil, and Mae began to close. Mae pushed at the creature swallowing her whole, but it was like pushing against a bear trap. Spikes pressed into her back, her legs, her shoulders, her arms. Sharp agony drew a ragged scream out of her throat as her blood was sucked up and pumped down into the tubes that ran to the door, mixing with the blood of the howling wolf and the screaming child.

The door began to open, hot white light pouring through the cracks and shattering the shadows of the room. And in that light, Mae saw her death.

Cedar Hunt lurched through the empty train car, blinking blood and sweat out of his eyes. His lungs felt heavy and full of blood. He cocked the trigger back on the gun and stumbled into the next car, parceling his breath so as not to pass out.

He lifted the gun and shot the first person he saw—Mr. Shard LeFel, who stood bathing in an unholy light coming up from the floor of the car. The shot caught Shard LeFel in the shoulder and knocked him flat on his back.

Cedar cocked the gun, fired again, this time aiming for the tall, skeletal figure of Mr. Shunt. He missed.

And then, just as sure as a watch running down, Cedar was

no longer a man. He was a wolf again. He lunged for Mr. Shunt, jaws, claws, and rage. Mr. Shunt was made of blades and hooks, razors and pain—too fast to catch his throat, too slick to snap his bones. Cedar tore at flesh that tasted of rotted blood, but could do no true damage to the Strange.

"Mr. Shunt," Shard LeFel yelled as he regained his feet and strode back up to the doorway. "Kill them. Spill their blood now!" Shard LeFel used the bladed cane to help him stand on the edge of the opening doorway beneath him, one boot at the threshold.

Mr. Shunt skittered away from Cedar's hold and flicked a lever on the device at the top of the doorway. The device lit up.

Screams of agony filled the room.

Cedar could not kill the three Strange creatures in time to save Mae, Elbert, and Wil, and he had no time to choose between them. Little of a man's reasoning filtered through the pain now. His mind was all wolf, and the wolf would kill the one Strange in front of him.

Cedar jumped over the door, past Shard LeFel, crashing down on Mr. Shunt before he could trigger another lever in the device.

Cedar snapped at Shunt's face, caught scarf and a hank of hair. Mr. Shunt unhinged and slipped free, then pulled up the gun that had fallen from Cedar's hand. Mr. Shunt aimed that gun at Cedar's head.

Then the train car exploded—walls bashed apart as if a boulder had torn through them.

"LeFel!" A great, hoarse bellow shook through the night.

Jeb Lindson had come calling.

Another wall shuddered from the impact of the huge matics Jeb swung like a child swings a stick.

Mr. Shunt turned the gun on Jeb Lindson. And squeezed the trigger.

The shot took Jeb straight through the middle of his head, leaving a trail of smoke spiraling up out of the hole.

Jeb smiled, bloody, charred, torn apart, and shredded so that he barely resembled the man he once was. He picked up one of the huge ball tickers and pounded it into Mr. Shunt, knocking him flat before turning toward his true goal, Mr. Shard LeFel.

Shard LeFel raised his cane. "You will not stand in the way of my revenge! You will not stop me!" He lunged. The silver blade pierced Jeb's ribs, clean out his back.

And the big man let out a huge wet chortle.

Shard LeFel's eyes went wide with horror.

"Can't kill a man more'n three times, devil," Jeb Lindson said. "Said it yourself. You plain can't kill me no more."

Mr. Shunt seemed just as shocked as Shard LeFel and stood, weighing his options. Cedar barreled into Mr. Shunt and tore into his neck, shaking and breaking it. Then Cedar ripped Mr. Shunt apart, limb from limb, stringing bone and guts and metal out of him like pulling the meat out of a crab, until Mr. Shunt stopped moving, stopped twitching, stopped ticking.

It took no more than a minute before Mr. Shunt was reduced to a mess of cracked bits. It took a few seconds more before Cedar could reclaim enough of his mind to realize Wil, Mae, and Elbert were still trapped. Trapped by the Strangeworks.

Cedar attacked the first Strange, sinking teeth into its head and throwing himself backward, twisting off the head with the strength of his jaw.

The Strange wriggled and shrieked and sprang open like a popped seed. From that bloody mess, the little child Elbert tumbled out onto the floor.

Cedar paused just long enough to be sure the child was breathing, then ran to the next Strangework.

"No!" Shard LeFel screamed. "Release me. Fall to the ground and worship me."

Cedar glanced at him. The door was closing, and Shard LeFel was not walking through it. Jeb Lindson was there instead, big hand wrapped around Shard LeFel's throat, holding him one-handed in midair above the door. With a vicious smile, Jeb Lindson lowered Shard LeFel just enough, the tips of his boots slipped into the door, before he yanked him up again.

"Only gonna do one thing, devil," Jeb said. "Gonna kill you, me, and this dead iron. And it's only gonna take me the one time."

Jeb used one hand to smash the ball matic into the Holder at the head of the doorway.

The Holder exploded in a roll of thunder and a blast of lightning. Seven distinct bits of the device flew straight up into the night and then whisked across the starry sky faster than anything on this earth.

Cedar was on the next Strangework, biting, killing, twisting, destroying, until it disgorged his brother, Wil, who was broken, bloody. But he still breathed.

Cedar Hunt wasn't done killing yet.

He threw himself at the last Strange. And this time, it was Mae who fell from the monstrous creature, Mae who took a hard, shuddering breath, pulling the gag from her mouth and the barbed wire from her throat.

Jeb Lindson lifted Shard LeFel away from the closed doorway in the floor, his huge hand crushing LeFel's windpipe. Jeb Lindson laughed and laughed, his ruined face drooping with the effort to smile as he dragged Shard LeFel behind him over the rubble of the train car and down to the ground outside.

Shard LeFel scrabbled, reaching for the door, reaching

for the stairs, trying to scream through a throat that could do no more than gurgle.

And then Jeb stopped laughing. "For Mae," he breathed. "*My* Mae."

Jeb pounded LeFel's face methodically with his fists, breaking his beautiful features, snapping his elegant neck, cracking his graceful back, then every other bone in his body, before crushing his skull and digging his brain out with his knuckles. Just for good measure, he pounded the bloody scraps of Shard LeFel with the metal ticker, until all that remained of him was pulverized into a fine mash.

"Mr. Hunt?"

Cedar looked away from the bloody spectacle.

Rose Small stood on what was left of the platform, her rifle smoking, her goggles pushed up, little Elbert hugged close against her hip. She was dirty, singed, a little bloody. He didn't think he'd ever seen her smile so brightly.

Rose assessed the damage to the railcar. "Don't know if you can jump down, and I wouldn't advise you to drop too close to Mr. Lindson. He's of a powerful single purpose right now. Can you make it here to the platform next to me?"

Cedar took a step, looked back at Mae, who had somehow pulled herself up on her feet and was walking, a bit dazed, toward Rose. Cedar nudged Wil until his brother gained his feet and blindly followed him. The door in the floor was closed, the white light gone. Cedar knew he'd need to break that door, maybe burn it down, but could not summon the effort, nor could he begin to think of the method to do so.

He was suddenly very tired, very much in pain, and very hot. All he wanted to do was lie down and lose himself to the soft, luxurious promise of sleep. What was wrong with him?

He glanced at the sky behind Rose Small. It was no longer dark and star-caught, but instead blushing with pink.

How had dawn come so soon? Rose was helping Mae to sit, and looking over both Mae's and Elbert's injuries.

Dawn was on its way.

Rose glanced over her shoulder and smiled. "That's good, Mr. Hunt. You're almost there. Mae and Elbert are torn up pretty bad, but they're mostly whole. A fair bit better than I reckon they should expect to be."

The slide of dawn and the grip of pain blurred Rose's words and made her seem far away. He wanted to go to Mae, to touch her and know she was safe, but he could not move. So he listened to Rose Small's words and knew they meant safety and tending. Cedar lay down to rest. Then the moon drained away, taking the wolf with it and leaving him free to be a man once again.

Rose Small did not avert her eyes as Mr. Hunt slipped his wolf skin and stretched out into his bare naked self. It didn't take long at all for him to turn from wolf to man, and he made no sound, gave no indication that it hurt.

He simply was looking at her from a wolf's eyes, then rolled his shoulders, stretched his legs, arched his back that had three bullet wounds clean through it, and was kneeling in his man form. Near as she could tell, he fell asleep right there. The wounds in his back started mending some, even as she watched, though they leaked a strange black oil.

She looked over at the other wolf, who regarded her with eyes the color of old copper. He limped over and laid himself down next to Cedar.

"I'm supposing you're not just a wild animal," Rose said as she took a step toward Cedar. "But seeing as how everyone here is still bleeding, I think we'll need to find some water and shelter before folks in town come looking for what all the noise was about."

She shifted the pack on her back, sliding her arm out of one strap. The wolf closed his eyes, and seemed to fall asleep just like Cedar.

"Well, don't that beat all?" Rose knelt and pulled her blanket roll off the bottom of her pack and unrolled the wool blanket—one that she had bought from Mae—over Mae and little Elbert.

At that touch, Mae seemed to come to, brushing back her hair with bloody hands, and fixing Rose with a clear-eyed stare.

"Jeb?"

"He's here, as much of him as can be." Rose nodded to where Jeb knelt, unmoving, above the gory mash that had just a moment before been Mr. Shard LeFel.

Mae moved the blanket so that it was wrapped around Elbert, and handed the boy to Rose. Then Mae walked down what was left of the train-car stairs, toward what was left of her husband.

"Husband? Jeb?"

Jeb raised his head. "Mae?" The word was a sigh, almost unrecognizable from what was left of his mouth.

"I'm here, my love."

Jeb struggled to stand, finally pushed onto his ruined leg and broken ankle, steadying himself with will alone.

Mae was smiling as if an angel had just descended from heaven and landed there in front of her.

"Oh, Jeb." She stepped right up to him and put her hands in his, while he looked down at her, love and devotion shining from his eyes.

"My Mae," he said. "To have and to hold."

Mae nodded. "Yes, love. Always." She glanced at his shackles, running her fingers along the cuff of one of his hands, looking for a way to release him, while he looked at her in adoration.

Jeb held perfectly still as she worked her hands around the shackles, but no matter what she did, she couldn't find a way to release them.

Finally, Jeb pulled one hand out of hers and gently placed a single finger beneath her chin, tipping her face upward.

"Mae," he said again. "My wife."

Even though her face was tipped, her eyes were closed. The gloss of tears ran a clean line through the blood on her cheeks. She took a deep breath and finally opened her eyes.

Sorrow and pain cast fleeting shadows across her features as she studied the shredded remains of the man before her. Then she smiled.

"It's going to be all right, my love," she said, her voice hitching. "You're going to be just fine. We're going to be just fine."

The sky grew brighter, the sun pressing just below the horizon's edge.

Jeb shook his head and softly drew one thumb across her cheek, as if he had done so a thousand times before, wiping her tears away. "It is too late for me. Has been for some time. We know that."

"No," Mae said. "Don't say that."

"What should I say, my Mae?" he asked.

"That you'll stay with me. Always."

Jeb cupped the side of her face in his bloody hand. "To love and cherish," he said.

"I do love you," she said. "I will always love you."

"The vow," he said, his voice soft, sad. "Say the vow, my beautiful wife. To love and to cherish."

Mae searched his face. "To love and to cherish."

"Until death do us part."

"Until death do us part," she whispered.

Jeb took a deep, shuddering breath. "I love you," he exhaled, "always."

He bent to her, and she stood on tiptoe. They kissed gently, husband and wife for one last moment as the sun burned bright over the horizon.

Sunlight poured down over them, cloaking them in a golden veil while they kissed. Then Jeb Lindson faded away, shackles falling to the earth, until he was nothing but dust that glinted on the wind, gathered up and carried in a rejoice of morning birdsong, to the sky.

The widow Mae Lindson stood for a long, long while, face tipped up to the glow of the eastern sky, her eyes closed as if she could not yet find the strength to look upon the world now that her husband was no longer upon it.

CHAPTER THIRTY-THREE

ose Small knew the new day would bring new people out to find them. And if the town had wanted to burn Mae as a witch before, she knew once they got an eyeful of this mess, they wouldn't wait for a slow flame to kill her this time. It'd be the noose for all of them, and it'd be fast.

She had found the water barrels and washed up Elbert. He wasn't talking, but he didn't let go of her hand. Eventually, he'd seemed content to sleep while she kept him propped on her hip. The wolf and Mr. Cedar Hunt slept, and Mae finally let Rose lead her to one of the water barrels so she could wash her arms and face.

Rose walked back to where Cedar Hunt slept, and pulled her canteen from her belt and sloshed the water a bit. She uncorked it, took a long drink to soothe her smoke-burned throat, and steady her nerves.

"It's time we be going, I think," she said, though she didn't know who among them was listening. "We'll need to get little Elbert back to his family and the rest of you somewhere out of the town folk's eyes."

Cedar Hunt stirred.

He slowly sat, and Rose watched as a cool breeze brought him to realize he was naked, except for the blanket she had covered him with. He situated the blanket around himself so it covered him in a more civilized manner.

Rose did the proper thing and looked away until he got himself decent. When she looked back, Cedar Hunt had one hand on the wolf who was still drowsing, and was looking out across the rubble, taking in the damage around them. He looked sorely exhausted. Sounded it too.

"Clothes, and food, if we have them," he whispered hoarsely.

"I can find that for you. You'll be all right, then, here with the wolf?"

Cedar looked back at the wolf and a serene sort of ease crossed his face. "I'll be fine. The boy?" he asked, as if dredging deep dreams.

"Shook, but breathing. And Mae's whole too. Mostly." Rose nodded. Cedar Hunt's gaze followed to where she still stood near the water barrels, face tipped to the sky. He swallowed hard and looked away.

Then: "The Madders?"

Rose shrugged. "Ran off into the night as soon as that device flew into bits."

"Ah," he breathed. Cedar closed his eyes, and drowsed, sitting.

Rose shook her head. There was no one but herself to take care of things. It wasn't easy, but she managed to round up a horse and wagon and hitch them up, while still juggling little Elbert. Mae wasn't in her full senses, but climbed into the back of the wagon, and thank God and glim, Elbert was content to curl up with her.

It took a little more coaxing, but Rose got Mr. Hunt and the wolf into the wagon too. As a last thought, Rose set the railcar on fire—just the one that had held the doorway and those wicked Strange. She wasn't sure if there was enough fire in the world to destroy that evil, but wasn't about to leave it out here for folk to find.

She climbed up into the wagon, kicked the brake free, and flicked the reins, guiding the horse away from the rail.

The wide cleared area up and down the rail looked like a battlefield. Broken metal, steaming piles of gears, coils, and tubes, carved eerie shadows in the early-morning light. The still forms of dead rail workers sent a chill up her spine. That could just as well be her on the ground, could be Mae or little Elbert. She held tighter to the rifle and headed up the tracks and around the slight curve in the hill. She'd go to Mr. Hunt's cabin, figuring it was the only home among them that was still standing, and not in plain sight.

Birdsong, late to the morning, had started up slow, but now filled the air. Rose took a deep, full breath, wishing the new morning could clean her of the long night's pain and fear. But it would take more than a clear dawn to take away this horror. It had been a hard night. Still, her friend was alive, and so too were Mr. Hunt and Elbert. She was grateful for that. Grateful she had lived to see the day.

CHAPTER THIRTY-FOUR

Cedar Hunt swung down off his horse with a grunt, Elbert in his arms. The bullets had not been properly dug out, but Mae Lindson had done what she could to clean his wounds of the Strange black bugs and oil. There wasn't time for more. They'd all decided to leave town and head east together, but they'd gone first to Cedar's house to give Mae Lindson and Wil a roof while he brought Elbert back to town.

Well, while he and Rose Small brought Elbert back to town. The girl had refused to stay behind and had instead ridden alongside him, saying she'd stand up for his character against the crowd if needed. It had not gone beneath his notice that she brought along her shotgun and her goggles fitted tight against her bonnet.

Though she'd been cheerful about it back at the cabin, she'd had no choice but to cut her hair just below her ears, evening the ragged edge the fire had left behind. He couldn't help but notice how often her fingers wandered to tuck it behind her ears, or drop it forward to try to hide the burn on her cheek and neck, which had thankfully not blistered.

The townsfolk were riled up and skittery, holding to clumps in the street and talking about the happenings of last night—from the witch burning to the rail explosions, likely caused by some sort of malfunction of the strange matics and tickers under LeFel's lock and key. The townsfolk had quickly cleared out of Cedar's way once they saw him come riding. Word of the night's fight with the matics out on the rail had come to town, probably from the surviving railmen.

Cedar didn't know whom they had painted as in the right or the wrong, nor if any of the men had spotted Rose, the Madders, or Mae, and truth was, he didn't much care. He'd be riding east. East to see Mae Lindson safely to her sisters she'd left at the coven. Then east to find the universities, the scholars, the devisers, who might know of a way to break the curse he and his brother still carried.

Rose Small stubbornly insisted she wanted to go east too, and when both women had stood side by side against him, he knew there wasn't a man born who could convince her the road was no place for a lady such as she.

But looking around the town at the suspicious gazes the men and women cast at him, and in equal measure Miss Small, he got to thinking Hallelujah might not be a place for a lady like her anymore either.

They had ridden straight through to the blacksmith's shop, and word had preceded them.

The blacksmith strode down the main road, his wife beside him.

At the first sight of Cedar and the bundle in his arms, Mrs. Gregor cried out with joy.

Cedar was careful to hand the boy to her, after he dismounted, but Mr. Gregor interrupted his intent, and took the boy his own self. He unwrapped him and pulled up his shirt to reveal his back, scratched and weeping with small punctures, but not bearing the mark of the pentagram Rose Small had told Cedar had been carved into the Strange changeling.

"Papa!" the boy cried, catching the big man in a hug. It was the first word Cedar had heard out of him.

Mr. Gregor pushed him back gently and looked up at Cedar, then Rose. Then he looked quickly away.

"Elbert," the big man said gently. "This is important, now. Tell me your middle name."

"James. Like Uncle."

Mr. Gregor nodded. "That's right, son. That's right."

Mrs. Gregor sobbed, and pulled her son into her arms.

"Go on and take him inside, Hannah," Mr. Gregor said. "I'll be there soon."

Mr. Gregor waited until she was gone, the door not only closed but locked behind her.

"The boy doesn't seem to remember the last few days," Cedar said. "A blessing, I think."

"I can't be more grateful," Mr. Gregor said around a catch in his throat. "Mr. Hunt. Name your price and I'll give it to you gladly."

"I'm not a man who needs many things. And I'm set well enough."

"You must take some payment," he insisted.

Cedar didn't want to take anything for a job he had already gained so much from—finding his brother. "What happened to the changeling Shard LeFel brought you?" he asked.

Mr. Gregor looked down at his hands clenched together in front of him. "In the middle of the night, it was tearing through the house, wild. Crazy. When it struck Hannah and made her bleed, she thought it possessed by devils and began reading Bible verses while I held it tight and still. When daylight poured in through the window and touched him—it—he turned to a stock of wood."

He held Cedar's gaze, as if knowing how mad that sounded.

Cedar adjusted the hat on his head, catching his breath against the wound in his side and the other injuries that had not healed. They likely wouldn't heal any faster than a normal man's pains, since the change into wolf, and the quick healing it offered, was a month away.

"Well, then how about you pay me by giving me that stock of wood?"

If the blacksmith seemed surprised, he hid it well. "Follow me—I put it in the shop. I wasn't sure what else to do."

Cedar glanced at Rose Small. She shrugged. "I'm going with you." She marched off after Mr. Gregor, her horse following behind her.

Cedar walked after them, keeping a keen ear out for any sounds of trouble. But all he heard was the sounds of townsfolk, and the hammering of the men who worked for Mr. Gregor.

Mr. Gregor stepped into his shop, where four young men worked hammers and vises. "Take a break," Mr. Gregor said. "Take your supper early if you want. I'll tend the fires."

The men looked over, and gave Cedar Hunt a wary eye.

"Go on, now," Mr. Gregor said. "Before I change my mind and you'll get no break at all today."

The men caught up their lunch buckets and hurried out with little more than a nod to Rose Small, whom, Cedar realized, they must know nearly as well as Mr. Gregor.

Once the workers were gone, Mr. Gregor strode to the back of the shop and pulled the stock of wood from the corner shelf. It was wrapped in waxed cloth, a Bible pressed tight against it. He handed it to Cedar.

Cedar unwrapped the cloth, gave Mr. Gregor the Bible, and tipped the wood to the sunlight to study it.

It didn't look like a child at all. It looked like a branch that had been debarked and rubbed smooth with oil.

"What do you plan for it?" Mr. Gregor asked.

Cedar nodded at the blacksmith's forge that was hot enough to heat the sun.

"I think that fire will make sure the Strange can never use it again." Cedar held Mr. Gregor's gaze. Most folk didn't believe in Strange.

But sometimes, some folk opened their eyes and saw, harsh and clear, that the Strange were real. And saw the damage they could do.

"I'll tend the bellows," Mr. Gregor said.

He walked to the forge and pumped air over the fire until the coals stoked ruby hot.

Cedar threw the stock into the fire and watched as it burned as quickly as if it were made of paper. The blacksmith stirred the ashes, making sure there were no lumps of wood left.

"Do you think we'll have worries?" Mr. Gregor asked. "From those sorts again? That they might want my boy again?"

Cedar shook his head. "Don't reckon you will. Mr. Shard LeFel and his man, Mr. Shunt, are dead. They were the bringers of such things to this town. Make sure word of that gets told. He had dark things locked up in those railcars— any man can go on out and see what's left of them for himself. Those devices and matics were meant to kill. Now that Shard LeFel is dead, I think Hallelujah will continue on apace with no Strange happenings, though the matter of the rail will be something this town will have to decide."

Cedar pulled a tuning fork from around his neck and struck it against the heel of his palm. A sweet pure note sang out. "I'll be on my way, out of Hallelujah, out of the Oregon Territory. I'd like to give this to your son." He held out the tuning fork. "If ever this note turns sour, you'll know you and your family are in the company of the Strange."

"Mr. Hunt, I am the one who should pay you." Mr. Gregor walked across his shop and, on a high shelf, drew down a cast-iron safe. He worked the lock, then withdrew an item. He locked the safe, and turned.

"This is the Gregors' seal. Any who are friends of mine will be a friend to you, Mr. Hunt. Any who are family to me will be family to you." He held out a ring, cleverly carved with words upon the center, and a great bruin bear breathing fire across the outside.

"I don't think—," Cedar began.

"You'll take it," Mr. Gregor said. "It is the least I can give you for my son's life."

Rose Small, who had been silent all this time, spoke up. "It's a fine gift, Mr. Gregor. I'd wager you have family and friends scattered far and wide."

Mr. Gregor glanced at Rose and looked like he was going to say something else. But instead said, "That is the truth, Rose Small. You've always told the truth." He took the tuning fork and tucked it in his pocket, while Cedar placed the ring on his left thumb.

"I'm sorry for the way I treated you the other night," Mr. Gregor said.

Rose smiled. "We were all riled up. It's not a matter to me now, though I was sore angry at you then." She laughed. "But thank you."

"Suppose you'll come around the house for dinner?" he asked as they walked out of the heat of the shop into the cool afternoon light.

"No, Mr. Gregor," Rose said. "I'll be traveling too."

"Ah," he said, his hands behind his back. "Send me a postcard when you've piloted your first airship."

At those words, Cedar watched Rose Small light up. "I promise you I will. Might even drop it out of the hatch as I float over the top of your house on my way to China."

Mr. Gregor chuckled and glanced over his shoulder at his house, restless.

"Well, then," Cedar said. "We should be on our way, and I'm sure your son wants to see you. Good day, Mr. Gregor."

"You're a fine and decent man, Mr. Hunt. And always welcome in the Gregors' home for generations to come."

Cedar shook Mr. Gregor's hand, surprised at how that

offer brought a smile to his lips. It had been a long time since he had thought he had a place he belonged in this world. A place he was welcome.

"Thank you, Mr. Gregor."

Cedar swung up onto his horse, holding his breath against the shot of pain in his side. He pressed his elbow against the bandage bound there beneath his coat, hoping to stem the weeping of the wound.

Rose Small gave Mr. Gregor a huge hug. He patted her fondly on the back and looked up at Cedar. "See that you take care of her for me, Mr. Hunt."

Cedar nodded. "I'll do what I can. Though she's done a fair job minding her own self."

Rose Small hitched up into her saddle and gathered the reins. "Oh, I'm sure I'll be enough trouble to keep us both busy, Mr. Hunt."

"No doubt," he drawled.

They turned and rode down the main street a bit.

"Did you want to say good-bye to your parents?" Cedar finally asked.

He watched as Rose Small's smile went from a sparking hot flame down to a lantern's dim glow. "No, thank you. We've had our say. A whole lifetime of it."

As they passed in front of the mercantile, Rose's mother came out of the shop with a broom and started sweeping. When she noticed Rose riding past, she stopped and held one hand up, as if to wave. But Rose Small kept her gaze on the horizon, curiosity bright in her eyes, and a small smile curving her lips.

Cedar Hunt was glad it didn't take long to gather supplies, including Mae's mule, Prudence, whom they had found contentedly foraging in the forest. He wanted to start on the road today and get a ways from town before the people there decided they were to blame for the rail disaster.

His only concern was Wil.

Cedar finished checking on the mule, his horse, and the horse Rose had taken from the rail. They were on long leads beneath the trees, near enough they could make acquaintance, and far enough they wouldn't foul one another's lines.

That done, he stepped into his cabin, pulling his hat from his head as if he were entering a church instead of his humble shack.

There had never been so many people in his house. He paused just inside the door, not wanting to get in the women's way. Rose was packing the last of the foodstuff from his cupboard and Mae was sitting on the chest she'd dragged over to his cot, checking on one of Wil's many wounds.

Wil was still in wolf form and sleeping on the cot.

"I think this is about all that'll take to the road," Rose was saying. "Not much for herbs and medicine, though we can probably gather some as we go. Perhaps we can stop in a town or city for supplies. A city," she said, as if dreaming, "wouldn't that be grand?" She turned, saw Cedar standing with his hat in his hands looking at Mae, and gave him a curious frown. "Have you seen to the horses, Mr. Hunt?"

Mae looked away from Wil, and over at Cedar.

"I have," Cedar said. "They're about set to go."

Rose hefted up the two satchels of food. "I'll just take this out, then. Unless you need me for anything?" she asked Mae.

Mae was still staring at Cedar, though he pretended not to notice.

"Mrs. Lindson?" Rose said.

Mae seemed to come to. "No. I'll be fine. I'm fine. Go on ahead."

Rose nodded and walked up to Cedar, who stepped aside

so she could use the door. She gave him a look as she walked past, maybe a warning, maybe an encouragement. Since she also rolled her eyes toward Mae, all he figured was she was telling him to not bother the widow too much.

Mae had gone back to lifting and replacing the compresses on Wil's side. The cloths were not as bloody as last he'd seen them.

"How is he?" Cedar walked a short bit across the room and stopped halfway. The memory of her hands soothing his own wounds washed through his mind.

"Recovering more quickly than I'd thought," Mae said. "The curse at least gives him that."

She stood and Cedar could see the red line of scratches along the back of her neck, and the stiffness in her shoulders that hinted at more injuries beneath her long-sleeved dress. She'd spent the day working herbs to see to all their wounds, her own included, but it was clear she was near exhausted.

"Do you think he'll be up for travel today?" Cedar didn't know why he asked that. They'd already talked it over and decided they'd head out, even if it meant wrapping Wil up and putting him on a sled behind one of the horses.

"I think he'll be up in the next hour or so. To eat. Then we'll see how much more he can endure." Mae finally turned.

Her eyes were red, glossy with unshed tears, even though her voice was flat and steady. "I don't . . . I don't know how much more . . ." She shook her head.

"He'll be fine," Cedar said gently. He walked the distance between them and, after a moment's hesitation, rested his hand on her arm. "We're all going to be fine."

Mae stared at his shoulder, stiff, unbreathing. Then she stepped that much closer to him and placed her head on his chest, and her right hand on his arm, just as his was on hers.

Cedar inhaled the sweet scent of her, and swallowed hard. He held very still, not daring to comfort her, to pull her in against his body, to wrap his arms around her tightly and hold her as he desired, safe against the pain. There was no safety against this kind of pain, and the only comfort was time.

Mae cried, very, very quietly, while Cedar stared at the wall, holding his emotions under lock and key. Time was the only, and the kindest, thing he could give to her.

Finally, she took a deeper breath, held it, and let it out. Her hand clenched his shirtsleeve for the briefest moment, as she steeled herself to face the world again.

When she pulled back, her eyes were dry.

"Mr. Hunt," she began awkwardly, glancing from his tearstained shoulder to his mouth to the wall behind him, seeming uncertain of how to explain herself, "I didn't—"

"Do you need a hand waking Wil?" Cedar smoothly interrupted. He stepped around her, careful not to let his fingers linger against her arm, careful not to touch her again, for fear of what he might do. He walked over to the cot, placing his hand on his brother's side.

Mae didn't answer for a moment; then, "Yes," she said on a grateful exhalation. "He responds to you much better than to me."

Cedar called Wil's name and smiled when he opened his eyes. It was a marvel to him that his brother was alive, even though he was still under the curse's hold.

Mae brought out a slab of venison and put it on the floor. With the meat as encouragement, Wil stepped down off the cot and ate and drank. Then he walked a slow circle around Cedar, and a wider circle around the room, his limp easing some the more he moved. Finally, he glanced up at Cedar, copper brown eyes filled with a man's intelligence and curiosity.

"We'll need to be going," Cedar said. "Traveling away from here, traveling east. We'll go at your pace. Are you ready?"

In answer, Wil walked to the door and waited there.

Cedar took one last look at the cabin, his gaze resting on the heavy chain and leather collar pounded into the hearth. Mae and Rose hadn't asked him about it, though he supposed they knew very well what he'd used it for. His fingers strayed to the Madders' chain around his neck. He'd be more than glad to leave the heavy chain and collar behind.

Mae finished cleaning up and poured the last of the herb water over the coals in the fire. She dried her hands on her skirt, and came to stand next to Cedar.

"Well, then," she said. "Shall we, Mr. Hunt?"

Cedar took one last look at the cabin, then opened the door. Wil slipped out quickly. "Yes, Mrs. Lindson," Cedar said, "I believe we shall." He held his hand out, ushering her through the door, and then followed her into sunlight.

They had gotten three miles or so out of town when Cedar heard a clattering of wheels following them.

He looked back. A tinker's wagon, painted bright as a bordello bedspread, top-heavy with a crazy assortment of metals and gears and whim-wham, followed them. Atop the rattling monstrosity sat the Madders. Alun Madder smoked his pipe and held the reins of the two draft horses who pulled the contraption at a quick clip.

They pulled up behind Cedar, Mae, Rose, and Wil.

"Evening, fine folk," Alun called out. "Where you headed?"

"Down the road," Cedar said, leaning forward in the saddle a bit to ease the pain.

Alun chuckled. "We've been thinking we'd travel with you a piece."

"Oh? And why's that?"

"You still owe us a favor, Mr. Cedar Hunt," Alun Madder said with a wide smile. "And we've come to ask for it."

Cedar tipped his hat back and loosened the strap on the gun he kept lashed to his saddle. "That so? Seems to me your favors do nothing but bring trouble."

"We're looking for you to hunt for us."

"My time's previously committed, Mr. Madder. I have people to tend to and promises to keep."

Alun puffed on his pipe, considering. "We're patient men, Mr. Hunt, but you promised you'd find our Holder, and bring it to us."

Wil, who had stayed at Cedar's heel, pricked his ears up and whined.

"The Holder?" Cedar asked, searching his memories for what they had told him. "Don't know how I'd likely find it if I don't know what it is."

"The Holder is a device of seven pieces, made of the seven ancient metals. Each piece is a talisman, an artifact, a device to be used for good: healing the sick, blessing crops, bringing peace unto a land. When this New World was discovered, the Holder was brought here as a gift by like-minded men who wanted peace and prosperity for settlers and natives alike.

"But Shard LeFel caught rumor of it. He sent his Strange to sniff it out." Alun paused, his gaze lost to a distant time. When he spoke again, his voice was lower. "They killed for it, tortured for it, committed such horrors. Relentless, until they had stolen each and every piece. Then they worked their dark devising. The Holder is now a weapon of pain, plague, war. Each piece broken and remade Strange-wise, so that nothing but sickness, ruin, and chaos fall to any who find it. And if someone is clever enough to put those seven pieces back together again, then they'll be clever enough to understand the Holder can also be a weapon of a magnitude that has never been seen in these lands.

"We're of a strong mind to put an end to such things, Mr.

Hunt," Alun said. "And we're of a stronger mind you're the man who can help us do it."

Cedar glanced at Mae Lindson and Rose Small. Neither of them said anything, though Rose's eyes were wide. The decision would be his own.

"And"—Alun Madder's tone was light as he pointed the stem of his pipe at Cedar—"while we travel together, it'd only be neighborly of us to offer up the back of the wagon for anyone who grows weary. The wolf, perhaps?"

Cedar looked down at Wil. The Pawnee god had deemed to make Wil's curse different from Cedar's, though Cedar did not know why. For the obvious, Wil remained a wolf even after the full moon, and even in daylight. But perhaps less obvious, he did not seem overwhelmed with the killing rage of the beast. He was possessed of the sharp intelligence of both wolf and man at all times.

Wil looked up at Cedar and in his eyes was the agreement, the determination, to help find the Holder. Cedar nodded.

Wil trotted to the back of the Madders' wagon. Cadoc Madder quickly lowered a step from the back and Wil limped up it, and inside the wagon.

Alun laughed. "Looks like it's been agreed for you, Mr. Hunt."

Cedar sat back straight in the saddle and turned his horse to the east. "Just so long as our paths remain the same, I'll hunt your Holder for you."

"That's fine, fine," Alun shouted as he flicked the reins. "I have a feeling our paths will remain the same for a long time, Mr. Hunt. A very long time." He and his brothers laughed, and started singing a bawdy parlor song.

Cedar glanced over at Mae Lindson. She seemed caught in her own song, as if the wind carried words to her, her gaze set firmly east. He imagined it would take her a long time to recover from losing her husband, her home, and all that was dear to her.

He curled his fingers around the reins, to keep from reaching out to her, to keep from touching her. A fine woman like her didn't need a man encroaching on her grief. Not just yet.

"What thoughts are you keeping, Mr. Hunt?" Rose Small asked.

"It's a strange path life leads a person down. Never know how it will all turn round. For bad or good."

Rose thought on that a moment. "I suppose you're right. I'm looking forward to where the path will take me. Aren't you looking forward to your path, Mr. Hunt?"

Cedar made a point to stare at the horizon ahead, instead of where his gaze wanted to linger: on the beautiful Mae Lindson.

"Not so long ago, I didn't think I was," he said.

"And now?"

"Now I think I've changed my mind. Might be a thing or two I can look forward to."

"Finding the Holder?" she asked.

"I suppose."

Rose looked over at Mae, then turned an innocent look to Cedar, though there was a wicked sparkle in her eye. "Is there something else you're looking forward to?"

"I suppose."

"Don't reckon you'd tell me what?" she pressed.

"Nope. Don't reckon I would." He nudged his horse into a trot, then a slow lope, and began down the road to the east, and all the promise this fine land could hold.

EPILOGUE

Mr. Shunt sat cross-legged in the shadows by the shattered and burned train car, the last bits of him hooked, stretched, and sewn into place. It had been a slow and grueling process to piece himself back together, and he had used spare parts from the other Strangeworks to fill the holes Jeb Lindson and that cursed man Cedar Hunt had left in him.

His gray, gore-covered coat wrapped him from chin to boot, his face hidden beneath layers of silk and cotton and his stovepipe hat.

He was looking for something. Waiting for one thing more to finish his construction.

There. A dull glint, movement in the bloody soil.

He bent and plucked up a delicate silver dragonfly. He held it in his open palm, and the crystal wings shivered sparks of color in the late-afternoon light.

Such a precious thing. So rare. And now it had no cage to hold it.

Mr. Shunt pressed it into his chest, piecing it together, stitching it a new cage, just as he had pieced himself together anew. Then he took the iron key from his pocket and wound the dragonfly until its wings hummed.

Too great of a treasure to waste on that dead man. Now the dragonfly was where it belonged. Now Mr. Shunt would see that his own desires, his own hungers, were fulfilled.

And that which he wanted most was traveling east.

So east was where he'd go.

He strode down the rail, heading east on the dead iron rails, the sun a burning ember behind him, and all the land spread before him, like a feast of dreams.

Read on for an exciting excerpt from
Devon Monk's new Age of Steam novel,

COLD COPPER

Coming in July 2013 from Roc.

There were plenty of good ways to die. Cedar Hunt wiped ice off his face and pushed through the knee-deep snow, leaning against the wind. Some people said drowning wasn't bad; others said hanging was a peaceful way to go. But he had decided real quick that dying in the teeth of a blizzard wasn't any way to lay a soul to rest.

Cold just made him angry and anger fueled his determination to keep right on living.

"Mr. Hunt," Miss Dupuis called over the howl of the wind. "A river, I believe."

He looked back at the people following him as he broke trail through the drifts. Miss Sophie Dupuis was an acquaintance of the Madder brothers.

She looked like a French diplomat but was part of a secretive group of people who, as far as he could reckon, spent most their time taking the law into their own hands to try to rid the land of the Strange, those unholy creatures from myth and legend intent on killing good folk.

But now there was an even greater threat than the

Strange. The Holder—a Strangeworked weapon made of seven ancient metals—was scattered across this land.

Cedar had seen the destruction even just one piece of it had caused. It wiped out a town of people, left their bodies as playthings for the Strange, and nearly killed his friend Rose Small.

The remaining pieces of the device would do the same or worse. And if they fell into the wrong hands, they could bring the United States, and all within it, to its knees.

His instinct for the Holder's whereabouts had sent them north out of Kansas, heading up to Des Moines. But this snowstorm had fouled his senses.

"Which way?" he called out to Miss Dupuis.

She adjusted the compass in her hand and pointed west. They'd been hoping to catch a direction toward civilization for hours now, and following a river was their best hope of doing so.

Behind her loomed the Madder brothers' wagon, pulled by a team of mules. Alun Madder sat the driver's seat. A miner and deviser by trade, he was a bear of a man: heavy coat, wide-brimmed hat, messy curls of hair, and beard adding to the wild look of him. Even in the pounding snow, he kept his pipe hot, pulling cherry red coals from the bowl.

His two brothers, Bryn and Cadoc, were behind the wagon, pushing when the mules weren't enough to pull the sleds they had rigged up beneath the wheels. In the back of the wagon, out of sight, was the woman Cedar loved, the witch Mae Lindson. His brother Wil, who carried the same Pawnee curse as Cedar and currently wore a wolf's shape because of it, was also in the wagon.

The wind thrashed harder, picking up snow and ice. Cedar shivered under the onslaught.

If Mae Lindson hadn't cast a spell of warmth on his

hands and feet every few hours, he knew he'd have lost his fingers and toes yesterday.

It had taken Mae several attempts to find a way to bind warmth to skin without scorching flesh. He figured he'd carry the scars on the back of his wrists for years to come, but didn't regret a moment of the pain.

Because of her, they might make it to shelter. If shelter could be found.

One thing was certain: there was no turning around now. It was well past midday, and the path behind was blocked by fallen trees and piles of snow. The mules and horses struggled with every passing hour.

They were running out of daylight and running out of time.

Cedar tipped his head so he could see up from beneath the brim of his hat to where Miss Dupuis pointed. Nothing but snow and hills ahead, though he thought he could make out a downward slope.

"Are you sure?" he called back over the wind's howl.

"Yes. If the maps are correct, there should be a river there." Miss Dupuis's voice quavered. She was shaking even though she wore a long wool coat over her several layers of skirts, kidskin gloves, a rabbit-skin muff, and a rabbit-skin shawl across her shoulders. Her hair was tucked up beneath a woolen cap covered in a heavy layer of white that would not melt.

The compass in her hand burned a bloody red and let off enough heat to stay the snow from its surface. She'd shown him the contraption the Madders had devised—a combination of sextant and compass housed in an enameled case filled with sand that could be heated to keep the user's hands warm.

Now she tucked her palms into the furred hand warmer to keep her gloved fingers from freezing.

Miss Dupuis had refused the warming spell from Mae, knowing that every time Mae cast the spell, it drained Mae's strength.

"You should return to the wagon," Cedar said.

"Not yet. I'll watch for lights, town, rail. If we come on the river and follow the banks, we should see a town."

Cedar didn't waste breath arguing. Truth was, he could use a second set of eyes in all this white. "Shout if you see the river. I'd rather not find it by falling through the ice."

He adjusted his course west, every step sinking into snow up to his knees, despite the snowshoes he'd strung together out of strips of leather and willow. He'd fashioned the shoes a week ago, when he and Wil had first felt the weather taking a shift toward the worse.

Neither of them had expected this storm.

"Where you think you're going now, Mr. Hunt?" Alun Madder hollered from the seat of the wagon.

"Des Moines!" Cedar had been telling him that the city should be the nearest shelter for two days, but the Madders refused to believe him. Refused almost to admit Des Moines was a city that existed in the world at all.

He didn't know what nonsense they had in those stubborn heads of theirs, but ignoring a town didn't mean it wasn't there.

Alun let out a hard whistle and pulled the mules up short. Even Miss Dupuis's horse jerked at the sound and stopped, head drooping, grateful for the rest.

Alun lifted a lantern to better see through the snow, and sunset light slapped across his round, weathered face, revealing a beard white from snow, a bulbous nose stuck in the center of his close-set features, and glass-sharp eyes looking out from beneath bushy brows.

Quick tempered and quirky natured, Alun Madder was the eldest of the brothers. The blowing snow turned him into a ghoulish figure, as if the face of death itself was peering out at Cedar through a casing of ice.

"We will not stop in Des Moines," Alun said flatly.

Cedar was pretty sure that was the first time the miner had actually spoken the name of the town. But he didn't care to point it out. He didn't care in the least if the Madders acknowledged that the town existed.

"We will or we won't last the night." Cedar spaced his words like hammer strikes. "The mules are near dead. The horse too. We won't last long enough to dig our own graves. We stop in Des Moines."

"I say otherwise," Alun yelled. "And so do my brothers."

As if called to battle, the other two Madder brothers strode through the snow alongside the stopped wagon, both carrying geared-up shotguns against palms and shoulders.

Near freezing to death did a lot of odd things to a man's sense of reason. It was said some went raving mad, tore their clothes off, and ran through the snow naked while their blood turned to ice.

Maybe the cold had frozen up the Madder brothers' brains.

Maybe Cedar didn't give a damn about that.

"Do not stand against me, Alun Madder, and think you will win," Cedar said. "And do not think I will stand here and waste time fighting you instead of finding our path to salvation. If you have some device or matic you've bolted together that can change the weather or give us speed, I'll wait for you to bring it out here; otherwise I am going to find that city."

"A city of devils," Alun said.

"Good. I expect they'll keep the fires warm."

Alun scowled and returned to puffing smoke out of his pipe.

That was answer enough.

Cedar turned his back on the brothers and their guns and pushed through the snow down the next slope.

They could shoot him in the back for all he cared. He wasn't going to stand still in the middle of a blizzard and argue his heartbeats away.

After what seemed a long time, the mules let out hoarse brays, and the crunching hiss of the wagon's sled runners scraped through the snow behind him again.

Good. They were still following him.

The spell of warmth around him gradually wore away and the cold sank through skin down to bone. Hands, face, and feet went numb, but he pushed on.

It seemed all the world was ice and death. There was nothing but putting each foot down, one after another, breaking through to solid ground for the horse behind him, who left a path for the mules and wagon.

Cedar lost all sense of time to that rhythm, and soon the Pawnee curse showed him other things riding that storm. The Strange were thick in that wind. Ghostly fingers and teeth clawed at him, catching at his coat, his feet, his hat.

Angry. But not solid enough to draw blood.

He could kill the Strange, even in this ghostly form they took. It would make the world a much better place without them and eventually, if he killed them all, he might again regain a normal man's life. The curse he carried forced him to hunt and kill the Strange. All the Strange in the world. He suspected he'd breathe out his last days before that was done, and still not be free of the curse.

But he was too exhausted to fight them today. He ignored these Strange that plucked and wailed and bit. Life was all that mattered now. And life, for all of them, meant moving west.

Wil, beside him, growled. Cedar looked down, surprised to see his brother out of the wagon.

Wil's ears were flattened against his wide gray-and-black skull, his copper eyes the only flecks of color in the snow. Wil saw the Strange too, likely smelled the moldy green of them as Cedar smelled them, likely saw the flash of eyes and heard the trebled laughter warbling through the air.

The Strange couldn't do serious harm unless they took on a shape, a form, a body. As Cedar had learned firsthand, dead people were the clothing preferred by the Strange, though there were times they could inhabit other bits and matics.

He wasn't going to give them any corpses to waltz about.

"Don't," Cedar said to Wil. "There is no time to chase them. They'll lead you to your death."

Wil growled, but stayed close, snapping at the swarm of Strange, and holding them off as daylight drained away and the shadows deepened.

"Mr. Hunt," Miss Dupuis called out. "Please, Mr. Hunt. You must stop!"

The heat in her tone finally soaked through the cold that gripped his thoughts. Cedar stopped. Wil's teeth were dug in the cuff of his coat, and he was pulling backward, whining.

For good reason. They had reached the bank of the river. If Cedar had walked even three steps more, he'd have slid down the steep embankment and landed in the water.

The Madders behind him were talking—no, they were arguing, loudly—about ice and rivers and speed and something else Cedar couldn't hear except for the smattering of curses and the phrase "that devil," followed by words that must have been their mother language of Welsh.

"We've found the river," Miss Dupuis said.

Cedar lifted his free hand and rubbed his stinging eyes. His vision was blurred by the snow, his hand lifeless in the heavy gloves.

The river was not flowing. It was a frozen ribbon that

wound off to the northwest, black and dusty as an old chalk-board.

"Good," he croaked, his mouth and throat on fire. He needed water, he needed rest; but there was no time for either with night fast approaching. "Town won't be far."

"We're going to step back, Mr. Hunt," Mae Lindson said, "so the Madders can come through."

Cedar jerked at her voice. When had she climbed out of the wagon?

"Cedar," Mae said again, her tone stern, as if trying to pitch her voice over a fever snuffing out his senses. He supposed she wasn't much wrong to do so.

Along with the cold confusing his head, his ears were filled with the eerie voices of the Strange calling him. Pleading for him to follow.